KATIE MCINTYRE HITS A HOME RUN

KATIE MCINTYRE HITS A HOME RUN

WOMEN'S WORK
BOOK 1

MINDY KLASKY

PEABRIDGE
PRESS

This is a work of fiction. Any references to historical events, real people, or real locales are used fictitiously. Other names, characters, places, and incidents are products of the author's imagination, and any resemblance to actual events or locales or persons, living or dead, is entirely coincidental.

This book was previously published as *The C Word.*

Published by Peabridge Press
P.O. Box 42133, Arlington, VA 22204

ISBN 978-1-95018-452-1

Discover other titles by Mindy Klasky at www.mindyklasky.com

112822mkm

ALSO BY MINDY KLASKY

You can always find a complete, up-to-date list of Mindy's books (including books in other genres) on her website,

www.mindyklasky.com.

The Women's Work Series

Katie McIntyre Hits a Home Run

Jennifer Price Lives a Charmed Life

Emily Holcomb Bakes a New Cake

The Diamond Brides Series

Perfect Pitch

Catching Hell

Reaching First

Second Thoughts

Third Degree

Stopping Short

From Left Field

Center Stage

Always Right

True Love Classics

Harmony Christmas

Harmony Hearts

Harmony Hero

Small Town Daddy Dance

The Mogul's Unexpected Baby

To every person who has struggled during CoronaChaos
(and yes, I know that means "to everyone")

The Renaissance took place in chaos and plague.

Shiva Ayyadurai

PROLOGUE

In retrospect, the lipstick on Aaron's collar should have been my first clue.

"What the actual fuck?" I demanded, holding up the stained shirt he'd left on the bathroom floor. We were already late to our pre-wedding party at Jungle Bird, over in Chelsea.

He shrugged. "Goddamn morning show. They had me in Makeup for an hour. I swear to God, that woman was thirty seconds away from going rogue with an eyelash curler."

That made sense. A lot more sense than my fiancé cheating on me two weeks before our wedding.

Aaron complained about TV interviews all the time. All the guys did. They'd rather run the entire stadium than spend fifteen minutes under studio lights.

But New York loved its baseball heroes. And so did I. "Sorry," I said, tossing the shirt into the hamper. "Didn't mean to sound salty."

"*Sound* salty?" Aaron pulled me down beside him on our king-size bed. The tip of his tongue found the vulnerable curve behind my ear before he whispered, "You never have to worry about me. I love you." He teased the hem of my silk teddy with his wiry fingers. "I can't wait to marry you." His hand slipped beneath the lace of my matching panties. "I'd never do anything to risk…losing…this."

We were two hours late getting to the tiki bar. When we exited Aaron's Lamborghini, paparazzi swarmed the sidewalk. We posed for a few minutes, letting them snap their fill, Aaron calm and confident while I tried to keep my eyes from squinching closed. Finally, he settled his palm against the small of my back and guided me toward the bar and our waiting friends. Half the people inside said something about the high color on my cheeks, and I laughed like any happy bride-to-be.

~

My second clue was the text exchange he didn't bother to hide, a week before the wedding.

I'd promised to shut down my computer at eight. That would leave plenty of time to watch *Fast & Furious Whatever*—Aaron's pick, of course. At least I'd get to ogle John Cena.

But my editor's notes were a lot more extensive than I'd hoped. With three feature articles under my belt, I'd thought I had a better grasp of what *Press Box* wanted. Instead, I felt like I was back to cub reporting for *The Springfield Examiner*.

Aaron totally didn't get it. He said I was wasting my time with my little side gig. I didn't *need* to work. I should dive into the social events and charity gigs that kept all the other WAGs—wives and girlfriends—busy.

But he agreed to watch the hockey game while I took a machete to my opening graf. I didn't bother explaining to Aaron why every word had to be perfect. The trans woman I was writing about had faced enough hardship on the pro golf circuit. She didn't need the largest sports journalism site on the Internet screwing her over.

It was well after ten before I curled up next to Aaron on the leather couch in front of our mammoth TV. A quick glance confirmed New York was up by one, with less than a minute to play. Pittsburgh pulled the goalie as I shifted to a more comfortable position.

Aaron's ass buzzed.

He ignored it, eyes glued to the game. New York's rookie defenseman was hacking at the puck, trying to cut his way through a tangle of skates. The kid went down to one knee and lunged with his stick. He managed to snag the puck, jack-knifing his entire body to send the frozen rubber into the empty net for his first career goal. The arena erupted as the clock ran out.

Aaron's ass buzzed again.

I shifted so he could reach his phone. A bunch of the guys were at the game but Aaron had begged off, saying they only wanted to pick up puck bunnies. Now, I said, "Spare me. Juan needs help choosing between Bachelorette 1, 2, and 3."

Juan Gonzales was Aaron's best friend. Best man, too. They'd both been traded to New York in 2015, and after four years of turning double plays on the field, they could practically read each others' minds.

Aaron grunted as he glanced at the row of emojis from Lucky21: Banana, red lips, eggplant, pink lips, a spray of water drops, and a trio of bright pink tongues.

"Lucky21?" I asked, amused.

Aaron shrugged. "He shut down 21JuanGon. Too many exes with axes to grind."

"Hard to believe," I said. Almost like he heard me, Juan sent a line of fireworks, followed by a winking smiley face.

Aaron shook his head and slipped the phone into his pocket.

"Aren't you going to answer?"

"Those were boasts, not questions. My man doesn't need help getting laid. Speaking of which…" He waggled his eyebrows like a badly drawn cartoon character.

I laughed. "I'm sorry I took so long finishing up work."

Aaron's grin was wicked. "How sorry?"

"Um, what did you have in mind?"

He moved faster than I expected, flipping our positions. His hands planted beside my head and his forearms corded with muscle as he lowered himself for a kiss. I opened my lips before he did. He wedged his knee between mine, and his tongue slid home.

Juan texted again, but Aaron rocked against my hips. "Mmm," I said. "That game really got you going."

He growled, and I forgot about using my words. After, as I dozed off to a recap of New York's win, I realized I'd found the perfect way to avoid watching movies with never-ending car chases.

~

The third clue was so blatant even *I* had to see the truth.

"I'm really doing this," I said, taking one last look in the mirror. My wedding gown's sweetheart neckline plunged beneath the strand of pearls I'd borrowed from my grandmother.

Brittany reached out to straighten the comb holding my veil, tucking in an errant bobby pin. "You're gorgeous," she said.

I clutched my best friend's hand. "It's all going too fast! We haven't had two seconds to talk all day."

Brit's lips twisted into a familiar smirk. "That's what happens when you marry New York's most eligible bachelor. At the Waldorf. On New Year's Eve. Especially when he's a world-famous sportsball star."

A gulf of misgiving yawned beneath my ribs. "We should have eloped."

"Like *that* was ever going to happen. Stop that! Look at me. No. You are *not* going to ruin your mascara. Don't make me call the Sephora Dragon back in here!"

My laugh was shaky. I'd spent almost six hours in the

hands of the iron-willed stylist, submitting to a cuticle-shearing manicure, a pore-concealing mask, and more makeup than I'd worn in the rest of my life, combined.

Through it all, Aaron's mother, sisters, aunts, and cousins had cooed around me. Six of them were bridesmaids, dressed in gowns that ran the gamut from mushroom to parchment to champagne. I'd spent the better part of the past week with my soon-to-be family, enjoying a spa day the Thursday after Christmas, a family dinner on Friday night, the Saturday matinée of *Frozen*, an all-day brunch on Sunday, a day of shopping up and down Fifth Avenue on Monday…

By Tuesday morning—wedding day—I'd been *grateful* when my grandmother begged off from helping me get dressed. One fewer female relation in my face felt like a blessing. "Just skip lunch so your gown fits properly," Angel had said, pursing her lips over room-service coffee. "What?" she asked, in response to my exasperated huff. "I'm only telling the truth."

Brittany had kept me from ripping Angel a new one; she knew my grandmother well. She'd used the same diplomacy to finally drive my bridesmaids from the room where I'd been held hostage all afternoon. "I'm the maid of honor," she'd insisted, polite but firm. "I came all the way from DC, and I get five minutes alone with my best friend before she's yours forever."

Now, she dug through the detritus on the bed, finally coming up with her phone. "Come on," she said. "One last selfie, before you become Mrs. Aaron Henderson."

I made a face. Aaron and I had fought over my name for months. I'd finally given in last week, promising that I'd only keep Katie McIntyre on my *Press Box* articles. He seemed to think I'd be wrapping up my professional gig by the start of spring training. He was wrong, but it didn't hurt to let him think he'd won.

I caught my scowl in the mirror as Brittany thumbed her

phone to life. Before she could swipe to her camera, a dozen alerts flashed across the screen. "What the hell?" From her expression, alien spaceships must have materialized above the Empire State Building.

"What is it?"

Brit held up her hand, palm out in the universal sign for *Stop*. I craned my neck to see, but she angled the phone away.

"What's going on?" Annoyance was trumping my curiosity.

A head-shake this time, terse enough to pry a red curl loose from Brittany's hairspray helmet. She winced as she tapped the screen.

"Ooooh," came a moan that had nothing to do with alien spaceships. Well, maybe with alien probing… "Come on, baby… Give it to me, Santa! Give it to me hard!"

And then I heard a groan I would have recognized anywhere. I grabbed for the phone again. This time, Brittany let me have it.

For just a moment, nothing made sense. I was looking at my living room. At my leather couch. At my Christmas tree—eight feet tall, covered with colored blinking lights and dozens of ornaments, with an Instant Pot, a gravity blanket, and his-and-hers LL Bean boots still nestled beneath the branches because I'd been too busy with wedding crap to put away our gifts.

Our gifts. My gifts and Aaron's gifts. Mine. His.

My brain couldn't keep stuttering forever. I couldn't keep staring at the multi-colored lights, wondering why I hadn't put my foot down and said we needed white ones, plain ones, ones that didn't blink on and off like some manic video game.

I had to look at the woman sprawled on the rug in front of the couch. I had to look at the man plowing into her from behind—the man wearing a jaunty Santa hat and not a single stitch more.

Aaron.

"Katie—" Brit said, trying to wrestle the phone away. My fingers froze into claws.

I didn't answer. I just stared at the bobbing red hat and the tense white ass and the inevitable, porn-star-screaming conclusion.

The video started again, and Brittany finally succeeded in prying her phone free. She slammed off the volume and cut the picture before she tried: "Maybe it's a fake—"

"It's not a fake." A red-hot fuse kindled in my gut.

"Maybe it happened a while ago. Before he met you."

"It happened this week. After Christmas." I froze the fire before it could do any damage.

"Maybe…" But Brit couldn't come up with another lie.

My next breath sliced through my lungs. I pulled away from the phone, from the video, from something old and something new, something borrowed and something fucking blue.

Aaron had screwed a woman in our home, a week before our wedding. And he'd been stupid enough, or horny enough, or didn't-give-a-damn enough to record the whole thing. Or let the bitch record it. Whatever.

The frozen places inside me shifted and started to melt. But I needed that ice. I needed every sparkling crystal to hold my life together. I commanded my gel-polished fingernails to stop tearing crescent moons into my palms.

Lucky21. Juan Gonzalez, my ass. I had to hand it to Aaron. He was quick on his feet. And I'd bought the line about his teammate changing handles like a kid pouncing on a Mickey Mantle rookie card. Just like I'd swallowed his lie about the lipstick on his collar…

Lucky Fucking 21. The holiday elf begging for Santa's load hadn't seen twenty-one for a decade at least. And whatever surgeon had installed her triple-D snow globes ought to be sued for malpractice. Santa's Little Helper looked too top-heavy to stand.

"Come on," I said, stepping out of my Manolo Blahnik crystal-toe pumps. I gathered up yards of white taffeta and jammed my feet into the ratty Keds I'd worn to the hotel that morning.

"What are you doing?" Brittany asked, but she was already stepping out of her own high heels.

I looked around for my own phone. There it was, on the coffee table, with its sleek wallet case—a credit card, my driver's license, and an emergency twenty-dollar bill.

Well, this was an emergency. I grabbed it.

"Give me your phone." Brittany handed it over as I threw open the door to the suite. Aaron's oldest sister was bustling down the hall, her taupe bridesmaid's dress hiked up to her knees. "*There* you are," she said. "Mama was starting to w—"

I pushed past her without a word. I didn't have time for an elevator. Instead, I led Brittany to the stairwell. Three flights down. Out the door. Down the corridor.

I stepped into the ballroom, where every table was covered with fine china and polished silverware, ready for the guests to converge after the ceremony down the hall. Each centerpiece was a cluster of sweetheart roses gathered around an engagement photo of me with Aaron, along with one of our elegant letterpress invitations. Choking on a quick wash of bile, I grabbed one of the worthless invites.

The DJ stood at the front of the room, joking with three members of the band. I couldn't remember his name. We'd interviewed half a dozen guys for the job, and Aaron had chosen this one. He was the most expensive, of course.

"Ms. McIntyre," he said, straightening his tuxedo jacket the instant I stormed into view.

"Here," I said, shoving Brittany's phone toward him.

He took it by reflex. "What?"

"Play it."

"Um, play what, Miss McIntyre?"

I took a deep breath. Held it for a count of three. Felt the soothing comfort of ice stiffening my spine. "That phone has a video on it. I want you to play it on that screen. As large and as loud as you can make it."

The DJ shrugged. "I'll need a password for the phone."

"Brittany?"

"One, two, three, four," Brit said.

I whirled on my best friend. "Are you serious?"

Brit shrugged. "It's easy to type."

Back to the DJ. "One, two, three, four," I repeated.

He connected the phone to his computer with a cable that materialized from his tangle of sound equipment. "So, this is for your first dance with Mr. Henderson?"

"I want you to play it now."

He was confused. "Now?"

I eyed him steadily. "And start it over, when you get to the end. As many times as the family lets you." I dug into my wallet and came up with the twenty. "I wish I had more. Don't let them stiff you on your bill." I shoved the money into his palm before I dragged Brittany out the door.

A second ballroom at the far end of the floor was set up for the ceremony. My brother waited just outside, accompanied by the F5 tornado that was our wedding coordinator. Another Henderson family find.

"Katie!" Sean said, relief flooding his face.

"Sorry I'm late." I stopped short in front of him.

"Let's—"

"Nope," I interrupted. "Change of plans."

The wedding coordinator's gasp of horror ripped something free inside my chest, and I took my first full breath in weeks.

"What— Why—" Sean gulped before he trotted out his best older-brother tone. "You're not getting cold feet, are you?"

The wedding coordinator nodded like a bobblehead in a

hurricane. Her face spun into a frayed mask, equal parts impatience and knowing sympathy.

Sean *always* thought I was getting cold feet—when I changed my major, when I changed my college, when I moved to Springfield, and when I moved back home to DC. I hated his way of figuratively patting me on my head and telling me I'd grow up some day. He acted like he was thirty-six years older than I was, instead of six.

But this wasn't the time or place to dredge up all of that.

"No cold feet." I hitched up my skirt to show him my Keds. Wiggling my toes, I said, "In fact, my *feet* are comfortable for the first time all day." I reached out and straightened his boutonniere. He really did look handsome in his tux. At least Timothy would get to enjoy his husband out of hospital scrubs for one night. "Sorry to do this, but the wedding's off."

The wedding coordinator roared like a train. "The wedding is *what?*"

"Ooooh." A moan reverberated from the far end of the hallway. The DJ had a much better sound system than I'd imagined. Its vibrations freed something locked deep inside me.

"Sorry," I said, kissing Sean on the cheek. "Gotta run."

I grabbed Brittany's hand and we raced back to the stairwell. We laughed like kids playing hooky as we fled down the steps, squealing as we burst into the lobby.

I lost my veil in front of a line of hotel guests waiting to check in. I didn't wait for the uniformed doorman's assistance with the heavy glass and metal doors. Instead, I barged onto the street and pulled Brit behind me.

Paparazzi were waiting. Paparazzi were always waiting. "Katie!" one of them called, and then the entire pack started baying.

I paused for a moment, setting one hand on my hip and tilting my head to the perfect angle. I'd learned a lot in my time with Aaron.

But before the photographers could get their fill, I shoved the slightly crumpled invitation into the closest greedy hand. "Here's your ticket to the main event. Tell anyone who asks that you're a friend of the bride."

I took advantage of the confusion to dart in front of a businessman who was about to slip into a taxi at the curb. Before he could protest, I wrangled armfuls of white taffeta onto the seat, yanked Brittany in after me, and slammed the door.

"Where to?" asked the laconic driver. He probably had runaway brides tumble into his cab every day.

"Penn Station," I said. I closed my fingers around my phone, grateful I had a credit card to cover the train fare. Then I turned to Brit, who was laughing so hard she could barely breathe. "Sorry about that," I said. "I guess I owe you a phone."

1

KATIE

I sipped my sparkling water and huddled closer to the red-tinged patio heater, pretending the woman who approached was the most fascinating hostess in the world.

It was ridiculous for Heart Foundation International to host an outdoors fundraiser in March, in Washington DC. And it was *absurd* for the charity to partner with professional baseball, dragging a hundred players from the relaxed spring-training sunshine of Florida and Arizona to a formal dog-and-pony show in the nation's capital. But it was downright *outrageous* to position speakers at all four corners of the National Gallery of Art's terrace, blasting "You Gotta Have Heart" from *Damn Yankees,* over and over and over again.

I was going to hear the song in my nightmares. If I didn't freeze to death first.

The Foundation's president seized a heart-healthy tofu-dog from a passing waiter's tray as she exclaimed, "Katie McIntyre! What a pleasure!"

I should have been flattered. The polished executive could be reaping valuable donations by chatting up baseball's most eligible millionaires, not to mention the lawyers and lobbyists who were drooling over their sports idols.

But estrogen called to estrogen across the crowded terrace. I was being blatantly cold-shouldered by ballplayers who had been my friends just three months ago. Even my fellow journalists were giving me a wide berth, as if the jilting of Aaron Henderson might be contagious.

Contagion. It was on everyone's minds.

"Thank you," I said. "What a lovely view!" I gestured toward the Capitol, visible at the end of the terrace. The less said about the giant boulder—er, refined masterpiece of contemporary sculpture—beside me, the better. The rock, the pile of silver rods gleaming like a giant's game of Pick-Up Sticks, and the two-story-tall bright blue rooster… I was never going to understand modern art.

The director beamed. "We're so fortunate to get this event in tonight. I'm afraid our string quartet backed out at the last minute." She lowered her voice to a strained whisper. "COVID, you know."

That explained the endless Broadway chorus. I managed a sympathetic laugh. "As long as no one coughs, we should all be fine."

"Well, they canceled SXSW yesterday." The president frowned. "And I think Seattle's had a dozen deaths."

Great cocktail party banter. But the entire country *was* on edge. It felt daring to attend a party. Reckless, like a kid sneaking out past curfew.

"We'll get a handle on this," I said. "A couple of weeks of…what are they calling it? Social distancing. Flatten the curve, and we'll be fine."

What else was I going to say? *Hope you got toilet paper last week, because the shelves are bare now.*

Gamely, the charity director followed my lead. "Starting

on Monday, our people will be teleworking. But I guess you already do that, writing for *Press Box?*"

I should be pleased that she knew me as more than Aaron's plus-one. After all, I'd accepted the invitation as part of a couple, four months ago. A lifetime ago.

It was hard to believe how quickly life could change.

But I'd decided to attend on my own. I had every right to be at this party. And I might come away with the perfect scoop for a *Press Box* feature. Wouldn't *that* piss off Aaron, who'd never believed my writing was serious?

Besides, I had to venture back to the world of professional sports at some point. That, or find a new job. So why not make my return in my own hometown?

Right now, my ex was holding court beneath the giant chicken. A dozen of his buddies were flashing V signs and taking selfies as they juggled their microbrews.

So much for spring training. But the guys were still a month away from the regular season. They could cheat for one night. Not as bad as cheating on your fiancée. Ba-dump-bum.

Aaron's sex tape had gone viral after I dumped him. I'd heard that he'd spent a fortune getting the thing off a million servers, but the Internet never forgot. Now, I shifted my angle to block out Aaron and his jostling teammates, focusing instead on the foundation head. What were we talking about? Right. Working from home.

I started to make a breezy—if delayed—response, but I was cut off by the director's murmur. "Will you excuse me?" Then, before I could reply: "Senator! Senator Jackson! I'm so glad I caught you!"

So much for girl power.

I was left alone, clutching my glass of fizzy water like a lifeline. I didn't trust myself with alcohol—not tonight. Not at this first public outing since…New York. Not with Aaron surrounded by his crew.

Maybe I hadn't thought this through.

I felt like a gawky tween wallflower at a bar mitzvah party. At least I wasn't wearing braces. And I'd long out-grown my training bra.

I was more grateful than ever that I'd dragged Brittany to half a dozen stores until I'd found tonight's perfect dress—a strapless silk sheath, midnight blue, flowing all the way down to my ankles. I'd splurged on silvery sandals—no Manolo Blahniks, but *I'd* paid for them instead of relying on one of Aaron's guilty gifts.

Aaron. Again. There were dozens of other people at this party. I just had to find one of them to talk to. Gulping the last of my drink, I barely avoided disaster when the ice cubes tumbled to the rim of my glass.

The guys by the statue were getting louder. Some genius had just realized that *cock* was a synonym for rooster. They were clinking beer bottles and egging each other on to worse and worse puns.

Juan Gonzalez broke away from the pack. A couple of guys called out: "Get one for me! I'll have another!" Aaron added, "Count me in!"

Juan was heading for the bar, directly behind me. For a split second, I considered diving into the scrum of lobbyists by the boulder to avoid talking to him.

But I hadn't backed down from a fight since I was tall enough to reach the Band-Aids in Angel's bathroom medicine cabinet. I planted my silver-wrapped feet and drew myself up to my full height. My glass was ice beneath my palm.

A sudden silence fell over the partygoers. Maybe the speakers had finally burned out on their endless loop of "You Gotta Have Heart." Maybe there was just a natural pause in the ebb and flow of cocktail-party chit-chat. But it felt like the entire assembly—lawyers and lobbyists and baseball players and charity foundation hosts—had simultaneously caught their breaths, gawking at an accident about to happen.

I riveted on a smile and met the familiar dark eyes of Aaron's best friend. "Juan," I said, careful to keep my voice cordial.

"Out of my way, *puta*."

My spine stiffened, and I raised my chin. If we hadn't been the center of attention before he spoke, we definitely were now. I heard a car brake on Pennsylvania Avenue, three stories below.

"No need to do Aaron's dirty work," I said, glancing at the now-silent cluster of ballplayers. Sure enough, my former beloved was staring at us, his jaw set in the hard line I knew from every stupid fight we'd ever had. I told Juan, "He's a big boy. Picked out his own Christmas present and everything."

Juan sneered before the words were out of my mouth. "My boy wouldn't've gone shopping if you gave him what he needs."

"That's not f—"

Fair. I was going to say fair. But I didn't get the chance because Juan shoved past me, barely taking time to call over his shoulder, "Your free ride left the station, bitch. Game over, *coño*."

2

KATIE

Holy crap.

I translated the Spanish easily. Anyone who'd spent any time at all in a professional locker room could bridge the gap. In one minute flat, Juan had hit the trifecta: whore, bitch, and—without blinking an eye—the C word.

All three epithets drove me absolutely, freaking, bat-shit insane. They were only leveled against women—usually, women who stood up for themselves. Like *shrill* and *strident*, they were weapons meant to keep nice girls in their place.

I wasn't a nice girl. Something hard and hot ignited in my belly.

Juan's teammates were frozen beneath the rooster. Their mouths gaped in astonished Os. Their eyes bulged with excitement. The flames licked higher beneath my sternum.

No. *Most* of the guys were stock-still. But not Aaron. Aaron stood a little straighter. He narrowed his eyes. He nodded once, then jutted his chin toward Juan. *Thanks, man. Thanks for having my back.*

The fire inside me roared.

I threw a wall of ice around it. I had to block the flames. I had to keep myself—and everyone else—safe. I couldn't afford to be angry. Not here. Not in public. Not ever.

And what the hell did I care about Aaron's reaction anyway? I'd spent the last three months rooting out every remnant of Aaron Henderson from my life.

Okay. I'd wasted the first week, sleeping on Brittany's couch, indulging in a lifetime's worth of Ben and Jerry, mac and cheese, and gin and gingers.

But then I'd pulled up my big-girl pants.

I'd sent a formal letter to Aaron's agent—actual paper in a sealed envelope with a stamp and everything, sent certified, return receipt requested. I'd demanded my computer, my clothes, and the rest of my belongings. The guy must have realized I wouldn't hesitate to call every friend I had in the press because a dozen boxes arrived by overnight courier.

I'd found an apartment in DC, a sublet from one of my *Press Box* colleagues who was heading to Tokyo for a head-start on Olympics coverage. I'd filed a story the day I was supposed to return from my honeymoon in Fiji, and I hadn't looked back.

Until tonight. Until I caught myself hoping that—somehow, some way, some idiotic way—Aaron would take my side. He'd put Juan in his place. He'd *defend my honor*.

I snorted at my gullibility—an actual noise, scraping through my nose. Real ladylike. Angel would've disowned me if she'd heard.

Screw it. I could defend my own fucking honor. Clearing my throat, I offered a silent apology to Señora White, my tenth grade Spanish teacher. And then, with a flawless Castilian accent and precise Venezuelan vocabulary, I said, "*Chúpame mi verga inexistente, cabrón.*"

The crowd might not be fluent in Spanish, but they got the gist. Juan's fingers folded into tight fists, and his neck bulged above his starched white collar. I refused to glance toward Aaron. I was never making that mistake again. I felt the weight of hundreds of eyes, like a physical pressure crushing my windpipe.

"And that's a home run for Katie McIntyre!"

I was forced to glance toward the man who stood closest to the giant game of Pick-Up Sticks. Six-four. Two twenty. Dark brown hair, short enough to stay in place without gobs of sticky product. Scruff on his cheeks long enough to say it was intentional. His blue eyes looked almost silver as he took a single step toward me.

Jason Price. Southpaw closing pitcher for the Raleigh Rockets. I knew who he was, of course. Anyone who'd watched the Rockets' unlikely World Series win the year before knew the Professor.

But I sure as hell didn't need him saving my ass, here on the National Gallery terrace. Before I could say as much, the speakers flared back to life, twice the volume they'd been before. *"You Gotta Have Heart!"*

The damned Yankees broke the spell. Juan stormed over to the bar, holding up four fingers to request his bottled microbrews. One of the lobbyists hooted, staring at me like he'd just been given a Spanish-English dictionary. The Foundation director shot me a filthy look before she sidled up to a nearby judge.

I was shaking—just a little, like I'd done two Pilates classes back to back. A circle cleared around me as the party guests collectively decided I didn't exist. I took a deep breath. Another one.

And I realized I couldn't let it go. I couldn't let Juan get away with calling me a c—

"Come on, Killer." This time, Jason Price's baritone was pitched just for me. While I'd been watching my social life disintegrate into dust, he'd crossed the terrace to my side. "Walk it off," he said. "Take a win when you get it."

I whirled to put him in his place.

3

JASON

Well, shit. She sure as hell wasn't backing down.

Let her take on the entire New York team and half of DC's fundraising elite. No skin off my ass.

I shrugged and started toward the glass door that led to the elevator lobby. I'd already done what I could for HFI, making the rounds of potential donors, talking up the charity's cutting-edge science. After siding against Gonzales and the other New York jackasses, I'd just be a distraction for the rest of the night.

Time to head back to my hotel room. Raid the mini-bar for a nightcap. Dive into the books I'd picked up that afternoon, like this was any other night in any other city on any other road trip.

That's what I meant to do. But Katie McIntyre got to the door before I did, and all my good intentions vaporized.

She had one hell of a stride, even in those silvery sandals, with heels that looked like registered weapons. She held herself stiff as a statue, not looking left or right as she cut through the crowd. And she totally rocked her blood-red nail polish.

Her biceps flexed as she yanked the door open. "After you," she said, gritting out the words like a declaration of war.

Whatever. My manhood wasn't actually threatened by a woman holding a door. Once we'd cleared the terrace, she stormed around me and pounded the crap out of the button for the elevator. When it arrived, she let me go first there, too.

But she wasn't made of stone. I heard her deep, measured breaths, inhaling through her nose and exhaling through pursed lips painted to match the exact shade of her fingernails. I wasn't stupid enough to stare, but green eyes glared at mine in the watery reflection of the elevator doors, daring me to fuck up.

She didn't say a word until we stood outside, with the March wind whipping around a massive Henry Moore statue. A couple of photogs stood by the door, but this was DC. They were waiting for politicians.

Nonetheless, she kept her voice down as she led the way toward the street. "Thanks. You were right. Leaving was the right thing to do."

"Gonzales is an asshole. No scoop there."

She snorted a little, like one of those unbroken horses in a western movie. "Scoop?"

"Don't you write for *Press Box*?"

She seemed surprised. Most of the crowd upstairs probably knew her as the woman who'd handed Aaron Henderson his balls three months ago. But that was a shame, because last month she wrote a damn good story about that football quarterback rehabbing his broken leg. She hadn't shied away from the gruesome injury. Hadn't been sentimental, either.

She'd been professional and cool and efficient—exactly how she looked now, prying her phone out of her ridiculously tiny purse. She tapped the screen and muttered, "Dammit!"

"Got a problem?"

"My phone's dead. It hasn't been charging right."

I glanced toward Pennsylvania Avenue. There should have been plenty of cabs on a Saturday night, but not one was in sight. The virus was making everyone crazy.

She probably wouldn't let me put her in a cab anyway. That might resemble a sign of weakness. And she sure wouldn't let me call a Lyft. She wouldn't give up her home address that easily.

Suspecting I was in serious danger of being de-nutted on the spot, I said, "Look. I'm staying at the Monaco." I talked fast so she didn't have time to misunderstand. "The front desk'll have a Lost and Found, and you can borrow a charger. Let me buy you a drink while you wait. Prove that not all baseball players are jerks."

"I don't think all—" She cut herself off. I watched her try to come up with a better solution for her dead phone.

I said, "There's a cab stand in front of the hotel. You can get one there, if you'd rather do that."

I couldn't read her mind, of course. But she came to some decision, nodding once. "Let's go."

She didn't need me to lead the way. As we reached the first traffic light, she gestured up the empty street. "It's really weird. Usually, there are tons of people out here on a Saturday night."

The light changed, and I picked up my pace to match hers. "When I checked into the hotel, they upgraded me to the Presidential Suite. The manager said half their reservations have canceled."

She gave me a smirky sort of smile. "That must happen to you a lot. Upgrades."

I shrugged. "I usually travel with the team."

For the first time since she'd faced down Gonzales, she looked a shade less confident. "Wait. Are the other guys staying at the Monaco?"

I shook my head. "They're at the usual place, down by the ballpark. Bad habit, I guess."

"And you don't have bad habits?" She slowed her pace just a little and her lips curved into a taunting grin. She knew damn well what she was doing with her tone.

My gut tightened, and for a moment I imagined how it would feel to take down that fancy twist in her hair…

And get a hard knee to the crotch. She'd probably slam the heel of her hand into my nose for good measure, right before she jammed her fingers into my eyes. I knew damn well her teasing tone didn't give me the right to paw her like a souvenir from the museum gift shop. But I couldn't help where my Neanderthal man-brain went.

"I've got plenty of bad habits," I said easily. "But staying in a crappy hotel just because it's familiar isn't one of them."

She grinned again. "How enlightened."

We got to the hotel too soon. A trio of cabs waited out front, and I braced for a curt goodbye. But she glanced at the hotel's stylized sign and laughed—a single, amused bark. "You've got to be kidding me."

I followed her gaze. The hotel's bar was called Dirty Habit.

She turned away from the taxis. "Bad habit. Dirty habit. Close enough," she said. "One drink."

I detoured long enough to get a charging cord from the front desk clerk, and then we entered the bar together. Without asking, she headed toward the booth in the farthest corner. It was like she understood how to avoid a crowd of bat bunnies or—worse—a scrum of armchair pitching coaches who wanted to talk about how I'd hung a slider over the plate to that left-handed son-of-a-bitch…

Which, of course, she *did* understand. She'd been engaged to Aaron Fucking Henderson before she'd left him to the mercy of the tabloids.

I wondered how many times Henderson opted for the least

visible table. That didn't seem his speed. But she slipped into the booth, taking the bench facing out without my asking. The server came over to take our order.

"Club soda with lime," she said.

"Glenlivet," I said. "Neat." That made it easier to measure how much alcohol I was sneaking past spring training's restrictions.

The server started to walk away, but Katie called her back. "On second thought, I'll try a Rice 'n Roses. And could you plug this in behind the bar?"

I glanced at the menu card on the table as she handed over her phone. She'd opted for vodka and sake with lychee and rose. Sophisticated. And maybe a bit festive. For the first time since we'd left the museum, her shoulders weren't stiff with military precision.

"So," I said, after the server left. "Remind me never to make you angry."

Her eyebrows rose, making her look surprised. "I don't get angry."

"My mistake. You were just making cocktail party chatter with Gonzales."

"I was embarrassed. And frustrated. But I didn't lose my temper. I knew exactly what I was saying."

"Fine, then. Remind me never to embarrass you."

"I'm willing to bet there's nothing wrong with your memory."

Memory. She said *memory*. But the caveman part of me that already wondered what she'd look like with her hair down flexed and showed off like she'd told me I was ripped. I made a point of asking about her connections to Heart Foundation International, and we talked about nothing until the server brought our drinks.

Once we were alone again, I saluted her with my Scotch. "You've got one hell of a Spanish vocabulary."

She laughed. Her head tilted back and her neck stretched,

and Neanderthal-me wanted to say something else just as witty and entertaining. "My brother's first boyfriend was a Venezuelan exchange student. They had a…rocky relationship."

"Makes me wish I had a brother. I was stuck learning Spanish the hard way. *Mi burro es muy perezoso.*"

"Are you an only child?" she asked.

"Nope. I've got five sisters." I braced for the usual surprise, but she only nodded shrewdly.

"So that's where you learned to let a woman open doors for herself."

"If she wants to. Sure."

"Where are you in the order?"

"I'm the baby. Mom swears she and Dad would've kept going, if I'd been born a girl."

"Your *mom!* I thought fathers got hung up on that."

"You haven't met my mother. She wanted someone to keep her company at football games. Or baseball. Soccer, in a pinch."

"Where'd you grow up?"

"Killeen, Texas."

Somewhere between the first sip of her drink and now, she must have made a decision, because she raised her foot to my bench. She planted her toes next to my thigh, and her unblinking eyes told me she knew *exactly* what she was doing. "You don't sound like it."

"I'm on the road a lot," I said. "Nine, ten months a year. I never stay in one place very long."

I meant it as a warning. Just to make sure we were both on the same page. The words eased something in my chest, a tightness I hadn't realized was growing. And that wasn't the only tightness I felt. The zipper on my tuxedo pants felt like it was made of lead.

She reached across the table and dusted her fingernails against the back of the hand that held my drink. "That must be hard," she said.

Traveling. *Travel* was hard. My mind was in the gutter.

But she was flirting, too. That's what her fancy drink meant, what her foot was saying, what the hot little pads of her fingers were telegraphing into my hand.

"So tell me," she said, after matching the perfect lipstick print on her glass and taking another sip. "You've been a lot of places. What's the most romantic city in the world?"

She pressed her foot closer to my thigh, but her calm, green eyes said she'd heard my warning. I wasn't long-term-relationship material. But she wasn't backing off.

So I dropped the hand that wasn't holding my drink and curved my fingers around her ankle. "Hamburg," I said.

There was that bark of laughter again, short and sharp and smart like a fox. "Germany?"

I nodded, trying to look sincere.

"I have *never* heard Hamburg called a romantic city."

"What would *you* say?" I pretended to sound perplexed.

"Paris? Rome? Venice? Just to name three, off the top of my head. How is *Hamburg* romantic?"

"I was an exchange student there, when I was fifteen. I kissed my first girlfriend at Miniatur Wunderland. It's more than just the world's largest model train set, you know."

She threw back her head and laughed—really laughed—for the first time that night. The sound kicked another load of steel into the distraction between my legs. "Well if *that's* the standard we're using, then the most romantic place state-side is the parking lot behind the Vienna Inn hot-dog stand."

"Vienna?" I asked.

"It's a suburb of DC. Half an hour from here."

"Your first kiss was over hot dogs? Please tell me he skipped the onions and relish."

"Good girls don't kiss and tell."

"So you're a good girl?"

I waited to see how she'd play it.

Her foot shifted closer to my thigh. She picked up her drink and downed a quick swallow before pressing the pulse point in her wrist against the ice-chilled glass.

And the goddamn server came back to the table. If I were another kind of guy, she would have lost her tip as she smiled and asked, "Another round?"

Katie shrugged back to normal before I did. "Just my phone, please. When you have a chance."

Fuck. There was my answer—and I'd barely figured out the question I wanted to ask. But the lady had made herself perfectly clear. I pulled my wallet out of my breast pocket and handed over my room key to pay for the drinks.

Katie slid her foot to the ground. She positioned her glass precisely in the center of her cocktail napkin. She fiddled with her discarded straw, tying it into a single tight knot.

Neither of us said a word before the server returned. She placed the phone in front of Katie and the bill in front of me before retreating with a professional smile.

Katie stared at the black glass screen as if she'd never seen a cell before. She licked her lips. She glanced out the door of the bar, toward the hotel lobby and escape. "Jason," she finally said. "I..."

But she didn't end that sentence. And she didn't put her phone back in her purse.

So I decided to take a gamble.

I pushed my key card across the table. "Presidential Suite. Top floor. I'll get another key at the front desk and wait for you upstairs."

She stared at me as if I'd spoken a foreign language. Not Spanish. She had an excellent grasp of Spanish.

I climbed to my feet, grateful that the tent in my trousers had yielded to the idiot chance I was taking. I considered leaning over and claiming the kiss I'd been thinking about from the moment she knocked Gonzales flat on his ass.

But I minded my manners and kept my hands to myself.

And I kept my voice perfectly even as I said, “No pressure, Killer. Your choice.”

Still, my heart beat faster as I crossed the lobby to get a replacement key. I knew exactly how I wanted her to choose.

4

KATIE

No *pressure.*

Yeah. Right.

My most intimate contact in the past three months had been with my doctor, when I submitted to the humiliating STD test Brittany had convinced me was absolutely necessary. But I'd been turned on by Jason Price from the second he'd called me *Killer,* back on the terrace.

He'd backed me up there. And he'd given me space after, even when my idiotic phone ran out of juice. Half the men I knew would have used the opportunity to give me a sleazy invitation to their hotel room. "Just to charge up, heh, heh." Is that what they're calling it these days?

Nope. Jason had kept his mouth shut. And now I was more than a little obsessed with that mouth. With his lips anyway, how they crooked into a self-deprecating smile when he talked about Hamburg. And his hands too, his fingers flexing around his glass…

My breath caught in my throat.

Bottom line—I liked the look of him. Liked the idea of him. Maybe even liked *him*. On a practical note, I was pretty sure he'd know *exactly* how to drive Aaron out of my brain forever. And best of all? He'd already told me—no strings attached.

I picked up the key.

The elevator waited in the lobby, door open, a sign from the universe that I was doing the right thing. I swiped the key to bypass security and pressed the button for the top floor. I wasn't sure if the elevator caused my belly—or something notably lower—to swoop.

The room was labeled: Presidential Suite. I touched the card to the reader, and a light flashed green. I barely heard the mechanism trip inside the door.

Your choice.

I could still leave. I could take my recharged phone and get an Uber. I could go home and call Brittany and tell her all about this crazy night.

Screw that. I pushed into the room.

He waited by the window. He'd taken off his tuxedo jacket and hung it over the back of a chair, covering the collar with the folds of his cummerbund. He'd lost the shiny black shoes too, along with his socks. His feet were bare on the thick carpet. His shirt cuffs were folded back, crisp white linen underscoring the strength of his forearms. He'd stripped his tie straight, letting the black diamonds dangle on either side of his throat.

"I wish you hadn't done that," I said, as the door clicked closed behind me.

"Done what?" he asked calmly, without the smirking victory another man, Aaron, don't-think-about-Aaron, might have shown.

"Undone your tie," I said. "I wanted to do that."

He waited for me to cross the room. He let me drop my

purse onto the coffee table. He raised his chin, just a little, so I could trace a painted fingernail over the ridge of his Adam's apple.

I kissed him first. Leaning forward, I tilted my head to find his lips. The first touch startled me—his mouth was softer than I expected. A hell of a lot more welcoming. My surprise became a needy little mew that embarrassed me and almost made me stop.

But his palm spread across the back of my head, inviting me closer. I unlocked tiny muscles in my neck that I hadn't realized I was holding tight. His fingers spread, just enough to let me know he'd hold me steady. I parted my lips.

I'd been right. This man knew *exactly* what to do with his tongue. I shivered in reaction and gave him more access. Or maybe I shivered because part of me had been terrified to do this. Part of me had feared I'd never want to kiss a man again. That no one would want to kiss me.

A bubble of laughter rose from the same soft, swoopy space that had turned over in the elevator. He pulled away, just enough to touch his forehead to mine. "What's so funny?" he asked.

"I'm glad you skipped the onions and relish."

He laughed and pulled me close for another mind-searing kiss. This time, he strayed from my lips to find the pulse point below my jaw. He did something with the tip of his tongue that made me moan—actually *moan*—and when he scraped his teeth against the same tender spot, my legs began to tremble.

His hands were on my hips, then my waist, then spread across my back. He held me as I melted, as I pressed into him because he was what I wanted, and he made me feel so damn good.

I pulled his shirttails out of his waistband, discovered he was wearing an undershirt and liberated that too. His shirt was fastened with studs, not buttons, and my fingers fumbled the first one, the one closest to his throat. "I hate these things!" I said.

But he didn't help me. Didn't take away the fun, the feeling that I was unwrapping my very grown-up present.

The thought froze me. Present. Christmas present. Santa. I saw Aaron bouncing behind that woman, pumping her like she was a sex doll…

Jason's fingers folded around mine. His heart was beating fast but even, steady beneath the edge of my hand. "Katie," he said, and my name sounded like a lifeline.

There was an offer there, same as in the bar downstairs. I could step away. I could laugh and pick up my purse, head out the door to the elevator. No harm. No foul.

I shook my head, one tight twist to remember what I really wanted. Not what society expected me to do. Not what the tabloids craved. Certainly not what Aaron and his buddies thought—that I'd pine away for my asshole ex the rest of my natural life.

"I want to be here," I said, to myself and to Jason and to everyone in the world who thought they had a say in how I should behave. "I want you."

He grinned at that, a quick flash of hunter's teeth. I knew the expression—a confident athlete, certain of a win. "In that case…" He worked the stud easily, popped another one free, then pulled both the pleated tuxedo shirt and the smooth undershirt over his head, removing them together.

I glimpsed a scar inside his left elbow, a white crescent that stood out against his taut, tanned skin. He'd had ligaments repaired; I'd read about the surgery when he'd carried the Rockets to their World Series win.

I wanted to touch it. I wanted to touch *him*, all of him. To taste him. To feel him against me, around me, inside me. I pulled him toward the bedroom.

The man was good with a zipper. With buckled sandals

too. My strapless dress meant he didn't have to mess with a bra.

Which only gave him more time to pay attention to my breasts. He sat on the edge of the bed, knees spread, the black fabric of his trousers stretched tight across an impressive erection.

I stood in front of him, naked except for the simple black thong I'd offered up on the altar of Visible Panty Line. My breath was coming fast now, in quick, sharp pants, like a sprinter after a record-setting run.

He slipped his hands beneath the thin cotton edge at the back of my thong, cupping my butt and pulling me closer. He squeezed my ass as his lips closed over the tip of my breast. The dual sensations rocketed along my spine, igniting my nerves like wildfire. He sucked hard and I clutched his shoulders.

My knees quivered. His right hand splayed across the small of my back, anchoring me, giving me a base. His clever left hand slipped past the soaked triangle of fabric between my legs, stroking me, spreading me, finding my slick, swollen nub.

He switched his attention to my left breast, grazing the hard tip with his teeth. The hint of roughness sparked an electric line to the hot, wet pearl beneath his fingers. I shifted my weight and closed around his wrist, riding him hard. His fingers slipped inside me, curling, scraping, echoing the repeated rake of his teeth across my nipple.

"Oh my god!" I cried, crashing hard against his hand. "Oh, Jason… Oh my god…" Even as I tumbled into red-black velvet, I knew sex was never this easy. My body was never this responsive, even when I touched myself. But it certainly was tonight, with Jason Price.

He held me while I shuddered, waiting until my liquid legs could bear my full weight. But then, when I least expected it, he pulled on my breast again, lips and tongue and teeth teasing me, stretching me, shooting liquid heat into the single pulsing point of my nipple until I bloomed and spread into a second, even deeper orgasm.

My voice was raspy when I swam back to the surface. "Not fair," I said. "It's your turn."

His smile was lazy, even as his thighs tightened around mine, scraping my over-excited flesh with the taut fabric of his trousers. "No turns," he said. "Just what we want. When we want."

I wanted to see him naked. I wanted to curl my fingers around his cock. I wanted to feel him pumping hard inside me.

But… "I don't have a condom."

"Fortunately for both of us, I'm a little more prepared than I was in Hamburg." He climbed to his feet.

I watched hungrily as he crossed to the bathroom. I heard him rustle for something. A glass clanked on a marble counter.

When he returned to the bed, he displayed a strip of golden foil packets like an Olympic victor's laurel wreath. I took advantage of his occupied hands to relieve him of his suspenders and pants.

He wore boxers, black silk. I didn't waste time admiring the view. Instead, I added his underwear to the tangle of clothes on the floor. I pushed him back on the bed and tugged the first foil square from his fingers. I intended to put each one to perfect use, for all that remained of the night.

And that's exactly what we did.

5

KATIE

The smell of coffee filtered into my dreams. I rolled over and scrunched my pillow into a more comfortable position, stretching my toes toward the foot of the bed. Tiny protests whispered down my thighs, the long muscles protesting overuse.

Blearily, I opened my eyes and blinked hard to bring the nightstand into focus. The clock claimed it was 11:17. *Impossible!*

But bright light shimmered against the edges of the blackout curtains. And, looking out the bedroom door, I could see the suite's living room flooded with brilliant sunshine.

I pulled myself upright and felt the soft ache of well-worked abs. My dress was tumbled on the floor with Jason's tuxedo pants. I stepped over the tangle on my way to the closet. Sure enough, a white linen robe hung on a padded hanger, its belt tied in a professional square knot. Terry slippers glinted inside a plastic bag on the closet floor.

I shrugged into the robe but opted for bare feet. Running my hand through my hair, I made a much-needed trip to the bathroom.

After, washing my hands, my attention was drawn to the black leather Dopp kit on the counter. I peeked past the zipper and found a jumble of toiletries—shampoo in a bespoke translucent bottle emblazoned with a strong, masculine J, shaving cream and a travel razor, a monogrammed plastic box for soap. A transparent kit was ready for medical emergencies, complete with Band-Aids, Tylenol, and half a dozen pills in silver packets. I tried to picture Jason using the tiny sewing kit and failed miserably, no matter how nimble his fingers had been the night before.

A miniature tube of Crest stood at attention in one of the hotel's glasses, beside a collapsible toothbrush. I squeezed a blue-green line onto my index finger and scrubbed my teeth and tongue, rinsing the sink clean when I was done.

My grin in the mirror was bemused. A washcloth took care of the worst of my smudged makeup. My lips were soft and a little swollen.

Enough. Time to face the music. Men could be such wusses about hooking up.

Jason's legs stretched in front of him on the couch, and his back was cushioned by throw pillows. He looked up from a book. *The Meditations of Marcus Aurelius.*

Okay. Not what I expected from a major league pitcher. But since his nickname was Professor, I shouldn't have been surprised.

He'd pulled on his boxers, but every other inch of skin was on display. I favored him with a not-so-mock leer. "You seem pretty determined to keep us from checking out on time."

He laughed and nodded toward the Keurig on the kitchenette counter. "I left you one coffee. Room service should be here by noon. I ordered French toast for you, but I got an omelet if you want to trade."

I snapped a pod into the coffee maker. "What kind of omelet?"

"Egg whites," he said, rising from the couch. "Plain. With dry wheat toast."

Of course. He was still in spring training, no matter what (or who) he'd indulged in last night.

I wrinkled my nose as he settled his hands on my waist. "You can keep the omelet. But do you think they'll bring those little pots of jelly? I'd do anything for one of those."

I felt his laugh more than heard it as he leaned in for a kiss. "Anything, Killer?"

A sharp buzz interrupted my reply.

Jason pulled away. "Your phone's been going off like crazy for the past two hours."

"You've been up that long? Why didn't you wake me?"

His eyes glinted. "I figured I was the reason you were sleeping in."

Another buzz matched the wheezing of the coffee machine as the brew cycle finished. Doubt rippled through my gut for the first time that morning. What had Juan Gonzales done after we left the party? Had Aaron fed me to the tabloids?

As if Jason had read my mind, he said, "Someone at the gala must have tipped off the paps."

I grimaced and tapped the screen to collect my bad news. Notices scrolled down the glass, one after another. Brit had sent the last one.

BRITTANY

Good time to call?

But every other text was from Sean. My brother had texted me every ten minutes since 2 a.m., with the precision of a metronome. Each message was identical.

SEAN

Call me. Now.

I twisted my wrist so Jason could see. "Um, I think I need to call my brother."

He frowned as I punched the number. I wanted to tell him not to worry. Sean had never met a molehill he couldn't turn into a mountain. I still couldn't believe my brother was an emergency room physician. Washington Memorial could fuel the entire hospital off his nervous energy.

He answered on the first ring. "Katie."

"I had my phone off," I lied, trying to ignore the stab of nerves beneath my breastbone. *Sean was just being Sean.* "I just got your—"

"It's Angel," he interrupted. "Oak Grove called in the middle of my shift. She fell last night. Just after midnight."

6

JASON

Katie's expression changed in a heartbeat. One moment, she was an annoyed little sister, reporting in because her over-protective brother wanted to micro-manage her life. The next, she was a frightened woman, stammering out a series of incomplete questions. "Is she— I mean… Where—what happened?"

She reached behind her to find the arm of the sofa. Lowering onto the cushion, she clutched her phone so tightly her knuckles went as white as her robe.

That goddamn robe… When she'd walked into the living room, I'd figured it would take me about one minute to get her out of the thing. I could be generous—give her two minutes. Let her gulp half her coffee. But then I'd tug the belt that was already slipping free. I'd catch my hands in that hair that was so black it looked almost blue in full daylight. I'd bury my face in the curve above her hip, re-visit the sensitive spot

I'd found behind her right knee, and scrape my teeth along the inside of her thigh…

Shit.

Katie was finally clearing her throat, responding to whatever her brother had said. I stood by the coffee maker like a jackass, my underwear hiked in front of me like I was a fifteen-year-old boy.

I headed into the bedroom.

Whatever her brother's news, a reprise of last night was clearly off the table. Irritation crackled in Katie's voice. "Well, I can't change that now. Where should I meet you?"

So much for room service, too.

As Katie shifted to placating noises, I retrieved my duffel from the closet floor. Clean boxers. Faded jeans. A blue windowpane shirt, as much a uniform as the one I wore for the Rockets. I finished my camouflage with a generic black ball cap, pulling the bill low over my eyes.

I was dropping my phone and wallet into their respective pockets when Katie wrapped up her call. "Okay," she said, exasperation breaking the word in two. "Half an hour. No, I can't—" She swallowed hard and repeated firmly, "Half an hour, Sean."

I waited for her to end the call before I spoke from the bedroom doorway. "Bad news?"

"My grandmother. She fell last night and broke her arm. She's in assisted living, but they say she has to go to rehab before they'll let her back in. Sean says a nursing home isn't safe right now, because of the coronavirus. The hospital isn't safe either, and she has to get out of there *now*, and she can't come stay with me because I've only got one bedroom, so that means she has to go to Sean and Timothy's, but they can't take care of her, because who knows what Sean'll bring home from the emergency room, so I—"

She must have realized she was babbling, because she stopped mid-sentence. Closing her eyes, she lowered her phone to her lap. She took a single deep breath and exhaled on a count of ten, the same way she had in the elevator after pile-driving Gonzales.

When she opened her eyes, she was calm again. "Sorry about that." She stood and tugged her belt tight. "I guess this means you get the French toast *and* the omelet."

I laughed, because that's what she needed me to do. "Get dressed," I said. "I'll go downstairs with you."

"You don't have—" she started, but then she cut off her protest. "Thanks." She picked up her ridiculous excuse for a purse and marched into the bedroom, closing the door with a note of finality.

It didn't matter. It really didn't matter. Even if I'd gotten her out of her robe for a morning-after tumble, room service would have interrupted us. And after breakfast, I still would've had to hit the road.

Jen had a car coming for me at one. I was flying commercial back to Coral Crest since I'd missed the morning's charter flight, the one Major League set up to support its partnership with the Heart Foundation. At least the fundraiser meant we were playing a night game—almost unheard of for spring training. I'd get to the park on time if I left in the next ninety minutes.

I couldn't have spent the rest of the day in bed with Katie McIntyre, even if she weren't fielding a family disaster.

A knock at the door signaled the arrival of breakfast. Brunch. Lunch. Whatever. I waved the waiter in and let the guy roll his cart over to the table by the window. I passed, though, on the dramatic reveal of the meals beneath their polished silver domes. Instead, I dug around between the plates and glasses, picked up the black leather portfolio, and signed the bill, automatically adding a twenty-five percent tip. The waiter was heading back to the elevator by the time Katie opened the bedroom door.

Her dress looked fine after its night on the floor. I caught myself checking for the faint line of her thong as she retrieved her abandoned coffee, ankles rock-steady in her sky-high heels. When I found no evidence of the scrap of lace, I wondered if she was going commando.

She'd put on fresh lipstick. Done something with her hair too, twisting it to get it off her neck. She looked fresh. Composed. Like she'd actually gotten a full night's sleep, which was literally a fucking lie.

"Ready?" I asked, because one of us had to say something.

She nodded and led the way out of the suite.

Waiting for the elevator, she fiddled with her phone, tapping an app to summon a car. The door chimed, and she caught her breath in an exasperated huff before she punched the button for L.

"What?" I asked, because it seemed like I'd pretty much forgotten how to carry on a real conversation, the kind with complete sentences, including actual subjects and predicates.

She pursed her lips as we stepped into the lobby, and she stabbed again at the phone. "It says it'll take twenty-three minutes to get a car here."

I shrugged and followed her outside. "Take a cab." I opened the rear door of the first red-and-gray taxi waiting in front of the hotel. Before she could protest, I passed a couple of twenties to the driver through the front window.

"Jason—" she started, but I cut her off.

"Give me your phone."

I was a little surprised that she complied, and I tapped in my number quickly, before she could change her mind. Almost immediately, I felt the answering buzz in my pocket. "There. Call me when you get a chance. Let me know you're okay. That your grandmother is too."

"I'm sorry," she said, taking her phone back. "This isn't how I planned this morning to go."

"You planned this morning? I should have known." There. That's what I wanted to see—the defiant raise of her chin. I leaned in for a quick kiss, just a brush of my lips against hers, because we didn't have time for more. "Go," I said.

Hiking that indecent dress above her knees, she climbed into the cab. I was about to close the door and send her on her way, when I remembered I had one last thing to give her. I reached into my pocket and extracted the tiny jar of marionberry jam that had come with room service. "Hold onto this. It's down payment on a real breakfast."

She laughed as her fingers closed over the gold and glass. "Enjoy your omelet," she said.

"Where to?" the driver asked as Katie settled into place.

"2115 Kensington," she said. "In Arlington."

The driver nodded and shifted his car into Drive. I closed the door and gave the roof two staccato taps.

She didn't look back as the cab drove away. I somehow suspected Katie McIntyre didn't look back at anything. Or anyone.

Hunching my shoulders, I headed upstairs to eat my cold egg-white omelet.

7

KATIE

I ushered Brittany into the kitchen, keeping my voice low as Angel napped in the ground-floor master bedroom of my brother's McMansion. "Thank God you're here!"

"Let me get this straight," Brit said, setting a bag of groceries on the counter. "Your brother, an actual medical doctor, thought *you* were qualified to make dinner for your ailing grandmother. Has he even *met* you before?"

I scratched my temple with my middle finger, but my heart wasn't in it. Brittany and I both knew that nuking a frozen dinner was the extent of my cooking prowess. That, and pouring a bowl of cereal. Toast, in a pinch. If people liked it burned.

Sean's parting words that afternoon had been that Angel needed three square meals a day. Her recovery depended on it. Good food, good sleep, and assistance with all the activities of daily living, like getting dressed and using the toilet.

And with Sean potentially exposed to COVID in the

emergency room every day, there was no way he could provide those services. Timothy either, because he was exposed to Sean. So my commanding older brother had mandated a switch for the foreseeable future. Angel and I were living in a luxury single-family home in the suburbs, while Sean and Timothy holed up in my too-small-for-two sublet downtown apartment.

I'd waited until Sean's car pulled out of sight before I called in reinforcements. Brit could make a feast fit for a queen out of an egg, a fistful of wilted lettuce, and the scrapings from an almost-empty jar of peanut butter. Don't ask me how I knew.

"I'll get things under control by tomorrow," I said. "But today has been *nuts!* D-Day took less organization."

Brit laughed. "Come on! All you had to do was grab your phone and throw a few things into a suitcase."

"That's all *I* had to do. But Sean and Timothy packed like they were moving to Outer Mongolia. And we had to swing by Angel's place at Oak Grove to pick up her stuff. And Lucifer."

"Lucy!" Brit's face softened, and her tone went goo-goo ga-ga. "Where's the widdle sweetheart?"

"Napping with Angel. With any luck, my grandmother'll roll over and smother that hairless demon."

"How can you say that about the sweetest cat in the world?"

"In the fifteen minutes it took to bring Angel's stuff in from the car, that animal peed on my pillow, crapped on my purse, and puked on my jacket."

"Maybe if you called her by her *real* name…"

I didn't hate all cats. Just the ones who hissed at me for no reason. Who broke off their contented purring when I walked into the room. Who followed me with unblinking eyes, naked tail twitching as if I were a prize kill at the Serengeti watering hole…

I sniffed, still aggrieved. "Sean didn't even give me a chance to clean up my stuff. He told me to throw everything in the laundry room, and then he sent me out to buy Purell and Clorox wipes."

"Where'd you find those? I thought they were totally sold out."

"Yeah. Five stores later… Sean finally drove over to Memorial and took some from the supply room. He made me promise I'd gel up every time I come in the house. That, and a twenty-second hand-washing every two hours. I have to wipe down surfaces three times a day."

Brit laughed at the overkill. "I don't see your mask." Her voice was heavy with mock scolding.

I frowned. "He says we don't need them. The CDC issued some report saying they weren't helpful for regular people. Save the masks for hospital staff."

She smirked. "Everyone's over-reacting. In a week or two, everything'll be back to normal."

"Maybe… But Sean says he's never seen patients sick like this. And Angel…"

I wasn't superstitious. But it felt like bad luck to repeat what Sean had said. My grandmother had three strikes against her: the heart attack she'd had last year, her asthma, and her age.

It was hard to believe that when Sean was born, Angel had insisted fifty was too young to be called "Grandma." My parents had humored her when she chose her own nickname. It had stuck when Sean and I moved in with her twenty-two years ago, even if I consistently brought out her least angelic demeanor.

"Enough," I said, decisively changing the topic. "What's for dinner?"

Brittany settled a protective hand over the groceries. "Nope. You go first. How was the party? Did Aaron *die* when he saw that dress?"

I blushed.

I *never* blushed. Blushing was for shy, quiet girls who always followed the rules and never, ever… My brain flashed to Jason's tongue, hot and hard and slick.

"Oh my God," Brit squealed. "You fucked him!"

"Shhh!" I hissed, glancing over her shoulder toward Angel's room. "Not Aaron."

"Then who?" Brittany's stage whisper could have reached the last row of Rockets Stadium.

Before I could respond, my phone buzzed. I snatched it off the table mid-vibration. Crap. Just another text from Timothy. So far, my brother-in-law had sent photographs of the computer router in his office (each individual wire and switch annotated for my benefit), a screen capture of settings I was supposed to configure on my computer, and another listing of all the privacy options on my phone. He was a little obsessed with network security.

Oh goodie. I was supposed to make some changes to my laptop's DOS shell, whatever the hell that was.

And I thought I'd gone overboard, pointing out to Sean that the extra sheets for my double bed were in my hamper. And telling him he'd have to buy laundry detergent, because I ran out last week.

Brittany laughed as I put down my phone with an exasperated sigh. "No text from Mr. Good Times? Tell me it's not Juan. Please tell me you did not fuck Juan Gonzales."

"I did *not* f—"

"Katie?" The querulous question came from the doorway.

I scrambled to my feet. "Angel! What are you doing out of bed?"

My grandmother swayed on unsteady feet, awkwardly resting her good arm against the door frame. A splint swaddled her right arm from her palm to her elbow. She had to wait for the swelling to go down before they could make her a cast.

"I heard voices," Angel said. "I thought the boys were back from their camping trip."

I laughed uneasily as I guided my grandmother to the closest chair. "Nobody's camping, Angel. Sean and Timothy are staying at my apartment. We traded places, remember? So I can help you while Sean works at the hospital?"

Maybe her meds were off. The orthopedist said she had a low tolerance for pain, and he'd prescribed something pretty strong.

"I want Sean," Angel whined, turning his name into two syllables.

And people in Hell want ice water.

Angel always wanted Sean. He'd been her favorite from the second he was born; she'd barely noticed me, her second grandchild. She said Sean had an old soul. She said she could see so many stories in his eyes. They'd shared a gag-worthy bond even before Mama ran away. Before Daddy died.

Brittany stepped into the breach before I could dig up a patient answer. Smiling cheerfully, she said, "Hello, Mrs. McIntyre."

Angel's attention snagged on Brittany's tattooed biceps. "Are you the new girl?"

"Angel! You know Brittany. She's my best friend." My grandmother blinked. "The one who works at Two Girls and a Radish." Angel didn't seem to recognize the name of the upscale restaurant where Brit toiled behind the bar. "The one who makes donuts."

"Oh, donuts!" Angel said, with all the joy of a pre-tantrum toddler. "I love donuts!"

"Everyone loves donuts," Brit said. That's why she wanted to open a bakery specializing in the deep-fried treats. She was still in the planning stages, developing a full roster of signature items, both sweet and savory. So far, I'd put the kibosh on Mint Durian Cream and Chocolate-Glazed Chicken Pot Pie.

But I'd been an eager supporter of Brit's more mainstream efforts.

Now, Brit fished out a container with her latest trial flavor. My hand twitched toward my phone. Maybe I should call Sean, just to make sure Angel's disorientation was normal. But he was probably beat, snagging his own exhausted sleep before he headed back to the hospital for another all-night shift. And I was perfectly capable of taking care of things here.

But Angel's pupils were huge. And she really *didn't* seem to recognize Brittany…

Before I could make up my mind, my phone buzzed again. Timothy. I should double-check the privacy settings on all my apps and delete access to my location unless it was absolutely necessary for them to function. Good to know.

Leave it to Sean to marry the most uptight software designer on the planet. But they were happy together. And they *did* have a cool house.

I returned my phone to the table. I could handle this. Angel could snack on a donut. Brit would make us a real dinner. Then I'd get my grandmother settled back in bed, in hopes that she'd sleep through the night.

Brittany opened her plastic container with a flourish. "Ta-da!"

"Well, that doesn't look like any donut *I've* ever seen!" Angel said.

It didn't look like a donut I'd seen before, either. I recognized one of Brit's staples—a narrow Maple Madness bar, generously frosted and filled with vanilla cream. And those looked like her special Brandy Beach Balls, covered in a boozy glaze and injected with rich custard. But Brit had molded the three pieces into one before dropping them in her fryer. And she'd carefully rolled the Beach Balls in chocolate jimmies after they were glazed. She'd overfilled the Maple Madness bar, so it looked exactly like a rigid, spurting—

"Brittany?" I asked. "Can you help me get some plates?"

Brit popped to her feet with a cheeky smile. "Sure."

"This feels like a special occasion," I said. "Let's get something from the butler's pantry."

See? Another good thing about Sean and Timothy's home. It had a genuine butler's pantry, where I could drag my best friend, back her against the granite counter, and demand, "What the hell were you thinking?"

"I wanted to celebrate whatever happened at the party, *which you still haven't told me about.* You didn't fuck Aaron, and you didn't fuck Juan, so who—?"

Afraid that Brittany's volume control was dangerously close to breaking, I said, "Jason Price."

She gave me a blank stare. "Does that name mean anything to me?"

"He's the Rockets' closer."

"That's some important sports thing, right? Here we go again…"

"No," I said, resolute. "We aren't going anywhere. It was just a hook up. Juan was a supreme dick last night, and Jason had my back."

"Had your back…" Brittany gave a lewd grin. "I didn't think you were that kind of girl."

"Brit—"

"I'm not judging! If you'll recall, *I'm* the one who said you needed to get some." She dropped her glib tone. "Seriously. I hope this gets you over Aaron. You need to believe your career is worth more than some sportsball asshole."

What I needed was a best friend who didn't spend her spare time reading self-help books. But instead of complaining about Brit's compassionate insights, I just made a rude noise.

She said, "Whatever. You had fun?"

"Yeah." And there was another flash-memory, a ripple of sensation down my spine as I remembered what Jason had done with his fingers as I arched my back and pressed against his naked chest.

"Katie?" Angel called from the kitchen. "Can you bring another plate? It looks like Lucy's decided to join us."

Perfect. Because what could be better than sharing a dick-shaped donut with my best friend, my grandmother, and a devil cat? "I'm coming," I called, grabbing a stack of platinum-edged dessert plates.

"Is that what you said last night?" Brittany whispered with mock curiosity.

"Oh yes," I said as I herded her back toward the kitchen. "Multiple times."

As Brit began to unpack all the ingredients for a healthy, balanced dinner, I took a knife out of the drawer by the dishwasher. Dividing the obscene donut, I tried not to wince as pastry cream oozed from the wound.

8

JASON

I prowled from the garage to the kitchen, flexing my fingers and trying to stop the internal replay of my ninth inning breakdown. I'd given up a bases-loaded homer to Atlanta's clean-up hitter. We lost, six-three.

It didn't matter. It was just spring training. A chance to get into shape. Skip could look at the rookies, figure out who'd make the regular season team. As a veteran coming off a World Series win, I didn't have to worry.

Bullshit. I'd fucked up.

No one had looked me in the eye and said my head wasn't in the game. But I'd been the last guy to get to the park. I'd skimped on my standard pre-game routine—the stretches I did before I ever hit the bullpen. I couldn't get loose, no matter how many practice pitches I threw. The scar on my left arm itched like a mother.

The Mind-Fuck had me bad.

Spring training was always a bitch. I could manage a

week, two, three, staying in one place. But push it a few days more, and my concentration blurred. By the end of week four, I couldn't sleep through the night. Another week after that, and I lost my temper at stupid things, twitching like a dying eel when I had to carry on normal conversations.

When I was a kid, I was lucky; the Mind-Fuck hadn't burrowed into my brain yet. It only started in college, beating me down by the end of every quarter. But now that I was on the road for half of every baseball season…

It was like I'd lost my resistance to some disease. Drinking left me too fucked up to function. Screwing my brains out made me more hopped up than before. I could exhaust my body with exercise, but that only knocked the fucker out for a few hours.

The only way to truly break the Fuck was hitting the road. Getting in a car helped, but the real solution was flying somewhere. Something about the zombie shuffle of airport travelers, the hum of anxiety over late arrivals and canceled flights, the recycled air whooshing into high gear as a plane door closed… It was torture for most people, but it short-circuited my broken brain.

So, I should have been fine. The trips to and from DC should have reset my breaker. Now that I was back in Florida, standing in my own kitchen after a nine-inning game, I shouldn't be twitching like a worm on a hook.

Too bad my body hadn't received the message.

I reached for my phone. It was almost midnight, too late for the text I craved. I shouldn't be thinking about Katie McIntyre—about her badass attitude, her killer green eyes, and the sound she'd made when I circled my thumb around her c—

"Jason? You're home late."

I had to clear my throat twice before I could answer. "Jen?"

I dropped my duffel in the kitchen and stalked into the

living room, where my sister was rousing herself from the overstuffed chair beneath the reading lamp. She had a glass of that pink wine she liked, and the face of a serial killer leered from the true crime book in her lap. "Welcome home," she said, swinging her feet from the ottoman.

She wore her standard uniform—a white broadcloth shirt tucked into ironed khakis. Her straight brown hair was pulled into her ever-present ponytail. Her feet were tucked into—what did they call them? Ballet shoes? Something flat. Practical. She wore small pearl earrings.

I sank onto the couch. The reading lamp reflected off the sliding glass door, so I couldn't see out to the pool. "Were you waiting up for me?"

"Not really. I came over to drop off groceries and water the plants. The dendrobium was getting root-bound, so I took it out back to repot it."

"Dendrobium?" I asked, like I cared which plant she was talking about. She was the one who always wanted to make my Florida place a home. Raleigh, too. What did I care? I owned houses in both places, but I didn't need either one to look like a magazine spread.

"The orchid on the kitchen counter." When I shook my head, she said, "The one with purple flowers. And then, I had to trim the leaves on the peace lily." She forestalled my question by pointing to the monster in the corner, with its phallic white flowers and dark green foliage. "And then I saw that the ficus—" She waved at the tree. Why didn't she just say the tree? "—still has red spider mite, so I washed it down again."

"Thanks," I said. I didn't give a damn about the houseplants. But Jen did. And if she wanted to spend her time washing a dendrobium lily and repotting a spider tree, that was her prerogative.

"Yesterday's mail is on your desk," she said. "I paid the bills. There's an invitation to a golf tournament in San Diego, and the team sent information about the Blast Foundation gala."

"Thanks," I said again. The bills would be marked with her neat transaction numbers, red ink in the upper right corner.

"Mary Ann Dixon called."

She was the wife of my college baseball coach. She checked in once a month or so, keeping me in the loop on how Coach was doing. "Anything changed?"

"Not really," Jen said. "They started Stan on an experimental drug. She's worried the side effects will be too bad for him to stay in the trial."

Fuck lung cancer.

Jen slipped something from beneath the back cover of her book. "I bought a card for Dad's birthday. I already wrote a note from both of us. You just have to sign."

Jesus Christ. She'd trapped me, and she knew it. I had absolutely no intention of acknowledging our father's birthday, just like I had no intention of calling home, of going to visit, of doing anything at all that might be construed as making peace with my old man.

But I wasn't going to shit all over her efforts. She'd just need to go out and buy another card, one to send just from her. So I took the pen she handed me and scrawled my name at the bottom of her note.

"You're a pain in the ass," I said, passing the card back to her.

"That's why I'm your favorite sister."

I blew air through my lips, but I didn't contradict her. Instead, I leaned my head against the back of the couch and stared up at the ceiling. "I carried the tux home with me. It's in my bag."

Usually, I shipped clothes back to the house—to Florida for my rare trips during spring training, to Raleigh during the regular season. If I was going to be on the road for more than a couple of days, Jen sent clothes on ahead. I liked to travel light.

"I'll drop it off at the cleaners tomorrow," she said. "There are mangos in the fridge, and I cut up a pineapple." I could see into the kitchen, where she'd also filled the fruit bowl on the counter. Oranges and just-ripe bananas and those apples I loved.

Everything seemed normal. Like newspapers weren't screaming about the pandemic, acting like zombies were stalking the streets of Coral Crest. Like guys weren't standing around the locker room, spouting rumors they'd heard, that Arizona was shutting down the Cactus League, that all of spring training was about to go on ice.

I caught myself scratching my scar again. Taking a deep breath, I told the Mind-Fuck it could go to hell.

"How was your flight?" Jen asked without a hint of criticism, even though she must have scrambled for my reservation after I missed the morning charter.

She had to wonder why I'd changed plans. Despite all appearances to the contrary, Jennifer Price Parker *was* only human. But in the seven years she'd worked as my assistant, Jen had never asked a single question about my personal life.

And I'd returned the favor.

It had to be rough on her, widowed at twenty-five when the husband everyone thought she should have dumped in high school was crushed by his ATV. No kids, no cash, no career—unless you considered working in Accounts Receivable at Dad's factory a calling.

She'd volunteered to help me for a couple of weeks when I had to fire my first assistant for selling unauthorized memorabilia, and the arrangement had stuck. I paid her a generous salary, along with health, dental, and vision. She got four weeks of leave, but she only took it off-season, between October and February. I paid for her Subaru Outback.

The system worked for both of us.

"Strange," I said, finally answering her question about my flight. "National was a ghost town. No lines at security, and the plane was only half full."

"This virus thing. It'll get worse before it gets better."

Her voice was completely noncommittal, but I caught her quick glance toward my knee. I realized I was drumming my fingers there, tapping out a quick rhythm in triplets. Goddamn Mind-Fuck. I forced my palm to lie flat on my jeans.

She went on, as if she hadn't noticed. "The lines were long at Publix. People were stocking up like they were about to ride out a hurricane."

Before I could respond, my phone pinged. I wasn't sure which of us was more surprised. I always kept it set to silent, but I'd wanted to make sure I didn't miss a text from Katie.

My gut tightened as I pulled the cell from my pocket. If it wasn't Katie, I didn't care who wanted me after midnight. And if it was Katie, I didn't want to respond in front of Jen's perceptive eyes.

202 area code. Katie.

Jen picked up her glass of wine and her book. "I'll leave you to it," she said.

"Want to sleep here?" I asked, because she kept a room at the far end of the house, and that was the polite thing to ask, and because my phone was burning a hole in my palm, and if I didn't start typing back now, right now, Katie was going to think I was asleep, or out with the guys, or that I didn't give a damn.

Jen shook her head. "Looks like you could use some privacy."

My phone pinged again, the built-in reminder sounding like a gong.

"I'll get your tux on the way out," Jen said.

I thanked her, but my eyes were already on my phone as she headed out to the apartment I rented for her, the two-bedroom she said was more space than she needed. I barely heard the Outback's engine start up.

KATIE

That last pitch was down and in. No way Ruiz should have gotten to it.

She dove right in, like we'd been carrying on a conversation for hours. But the last thing I wanted to talk about was fucking up the game. I considered putting my phone away and falling into bed like a good little boy. Instead, I stretched out on the couch and typed:

JASON

I was distracted, thinking about how you looked when I

—

Asshole move. I backspaced and tried again.

JASON

How's your grandmother?

Fine. Sort of. Broken arm, two bones.

I sucked a quick breath between my teeth. Sounded painful for anyone, but for an old lady…

JASON

Compound?

No. She's lucky, I guess. Cast in a week. I'm staying with her at least until then. At my brother's.

2115 Kensington. In Arlington. Not that I was a stalker or anything. I typed quickly to prove I could be a compassionate friend.

JASON

You must be exhausted.

Too wired to sleep.

My brain suggested a number of diversions, and my dick weighed in with immediate approval. Before I could be a jackass, though:

KATIE

BRB

I waited a minute. Then a few more. I began to worry, thinking about everything that could go wrong with an elderly patient in the middle of the night. I started to tap the phone screen, to call Katie, but if something really bad was happening, I didn't want to distract her. I forced myself to count prime numbers, to distract my Mind-Fucked brain.

I'd just gotten to 157 when the three floating bubbles finally danced on my screen.

KATIE

Sorry about that.

Everything okay?

Angel's cat was screaming down in my room.

Poor pussy. No, I wasn't going to type that. What sort of dickwad would even *think* that?

JASON

The cat's okay?

The cat is a jerk.

Bubbles floated before I could type a response.

She peed on my pillow.

More bubbles.

She puked on my coat.

And it's not just the cat.

I made coffee.

Not coffee.

For company.

Makes triple espresso masochists.

Macaroni.

MACCHIATOS.

Doesn't make coffee.

Spilled water all over counter.

Almost electrocuted myself.

Brit laughed at me.

Angel laughed at Brit.

Angel couldn't get to the bathroom.

Arm in sling.

Angel wet pants.

S and T have 3.5 baths.

2 rolls of toilet paper.

In entire house.

Went to store.

No TP in all DC.

Time to ration.

Angel sleeping in S and T's room.

Guest room in basement.

Guest room smells like cat pee.

Need to hear Angel.

Worried she'll need to pee during night.

Sleeping on rock hard couch.

Or trying to.

Crick in neck.

Too much caffeine.

Don't usually talk about pee this much.

I shouldn't be laughing, but I couldn't help it. Not when I knew she had to be reasonably safe and secure—if overwhelmed—or she wouldn't be typing to me in the middle of the night.

JASON

Go pee.

And then, after a minute:

KATIE

I'm back.

Can I call you?

Can't talk. Don't want to wake Angel.

I wanted to hear her voice.

I wanted her to know that I felt bad she'd needed to leave before breakfast. I wanted to say that if I'd had a choice, I would have spent the rest of the day with her. I wanted to tell her I didn't hook up with just anyone. At least I usually took my dates to dinner. Got to know them over a rare steak and a decent bottle of wine.

But I typed:

JASON

Got it. Can you get some sleep now?

???

Try.

I will.

Thanks for listening.

Any time.

Night.

Good night.

I waited for more bubbles to surface. I wanted her to type something else, but I had to admit it was probably best that she didn't. Maybe she actually *would* fall asleep on the rock-hard sofa. Maybe everything would be better in the morning.

Well, there was one thing I could do to help with that.

I opened the long-running message thread I kept with Jen.

JASON

Pls send a mega-pack of toilet paper to 2115 Kensington, Arlington VA. Overnight delivery.

I was already in my bedroom when my phone pinged. For just a moment, I thought it was Katie. Maybe she'd found a corner of the house where she could talk without disturbing her grandmother.

Of course, it was my sister.

JEN

Extra soft or extra strong?

Katie was both.

Jesus. Last night must have melted whatever excuse I had for a brain. What the hell was I thinking—comparing Katie to *toilet paper?* If the guys on the team found out about this, I'd never hear the end of it.

JASON

Soft. Thx.

Katie McIntyre was strong enough for anything.

I stripped to my boxers and climbed into bed. Half a dozen books sat on the nightstand, each holding a brightly colored bookmark. I started to reach for the top one but changed my mind and turned out the light.

As I settled onto my pillow, I realized the Mind-Fuck had finally retreated.

9

KATIE

I woke up with a sick lurch at 6:07 on Monday morning.

I'd barely slept since turning my light out, well after one a.m. I kept slipping into weird half dreams, where endless blue windows scrolled up my phone screen, each one filled with a text about pee.

That was me—sex goddess extraordinaire. Swear like a Venezuelan sailor at a fundraiser gala, do my impression of a nymphomaniac on a prison day pass, then text about pee for half an hour straight. It didn't *get* any sexier than that. At least I hadn't launched into a diatribe about getting my period.

Thank God Jason was just a hook up. He was part of getting over Aaron, like the ice cream and carbs and liquor Brittany had poured down my throat the week after we got back from New York.

With that justification devoutly made, I was half-way back to sleep when I remembered *Press Box.* With all the chaos of settling into Sean and Timothy's house yesterday, I'd completely forgotten about my job. I needed to email my editor and beg permission to work from home for a couple of weeks.

Maybe I'd accidentally forgotten on purpose. I'd only been working for Martin since I'd relocated to DC. He was a pain in the ass about bending the rules, especially when it came to office absences. He remained unswayed by arguments that it *was* 2020, that articles could be written anywhere, and that *Press Box* technology was clearly up to the task of supporting telework. He definitely didn't care that my prior editor had regularly let me work from home.

It turned out, though, I didn't have to plead. Email waited in my inbox, from Martin's boss.

From: Peter Chatham, Editor-in-Chief

To: All Staff

Re: Telework

Due to the emerging coronavirus, all Press Box employees who can complete their work from home are expected to do so, effective immediately. IT is available to assist you with uploading and using our enterprise license on the Zoom platform for cloud meetings. At this time, no deadlines are shifting. We will continue to provide our usual high quality content to help our subscribers during this difficult time.

That was the last time for hours that I thought about Martin, *Press Box*, and my article about a new tennis phenom from Madagascar, because Angel called out from the master bedroom.

She didn't *call* exactly. It was more like she moaned. I was instantly on my feet and in the bedroom.

"Angel?" I asked, approaching the bed. I'd ensconced my grandmother like an empress the night before, building one wall of pillows to cradle her back and another to block her from twisting onto her side as she slept.

A sharp hiss came from Angel's knees, followed by a guttural yowl. Lucifer leaped from the comforter to my feet, narrowly missing an eighteen-claw landing.

"Jesus!" I shouted.

"Sean?" Angel's voice emerged from the mountain of pillows, tiny and quavering, like a child confronting every monster that had ever lived under a bed.

"It's me, Angel. Katie."

"I want Sean."

Yep. Got it. "Sean's at work, remember? You and I are staying here for a few days, until you're ready to move back to Oak Grove."

I crossed the room and pulled open the blackout curtains, figuring a little sunshine would help orient my grandmother.

"There we go," I said, shoving fake cheer into my voice. I turned back to the bed with an equally false smile and reached for the covers. "Let's get you up and into the—"

I stopped dead.

It wasn't just the *sight* of Angel, cowering against her pillows. She looked like she'd lost ten pounds overnight. Her damp hair clung to her scalp, sweat turning silver to dirty gray. Her cheeks were sunken, and her lips barely registered as thin, liver-colored lines.

And it wasn't just the *sound* of my grandmother. Angel whimpered in the glare of the sunlight. She seemed helpless and afraid, her little cries smothered by rapid, open-mouthed panting.

Mostly, it was the *smell* that rose from beneath the covers. It didn't take a nursing degree to figure out that Angel had been doubly incontinent during the night.

"Holy—" I cut off my exclamation when she cowered. Instead—heart pounding but determined to show I wasn't upset—I said, "You poor thing! Why didn't you call me?"

"I didn't want to bother the nurse."

My heart twisted at my grandmother's confusion. "There's no nurse, Angel. Just me."

"Katie…"

"That's right." My mind was racing. I needed something to cover her splint in the shower. And there was no way Angel could stand unassisted against the spray of water. I'd have to go in with her. Even then, she'd need a place to sit… "Can you wait here?" I asked. Then, remembering Sean's final instructions the night before, I said, "Let me get your pills, and then we can take care of everything else."

The medicine was jumbled on the bathroom counter where I'd left it the night before. I read all the labels, triple-checking against a note in my brother's angular handwriting to make sure I had the right meds at the proper dosages. I filled the convenient toothbrush glass at the sink and then watched my patient swallow each pill.

Angel's throat worked hard, even with the water. When she'd finally managed the last tablet, I said, "Drink the rest of that water. Excellent. Now give me a moment to get everything organized?"

Angel gave a tentative nod. I walked double-time to the kitchen. A trash bag could cover the splint. I could bring in one of the aluminum chairs from the back deck…

A blood-curdling yowl froze me on my way to the sliding glass door. Lucifer crouched on the center island, hairless back arched, ridged face stretched into a spitting frenzy.

I recognized a priority when one screamed at me. Cans of cat food were stacked beside the toaster, where Sean or Timothy must have left them. I pulled the ring on the closest one, instantly silencing my mortal enemy. The stench of Salmon Soufflé was nearly as repulsive as the mess in the bedroom. Lucifer pounced from the center island like a lioness bringing down a gazelle. I snatched my hand back before it became part of the kill.

One crisis averted. And Angel looked slightly better when I came back to the bedroom; either her meds were kicking in, or the glass of water had taken the edge off her dehydration. Still, it took more than an hour to accomplish a splint-protected shower.

Breakfast came next—a scrambled egg and a slice of buttered toast. The egg somehow ended up both runny and burned, and the rock-hard butter tore the barely browned toast, but none of that mattered because Angel spilled half the food down the front of her clean shirt, then declared she was full. Desperate for coffee, I settled for tea, because I couldn't face doing battle with the leaking coffee-making Terminator on the counter.

Next came the sheets. Wrestling the heavy Egyptian cotton off the gigantic bed, I felt like Cinderella. At least the mattress pad had done its protective job. I carried the bundle into the laundry room, where I tried a dozen different combinations of arcane settings before I got the washing machine to work.

I was lucky that Angel was content to sit on the couch that had served as my granite bed. She stroked Lucifer with her good hand, carrying on a one-sided conversation with the cat, who purred loudly enough to drown out the talk show on TV.

Taking advantage of Angel's distraction, I headed back to the bedroom. I opened the windows to let in some cold spring air. Clean sheets were in the linen closet, and soon I was clambering over the bed, trying to stretch the fitted sheet over the extra-deep mattress. Two seams ripped, but I couldn't bring myself to care.

Narrowly averting yet another disaster, I took care of Lucifer's litter box in the laundry room, scooping clay clumps into a plastic bag. The cat was already making a deposit in the bed of gray litter by the time I finished washing my hands.

Swearing under my breath as I realized how late it was, I hurried down to the basement to retrieve my computer from the guest room. I was hours behind schedule, but I still took a few minutes to douse half my worldly possessions with Nature's Miracle, trying to banish the stench Lucifer had created the day before.

When I finally checked in at work, I found that Martin had sent me a new assignment—an article comparing the current virus outbreak to zika and the Brazilian Olympics. He'd already sent two follow-up emails, each more urgent in tone than the last.

Exasperated, I replied to the most recent message, saying I would start my research immediately. The lie made me feel like a little kid. I remembered how Aaron used to patronize me when I told him about work, like he was patting a toddler on the head in thanks for an imaginary meal cooked up in Barbie's dream kitchen.

Screw that. I skimmed the other updates in my inbox, mostly from wire services.

Basketball was heading toward playoffs. Hockey, too. College hoops was frantic with conference tournaments. I skimmed a dozen stories I didn't have time to study in depth. Then one reached inside my belly and twisted, hard.

Can Rockets Reach Again?

The usual pre-season hype was illustrated with a photo of Jason Price.

I'd seen the picture before. He was throwing his final pitch of the World Series, a curveball that broke hard at the last possible second. His entire body was extended—left toes dug into the rubber, right foot landing halfway down the mound. His left arm stretched behind him, the ball caught between his fingers. His gloved right hand reached toward the mound.

It was baseball. But I'd felt that same perfect balance as he hovered over me in bed, every muscle ratcheted tight, every nerve firing as he held back, waiting for me.

The phone rang.

Not my cell, the landline. I was so surprised that it took me a moment to find the handset on the far nightstand. I reached it just as a third ring cut off, halfway through.

As I closed my computer and headed upstairs, my stomach rumbled. A quick glance confirmed it was almost 1:00. I'd been awake for seven hours, and all I'd accomplished was a shower, a nearly inedible breakfast, and making a bed.

"I told you, dear. I'm fine," Angel was saying into the phone as I returned to the living room. "You worry too much."

And she *did* sound fine—calm and reassuring, with the acerbic bite I expected from the woman who'd raised me. Maybe she'd just been exhausted earlier. In pain, too. She was on new meds. No wonder she'd been a bit confused. Anyone would be.

The next two weeks couldn't possibly be as bad as this morning had been.

"She's right here, dear. Just a moment." Angel handed over the phone with her customary little frown, as if she'd bitten into a scone expecting sweet apricot preserves and encountered orange marmalade instead. "Your brother," she said.

"Sean." I spoke into the phone, hoping my tone hid my apprehension.

"What the hell, Katie?"

I gave Angel a tight smile and shouldered the handset, moving into the kitchen for some semblance of privacy. "What's wrong?" I asked, risking my right hand to shoo Lucifer off the kitchen island.

"You had *Brittany* over last night?"

My brother had hated Brittany from the moment they'd met. She and I had been seniors in high school and he was in his second year of med school when she asked him to forge a doctor's note to get her out of an English Lit test. She'd told him to write that she had a raging case of creeping neogophilus, and he'd gone ballistic at the idea that anyone would invent pretend diseases when people were dying of real ones every day.

Fun times.

I defended my friend now. "She came by to fix dinner. And she brought a donut to um, cheer up Angel."

"Forget for one goddamn minute that no one needs to eat those fat bombs."

"I—" I tried to interrupt but Sean was on a roll.

"I didn't give up the comfort of my home for you to hold a circus for our immuno-compromised grandmother."

"I wasn't holding—"

"How many people come into Brit's bar in a single hour, Katie?"

"It's a restaurant, not—"

"And she probably took Metro to the house. Who stood next to her on the platform? How many people were in her car? How close did people get on the escalators?"

"Sean, I know you're worried—"

"It's here, Katie. This virus isn't just some story that's going away in twenty-four hours."

"You said if we washed our hands for twenty seconds, Happy Birthday—"

"That's not enough. Don't go out unless it's absolutely necessary. Don't bring anyone in. That's the only way to flatten the curve."

I followed the news. I knew that limiting exposure was the key to spreading out demands on the medical system. On hospitals. On doctors like Sean.

The government hadn't made anything official yet. But Sean had been in Memorial's emergency room for the past week. He might know even more than the government. After all, he'd moved his husband into my dinky apartment to keep Angel safe. To keep me safe, too.

"I'm sorry," I said, meekly.

"Promise." Now, he wasn't angry. He was tired. And maybe, just a little bit, scared. And that made me terrified.

"Yeah," I said. "I promise."

"So how's Angel really doing?"

I could tell him about the chaotic morning, about jumbled meds and soiled sheets and a killer cat who would just as soon devour my toes as curl up next to her mistress. But Sean was coming off a shift, and I was a grown-up who could handle a few setbacks, and really, what was he going to do if he knew? So I told him everything was fine and I had everything under control, and he really, truly didn't have to worry.

After I hung up the phone, I set about making lunch, trying to convince myself I'd told the truth.

10

KATIE

Monday afternoon went more smoothly than the morning, mostly because Angel napped and I was able to call into my meeting with Martin on time. Dinner was soup out of a jar, some organic blend from Sean's pantry, with a hand-drawn label and vegetables I'd never heard of. I would have been perfectly content with Campbell's chicken noodle.

Angel went to bed early, but I spent the evening scrolling through my newsfeeds obsessively. Rudy Gobert had flipped out at a basketball press conference, licking all the microphones and saying the virus was a hoax. The clip had already been turned into a dozen memes.

I thought about calling Jason. Or texting him, at least. But that would force me to confront the Great Pee Debacle. What the hell had I been thinking?

But that was it. I hadn't been thinking at all.

Instead of calling, I gave myself a pep talk. We'd hooked up. We had some good—*great*—sex. We'd blown off a little steam. That didn't mean I had to follow him around like a lovelorn groupie.

Besides, he was perfectly capable of texting me.

I fact, I wouldn't text back, even if he reached out first. I wasn't falling for another ball player. Not after Aaron.

I finally set aside my phone and tried to fall asleep on the couch. I'd padded it with the comforter from the guest room, but Lucifer had wasted no time expressing her disapproval of my decorating skills. At this rate, I should buy stock in Nature's Miracle. At least I got my exercise in, sprinting to the washing machine three separate times when the drum was set off-balance by the heavy load.

Just another perfect night in paradise.

I was practically a zombie on Tuesday morning. Wake Angel. Rejoice in clean sheets. Get her showered. Get her dressed. Breakfast. Plant Angel in front of the TV. Retreat to the kitchen to stare at my computer, too exhausted to *read* hard-hitting journalism, much less write it.

Brittany called half-way through my cup of milky, disgusting tea.

"I know exactly what you should do," she said, as if we were already in the middle of a conversation.

"Clone myself before Martin sends me a pink slip?"

"Whoops! Can he see you're on the phone now?"

"Only if he's spying through my computer's camera. We're working from home for the duration."

Brittany gave a low whistle of appreciation. "That must drive Mr. Stick-up-his-ass crazy."

"So far, he's checked in three times, demanding immediate responses to idiotic questions. I guess that's his way of making sure I'm not blowing off my work." As if to prove I was telling the truth, my computer pinged with a new email.

"What's he want this time?" Brit asked.

I checked my inbox and groaned. "That wasn't Martin. I think Timothy's having a breakdown, now that he's seen the half-ass computer set-up at my apartment. He just sent an article about the dangers of Trojan horses."

She perked right up. "Trojans?"

"Horses. You know, the computer thing. Like I've got time to read every article he sends me. I barely managed to get breakfast on the table before Martin was filling my inbox."

"I hope you stayed in your safety zone and poured a couple of bowls of cereal."

"I beg your pardon!" I feigned true insult. "I'll have you know I made fried eggs and toast!" Brittany didn't have to know the eggs had resulted in a previously undiscovered form of rubber, or that my efforts to avoid yesterday's barely warm toast had yielded today's charcoal bricks. My computer dinged again before I had to confess or lie.

"Timothy or Martin?"

I checked. "Door number three. Sean. He's been sending his own reminders, about hand washing and Clorox wipes and taking Angel's temperature every two hours."

"Overkill, much?"

"Well, she's running a fever, but it's under a hundred. He's pretty sure it's just a response to the broken arm, but he doesn't want to take any chances."

"Yeah. Or maybe he's a paranoid control freak."

I winced. "So now is as good a time as any to say he doesn't want any visitors in the house. Um, including you."

Brit laughed. "Right! Because you should totally be trapped there on your own, without even a donut to make things better."

No reason to tell her what Sean had said about the health attributes of Brit's prized creations. "He's serious."

"He just hates me because of the creeping neogophilus thing. You're not *listening* to him, are you?"

"It's his house. And he is a doctor. I mean, *I* think it's ridiculous…" I trailed off. I *had* thought it was ridiculous. But the more I read panicked reports online, the more I was beginning to think the virus was actually a serious threat. The Ivy League had canceled its basketball tournaments. Sure, they couldn't hope for more than a twelve-seed next week, but it was chilling to think they'd drop out of the March tournament completely.

"I bet you'd open the door for Jason Price," Brittany said with a sly twist to her voice.

"That would require Jason Price to fly up here from Florida."

"Have you asked him to?"

"Of course not! He's a *baseball* player," I said. And then I remembered she probably wouldn't know the significance of the calendar to a Rockets pitcher. I risked sounding like I was explaining to a two-year-old. "He's in the middle of spring training."

"But you've talked to him."

"Not exactly. We texted Sunday night. But after that, nada." I made sure my voice was casual. "I was just using him for his body."

"I looked him up online. There are a lot worse bodies you could use."

There were. But I wasn't going to think about that. Just like I wasn't going to think about purple hippos or green elephants or glittery white unicorns that farted rainbows...

Before I could reply, Angel called from the living room. "Katie? It's just about lunch-time, isn't it?"

I muttered a curse—but better lunch duty than bathroom duty. I called out, "Give me a few minutes, and I'll bring it out there." Then, to Brittany, I said, "Gotta go."

"Wait! I actually called for a reason. You know I couldn't find toilet paper the other day. But the stores must be keeping some for people who get deliveries. Why don't you schedule a load of groceries? Book it with the store directly or use one of those services."

"That's a great idea."

Brit said, "See? I can do more than make dirty donuts."

"Hey," I said, even as I pulled up the website for the closest grocery store. "You and me. We're okay?"

"Of course we're okay. But your brother is a big baby, and you can tell him I said so."

"It's just a couple of weeks. Then, I'll be back home and we can go out for martinis and sushi—my treat."

"I'll hold you to that."

Hanging up, I turned my full attention to my computer screen. The closest grocery store didn't have any delivery slots for the next two weeks. I tried another one. Same result. I checked on the services, the ones that sent personal shoppers into stores armed with complete shopping lists, but they were fully booked too.

So much for Brittany's brainstorm.

What had Sean and Timothy been thinking, with two rolls of TP in the entire house?

They'd been thinking they could run out and get more any time they needed to. They'd been thinking things would continue, same as ever, without the novel coronavirus turning life upside down.

I'd have to solve the toilet paper crisis later. For now, there was lunch to prepare.

Sadly, it turned out that sardines weren't a good substitute for tuna, even though they were both canned fish. And the afternoon went further downhill when Lucifer decided to yowl through a Zoom meeting with Martin and the rest of my team. Angel's pain meds wore off sixty minutes before she could take her next dose, and Sean answered my frantic text with an unsympathetic, "She'll have to tough it out. It's only an hour." Timothy sent tutorials for setting up a firewall—just in case I didn't have anything else to do in my free time.

At least I managed to send Martin two short articles. And I couldn't ruin dinner. I heated a jar of artisanal vodka sauce and poured it over the hand-shaped gemelli I'd found in the pantry. The guys had an unbelievable supply of high-end food—tiny jars of tapenade and chutney, at least six kinds of preserves, and a vast array of other gourmet treats from brands I'd never heard of.

I thought about the little pot of jam Jason had pressed into my palm as he handed me into the cab at the Monaco. It sat on my nightstand now, making me smile every time I ventured into the guest room. I should text him, just to say I missed him.

But what the hell was he supposed to say to that? And how would I respond?

Instead, I got Angel settled for an early bed-time. After she was asleep, I turned on the TV, leaving the sound low so I didn't disturb her. I flipped between hockey and pro basketball and college tournaments, pretending like everything was absolutely, one hundred percent normal. I tried not to notice the abundance of empty seats in arena after arena after arena.

11

KATIE

The toilet paper fairy arrived Wednesday morning.

I opened the front door to pick up the newspaper—Sean and Timothy were old school and got the *Banner* in print—and I was greeted by the sight of a corrugated box the size of a small bus. Thanks to another night on the Sofa of Suffering, my back was killing me, but I hefted the carton over the threshold and pushed it down the hall to the kitchen. I wondered what the guys were expecting.

I was astonished to find my name on the box's address label. The tape yielded to the blades of kitchen shears. Inside, I found a lifetime supply of toilet paper—forty-eight rolls of snow-white perfection.

What the hell?

A slip of paper fluttered to the ground as my grandmother shuffled into the kitchen. She'd managed to drape her robe over both shoulders and she'd slipped her feet into fur-lined mules. Progress.

I scooped up the paper before it could send her flying. "Angel! You shouldn't be walking alone."

Her mouth shrunk to a bitter plug. "I broke my arm, not my leg." I was so relieved to hear her usual biting tone that I dropped the argument immediately—even when she sniffed like she'd just discovered a full gallon of spoiled milk in the fridge. "And *what*, in the name of all that's holy, is *that?*"

"Toilet paper," I answered dutifully.

She made a face. "Don't get smart with me. Who sends a box like that?"

Exactly what *I* was wondering. I looked at the receipt in my hand. *Compliments of Jason Price.*

I read it twice, to make sure I wasn't hallucinating. *Jason had sent me toilet paper?* What the hell kind of gift was that?

But I knew exactly what kind of gift it was. A perfect one. The one thing I truly needed. He'd listened to me—well, he'd read my texts—and he'd solved my biggest problem.

"Well?" Angel asked.

Growing up, I'd had time to master hundreds of Angel's rules. Nice girls didn't show their shoulders in summer tops. They didn't wear ankle bracelets. They didn't pierce any part of their anatomy, at least nothing more than a single hole in each earlobe. And they absolutely, positively *never* accepted a gift from a man who wasn't a father, a brother, or a beau.

(Of course, nice *boys* could bring home a succession of boyfriends without ever raising the slightest hint of condemnation. Angel had treated every one of Sean's love interests like a king. Or, rather, a very spoiled prince. Double standards R us, in Angel's household.)

"Young lady," Angel said, immediately throwing me back into the emotional whirlpool of junior high. "I asked you a question."

Of course my father hadn't sent the toilet paper from beyond the grave. I could say Sean had, but if Angel said anything to him there was a better than fifty-fifty chance he'd go all Boy Scout and insist on telling the truth. That left…

I looked Angel in the eye and said, "It's from my boyfriend."

"Boyfriend! This is the first I've heard of any—"

In for a penny… I cut her off with a gambit I'd perfected in high school. "I *told* you about him, Angel." Over the years, I'd invented hundreds of conversations with my grandmother, ones she'd "forgotten" in the rush of day-to-day life. I only felt a twinge of extra guilt when I thought about how disoriented Angel had been the day before.

"What's his name?" she spluttered, just like when I'd "reminded" her she'd promised me a twenty to meet Brittany at the movies, or she'd granted permission for Senior Skip Day, or she'd said I could break curfew for an especially cool party.

It wasn't nice to lie. But I figured that was the one benefit I got from Angel's preferring Sean over me. She never forgot a single thing *he* said, but I had a lot more rope to work with.

"Jason," I said.

By Angel's standards, the things Jason and I had done at the Hotel Monaco practically made us *married.* I had every right to turn him into a fake boyfriend. Especially when he was never going to find out about my fib.

"Jason who?"

"Jason Price," I said, with just a hint of irritation, as if we'd discussed my dating life a hundred times before.

"I want to meet this Jason Price, who thinks toilet paper is a perfectly acceptable gift for a young woman."

"Well that's too bad. He's in Florida."

Angel's suspicions ignited again. "Your boyfriend lives in Florida?"

"He's a baseball player, Angel. This is spring training."

"A base—" She cut herself off. "You didn't learn your lesson last time?

"Jason is nothing like Aaron!" I answered with a lot more heat than I'd planned. So much for my brilliant plan. I went on the offensive. "You've been standing far too long. I want you sitting at that table while I make us both some breakfast."

"Could we please just have some cereal?"

I should have protested that Angel needed protein to help her bones knit. But I was no more ready to face new forms of inedible eggs than she was. Besides, cereals were fortified, weren't they?

I edged my way around the mammoth block of toilet paper and took down two bowls for the organic, non-GMO, stevia-sweetened corn flakes I'd found on the top shelf of the pantry. It was the first breakfast we both polished off, every last bite. But it wasn't enough to make Angel forget to interrogate me about my new so-called boyfriend. I was in for a very long morning, and I had no one to blame but myself.

12

JASON

I was pulling into the player's lot when the hands-free system announced, "Phone call from Katie McIntyre." Grinning, I considered answering with the first thing that popped into my head: *I was up half the night, thinking about ripping off every stitch of your clothing with my teeth.*

But the security guard was checking my ID, so I went for the slightly more conservative, "Hey there, Killer."

For a moment I thought the call had dropped, but that was just Katie hesitating. When she did speak, her voice sounded strained. "Hey," she said. "Um, I've got you on speaker. My grandmother is here."

Good thing I hadn't gone with my first choice. Sitting up straighter, I tried to sound like a choir boy. "Good morning, ma'am."

"Young man." I wasn't sure if she was agreeing with me that the morning was good or if she was framing a question.

Katie spoke before I needed to gamble on an answer. "We got your present. Thank you so much. It was quite a surprise." Her voice sounded brassy, like she was faking a smile and shouting through her teeth.

"I'm glad it got there," I said, easing into my usual parking space. "I wanted Monday delivery, but shipping was delayed."

"You shouldn't have sent it at all." More of that fake brightness. I wondered if someone was holding a gun to her head. "But if there's one thing I've learned from Angel, it's that a girl should be grateful for gifts from her boyfriend."

Boyfriend.

Well, *that* came out of left field. We'd spent one—admittedly mind-blowing—night together. We'd exchanged a few texts. I'd sent her a box of toilet paper. Not exactly *Romeo and Juliet*.

Wait. Katie had just called herself a girl. I was willing to bet a year's salary she didn't go around infantilizing herself on a regular basis. And I'd bet another year's pay she didn't make a habit of placing calls with her grandmother on the line.

For some reason, Katie's grandmother thought I was Katie's boyfriend.

I didn't know anything about the woman, aside from the fact that she'd broken her arm. Well that, and she had a mean cat. A weak bladder too.

But Katie was dealing with enough crap, so I decided to play along. "Only the best for my girl." I put a tiny emphasis on the last word, like I was speaking in code. *Copy that, secret agent. I've got your six.*

The Katie McIntyre I'd met in DC would've managed a remote castration for my patronizing tone. But the Katie on the phone sounded relieved as she said, "Thank you so much for understanding."

I didn't need an Enigma machine to tell me she was grateful I wasn't calling her on her lie. So, what would a smitten boyfriend say to the girl he loved, with her grandmother listening in? I went for the innocuous: "You two are doing okay?"

"We're fine. But you know how Martin is."

I didn't know *who* Martin was. But I made some noncommittal grunt.

"He's assigned me three new stories since Monday."

Ding, ding, ding! Martin must be her editor. But just in case Martin was a tyrannical instructor in a short fiction seminar she was taking, I kept my reply neutral. "You wouldn't have it any other way."

"You know me so well," Katie said with a laugh. At least I guessed that's what that strangled gulp was supposed to be. "Well, we won't keep you," she went on. "I just wanted to say thank you for the toilet paper. You've got a 1:00 start today, right?"

I grinned. She might be faking our relationship, but she cared enough to check the Rockets' schedule. "I'm at the park now."

"Can I call you tonight?"

"That would be perfect." I loaded the words with enthusiasm, because that's what a real boyfriend would do. Honestly, it wasn't hard to fake. "Have a good day…" Shit. What was I supposed to call her? She didn't seem the *sweetheart* type. Babe? Only if I wanted a quick jab to the man-parts, the next time we were in the same room. I hastily tacked on the best thing that came to mind: "Killer."

Katie laughed—an open, clear sound unlike the rest of our dual-level conversation.

I grinned in response as I went for the fake-boyfriend gold. "You too, Mrs. McIntyre. I hope you have a lovely rest of your day."

Katie said goodbye and started to hang up, but not before I overheard her grandmother say, "What a nice boy!"

Grinning, I climbed out of the car. I'd played along. And that meant Katie owed me. I'd have fun extracting a reward, somewhere down the road.

13

KATIE

I lurked outside Angel's bedroom, listening for the soft snores that announced she was soundly asleep. Maybe it was the pain meds or maybe it was just old age, but she had once again headed to bed before eight. I didn't know if I should worry or just be grateful I had a little time to myself.

Either way, I felt guilty.

Sighing, I tiptoed into the kitchen. I'd prefer to take my phone downstairs to have some true privacy, but I didn't want to be out of range if Angel woke and needed me.

I sat on the edge of one of the ladderback chairs, hesitating before I tapped the button to launch my call. I wanted to talk to Jason; I really did. But I was utterly mortified for having faked our relationship. Was it worse to avoid calling him now? Would that be even creepier?

He answered on the first ring. "Hey, Killer! Who's listening in this time?"

"No one." I fought a fresh surge of embarrassment. "Just me."

"Why are we whispering?"

"Angel's asleep, and I don't want to wake her."

"Even to let her listen in on a conversation with your *boyfriend?*"

"I'm really sorry about that. She, um, jumped to conclusions, and…" *Okay. I led her right up to the cliff edge of conclusions. And then I pushed her over.*

"You're afraid of your grandmother!"

"I'm not *afraid* of her! I respect her."

"I don't believe it. You face down Juan Gonzalez without a second's hesitation, but a sweet little old lady…"

"Angel is *anything* but sweet." I realized how bad that sounded, and I started to rephrase, but there wasn't an easy save. Angel *wasn't* sweet. She'd never been a cookie-baking, lap-cuddling, forehead-kissing grandmother.

She was more like a drill sergeant. With a vendetta. And a loaded pistol.

Giving up on redeeming my reputation, I said, "Forget about her. At the rate her memory's going, she won't remember you tomorrow."

"And after I sent such a great *boyfriend* present…"

I grinned, despite the ever-present flicker of concern about Angel's memory, about my grandmother's health in general. "You're my hero," I said in a mocking tone. And then, because I wanted to avoid anything else that might sound remotely girlfriend-y, I retreated into neutral territory. "I bet the whole team said that this afternoon."

I'd checked the box score right before dinner. Jason had saved the game on a double-play, catching a line drive back to the mound and whipping it to second to make Atlanta pay for a badly executed hit and run.

"I had a choice," he said in an easy, self-deprecating tone. "I could catch the ball with my glove or my face."

"*Press Box* chose it for Play of the Day. You're on the website's front page." And I'd watched the video clip half a dozen times, including the slow-motion repeats, which looked like ballet.

"Might as well go out in a blaze of glory," he said.

"What do you mean?" My voice ratcheted up half an octave without my giving it permission. Had he been injured on the play?

Before my quick rush of adrenaline faded away, he asked, "Off the record?"

"Sure." I agreed without hesitation. But what the hell did *that* mean? Was I really willing to check my press card at the door for Jason "The Professor" Price?

In three years of dating, Aaron Henderson had never once asked to talk off the record. Apparently, it had never crossed his mind that I might do my freaking *job* and report on anything he said.

Ultimately, the joke was on me. Because I never *did* write about the secrets I heard, sitting at Aaron's side. I executed my own little gag order, for the good of my relationship. And look where *that* had gotten me.

Jason had no reason to know my self-doubt as he said, "It's all still rumor. But word in the clubhouse is, spring training will shut down tomorrow."

"But the *season* will start on time." I said it like a fact. It was one thing to cancel a few friendly match-ups as everyone shook the rust off after a few months' break. But there was big money on the line for the regular season—tickets, concessions, and merchandise across the league.

"That's the plan. But when they start, they'll only let in essential personnel. No fans or media."

"Damn," I breathed. No press conferences after the games? It wouldn't affect *me*—I wasn't covering the day-to-day grind of the season. But how would my fellow journalists file stories?

Somehow, the looming restrictions made the virus more real than all the shortages in grocery stores.

I started to cradle my phone to my shoulder so I could grab a glass of the quite-nice rosé Sean and Timothy had left in the fridge. The motion, though, tweaked one of the couch-irritated nerves in my neck. I cut off an involuntary groan at the ice-pick jab and gave up on the idea of multi-tasking.

"That didn't sound like the good kind of moan," Jason said.

In a flash, I was melting beneath the combined pressure of his tongue and his broad palms, sighing his name against the Hotel Monaco's silken sheets. I blinked hard to restore my attention to Sean and Timothy's camera-ready kitchen.

Angel. My grandmother was in earshot. I couldn't say—or do—half the things I wanted. And I shouldn't want to do any of them at all. Jason Price was not my real-world boyfriend.

"I'm fine," I said. "Just a crick in my neck. My brother's sofa looks a lot better than it feels."

"No guest room?" His voice was sympathetic.

"Not close enough to hear Angel if she needs me."

"Why not get a baby monitor?" The suggestion was off-hand, as if he were talking about pitching warm-ups. Why not throw a few curveballs? Have you thought about a slider? How's the fastball today?

"Um, because I never even thought of that."

"Baby monitors are like cell phones when the Price family gets together. Between them, my sisters have thirteen kids. Want me to send you one?"

It would be so easy to say yes. I wouldn't have to think about features, about ranges, about whether the package came with batteries included. He was offering to help. To take care of me. The mere fact that he'd *asked* felt warm and comforting, like stepping into brand new socks.

But I could take perfectly good care of myself. And. Jason. Price. Was. Not. My. Boyfriend. "No thanks. I'm sure *those* aren't flying off the shelves in corona panic. I should be able to find one around here. But thanks for the idea. It's a good one."

"Have it your way."

I couldn't tell if he was upset. Aaron would have been, if he'd suggested something, and I'd stubbornly refused to follow his lead.

It would be a stupid thing to fight about. But I *should* see if I could order one for next-day delivery. And I still had an article to write. That was the joy of working from home, right? I could make up for all the Angel-related breaks I'd taken during the day by writing long into the night.

"I should let you go," I said. *I don't want to hang up. I want to keep talking, all night long, like a kid up past my bedtime.*

"Sleep well," he said.

"Good night." *I wish you were here, so I could rip your clothes off and throw you onto the floor and have my wicked way with you. In a perfectly normal, non-boyfriendly way, of course.*

"Good night."

He cut the call before I could slip up and say something I'd truly regret.

Schooling my mind to a more professional bent—which, let's face it, wasn't difficult, because my mind had been anything *but* professional by the end of that call—I retrieved my computer from the living room. A quick check of my work email showed no major developments. The wire services, though, were on fire.

Professional basketball playoffs were canceled. Just like that, in the middle of televised games. Gobert, the player who'd screwed around at the press conference on Monday, had tested positive for the virus. Every team in the league was benched.

Basketball was the story of the night. But I was far more intrigued by baseball. I put Jason's name into a search engine.

I already knew the basics of his career, and he'd hinted at

a little more. He'd grown up in Texas. He had five sisters. Thirteen nieces and nephews. He read a copy of Marcus Aurelius's *Meditations* for fun. He looked sinful in a tux. Out of it, too.

Google quickly fed me more facts. He'd played his way onto the baseball team at Carver University; he hadn't been lured with a scholarship, recruited for his throwing arm. He'd majored in Philosophy. There was a famous picture of him with legendary coach Stan Dixon, taken right after Carver won the College World Series. Both men clutched each other in pure joy, their heads thrown back at perfect complementary angles. Their mouths were open as they shouted something lost to time, and tears glistened on their cheeks.

I'd read something about Dixon a while back, something not directly connected to Carver, to baseball… A quick search pinned down the facts. He'd been diagnosed with Stage IV lung cancer a year ago, and he'd taken a leave of absence from the school he loved. Follow-up stories had begun to take on an elegiac tone.

I dug deeper and found more articles that referenced Jason and his coach. Several pieces quoted Jason saying Dixon was like a father to him. My heart ached for the sorrow he seemed bound to suffer, probably sooner rather than later.

I read a few more articles, and I found a lot more photos. Several made my insides ripple as I remembered our crazy night at the Monaco. Ultimately, I realized what I hadn't said in our earlier conversation.

I waited until I'd settled onto the Couch From Hell before I once again took out my phone. It was too late to talk; I wanted to make sure Angel got a full night's sleep in the next room. But I texted:

KATIE

Hey. I've been meaning to say, I had a really good time when you were here. A lot of guys wouldn't have backed me up at the Foundation thing. I like that you didn't try to take control, that you let me be me. And the sex was pretty hot too.

I hit Send and was rewarded by a trio of bubbles.

JASON

Who is this?

I laughed.

KATIE

Seriously. When all this virus stuff is over, I'd like to see you again.

I'd like that too.

I really am sorry about the fake boyfriend stuff.

I'm not.

Okay. I just wanted to get that off my chest.

No! Don't type what you were going to type!

What was I going to type?

We both knew I'd left myself perfectly set up for a "chest" gag. But, yawning, I chickened out.

KATIE

Good night, fake boyfriend.

Good night.

He didn't add "fake girlfriend." Was that because he thought the game was stupid? Or was he thinking like I was, that there might possibly, just maybe, be a hint of something more between us?

I wasn't going to find out by sending more texts tonight. I put my phone on the coffee table and tried to find a comfortable position on the torture couch from hell.

14

JASON

I stood by my locker, shaking my head as Cruz spun out another lie about the waitresses at Martinis. "I'm telling you," the catcher said. "Three of 'em, just waiting for me when I hit the parking lot."

"You're full of shit," Green said.

"No, no, no!" Cruz protested. "And these ladies were *really* friendly. To me and to each other, if you know what I mean."

We were all grown men. We knew exactly what he meant.

He'd said the same thing about the babes at Jack's Crab House two nights ago. And the *zorras* waiting by the players' parking lot after the game the night before that. And the *putas* who hung out at his apartment's pool over the weekend. So really, all things considered, the "ladies" at Martinis were getting a lot of respect.

If Katie were here, she'd put Cruz in his place.

God, I'd been a jerk last night, offering to buy her a baby monitor. Like she wasn't capable of shopping online like a grown woman. Like she needed my protection. Or worse, my cash.

I knew why I'd done it. It felt like something I *could* do. Or ask Jen to do. Shit. Everyone was feeling the pressure, all the guys in the clubhouse. The walls were closing in around us. Every time Skip came through the door, tension jolted through the locker room.

We were stuck, waiting to see what the league did. We didn't have any say in the matter, but our lives hung in the balance—everything we'd be doing for the three weeks till Opening Day. Hell, after that, too.

So if I could tap a couple of computer keys and splurge on same-day shipping for a simple electronic device? That would have felt like taking back control.

A sudden silence blanketed the locker room. Cruz cut off his boasting mid-syllable. As I turned around, the guys around me froze, like we all faced a firing squad.

Zach Ormond didn't bother clearing his throat. A former catcher who'd taken a job in the Rockets' front office, he'd always been a team leader. He had our attention before he got out one word.

"Major league is shutting us down," Ormond said. "As of four o'clock this afternoon, spring training is canceled. The current plan is to start the regular season two weeks late, on April 9."

We shouldn't have been surprised. Pro basketball had gone out yesterday. College ball canceled earlier this afternoon. Everyone knew hockey was on the brink.

But the locker room still exploded with casual profanity directed at the league, the owners, and anyone else in power. The most succinct response, though, came from DJ Thomas, the pitcher who'd been set to go this afternoon. "Fuck corona," he said, throwing his glove into the bottom of his locker as if it were one of his lethal fastballs.

Ormond let the guys vent for a few minutes before he said,

"We don't have a playbook for this. The park'll be on lockdown after tonight. We'll keep you posted on when you have to report back. If you need help with flights home, Marty's in his office."

I had it easy. I could stay in Coral Crest without worrying about landlords or penalties for breaking a lease. Shit, I could lock the door and head up to Raleigh this afternoon. Jen would take care of shutting down anything that needed shutting down and follow me north when she was done. But a bunch of the guys lived farther away—Texas or Arizona or California. At least a dozen lived in other countries.

Sitting there, listening to everyone bitch about something they couldn't change, I felt the white scar on my elbow start to pucker. Goddamn Mind-Fuck. I'd only been in Coral Crest for four days. My twisted brain shouldn't start screaming to hit the road for a few weeks at least.

I curled my fingers into a fist as the guys got louder. Some wanted to know if the team would charter a flight up to North Carolina. Others wanted something set up for Santo Domingo. Translators were helping a couple of rookies, and I remembered we had a couple of guys in camp from Japan. That Korean pitcher, too.

Ormond was doing his best to field questions, but all he could really do was repeat that he didn't know anything more than he'd already told us. The guys just got louder.

"Shut the fuck up!" Thomas shouted over the din. He'd retrieved his glove from his locker, and he slapped it against his thigh as he fought to be heard.

The guys quieted, at least a little. "Why do we have to go anywhere?" Thomas asked. "We all planned on being here through the end of the month. Everyone renting a place is paid up. If you own your home, what difference does it make? Let's stay put. If the league comes to their senses and lets us back in early, we'll be one step ahead of everyone else."

Ormond looked like he was surrendering, holding up his

hands. "The team can't order anyone to do that. Officially, we shut down in two and a half hours."

"Sure," Thomas said. "*You* can't order us. But we can take a vote. As a team."

I didn't want to vote. With almost a month before the regular season's rhythm of travel, I wanted to hit the road. I could drive where I wanted. Fly. The Mind-Fuck was humming louder.

"Who's in?" Thomas asked, raising his own right hand.

Two thirds of the team reacted immediately, shooting up arms like high school kids begging for hall passes. A few stragglers saw which way the vote was going and jumped in.

I didn't want to do it. I wanted to get away. Maybe go back to DC. To an address I'd already memorized, in suburban Virginia.

But the guys needed to take control. They needed to do something to prove we weren't all sitting ducks. Thomas's vote was the same thing I'd tried the night before, when I'd offered to buy the baby monitor. He was carving out a slice of order in the middle of coronavirus chaos.

Only an asshole would keep the count from being unanimous. I raised my hand.

There. I was stuck in Florida. And it was my own goddamn fault.

15

KATIE

The end of sports hit like a hurricane, and *Press Box* sat in the eye of the storm. Martin ordered all of us to set aside our long-form articles. The website needed content fast. Multi-billion-dollar industries grinding to a halt overnight meant thousands of people were affected—players, of course, but everyday workers too, the ones who usually kept stadiums, casinos, and TV broadcasts running smoothly.

I felt like I had a purpose, like my reporting actually meant something, like it could help real people in the midst of the COVID crisis. I didn't mind staying up late and waking up early. I didn't mind pinning down quotes for article after article. My work mattered.

But for the first forty-eight hours, I didn't have a chance to *think* about calling Jason. Between fielding Martin's requests 24/7, taking care of Angel, and managing my brother's house, I barely had time to grab a couple of hours sleep.

I *did* hear about the Rockets' team vote, about how they

were sticking together in Florida. All for one and one for all. With every major news outlet looking for something—*anything*—to check the "feel-good" box, the Rockets got plenty of press.

Jason was busy. I was busy. Neither of us needed me to turn our hook-up into a marriage proposal. And after those first couple of nights when I was legitimately too busy to talk, it was easier not to reach out. Another couple of nights went by, and it would have felt stalkerish to check in.

But Angel, of all people, had other ideas. My grandmother was smitten with my ersatz boyfriend. She asked about him every morning, just assuming I'd stayed up late the night before, talking to my true love. Every time I got a text, she wanted to know if it was from him. Once, my phone rang during *Jeopardy!* and she muted Alex Trebek—a concession I hadn't seen in twenty-two years.

Honestly, that *Jeopardy!* stunt worried me almost as much as her fogginess had, those first couple of days after she'd left the hospital. But she seemed a lot more focused now. At least, she found a lot more to criticize. My pink yoga pants made me look bloated. My hair could do with a trim. My fingers looked stubby when I wasn't wearing nail polish.

Whenever I fired back a smart-ass reply, she insisted she was only telling the truth. Angel was back to her usual form.

No wonder I made time to talk to Brittany every day—on the phone, of course, instead of sitting at a bar sipping outrageously priced cocktails with punny names. We usually grabbed a few minutes in the afternoon, before she had to report for work.

"What do you think of a bacon-pineapple donut?" she mused, a week into the sports blackout. "Maybe with a coconut cream filling?"

"I think you've found my hard limit on bacon. Don't quit your day job."

Brit laughed grimly. "My day job might quit me. There

hasn't been a line to get in for the past week!" Two Girls and a Radish was legendary for its no-reservation policy and for the nightly queue that stretched around the block.

"And me, stuck at home with Angel." Like I had hundreds of dollars to drop on a restaurant meal.

"How'd this morning's appointment go?"

"The doctor kept us waiting almost an hour, even though we were the only people there. When they finally called us back, Angel let him know she was pissed. Excuse me. *Peeved.* But he took new X-rays, and he put in her in a cast. She's sulking now."

"Why?"

"Who knows?" I sighed. "Because she's tired and her arm hurts. Because she's stuck here with me, instead of with Sean. Because she's lonely and misses her friends, and she can't go back to Oak Grove until she can manage all her ADLs."

"ADLs?"

"Activities of daily living. Showering and dressing and bathroom visits. And scooping Lucifer's litter."

"Lucy!"

I gritted my teeth. Somehow that damn cat had everyone fooled. "*Lucifer* knocked the baby monitor off Angel's nightstand three times last night. I finally cranked the volume up and put it at the back of her dresser. I don't *think* that miserable excuse for a cat can reach it there."

"Have you ever considered that Lucy might behave better if you showed her just a hint of affection?"

"I'm feeding her twice a day. Isn't that enough?"

"Poor widdle sweetums. I'd make her tuna donuts, if Sean would just— Wait! Do you think tuna—"

"No." I cut her off and tried to un-think the suggestion. "Definitely not. You need to forget about savory donuts completely. Seriously. You'll thank me, down the line."

Brit started to grouse, but I cut her off. "I've got to go. Timothy just pulled up with groceries."

"Ready to put on your haz-mat suit?"

I laughed and ended the call. Sean's rules *were* a little extreme. We'd spent the better part of the past week negotiating them.

Timothy had lobbied for daily drop-offs, but Sean insisted it was essential to keep shopping trips to a minimum. They'd settled on once a week, which was fine with me.

In keeping with The System, I'd already cleared the kitchen table, removing the morning's newspaper, the placemats, and the hand-crafted salt- and pepper shakers. Now, I pulled on rubber gloves and opened the container of Clorox wipes.

"Incoming," I sang to Angel, as I sailed through the living room on my way to the front door. My grandmother barely stirred from her Hitler documentary on the History Channel.

Per our agreement, Timothy had left the grocery bags on the porch and retreated to the sidewalk. He gazed up at his house like a parent watching a newborn in the NICU.

"Thanks!" I called from the doormat.

"You guys are doing okay?" Timothy asked. "You didn't have Swiffer pads on your list, but I got some, dry and wet, both."

"Perfect," I said, faking enthusiasm because I *was* staying in his house. I hoped he wasn't going to transfer his obsession about computer safety to housekeeping.

"Sean wanted me to remind you—"

"I know. I'll wipe down every box, can, and bag. And let the canned goods sit for at least a week. You know, my hands are starting to chap."

He gave me a sympathetic grin. "That's why I slipped in a little something extra. There's a tube of Kiehl's Ultimate Strength in one of those bags."

"I *knew* there was a reason my brother married you." Actually, there were dozens of reasons Sean and Timothy had tied the knot. They were perfect for each other.

"Let me know if I missed anything on your list," he said.

"I will." But I was certain he hadn't forgotten a thing. "Give my love to Sean. He's doing okay? You both are?"

"We're fine. He's tired. You know me. I always work from home, so I'm trying to pick up the slack." I was pretty sure nothing had ever been *slack* in Timothy's life. "Go on," he said, nodding toward the bags. "Get those inside. You don't want the ice cream to melt."

I definitely didn't want the ice cream to melt. Even if I felt stupid, hurriedly wiping bleach over every square inch of the carton. The decontamination protocol took almost half an hour, and I was wilted by the time I'd put everything away.

But that night, I opened a familiar red-and-white can of chicken noodle soup for dinner, smiling as I pictured Timothy's face when he'd put it in his cart.

And so one day slipped into another for a second week of the new hit show, *Life at Sean's House*. Angel grew more sullen, but she said her arm didn't hurt. My brother texted each morning, wanting a full report on our grandmother's condition. Brit checked in each afternoon. Martin demanded article after article, editing each with a river of virtual red ink.

And then the world stopped.

The email hit my inbox at 5:00, at the end of the official work day.

From: Peter Chatham, Editor-in-Chief

To: Katie McIntyre

Re: Status of Press Box

Date: March 23, 2020

In the past month, the novel coronavirus has presented greater challenges to our organization than we have ever faced before. I regret to inform you that, effective immediately, we are obliged to terminate your employment with Press Box.

. . .

There was more—an assurance that my firing wasn't based on my performance, a promise of a reference should any be requested, an email address for Human Resources, along with the recommendation that I should seek unemployment benefits.

But the headline was crystal clear: I had just lost the only job I'd ever loved.

16

Commonwealth of Virginia

Office of the Governor

Executive Order Number Fifty-Three (2020)

I order the following:

Effective 11:59 p.m., Tuesday, March 24, 2020 until 11:59 p.m., Thursday, April 23, 2020, all public and private in person gatherings of 10 or more individuals are prohibited…

Closure of all dining and congregation areas in restaurants, dining establishments, food courts, breweries, microbreweries, distilleries, wineries, tasting rooms, and farmers markets effective 11:59 p.m., Tuesday, March 24, 2020…

Closure of all public access to recreational and entertainment businesses, effective 11:59 p.m., Tuesday, March 24, 2020…

Memorandum

From: Steven Johnson, Sports Section Editor, *Washington Banner*

To: All Sports Section Staff

The *Banner's* ongoing coverage of the coronavirus pandemic is affecting all departments of our paper, the newspaper of record in Washington DC. Many of you have volunteered to help out with virus coverage and we thank you for your initiative. Readership remains at an all-time high on our website, and we will continue to provide the superior analysis, opinion, and investigative news for which the *Banner* is known. Nevertheless, with no major sports being played at this time, we are unable to fill a separate Sports Section for the foreseeable future. Therefore, effective immediately, Sports will move inside the Lifestyle Section, with an expected footprint of two pages. This change is only temporary, until the current crisis has ended. Thank you for your ongoing support.

~

Programming Guide

Channel 720 Baseball World

Back-to-back World Series coverage, featuring all televised games from 1947 to 2019.

~

Programming Guide

Channel 721 Sports Kings

Hockey analysts Jean-Pierre Laurent and Tug Wilkinson call a live game, played through the Hockey Cup 2020 computer game platform.

~

Commonwealth of Virginia

Office of the Governor

Executive Order Number Fifty-Five (2020)

March 23, 2020

I order the following:

All individuals in Virginia shall remain at their place of residence…until June 10, 2020.

17

JASON

There was one problem with DJ Thomas's master plan of keeping the team together in the hope that spring training would miraculously get back on track: we might die of boredom before we ever returned to the park.

No team practice. No workouts. No shooting the shit in the locker room, listening to Cruz lie about the women he'd supposedly dragged back to his cave.

If I wasn't going to the ballpark because it was too risky, I sure as hell wasn't heading out to the bars and restaurants on the Ave. Not when every news report led with rising tallies of coronavirus infections and deaths.

I *did* buy a couple dozen gift certificates, hoping the infusion of cash might help local restaurants stay afloat. I'd redeem them later, when the virus had been beaten back.

Jen worked her usual magic, setting up grocery delivery from Publix. She came over to the house at nine every morning, taking an hour to handle paperwork and to water the plants, but she didn't stick around—even when I tempted her with classics for lunch, like my world-famous grilled grouper linguine.

So, I had plenty of time to stay in shape. My treadmill took a five-mile beating every morning. I lifted weights, the same as I would at the park. I threw a bucket of fastballs into a net in the back yard, retrieved them and repeated the drill with curveballs, then sliders. I took advantage of the pool.

And I spent way too much time on my phone.

It was easy to get lost on Instagram, thumbing past everyone's lies about their perfect families, perfect houses, perfect lives. I read the *News & Observer* every day, cover to cover like I would if I were back in my Raleigh house. For the first time in months, I caught up on all the back issues of *The Atlantic, The New Yorker,* and *The Economist.*

And I checked *Press Box* every hour. Sure, I was following their general coverage of the pandemic, about how the virus affected athletes, owners, and fans around the world. But I started each morning with a scan for Katie's name, and I devoured her stories first.

I wasn't obsessed. She was just a damn good writer.

Okay, I was a little obsessed. But we hadn't talked since I'd fucked things up by offering to send the baby monitor. Now, almost two weeks later, I couldn't even remember why it seemed like such a big mistake. She hadn't hung up on me. We'd talked like normal people, even after I started waving my wallet around.

She'd even texted that night. She'd had a good time at the Monaco—which was great, because that night was pretty much burned into my brain on a permanent loop. But, signing off, she'd gone out of her way to remind me I was only her *fake* boyfriend.

I got the message. She was up for a quickie the next time I was in town. I shouldn't plan on anything more.

Fact: if she'd wanted to call, she could have, anytime in

the last thirteen days. At least I knew she was safe and healthy because she filed a new story every morning. Sometimes two or three.

All of my justifications kept me sane until I tapped my phone on Tuesday, calling up *Press Box* for the first time that morning. A tasteful, black-trimmed notice filled the screen:

Effectively immediately, Press Box's standard coverage is on hiatus due to the coronavirus pandemic. As a subscriber, you are invited to enjoy our archive of prior articles at no additional charge.

I'd already enjoyed the archive, at least all of Katie's articles.

By noon, I'd gone to *Press Box* half a dozen times, usually without even realizing I was heading over to the site. The notice never changed, but I realized how addicted I was.

Fuck it. I didn't get to be a World-Series-winning closer by sitting on my thumbs. I hit the green phone icon.

One ring. I should hang up. I could say I butt-dialed if she ever called back.

Two. I cleared my throat, wishing I had a glass of water nearby.

Three. I took a breath and braced to leave a message. I should have thought up something clever before I called. Or at least something slyly seductive.

"Hello?"

That wasn't Katie's voice, not by several decades. So much for sly seduction. "Mrs. McIntyre?" I asked.

Suddenly I wondered what stories Katie had been telling her grandmother. In Mrs. McIntyre's world, were Katie and I still dating? Maybe I'd broken up with her. Maybe she'd broken up with me, after I pissed her off by doing something stupid. Maybe we were engaged.

"Jason!" Mrs. McIntyre sounded thrilled. So Katie and I

were still together. Even more importantly, Katie must still have my name in her contacts, because her grandmother couldn't possibly recognize my voice. That was a good thing, wasn't it?

Mrs. McIntyre said, "Katie will be so pleased you called. And how are you this fine afternoon?"

Wondering why you're on the phone instead of Katie. But I wasn't a total ass, so I pushed a smile into my voice and said, "I'm fine, thank you. And you?"

"I'm well," she said. "But Katie received a bit of bad news this morning. She's been laid off." The last two words were delivered in a grave whisper—the same tone my own grandmother would have used to say someone had cancer.

"That's actually why I'm calling," I said, hoping the hint would be enough to get the phone into Katie's hands.

"She'll bounce right back. She always does. When Abigail left, I thought poor Sean's heart would break. But Katie just pretended nothing had happened. She wrote in the word 'grand' on the Mother's Day card she'd already made in school and gave it to me like that was her plan all along."

I'd wondered why Katie and Sean were responsible for their grandmother's care, and now I knew. Somehow, I suspected Katie didn't tell a lot of people about her mother leaving—when she was pretty young, if she was still making cards.

It was my turn to talk again. I tried for something neutral, so I didn't pry up more of Katie's secrets. "She's a strong woman."

"When my son died, her father… Well, Sean had nightmares for weeks—about hospitals and doctors and all that. But Katie never said a word."

So much for my grand master plan. With Mrs. McIntyre on the line, Katie's privacy was doomed.

How old was she when she was orphaned? I could ask, but I suspected that—as Katie's boyfriend—I was already supposed to know. Time for another platitude: "Grief affects different people in different ways." I waited a few seconds, hoping my silence would sound respectful, and then I asked, "Is Katie around by any chance?"

"She just stepped onto the porch. Sean's husband is dropping off groceries. He's doing all our shopping you know. Because of the coronary—, the corollary—, the what-do-you-call-it, the C word."

"Coronavirus," I supplied. How long could it take to bring in a few bags of groceries? Hadn't I been talking to Mrs. McIntyre for a century already?

"I'm actually glad she isn't here." Her voice had become conspiratorial.

That makes one of us.

She went on. "I've been wanting to call you."

At least one woman in the McIntyre household did.

Her voice dipped even further, and I understood we were sharing a secret. "You've been a very naughty young man."

Mrs. McIntyre didn't know the half of it. But all of my naughtiness had been conducted at night, in the privacy of my own bed, as I replayed my stay at the Hotel Monaco with Katie.

Right. That probably wasn't what she had in mind. "How's that, Mrs. McIntyre?"

"A beau should be *attentive*. I understand your not coming to the house, but you should be phoning my granddaughter on a very regular basis."

I couldn't let my reputation go to hell, even to preserve my supposed girlfriend's goodwill with her grandmother. "I don't mean to disillusion you," I said. "But Katie and I usually talk when you aren't around to hear us. When you're taking a nap. Or after you've gone to bed."

The old woman actually cackled in delight. "Aren't you two clever! I'm impressed by how well you've kept things under wraps."

Not nearly as impressed as I am. I wondered what Katie and I *would* have talked about, if we hadn't been lying through our teeth.

How long could it take for her to wrap things up with the grocery delivery? Shouldn't she be back in the house by now? "Mrs. McIntyre," I started to say, ready to ask for Katie to call when she had a chance. But the old woman cut me off.

"There's Katie, coming in now. I don't want her to think I'm talking behind her back. I'd hate to disrupt any of your *private* conversations. Bye now!"

Before I could shout a protest, the line went dead.

18

KATIE

I stood in front of the refrigerator, a little overwhelmed by the full shelves. My hands were still raw from the bleach I'd used to wipe down all the containers after Timothy dropped off our groceries. The ritual had actually been soothing. It had given me something to do besides reach for my phone.

Yesterday, I'd been glued to the screen, reading the cascade of emails from my fellow cast-adrift journalists. We'd all been shocked. Horrified. Panicky.

By the end of the day, though, those emotions had given way to anger. My morning inbox was filled with demands. Who did Peter Chatham think he was? What was *Press Box* going to do once the pandemic was over? Who would work for them in the future, knowing the crappy decisions they were making now?

I couldn't join in the rage. Instead, familiar ice filled my belly. I recognized the wall I threw up between my thoughts and my feelings.

It was hard to keep that cool separation in place. Every new email put a chink in my armor. Every fresh text made me twitch. By mid-morning, I'd instituted a strict no-cell-phone diet—just twenty-four hours, to get my head on straight. The fact that it was hard to do meant it was necessary.

I'd used the rest of my day to scour the house. I'd washed out Lucifer's litter box, completely changing over the clumpable gray clay. I'd scrubbed the kitchen appliances until they gleamed, even the inside of the microwave. I'd thought about sending Timothy a photo of the newly straightened wires leading to the router in his office, but that would have broken my phone embargo.

No wonder my hands were raw. I flexed my fingers as I asked my grandmother, "What do you think? We've got four types of cheese and three boxes of crackers. Why don't I peel an orange and slice an apple, and we can have a picnic for dinner?"

"Picnics are so romantic," Angel said, turning the last word into a three-part song.

Crap. She must be having another reaction to her meds. Just this morning, she'd taken her last heavy-duty painkiller. I was braced for—perversely *hoping* for—the return of my usual Angel, the one who relentlessly dragged me, then defended herself by saying she was only telling the truth.

I'd caught glimpses of her in the past two weeks, but lately Angel was even more withdrawn than when she'd come home from the hospital. Half the time, she didn't even answer my questions as I made casual conversation. Sean insisted she'd passed her hearing test with flying colors at her last physical. He'd reviewed her list of meds and said there shouldn't be any conflicts.

He'd reassured me by saying he'd be more concerned if Angel *weren't* a little off. She'd broken her arm, proving she was actually mortal. She was reliant on another person for the first time in her adult life. And she was locked inside the house because a deadly disease seemed to be targeting her precise demographic—older people with multiple pre-existing conditions.

Who wouldn't be depressed?

But she'd been more alert today. Three times during the afternoon, I'd caught her grinning at the TV, like she was sharing some private joke with the *Law and Order* detectives. She'd carried on a spirited debate with Lucifer about the relative merits of Ben Stone and Jack McCoy.

I was thinking too much. I should accept small victories—my picnic idea was a hit. I didn't need to cook, and Angel didn't need to submit to the demeaning necessity of my cutting her food into bite-size pieces. Win-win.

I started ferrying food to the table as Angel retrieved silverware from a drawer. It wasn't until I was excavating a jar of imported olives from the pantry that I realized my grandmother was humming.

"What's that song?" I asked.

She broke off her tune with a sly grin. "'If Ever I Would Leave You,'" she said. "One of my favorite love songs."

I started to point out that *Camelot* was about *doomed* love, but that wouldn't gain me any Good Granddaughter points. Instead, I said, "You seem to be in a great mood tonight."

"Why wouldn't I be?" Angel asked, apparently without taking offense.

Before I could reply, Lucifer crossed the kitchen and wove a figure eight between my ankles without expressing a single claw.

Aliens must have invaded. They'd replaced my grandmother and her cat with pod creatures.

It was possible.

This *was* 2020, after all.

Unnerved, I opened my brother's wine cooler. After an

unfortunate encounter with a high-end French burgundy my first week in the house, Sean had given me strict instructions about which bottles were fair game.

"What do you think, Angel? Are you up for a glass of wine?"

"A jug of wine, a loaf of bread, and thou," Angel quoted. "What a shame *your* 'thou' can't join us."

On second thought, wine was a really bad idea. Angel already sounded drunk. I closed the door and turned back to the cheese I'd already set on the counter. Lucifer jumped onto Angel's lap as I said, "You're not making sense."

"I don't mean to disillusion you…" Angel didn't finish the sentence. Instead, she just chuckled and stroked her cat, like the indulgent sort of grandmother who baked cookies and gave her grandkids comic books and kept a box of colored chalk specifically for the decoration of her driveway, no matter what the neighbors might think.

"Disillusion me about what?" I finally prompted, when it became clear she wasn't going to finish the sentence on her own.

"That's what *he* said." Angel's eyes grew round, as if she were surprised by her own reply. "Whoops!"

"Whoops, what?" My question was equal parts concern and annoyance.

"Well, fine," Angel said. She leaned over and spoke to Lucifer, like a child confiding a secret to an imaginary friend. "She'll find out tonight, anyway. When she and her beau have their *private* conversation."

"Me and my…"

Angel gave me a slightly defiant smile. "I spoke with your young man this afternoon." And then, like a parent prompting a forgetful toddler: "With Jason?"

I wasn't expecting *that* wash of quick heat over my cheeks. Good thing I was already wrestling with the plastic wrap on a sizable chunk of Port Salut. It was ridiculous, the way stores wasted plastic. They could have used half as much and still kept the cheese fresh. And they wrapped it so tightly that the soft buttery center was oozing past the woven red rind. Who thought *that* was attractive?

But Angel was waiting so I had to say *something*. I finally croaked, "With Jason?"

"I forgot to give you the message earlier." She actually sounded apologetic.

No. I was *not* going to get excited about a missed phone call. I would *not* regress to high school, when the mere *thought* of a crush looking at me across a crowded classroom was enough to send me spiraling into daydreams. I refused to seize my grandmother by both arms—good one and bad—and shake her until she'd repeated every single syllable of her conversation with Jason Price.

Instead, I focused on our picnic fare, assembling a tray with cheese and crackers and fruit and the pâté Timothy had delivered that afternoon. I added the olives, and a handful of rosemary-dusted Marcona almonds that looked like they'd cost my last month's pay with *Press Box*.

See? I could totally concentrate on the matter at hand. I was calm and cool and collected. I was a mature adult.

"Enough humming!" I shouted, cutting off Angel's rendition of "Some Enchanted Evening." "What did Jason say? When did he call?"

"When you were outside, getting groceries from Timothy. He'd heard about *Press Box*."

Great. Now he knew I was a failure. I wondered if Angel had told him she'd always known I wouldn't make it in the dying industry of journalism. I shouldn't let it bother me. It was only the truth.

But that wasn't my real problem. My *real* problem was that Angel had talked to Jason, alone and unsupervised. He had no idea I'd been lying to her for the past two weeks, feeding her stories about our non-existent relationship. He couldn't possibly have maintained my charade.

But he must have. Because Angel wasn't berating me for driving him off. She wasn't telling me no normal man would want a woman like me, a woman who loved sports, who swore too much, who was damaged goods after leaving her fiancé at the altar. She wasn't remonstrating with me about the *truth*.

So I thanked her for the belated message. I said I'd call Jason later. And I didn't cut off her humming "People Will Say We're in Love" as I cleared the table.

I did, though, declare my twenty-four-hours phone moratorium over the instant I'd tucked my grandmother into bed for the night. My hand actually shook as I pressed my back against the wall of precisely straightened throw pillows on my bed in the guest room.

My inbox was flooded again, and I'd received dozens of texts. But the only thing I cared about was the phone call that had come in mid-morning. Angel and Jason had spoken for over five minutes. I tapped his number, wondering what could possibly have kept them talking for that long.

He answered on the first ring. "Hey, Killer!"

The nickname hit me like a shot of adrenaline. "Hey," I said. "I'm sorry I didn't call you back sooner. Angel just gave me the message."

"Love means never needing to say you're sorry."

I just about choked. "Excuse me?"

"We're madly and passionately in love, aren't we? That's what gives us the power to carry on our improbable long-distance relationship in the middle of a pandemic."

He was teasing me. My brain knew that. But my heart must have thought he was serious, because it started pumping twice as fast as normal. "I'm sorry," I said again. "I should have told Angel the truth. But our white lie is one of the few things that's making her happy these days. And she was in such a great mood tonight—the best since I moved in. What did you guys talk about?"

My over-alert ears caught his hesitation—maybe only a second, but it stretched like hours. "She told me about your mother," he said. "Your father too."

"She had no—" I started to protest. I *hated* people finding out about my family. They always treated me differently after they knew. Like I was…fragile. Broken. I felt guilty when I saw those kind frowns, when I heard the soft murmur of awkward condolences, decades after the fact.

Better to cauterize Jason's unnecessary sympathy now. "It was a long time ago," I said. "I'm fine."

"Of course you are," Jason said, and his voice was miraculously unchanged. "But I get it. My dad died when I was twelve."

Okay. He couldn't know *exactly* how I felt. He hadn't done the things I'd done, lived the life I'd lived. But he would understand at least some of the feelings I hated putting into words, the sense that my life had been soldered together and I could never, ever forget the jagged joint where the old pieces fit into the new.

I said wryly, "Suckiest club in the world."

And I hadn't had a clue Jason was in it. His real father hadn't come up when I ran his name through the search engines—just Coach Dixon.

Jason didn't seem marked by his loss—sad or reckless or damaged. Which made sense. Because *I* wasn't sad or reckless or damaged because of *my* loss. Not in any way that showed up on the outside.

But maybe I *had* sensed something about Jason's past. Maybe our mutual experience with loss had made it so easy to be with him. To accept the crazy-hot attraction that had fueled our one-night stand. Maybe there was something deep, something secret—like a lost-your-parent pheromone—that had made him so irresistible.

He hadn't responded to my sardonic comment, and I didn't want this conversation to lapse into one of the standard, awkward discussions—about Father's Day or grief camp, about birthdays and Christmas and all those other horrible rites of passage. So I veered down another path. "I'll set Angel straight tomorrow."

"Why do that?"

It was a simple question. And there were a dozen answers, each more reasonable than the last. Most importantly: sane people don't pretend to date. Not in the real world. Not outside books and movies and madcap romcom fantasies.

But if I said that, I wouldn't have any reason to call Jason again. So I asked, "You're joking, right?"

"Not really."

Everyone said texting was awkward because you couldn't read a person's tone. That's why people sprinkled emojis across their phone screens, for clarity. Okay, and for fun.

I needed every emoji in the world to parse his two words: *Not really*.

Was he joking? Keeping himself entertained in the middle of a pandemic? Was this a charity mission to help heal a bitter old woman with a broken arm? Was he thinking something else, something about me? Something along the lines that our night at the Monaco might have been something more than a fun little no-strings diversion?

"What does that even mean?" I asked. "Dating. During a pandemic."

"Well, in the real world, I'd ask you over to my house. Show you around. Cook you dinner."

"So much for the real world."

"We can do it." He was clearly warming to the idea. "Friday night. We'll have something to look forward to for the rest of the week."

My laugh was grounded in frustration. "In case you've forgotten, we're on house arrest."

"We'll FaceTime. I'll take you on a tour of my house. And you can show me yours. Well, Sean's. I'll have dinner delivered, there and here. We can eat together, over the phone."

Was I crazy for thinking that sounded like fun? *Stir*-crazy, maybe. But I'd cleaned the house top to bottom that morning. I could keep it together for three days, to make a good impression. "You don't have to send dinner."

"I insist."

"But Angel—"

"She'll be our chaperone."

"With nine hundred miles between us, I don't think I need anyone guarding my virtue."

"I don't know. I've heard you're pretty easy."

My laugh was a single sharp bark. "I could say the same about you, you know."

"Fair is fair. So what do you say? Friday night. Seven o'clock."

"Seven," I said, and it sounded like a promise.

When I hung up, I was looking forward to something for the first time since corona turned my life upside down.

Because it would help Angel.

Right.

That was the only reason why.

19

JASON

I automatically set a bookmark in the Churchill biography I was reading when Jen came into the kitchen. A quick glance at the clock on the stove confirmed my suspicion. She was half an hour late.

Jen was never half an hour late. Anywhere. For any reason.

"What's up?" I asked.

She handed me a sealed manila envelope. My name was printed on the front in precise red ink. A note was pinned to the front with a bright purple clip. *Mary Ann Dixon,* it said. *9:50.*

"What's this?"

"She called on my personal phone."

"Is Coach—"

"He's fine," she said, before my brain could catch up to my suddenly roiled stomach. "He's getting an infusion this morning, four hours in the chair. They wouldn't let her back in the room because of COVID, and she wanted someone to talk to. I told her you'd check in later today."

I reached for my phone.

"She can wait," she said, jutting her chin toward the envelope. "Open that first."

I could tell from her tone I wasn't going to like whatever was inside. I slipped a finger under the seal and pulled out a dozen printed pages. A quick glance at the top sheet revealed the name of my agent, three phone numbers, an email address, and a street address. Other sheets gave me the details on my accountant, my broker, three banks, seven credit cards…

"What the hell, Jen?"

"I'm giving notice."

Shit. She was serious. I pushed back from the table and grabbed a coffee mug, filling it two thirds and topping it off with hazelnut creamer from the fridge. I stirred in a generous teaspoon of sugar, just the way she liked it, and handed it to her as I gestured for her to sit at the kitchen table.

"Did you have breakfast?" I asked, nodding toward my usual yogurt, complete with flaxseed, chia seed, and a handful of early strawberries. It was an invitation for her to join me.

"Did you hear me?" Jen asked.

"Yeah. I'm waiting for you to tell me how I fucked up."

"You didn't do anything."

"Then—"

"I'm going home."

"To Raleigh?" That would make sense. With spring training on hold, Jen could head north. It was probably time for her to start planting her garden. But she didn't have to *quit*, to head up to North Carolina.

"To Killeen."

Holy fuck. "What could you possibly—"

"Mom called. Dad's converting the factory to make face

masks for healthcare workers. She's worried about him. He hasn't come home in a week."

"He's on a bender," I said flatly.

"I don't know. I don't think so. I think he really is trying to pivot. Trying to help."

"Of course, there's not a lot of demand for hockey visors in March," I said skeptically. Or shin guards. Or football pads. Or any of PriceGuard's other protective gear, in the middle of a pandemic.

"Don't be an ass," Jen said.

I'd lied, talking to Katie last night. My father wasn't dead. But after the shit he'd pulled all my life, he might as well be. The first time I'd wanted to kill him was when I was twelve, when we won the Little League World Series and he'd been too drunk to make it to the final game. But that was far from the last…

And now he was taking Jen away from me.

"So how does this work, exactly?" I asked, calm and analytical, like I wasn't raging inside. "You print out a record of my accounts and leave me high and dry, just because Dad snaps his fingers?" I watched Jen's throat bob as she drank her coffee without concern. I wasn't saying anything she didn't expect to hear. Still, I had to add, "And what do you think will happen when he's got the line running smoothly? How long before he kicks you out on your ass and hires some drunk down on his luck?"

She sighed in frustration. "Let's not have this fight, okay?"

"I'm not the one fighting. I'm just stating facts."

"Then let's not state those facts. Again."

But I was just warming up. My father thought he lived in some *Leave it to Beaver* wonderland, where my mother's only job was to keep him fed and clothed in a perfect, pristine home. My sisters could choose between nursing, teaching, or raising their own families. Anything else was a waste of time.

That was fine for Janine and Jackie—they liked being stay-at-home moms. But Joanie was "just" a nurse—Director of Nursing for a seven-hospital conglomerate in Los Angeles. And Jessica was "just" a teacher, although the university that made her president last spring would have said differently.

Jen was the biggest disappointment of all. She'd broken all the rules, liking math, getting an actual college degree in bookkeeping. And she'd used that degree to help out at PriceGuard when the old comptroller walked out on Dad's drunk ass. Only one year out of college, Jen had revamped the entire accounting department, updated the hardware and software, instituted a state-of-the-art inventory system. And Dad had busted her down to an accounts receivable clerk the first time one of his drinking buddies needed a job.

Those were facts. Not the amorphous emotions of a Little League kid whose dad was too drunk to come to the biggest game of his life. Not the well-seasoned disgust of a Carver senior whose father took out a full-page ad in the hometown newspaper after the College World Series, pimping PriceGuard's products like they were the reason we'd won. Not the disappointed hate of a major league veteran whose name and picture had been used repeatedly, without permission, to sell every piece of sports equipment a two-bit factory could churn out.

I said to Jen, "He's using you."

"Seems to be a thing, with Price men."

I just stared.

I paid her. I thanked her. I told her I loved her. "That's a low blow."

She ducked her head over her coffee mug. For the first time ever, I saw a gray hair woven into her chestnut ponytail. "You're right," she said, before she raised her chin. "And I'm sorry. But he's trying to do something good now. Something right. I can't do anything to stop the virus. But if one piece of PriceGuard equipment can keep a doctor alive to treat COVID patients…"

I wanted to argue. I wanted to tell her she'd be pissed off by her first day home, and ready to kill him by the end of the week. I wanted to say she should stay with me, that I needed her help, that I relied on her every single day.

But I could tell from the set of her shoulders she'd already made up her mind. And that meant we'd only end up in a fight.

Besides, the baseball season was shut down. I wasn't going anywhere for the foreseeable future.

So I pointed my coffee mug toward the purple flowers on the center island. "What happens to those after you leave? Do I water them every day?"

"Like you'd remember, before they shrivel up and die. I've already called Ms. Greenjeans to pick them up this afternoon."

"Who?"

"That's the name of the nursery over on Seminole." I must have looked perplexed because she gave a weary laugh. That's when I realized how exhausted she was. This decision hadn't been easy on her. Mom must have sounded really bad. Desperate, even.

Jen went on, as if she were explaining things to someone who'd just learned English. "They pick up the plants every year. I'll get them back next January, right before you come down for spring training."

"We board our plants."

Jen nodded. "You don't want the hassle of dealing with them whenever you head back to Raleigh. And it's not like you'll even notice when they're gone. You wouldn't notice if you were living in a bare rock cave."

"O—"

Okay. I started to say okay. But then I remembered I had a date on Friday night. I was taking Katie—and her grandmother, God help me—on a virtual tour of my home. I needed the place to look decent. Better than decent. I needed it to look perfect.

"Wait," I said. "I don't want them out of here before… I'll call Ms. Greenjeans before I go."

Jen eyed me shrewdly. "You don't want them out of here before what?"

"Hmm?" I tried to look nonchalant. My sister had been my assistant for seven years without a single hiccup, largely because we maintained a professional relationship. She didn't need to know about my personal life. Especially when I was positive that whatever Jen learned would be common knowledge among all my sisters within an hour.

"Hey," I said, as if an idea had just come to me. "What's the best bookstore in Coral Crest?"

"Don't change the subject."

"I'm not," I lied. But I'd been up half the night after talking with Katie, and somewhere between taking a cold shower and punching my pillow into a more comfortable shape, I'd come up with an idea.

For some reason, Jen believed me. Or, at least, she pretended to. She said, "Beach Reads. On the Ave."

"They do mail order?"

"Sure. You can call them or order through their website."

"And they're still open? Even with corona?"

"For now, anyway. They're doing curbside pick-up. I bought you nine books last week. Even *you* couldn't have finished all of them already."

I shook my head. "These aren't for me. We keep hearing about government shutting down non-essential businesses. Places like Beach Reads will be hit hard. I thought I'd order some books for friends and family. Send out a couple dozen now. Come up with another list next week, and the week after that."

"You've got a lot of friends," Jen said.

"Then Beach Reads can sell a lot of books. What do you think the kids would like?"

As I'd hoped, Jen got distracted putting together reading lists for our nieces and nephews. I considered asking her about the best service for ordering dinner for Katie and Mrs. McIntyre, up in DC. But that would lead me right back to the conversation about the plants, and why I wanted them around on Friday night.

How difficult could it be to order dinner? I'd figure it out.

In the end, Jen was the one who broke our just-formed truce. "Come home with me," she said.

"Jen..."

"Dad's going to meetings. And this retooling the factory, it's a big deal. He's doing a good thing—for his employees and for health care workers who need the protective gear."

"Throwing my picture on masks won't add to his bottom line. Not if he's selling to hospitals."

"Come on, Jase. Don't be like that."

I wasn't going to win this fight. But I also wasn't going to Killeen.

"I'll send a check," I said. I'd make it out to Mom, so I knew it would get where it needed to go.

"You can't just throw money at a problem and think it'll go away!" Jen said.

I *could* do that. I'd been doing that since I'd signed my first major league contract, and everything was going just fine.

Jen changed her tack. "You know you'll go stir-crazy here. Who knows how long things will be shut down?"

Just like that, she woke the Mind-Fuck. The tingle started at the base of my spine, and I ground my toe into the kitchen floor.

"One trip to Texas," Jen urged. "You don't even have to stay a week."

"No. I promised the team. We're all staying here until things open up."

Besides, I'd rather face the Fuck than give my father another chance to use me for his own good. To forestall further argument, I picked up Jen's sheaf of papers.

"Come on," I said. "Tell me everything I need to know to run my life."

She eyed me for a long time. I thought she was going to refuse. But then, because she was the one walking out, because I was the only person in the world more stubborn than she was, and because she loved me, she obliged. I didn't have to think about my father anymore.

20

KATIE

"What will you do with all your free time?" I asked Brittany. "Come on! Treat today like New Year's. What are your resolutions?"

Her moan vibrated over the phone connection. "New Year's? No wonder I'm hung over."

"You're hung over because this virus screwed you royally. And because your boss let you keep the bar open for your laid-off co-workers until closing time. And because you haven't been able to handle rum for as long as I've known you."

Brittany's moan turned to a gagging noise. "But Dark and Stormy seemed like such a perfect theme for the restaurant's last night..."

"Suck it up, buttercup." I was in a great mood. I'd awakened well-rested for the first time since moving into Sean's home. Angel had slept in, letting me enjoy a decent cup of tea—a phrase I never thought I'd use—without interruption.

Even Lucifer had politely waited for me to open a breakfast can of Tuna Tartare.

Okay. The rosy fish mush stank to high heaven. But even that odorous assault hadn't been enough to knock me back.

Nevertheless, Brit's announcement that Two Girls and a Radish was closed for the duration *had* taken me down a notch. "Come on," I urged her. "You really should make some plans. Think of this time off like a gift."

"Tell that to my landlord."

I winced. Sean wasn't charging me rent, and when *Press Box* shut down he'd offered to cover my sublet. Even better, my co-worker who actually had the lease on the apartment had decided to stay in Japan even after the Olympics were called off. He thought that was safer than coming home. So my housing situation was a hell of a lot more secure than it might have been.

"You'll find something before you have to worry about that," I said. My Pollyanna-sunshine voice wouldn't fool anyone for long. I rushed on to say, "I'm going to learn Swedish."

"Swedish!" I'd managed to make Brit laugh.

"You know how much I love those grim Scandinavian mysteries. Ever since I roomed with Astrid Andersson in college, I've wanted to read one in the original language."

"What's Swedish for serial killer?"

"I don't know yet. But I will! And I'm going to take up knitting, too."

"You've got to be kidding me. You won't sit still long enough for that."

I shrugged. "Lucifer will love having the yarn around. And it's something quiet I can do when Angel naps."

"Lucy!" Brit exclaimed, the way every person with a soul did, whenever that hairless demon was mentioned. "You could knit her a cat sweater. You know, like a dog sweater but…"

"For a cat. Right." I was thinking more like making a

human sweater, but whatever. "And I'm taking up baking, too."

Brit's shout of dismay wasn't exactly an endorsement.

"I can follow a recipe!" I said defensively.

"For peanut butter and jelly sandwiches. Maybe."

"I'm starting with chocolate chip cookies. The recipe on the yellow bag."

"I can't wait to see how *that* goes."

"You're supposed to be *supportive!*"

"I haven't forgotten the brownies you brought to book group."

"They shouldn't print high-altitude instructions on low-altitude boxes. Anyone could get confused."

"And those slice-and-bake sugar cookies you brought to Girl's Night In…"

"If they want all the cookies to be the same thickness, they should pre-slice them."

"And the birthday cake you brought to celebrate my turning thirty."

"Anyone could forget to add sugar!"

"I'm just saying this quarantine might not last long enough for you to master baking."

I would have protested further, but Brit was probably right. Time to go back on offense. "So, what are you going to work on? Tell me one thing."

"I'll develop a new donut recipe."

"Just one?"

"Three. Will that shut you up?"

I grinned. "Three's a good start. But none of those weird savory ones, okay?"

"And I'll figure out some sort of side hustle, too. Something I can do from home that doesn't cost a lot to start up and will earn me a thousand bucks a week. Think I can do that?"

"No problem," I said. Because that's what best friends

were *supposed* to do. Not criticize every little mistake someone might have made in the past.

There. We both had our work cut out for us. I never would have wished the coronavirus on anyone. But I was going to make the best of the time I'd been given by *Press Box*'s demise.

21

KATIE

"The bears are eating the children," I said, making my eyes go round as I stared into the mirror. "*Björnarna äter barnen.*"

I touched up my mascara as I practiced my first Swedish lesson. If worse came to worst in this pandemic, I could land a job as a stringer for the *Svenska Dagbladet.* They could hire me for the bear invasion beat. Good to have in my back pocket.

"*Alla vet att björnar är mycket smartare än barn; annars skulle våra städer vara fyllda med björnar i tråkiga kontorsjobb.*" The language program must have skipped ahead a few dozen lessons. Aside from my good friends, the bears, I couldn't make out a word in that passage. Scowling, I tapped the screen on my phone and shelved my mechanical instructor before I applied a slick of lip gloss.

I ran my hand through my hair one last time before returning to my tornado-struck bedroom. I'd arrived at Sean and Timothy's with a single suitcase crammed full of yoga pants and T-shirts, along with every pair of underpants I owned.

What? I'd argued with no one as I crammed the folded cotton into the empty guest-room dresser drawers. I was responsible for taking care of Angel. The less time I spent doing laundry the better.

Of course, that was one of my life mottos, even when I *wasn't* trapped in a suburban McMansion with my grandmother during a pandemic. I was a little ashamed of how much underwear I owned. And a little sad about how much of it was seamless, cotton, and practical.

This afternoon, though, I'd dug to the back of the drawer for a matching set of bra and panties. Lace. Black. With tiny red bows.

Not that Jason Price would have the first clue I'd put them on for him. That's what I got for asking Timothy to bring something date-appropriate from my closet in the sublet. He'd chosen the cashmere turtleneck I wore on job interviews, a Black Watch plaid skirt, opaque tights, and ballet flats.

I was pretty sure Timothy was enjoying a joke at my expense. Even a gay website designer couldn't be *that* oblivious to what women wore on dates. Or maybe he was sending a not-too-subtle message about appropriate dinner clothes with Angel at my side. As if I hadn't been worrying about that for the past three days.

Whatever. I hadn't managed to piece together a better outfit. Not that I hadn't tried. My bed was piled high in athleisure wear.

The doorbell rang, and I sprinted for the stairs. It took a few carefully aimed kicks to drive Lucifer from the front door, where three large bags waited on the porch. I called out thanks to the delivery man, who was just getting back into his car.

Passing through the living room, I raised the bags in a

playful salute to my grandmother, who was enthroned in her ample wing chair, watching the local news. "Dinner's here."

Angel's mouth twisted into a familiar frown. "What did you burn this time?"

"That's not very nice."

"I'm only telling the truth. You ordered delivery, so *something* must have gone wrong in the kitchen. Is the cookie sheet still soaking in the sink?"

"No. The cookie sheet isn't still soaking in the sink." I hoped my aggrieved tone hid the fact that I'd consigned the Calphalon tray to the trash that afternoon. Who would've thought oatmeal raisin cookies would turn to jet-black, insoluble stone in a mere fifty minutes? And why didn't the oatmeal company print its recipe on the canister with larger numbers?

At least the smoke alarm had driven Lucifer out of the kitchen. Even with the sliding glass door open to clear the air, the cat hadn't been brave enough to venture back in.

Anyone could have made that little mistake. Angel didn't have to be mean about it. I set my jaw and reminded her, "We're having dinner with Jason. Over FaceTime."

And just like that, my grandmother smiled. She reached her good hand to her hair, patting the lank strands I still hadn't mastered maneuvering into place with a blow-dryer. When she laughed, she sounded like a teenager. "Do I have time to change my blouse?"

I thought about saying no. But this was the first time all week that Angel had shown the slightest interest in her appearance. That had to be a good thing, right?

"Let me put these in the kitchen, and I'll come help you," I said.

I ferried the bags to the counter. I would have indulged my curiosity about their contents, but I feared Angel would overdo things in the bedroom. Maybe she'd try applying makeup. With her dominant hand still constrained by a cast, disaster would certainly ensue.

I only took two steps toward the bedroom before I pulled up short, barely avoiding Lucifer's thrashing tail. The cat was stretched across the precise geometric center of the kitchen. "Where did you come from?" I asked.

She yowled an extended note of dissatisfaction, but I didn't mind. Instead, I was grateful for the warning. I retraced my steps and collected the bags of food, putting them inside the microwave for safekeeping. This was one meal Lucifer wasn't going to ruin.

Foiled from consuming her early dinner, the cat accompanied me back to Angel's bedroom, weaving between my feet with such vigor that I needed to hop to safety three separate times.

Angel was scowling by the time I gained the bedroom. "Really, dear. I don't know what kept you. Your young man is expecting us at seven, right?"

Angel couldn't remember the dosage times for even one of her medications. She was shaky on the days of the week. And I was pretty sure she called me Abigail the other day, even though she'd covered quickly, saying, "You *do* have your mother's eyes."

But once she'd been reminded that Jason was joining us for dinner, she was locked in and loaded for *björn.* She'd laid a silk top across the bed, adding an Hermes scarf and a pair of gold earrings. Why the hell had Sean and Timothy even included that outfit when they sprang her from Oak Grove?

Lucifer jumped onto the comforter as Angel untangled a strand of pearls from her jewelry box. My grandmother clucked a scolding at the back of her throat. "Katie. I do *not* want cat hair on my blouse."

Well, it's a damn good thing your cat doesn't have hair, I thought, but I gamely tried to sound cheerful as I urged Lucifer away from the clothes. My first three attempts were as unsuccessful as every other effort I made to discipline that strong-willed menace. Just as I was about to add steel to my tone—and maybe the edge of my hand—Angel twittered, "Lucy, darling. Jump down now."

The cat obeyed immediately.

I gritted my teeth and helped my grandmother change clothes. I had to admit, the shimmering silk looked festive. We agreed to let Angel keep the cast close to her side beneath the top, leaving her sleeve empty.

I'd actually set the dining room table last night. Not that I'd been looking forward to my date, or anything. It had just been more convenient to rearrange the chairs—placing them both on one side of the table. And to spread out a tablecloth while Lucifer was sleeping with Angel. And to bring out Sean and Timothy's fine china when I didn't have an audience. Their crystal too. I'd even taken the time to polish two place settings of silver.

"How lovely," Angel said as she entered the dining room. I started to grin with pride, but my grandmother quickly qualified her praise. "Sean and Timothy registered for such beautiful patterns."

Yes, my brother and his husband had excellent taste. Yes, they'd succeeded in getting married, when I could only show a string of disastrous relationships. Yes, they were practically perfect in every way.

Like the dark cloud of my thoughts, Lucifer was back, doing her best to trip me as I escorted Angel to the table. That animal had an uncanny ability to predict exactly where I was going to step next. There must be some way for her to use her powers for good instead of for evil, but I sure as hell didn't know what it was.

Barely swallowing my exasperation, I said, "Why don't you have a seat, Angel? I'll get the food, and then we can call Jason."

I pulled out my grandmother's heavy chair. Or, rather, I

attempted to pull the chair. It snagged on something, catching hard after only a few inches.

"What the—"

Bending over, I peered past the yowling Lucifer to see what was obstructing the chair. The cat strutted in front of me, tail held high, as if she were the grand marshal of some parade. "Luci—" I barely refrained from voicing the last syllable, the one Angel despised.

But I thought it loud and clear when I saw that the legs of Angel's chair were wrapped in yarn. They were bound to the table leg on one side and to my chair on the other.

"It looks like Lucy got into your knitting!" Angel exclaimed. "Oh my! How much yarn *is* that?"

"Two hundred and fifty yards," I growled.

It wasn't even the damn cat's fault. I should have known better. I shouldn't have left a single thing I valued lying anywhere in the house. I tried to lift the chairs free, but the yarn was wrapped too tightly.

"Katie, dear," Angel said, apparently inured to Lucifer's proud wailing. "We really shouldn't keep your young man waiting." She raised her good wrist, showing off a dainty watch. "It's already five past seven."

I could argue. I could fight with the yarn. I could kneel down and wrestle with the chairs and the table, and probably Lucifer's four feet, eighteen claws, and mouthful of teeth.

But I knew when I was defeated. I made it to the kitchen in double-time and plucked the kitchen shears from the impressive knife block on the counter. Half a dozen sawing motions, accompanied by short, frustrated grunts as the rubber-wrapped handles gouged into my palms, and the chairs were free.

After helping Angel to her seat, I collected the strands of yarn—all two hundred and fifty severed yards—before Lucifer could make off with a prize. I deposited the entire mess in the kitchen trashcan, keeping Lucifer from eating it and precipitating a trip to the emergency veterinarian.

I started to press the heels of my hands to my eyes but remembered just in time to spare my mascara. Taking a deep breath, I counted to ten. Then, I rescued dinner from the microwave.

I was already late. I might as well take a moment and transfer the meal to the serving dishes I'd set out the night before. Curious despite my frustration with Lucifer, Angel, and the entire bizarre construct of First Date Night during a pandemic, I opened the nearest bag.

Chinese food.

Steamed dumplings. Minced chicken in lettuce wraps. Wonton and hot-and-sour soups in insulated containers. Bang-bang shrimp and beef with broccoli. Garlic chicken and twice-cooked pork. Hunan vegetables, with chunks of tofu. Container after container—enough for dinner tonight and meals for the entire weekend, with enough variety that neither Angel nor I would get tired of leftovers.

Nothing was fried, so it didn't get soggy in transport. Nothing needed to be cut with a knife.

It was the most thoughtful meal I'd ever seen in my life.

But one bag still sat on the counter, brown paper, too small for food. I opened it cautiously and peered inside. My laughter washed away the last of my frustration over the yarn.

I was staring at two chocolate truffles, each a single bite, perfectly formed and rolled in cocoa powder. And beneath them, in a clear plastic bag, was a fake-fur catnip mouse, complete with a frayed rope for a tail.

22

JASON

I suffered through dinner.

Okay, it wasn't exactly hazardous duty. But it was hard to maintain the veneer of—as Mrs. McIntyre put it so succinctly—a gentleman caller. I had to offer up mindless dinner-party conversation when I really wanted was to jump in my car, drive nine hundred miles, and jump Katie's bones.

Mu shu pork made a pretty sad substitute for *that*.

But I smiled and nodded and lied through my teeth when Mrs. McIntyre asked me how I'd met Katie. The fact that she asked meant Katie hadn't crafted her own cover story. She sure as hell wouldn't've told her grandmother that we'd fucked like monkeys an hour after we'd met.

I improvised. "I've been a subscriber to *Press Box* from the day it launched. And Katie's first story—" I took a slug of beer, giving her the chance to help me out.

Right on cue, she provided, "The one about the Texas school, Angel. Where they play co-ed flag football."

I nodded. "I've got four nieces living in Killeen. They'd give their entire collection of Barbie dolls to play Pee-Wee Flag."

Mrs. McIntyre looked amused as she speared a choice morsel of chicken with her fork. She leaned out of the phone's frame as she spoke baby talk to the cat I still hadn't seen. "Does Lucy want some num-nums? A widdle bit of chicken for the itty bitty cat?"

"Angel," Katie said, but her grandmother ignored the protest, turning back to me with an incisive look. "But you don't live in Texas now."

"No, ma'am. My main home is in Raleigh. But I'm in Florida now. For spring training."

Those eagle eyes turned on Katie. "I don't recall you saying you'd traveled to Raleigh lately. Or to Florida."

Seeing Katie stiffen at her grandmother's disapproval, I concocted an easy answer. "I've been coming to DC, ma'am. Whenever I can get a break from the team."

Mrs. McIntyre sniffed grudging acceptance of my lie. "And what have you enjoyed, while you've been here?"

The sound your granddaughter makes when she comes for the fourth time.

Yeah. Not the right boyfriend response. At least not when I was trying to make a good first impression. Instead, I said, "Politics and Prose is a favorite."

As I'd intended, I caught Mrs. McIntyre by surprise. "I didn't think you baseball players spent a lot of time in bookstores."

I bristled. Not at the assumption that ballplayers didn't read—I'd had years to get used to that. It was the *you baseball players.* She was lumping me with Aaron Henderson, which made me see red.

Once again, Katie saved me. "Jason goes to bookstores in every city he visits. He posts pictures of the books he buys on social media. It's sort of his thing."

My eyebrows flicked up in surprise. I hadn't realized she followed my Twitter feed. She flashed me a quick smile as she seized a bite of broccoli with her chopsticks. Before she popped it in her mouth, she offered her own lie to her grandmother: "One time when Jason was here, we rented those red bikes. I took him on a tour of the monuments."

If she was willing to play, I was happy to raise the ante. "The view from the top of the Washington Monument is amazing. But my favorite is the FDR. It's so quiet at sunset, with the light reflecting off the Tidal Basin..." I leaned forward, and whispered conspiratorially to Mrs. McIntyre, "It's a very romantic place to steal a kiss."

"Jason!" Katie protested, looking like a teenager caught after curfew.

But Mrs. McIntyre cooed approval. The rest of the meal was filled with meet-the-parents (*grandparent,* I reminded myself) small talk. I hadn't been grilled like that since high school, but I did my best to rise to the occasion. I told Mrs. McIntyre about growing up in Texas. I tossed off entertaining stories about my nieces and nephews. And as Katie broke out the truffles I'd had the driver pick up for dessert, I even waxed eloquent about the New Year's parades Dad sponsored every year in Killeen.

It was easy enough to put those parades in the distant past. Make them sound like a good memory Dad and I shared before he kicked his untimely bucket. It *had* been years since I'd gone to one. Since Dad decked out a flat-bed with the Rockets' red-and-blue logo and a banner: PriceGuard—The Rocket's Number One Choice.

I shouldn't have led with correcting his grammar, but the misplaced apostrophe pissed me off. That was just a warm-up for my explaining—for at least the hundredth time—that Dad couldn't use my team to promote his brand. Not without a contract.

Of course he'd fought back. Called me a pussy. Told me to man up and do something for my family, for once.

"Fine," I'd said. "I'll do something."

I'd grabbed the red paint Joanie was using to touch up the twins' wagon, and I'd corrected the apostrophe.

"Hey! I *bought* that banner!" my father roared.

"But you won't buy me!" I'd thrown the paint like a hardball, leaving a huge arc across the banner and the flat-bed and the driveway—a fucking arterial spray.

I still felt bad about scaring the twins. But I hadn't backed down. Not after a lifetime of Dad using me however he saw fit.

Fuck. No need to ruin Fake-Boyfriend Date Night with all that crap. So I kept things light, wrapping up a lie about the parade by saying, "Dad was a character."

Mrs. McIntyre intoned, "May he rest in peace."

Well, shit. It wasn't like I *wanted* him to die. And I felt a little guilty when I caught Katie's wistful smile. She had to be thinking about her own father, about something he'd done that was *worth* missing him. Something she had good reason to mourn.

Quickly, before I could think too much, I launched into another story, about Jackie's youngest trying to make real popcorn, on the stovetop and everything, which would have been a success if he'd remembered to put a lid on top of the pot.

That led to a story about Katie's brother making popcorn balls for a Boy Scout fundraiser, which led to tales about long-ago camping trips, which led to my exaggerating the dangers of tracing the Chisholm Trail.

I didn't realize how late it was until Mrs. McIntyre hid a yawn behind her cloth napkin. "Well," she said, with that tart little smile I'd come to expect from her. "Thank you for a lovely evening, Jason. It's time for Lucy and me to leave you two lovebirds in peace."

Katie asked, "Jason? Can you give us a few minutes?"

"Nonsense," Mrs. McIntyre said. "I'm perfectly capable of getting ready for bed by myself. Lucy can supervise." As if to prove her point, the cat yowled from the unseen floor as she pushed back from the table. "Good night, Jason."

I said good night, but Katie stared off-screen, worry carving a line between her eyebrows. "Let me just make sure…" she murmured. Then: "Angel! I'll get that comforter for you! Don't reach for it with— Angel! Jason—"

"Go," I said.

"I can call you—"

Hearing her exasperation, I cut her off. "I'll wait."

She didn't waste time arguing. Instead, she left her phone on the table, giving me a great view of the ceiling as she called out, "Angel! Don't even try to lift that!" Her cry was punctuated by a yowl from Lucy, which she met with a few sharp words that could have taught something to the guys in the clubhouse.

Carrying my dishes to the sink, I propped my phone on the backsplash before I turned on the faucet. What the hell was I doing? Sure, sex with Katie had been amazing. But I was pretty sure entertaining little old grandmothers for an entire meal wasn't the type of foreplay that got rave reviews in *Cosmo*. And I wasn't getting laid again anyway, not from nine hundred miles away.

Katie and I couldn't keep this game going on forever. Sure, Mrs. McIntyre might have perked up for me. But the old bird seemed plenty tough. She'd be just fine without the pretense of a love-match for her granddaughter.

The smart thing to do was break up over the next few weeks. Katie and I could have a "fight." Nothing major, just enough to get Mrs. McIntyre used to the idea that wedding bells weren't in our future.

I could engineer a silly argument by next weekend. And something more dramatic the next week. One more blow-up, and the whole thing would be over. Katie could call me out on some flaw—real or imagined. I'd be the bad guy.

Just like Henderson.

And Mrs. McIntyre would give Katie crap for making another shitty choice.

Fuck. We hadn't thought this through.

"Hey," Katie said, and I realized I was standing in front of my sink, letting hot water pour down the drain. "Sorry about that," she said. "I would have been back in half the time, but Lucifer kept trying to trip me.

"Your grandmother's a sweetheart." I turned off the water and reached for a towel to dry my hands.

"Yeah, yeah," Katie said. "You certainly have her wrapped around *your* little finger."

"It's amazing what good Chinese food can do."

"It was the real fur mousie for Lucifer. That sealed the deal."

"I *still* haven't seen that cat. I'm beginning to think you're both hallucinating her."

"She's curled up on Angel's feet right now. I could bring my phone in there."

"I'll take a rain-check." Huh. I guess we weren't breaking up. Not if I was making plans to meet Mrs. McIntyre's damned cat at some point in the future.

Katie realized what I'd said too. Her entire demeanor changed. She dropped her chin demurely and asked, "We're still on a date, aren't we?" She looked up through her eyelashes. "Weren't you going to show me your place?"

She knew exactly what she was doing—and it was working quite well. "You want to see my etchings?" I laughed. "Actually, there isn't a lot to see. I only live here a couple of months a year. The rest of the time, this place sits empty. Or my sisters use it as home base for day-trips to Disney."

"Still," she said. "I want to picture where you are when we talk."

"You asked for it." I flipped the phone's camera around. "Here's the kitchen. There's a refrigerator and a dishwasher and an oven and a microwave."

"You really know how to make things sound sexy," she said.

I laughed. "What am I supposed to say?"

"How about..." She lowered her voice to a sex-kitten purr. "There's a Sub-Zero." Her throaty whisper drew out a few more words: "And a... Miehle." She arched her back and tilted her head to a come-hither angle. "And that...right there...is a...Wolf."

Jesus Christ. My voice rasped as I said, "Is that like I'll huff and I'll puff and I'll blow..." I trailed off, because she'd succeeded in making me rock hard.

She laughed and shifted back to her normal voice. "That dendrobium desperately needs some water."

"What?" I asked, hitching at my jeans out of her line of sight.

"The orchid. The purple flower on the counter. The one with the brown leaves."

"You and my sister. You both have a fixation on that plant."

"What can I say? We women identify with fragile blossoms."

I snorted. "Right. Anyway, that was the kitchen." I carried the phone into the dark living room. The lights were on in the swimming pool outside. Okay, so maybe I *had* thought ahead, at least a little. Maybe I'd wanted to impress Katie McIntyre.

"Wow," she said. "I'd love to have a pool here. That was one of the selling points when I sublet my friend's apartment —it has a rooftop pool. But that's shut down now. Not that Sean and Timothy would ever take advantage of it."

I didn't care about her brother. My voice was husky as I kept the phone aimed at the pool. "I'm picturing you in a bikini," I said. "It's strapless, right? And cherry red? Tell me it's cherry red."

"Sorry, babe. I'm a one-piece sort of gal."

Babe. She was joking. I knew that. But the endearment snagged something deep inside of me, reeling me in slow and steady. I growled, "If you take off the top, a bikini is one piece."

"You do realize my grandmother is sleeping just down the hall?"

I turned the camera around to look her in the eye. "You closed her door, right?"

"I—"

"Don't lie," I warned.

"Yes, I closed her door."

"And you've got the monitor, in case she needs you?"

She dragged it into my field of vision. "I've got the monitor."

"Then I can say whatever I want. I can say it was murder watching you during dinner. I can say I started to slip up half a dozen times, telling you what I'd do if we were actually eating in the same room. I can say that right now, I want to kiss you, to see if you still taste like bittersweet chocolate."

I watched her throat bob as she swallowed, hard. Her pupils dilated, as if she were taking a hit off some designer drug. Sweet tension spun between us, the moments adding up as she considered her reply.

And I saw the exact instant when she chickened out. "What's that behind you?" she asked, squinting a little to make out something in the darkened room.

I gave her a heartbeat to change her mind—to laugh or clear her throat or even lick her lips. But then I brightened my tone about a thousand shades. "Can't blame a fake boyfriend for trying," I said. I switched on the lamp and moved to a better angle when the light reflected off the Plexiglas case she'd questioned. "It's my Carver jersey. The one I wore in the last game of the College World Series, senior year." I nodded toward the famous photo set inside the box. "That's me and Coach Dixon."

"You're a Lion, tried and true." The school's fight song started an insta-loop inside my head. Not exactly the soundtrack I'd been hoping for a minute ago. "And you majored in philosophy?" she asked.

She'd done some research. But she really wanted to talk about that now? She might as well dump a pitcher of ice in my lap. But I said, "Yep. Asking life's major questions. Like why a woman wants to talk about philosophy when she's supposed to be showing her so-called boyfriend around her home."

"You haven't finished *my* tour!"

"There isn't much more to see." I walked the phone down the hall, barely taking time to step through doors. "Guest room. Bathroom. Office. Home gym. Master bedroom."

I stopped there, framing her view of the bed—a sky blue comforter with stark white pillows. Jen had insisted I get something that looked more beachy than my place in Raleigh. I'd told her to buy whatever she wanted, so I ended up with rattan nightstands and a matching dresser, with some sort of abstract art on the walls. The books stacked beneath the lamp by my pillow were the only things remotely personal about the room.

Which Katie realized immediately. "It looks like a hotel."

"Thanks," I said dryly.

"I mean, not that there's anything wrong with that."

"Like I said, I'm usually only down here for spring training. I spend all day, every day at the park."

Just saying the words triggered the Mind-Fuck. My lungs compressed inside my chest like someone had crumpled them into a misshapen ball. I needed to clench my fingers, even though I was holding the phone. My legs twitched with the barely suppressed need to *move*, to get away from here, to be somewhere, anywhere else.

"Enough," I said, after I'd beaten back the urge. "I showed you mine. Now it's your turn."

That was a fatal miscalculation. She turned the phone away from her face and started walking me through her brother's house.

I didn't give a damn about the marble in the foyer or the chandelier framed by the stairs. The only thing interesting in the living room was the couch, and that was because I'd already spent a lot of time imagining Katie sleeping there, stretched out, curled up, her long legs naked as she tried to find a comfortable position.

The kitchen was a kitchen: granite countertops, a center island big enough to field dress a buck, and a sliding glass door that looked onto a pitch-black backyard.

Katie lingered in her brother's home office. Framed photographs covered one wall, so I dutifully met Sean and his husband, friends from their annual beach-house rental, the lawyer buddy who'd presided at their wedding. There was a formal photo of Mrs. McIntyre standing stiffly next to a man who had to be Mr. McIntyre, each of them closing claw-like hands over the shoulders of a little boy who was dressed in a sailor suit.

The image was too old to be Sean. "Your father?" I asked.

"When he was seven years old. There he is, all grown up." Katie moved the phone to another photo—two children, a boy and a girl, dressed in matching turtleneck sweaters and belted, acid-wash jeans. An intense man in a blue broadcloth shirt with a white collar, tucked into cuffed Chinos. A grim-looking woman in black leggings with an over-size tunic. All of them were posed against a professional white background, looking a little too tired. A little too stiff.

"How old are you there?" I asked.

"Five. Sean was eleven. It was Dad's birthday, and Mom

wanted a family photo. She left before we got the proofs. Sean had to choose which one to print up because Dad wouldn't touch them."

"Rough," I said, wondering about the rest of the story, whatever Katie wasn't telling me.

She was quiet a moment, and then she turned the phone back to face her. "There isn't really anything else to show you around here. I mean, it's not my house. It's Sean's."

"So much for my brilliant first-date idea."

"No!" she protested, loudly enough that any injury to my pride was salved. "It was a great idea. And it was a great dinner. Angel especially liked it. I haven't seen her so engaged in all the time I've been here. Thank you."

"You're welcome," I said, the verbal equivalent of shaking her hand. *I want the other Katie. Let me talk to the woman who made my fucking stove sound like an invitation to an orgy.*

"I guess I should let you go," she said.

You don't have to. You could keep me busy for hours. But I said, "It's been fun."

She hesitated a moment before she said, "I don't want to hang up first."

Then don't. Stay here and talk to me. Lean back on that couch and tell me everything you're thinking.

But if she stayed on the line, I'd be right back to the conversation she'd broken off, the one when she was looking out at the pool. I'd tell her exactly what I wanted to do with my mouth and my hands and my cock, and this time I wouldn't stop until she played along.

Which would be a real asshole move. Because she'd made it perfectly clear she didn't want any of that. Christ, she'd pretended to be fascinated by a framed college *jersey* to avoid that conversation.

"We'll hang up at the same time," I said. "One."

She joined me. "Two."

She reached forward to tap her phone, leaving me to say, "Three," alone.

Fuck it. I tossed my phone onto the bed and stripped off my clothes before I headed into the bathroom for a desperately needed shower. I turned the stinging needles to ice before I was done.

23

KATIE

I couldn't explain, even to myself, why I hadn't wanted to join in Jason's phone-sex games, especially when I was the one who got the ball rolling, joking about his kitchen. I'd certainly felt a tremor of excitement as he teased about my topless bikini. And after everything we'd done at the Monaco, we both knew I wasn't a prude.

I guess I wanted something more. I wanted to know we could talk to each other as friends. Pitiful as it sounded, I wanted to know he was interested in me for more than my body.

Maybe that's why I woke up with the idea for a new article: a profile of Jason Price, the philosopher king of baseball.

At first, I shoved the idea away. He was a World-Series-winning pitcher. Boatloads of ink had already been spilled about him. No one cared about the abstract ins and outs of ancient philosophy.

But as I waited for water to boil for my morning tea with

Angel, the idea wouldn't stop nagging. I remembered an article I'd read when I'd first checked out Jason online.

It was from the San Diego paper, a Sunday puff piece about Carver's baseball dynasty. Coach Dixon was quoted: "I've got thirty-six men on my squad, and twenty-two of them major in Contemporary Studies. Price is the first philosophy major I've ever coached. All that thinking *does* something to a man. He's got the lowest ERA of any college pitcher I've seen in my twenty-nine years of coaching."

Now, I scribbled a few words on the notepad beside the phone. Carver. Jason. Dixon. Automatically, I began to doodle around the edges of the page, adding hashmarks and swirls as I jotted down possible angles.

Who was I kidding? I wasn't writing for *Press Box* any longer. I didn't have credentials to get me past watchdogs. Even if my article ended up worthy of a Pulitzer, I didn't have a venue to publish it.

But that was exactly why I *should* write it. I was going to need a new job when we got to the other end of COVID. My clip file needed to be as strong as humanly possible, and this was exactly the type of story where I excelled.

Besides, it had grabbed me by the throat and refused to let me go.

"Didn't I ever tell you that ladies don't squint?" Angel interrupted my internal debate. I hadn't heard her come into the kitchen.

About once a day, every day, for the entire time I was in high school. "Ready for me to make breakfast?" I asked, instead of saying what I was really thinking.

"That would be lovely, dear."

Huh. That was the first thing Angel had said was "lovely" since I'd come to stay. Such success was worth pushing the extremes of my cooking abilities. "French toast maybe? With hash browns and bacon on the side?"

Angel pursed her lips. "Why don't we stick with regular toast?"

I had to admit that was the wiser choice.

Angel gestured toward the note I'd been making. "You'd better put that in a safe place before you start, dear. Are you outlining a new article?"

I swallowed my resentment that Angel thought I was capable of incinerating a scratchpad. After our last three weeks of living together, she had volumes of support for her suspicions. Instead, I asked, "How did you know this is for work?"

"Those drawings you leave around the edge." She sniffed a little, but she didn't expand on her implied criticism as I loaded the toaster with slices of bread. "What does that say?" she asked, craning her neck. "Carver? Are you writing an article about your young man?"

"How did you know Jason went to Carver?"

"You young people! You think you're the only ones who know how to use the Google machine."

"You're making my argument for me," I said, softening my criticism with a smile. "But yes. I'm thinking about doing a piece on Jason. I'd write it on spec. As a freelancer."

I braced for Angel's usual criticism, the type she'd levied against every one of my decisions from the moment I turned seven. But she said, "That's an excellent idea, dear. Use this odd time to your advantage."

I gaped. My grandmother was agreeing with me. And she'd actually called me "dear" three times in the span of two minutes. Last night's dinner had done something to her. Her most jagged edges had been smoothed. She'd been stirred out of her somber silence—her *depression*, if I was going to put an honest name to things. Angel was engaged for the first time since she'd come home from the hospital.

Jason had done that. With his Chinese food and his

amusing stories and his chocolate truffles and his catnip mouse for Lucifer…

And he had the same effect on me. I couldn't explain why exactly. It wasn't a physical thing—or not *only* a physical thing—because I felt it when we were miles apart. It was just easy spending time with him.

Maybe that was because we'd both lost our fathers at such a young age. People who'd never experienced such a loss couldn't understand how it shaped a person.

I felt bound to Jason because he'd been hurt the same way I had. I *trusted* him.

That did it. I was writing the article. I'd call him after breakfast and start interviewing him, with an eye toward finding a novel approach for my piece.

But first, I needed to make toast. I thought about retrieving the tiny pot of marionberry preserves from my nightstand. But no. I was saving that for something special. Not an ordinary breakfast on an ordinary day in what passed for ordinary life in the middle of a pandemic.

Even if my grandmother was thawing toward me for the first time in my adult life.

24

JASON

Katie called six minutes before I was supposed to log in to a team meeting on Zoom. "Hey," I answered, not bothering to scrub enthusiasm from my voice.

"Did I wake you?"

"I've been up a couple of hours. I wanted to get a run in before a team meeting at ten."

"Oh! I'll let you go."

"No," I rushed to reassure her. "I've got a few minutes."

She hesitated.

Ordinarily, I would have given her all the time she needed, but the team charged a thousand bucks for every minute we were late joining calls. "What's up?" I asked.

"I've-been-thinking-about-writing-an-article-about-you-and-your-time-at-Carver-and-how-it-turned-you-into-the-pitcher-you-are-today-but-I-won't-do-it-if-you-tell-me-not-to-even-though-I-think-it-has-the-potential-to-reach-a-lot-of-people-who-don't-usually-read-about-sports-and-I-think-I-can-really-do-it-justice-especially-because-I'm-not-tied-up-with-writing-for-*Press-Box*-now-but-if-you-think-it-would-be-wierd-we-can-just-forget-about-it-and-pretend-we-never-even-had-this-conversation."

"Wow," I said. "That's some lung capacity. Did you really get all that out in a single breath?"

"I've been thinking about it all morning," she said. She gave me a moment before she pressed: "So? What do you think?"

I thought it was a lousy idea. I hated talking to reporters. I hated feeling like I was pinned on a glass slide, trapped under a microscope. I hated being cautious about every word I said, making sure I only offered up the quotes I wanted to see live on in perpetuity.

I said, "I can't imagine why you'd want to write about me."

"So you're saying not to do it?"

"I'm saying you're a grown woman and you can do whatever you want. But if I were you, I'd find a topic worth my time."

"You're worth my time."

"I'm flattered. But seriously…"

"I am serious." And she was. She sounded like she was taking some oath of office.

"How would this work? Would everything I say be on the record?" Because that would pretty much put a bullet in the head of more conversations like last night's. No one needed to know I had a thing for cherry-red bikinis. Or that Katie had shot me down like an Olympic marksman.

I could picture her face growing even more grim, her teeth pinning her lower lip, her eyebrows drawing down before she said, "No?" That sounded like a question, but she corrected herself almost immediately. "No. I mean, I'll focus on your time in college. If I'm interviewing you, if I'm asking you specific questions about what happened, then we'd be on the record. But otherwise…"

That was fair. And it left me plenty of room to maneuver, if I wanted to get our late night chats back to beachwear territory. "Okay," I said.

"You'll let me interview you?"

"I should probably demand some reciprocal questions." I kept my tone light.

Like any good reporter, she pushed. "And you're okay with me doing some background research?"

I wondered how often she negotiated with the subject of an article, defining the range of her piece. But I'd read every word she'd ever published. A lot of those articles were about sensitive topics. Her subjects would have put up roadblocks, protecting their own privacy. I'd never heard a whisper about her violating anyone's trust. And athletes talked. I would have known if she had.

"Research away," I said. "But you're going to end up ditching the whole article before you ever finalize a word."

"How can you be so sure?"

"Trust me. I know how boring I really am."

She laughed, which should have been perfect. But I still felt a shiver of unease.

I shook my head. I would never get used to this part of being a professional baseball player. My life truly was an open book, in ways I never would have imagined before I signed my first contract with the Rockets.

Speaking of which… I glanced at the clock and saw that this chat had already cost me three thousand bucks.

"I have to run," I said. "I'll call you tonight?"

"I'll be waiting," she said, her voice suddenly soft.

Christ. She cut off the call on her end, and I scrambled to join my meeting, only to hear yet another round of how the owners wanted us all back in baseball at the earliest possible moment, just not before they could get paying fans in seats to watch us play.

As I heard the same old excuses, I wished I'd stayed on the line with Katie, all the late fines in the world be damned.

25

KATIE

After talking to Jason, I headed back to the kitchen to clean up from making breakfast. How could toast create so much mess? Okay toast, and tea, and fruit, and cheese, and a few slices of prosciutto from the deli drawer… I was really getting a handle on this cooking stuff.

I glanced into the living room to make sure Angel was watching her marathon of the original *Law and Order* before I called Brittany. She answered on the first ring, just as I started returning all the leftovers to the fridge. "So? How did last night go?" she asked.

I cast an eye toward the living room. "We had a good time."

"Angel's there?"

"Absolutely!"

"And she's in ear-shot."

"You know how things go."

"Well, crap," Brit said. "Can't you shake her?"

Before I could reply, Lucifer materialized in the precise center of the kitchen. The cat had an unholy ability to sit in the single most inconvenient place in the entire house. She extended one leg and began the delicate process of cleaning her butt.

"I wish," I said, nudging the cat with my big toe. Lucifer yowled as if she were being skinned.

"Lucy," Brit crooned.

At the same time, Angel called from the living room, "What are you doing to that precious cat?"

"Absolutely nothing," I said, using the side of my shoe to urge Lucifer toward her most worshipful human. The cat turned terrifying green eyes on me and stalked out of the room, displaying her newly cleaned butthole like a badge of disapproval.

"Why don't I just come over?" Brittany said. "You can tell me all the juicy details."

"I wish," I said again.

"No juicy details?"

"Sean would kill me if I let you in the front door."

"Thanks a lot!"

"It's not just you. You know that."

"I'm going a little crazy here."

I sighed. Of course Brit was going crazy. Brit was the most extroverted person I knew. COVID house arrest was bound to affect her more than it would most people. "I'm sorry. I knew it would be tough for you, as soon as Two Girls closed."

"Call me queen of the side hustle."

"What are you doing?"

"I signed up with one of those grocery delivery services, shopping for shut-ins. And yesterday, I put up flyers everywhere I could think of, advertising my new dog-walking service—Wag the Dog."

"Great name!"

"I've heard back from two people already. They must have been attracted to my fourteen years of industry experience."

"You've never walked a dog in your life!"

"Well, I dated that guy who liked to wear a choke collar in bed..."

"Brittany!"

"I got really good at snapping a leash on and off that thing."

I glanced into the living room, wondering if Angel was bothered by my shriek of laughter. Fortunately, a dead body had just been found on the stairs to a brownstone basement apartment. Angel was petting Lucifer, cooing reassurance as if the cat were traumatized by the crime.

"You are *terrible*," I finally said. And then I turned on the kitchen faucet, figuring it was better to waste water than to let Angel weigh in again on what I was about to say. "Listen. I'm writing an article about Jason."

"Does he know?"

"Of course he knows!"

"Then why are we whispering?"

Good question. I guess I didn't want Angel in my business any more than was absolutely necessary. Her good mood from earlier in the morning might have crystallized into her usual criticism of my every move. My whispering couldn't possibly be because I was afraid writing about Jason was a spectacularly bad idea.

"Katie?" Brit prompted. "I think that article is a spectacularly bad idea."

Sometimes it was terrible, having a best friend who could read your mind. I tried to deflect. "He agreed to it. But maybe I pressured him too much? Should I have waited a day or two after dinner before I asked?"

Brittany said, "How should I know? You haven't told me anything *about* dinner. I don't even know what you ate!"

"Chinese food, okay? Really good Chinese."

"Was the phone sex before you ate? Or after?"

"There wasn't any phone sex!" I squeaked. But not for Jason's trying. I cleared my throat before I said virtuously, "Angel was right there." I glanced up to see Detective Briscoe using his pen to open the victim's sports coat.

"Kinky," Brittany said.

"Come on," I said. "Seriously. Do you really think it's a bad idea?"

"I think you've already made up your mind. And I think you're one of the most determined journalists in the world. And I think *Press Box* is nuts for letting you go. And I think you should let me come over to make lunch for both of you, so you can tell me more about what happened last night. I'll make dinner too. And I'll cook a bunch of other things and put them in your freezer. I'll do all the dishes, too."

"Where were you when I was messing up the entire kitchen, making toast for breakfast?"

"I can come, then?"

"Nope. But I appreciate the offer."

"Fine," Brit said.

"Fine?"

"Be that way."

"We're still friends, though, right?"

Brit made a rude noise. "You're stuck with me for life. But I've gotta run. I have a tutoring session in ten minutes."

It was Saturday morning, and everyone I knew had meetings to run to instead of talking to me. "What are you learning?"

She laughed. "I'm not learning anything. I'm teaching."

"Teaching what?"

"Algebra."

"Wait. What? *You're* teaching math?"

"What do you think recipes are? I spend a lot of time figuring out how much flour to order and how much oil I'll need if I double a batch. I can solve for X with the best of 'em."

"You really *are* the queen of the side hustle!"

On the one hand, Brit made me feel like a slacker. On the other, her industriousness was sparking a new idea... The article about Jason was one thing; it would keep me busy for a short time. But I needed something bigger. Something more demanding. Something that would really build my journalistic muscles. Something like..."Maybe I should start my own newspaper."

"With a printing press? And all those cool trays of little pieces of type?"

"It's 2020," I pointed out. "I'll use a website."

"Would you publish sports?"

I shook my head, even though she couldn't see me. "No. I mean, if *Press Box* couldn't make things work... I need something different. Something unique." And then I had it, the perfect idea. "I'll publish good news."

"Good news?"

"You know, happy stories. About good things happening to great people. Random acts of kindness."

"Ohhh," Brit said, twisting her voice into a parody of ecstasy. "You'll write about puppies and kittens and unicorns farting rainbows."

"What a supportive friend *you* are," I said.

But I was already thinking about details. Timothy could help me throw together a website. I could publish short little summaries, bullet points really. Link to other stories, if I couldn't get actual interviews with people. How tough could it be to find a few stories about ordinary people doing positive things?

"Fine," Brit said. "You could call it the *Good News Gazette*."

"I bet that's already taken."

"Then the *Good News Guardian*," she proposed.

"The real *Guardian* newspaper would shut me down in a heartbeat."

"How about the *Corona Crier*?"

"That sounds depressing."

"Who's being supportive now?" she demanded.

But I was already interrupting her. "I've got it! *The Feel-Good Phoenix*." Phoenix. The bird that rose from the ashes of destruction—like we were all going to do once this stupid virus was under control.

"Not bad…" she said.

I was already picturing a masthead for the website. I could make it look like a real publication, mimic the countless newspapers and magazines I visited on a daily basis.

"I know you have a lot on your plate already," Brit said with a fake innocence that immediately made me wary. "But maybe you could translate everything into Swedish. Get your language lessons in that way."

"Ha, ha," I said.

"Or wait! You could *knit* illustrations for each story, little people and animals acting out whatever happened."

"I'll have you know I rolled an entire skein of yarn into a ball yesterday. Right before Lucifer ruined it."

"And, what else were you going to do? Bake? You could include a new recipe every day."

"For a best friend, you're not being very helpful."

"I'm *very* helpful!" she wailed. "I'm helping you fit in all of your COVID activities."

"Thanks," I said wryly.

"Now here's what *you* should do, to help me," Brit said. "Log in to the grocery delivery service and request me to pick up your order. Then I can come by, and we can talk face-to-face and you can give me all the dirt about last night. My Cheerful Shopper number is—"

"Brittany!"

"What?" she asked. "You can't blame a girl for trying."

I could. I could blame her for a lot. But she had me laughing, so I let her off the hook. And a few minutes later, when she headed off to teach some poor kid algebra, I started searching the web for some good-news stories I could publish in my very own online newspaper.

26

JASON

"Honestly," Katie said. "Angel thinks you walk on water. If you could bottle whatever you've got, you could make millions."

I *felt* her wince over the phone line. I was supposed to make some off-hand joke now. Pretend that my four-year contract with the Rockets wasn't public information. That a journalist with the premier online sports magazine had no way of knowing that I was bringing in nine mil a year.

Screw it. A belated over-the-top answer was better than nothing. "Today, your grandmother. Tomorrow, the world. What do you think? We could put my secret formula in the water supply, and I could have an army of women, ready to do my bidding."

"*Må vargar gnaga på alla dina förfäders ben.*"

"What's that?"

"It's Swedish. May wolves gnaw the bones of all your

ancestors. I think. Or maybe it's 'Please pass the lingonberries.'"

"Tell me again why you're learning Swedish?"

"I want to read grim mystery novels in the original."

"That makes perfect sense." I took care to keep my voice scrupulously even.

"Why *not* learn Swedish? If I ever attend a Nobel award ceremony, I'll be able to chat with my hosts."

"And you won't have to read the subtitles in Bergman movies."

"I've never actually seen a Bergman movie."

"What?" I was surprised. "What sort of liberal arts education do you claim to have? No *Seventh Seal?* No *Fanny and Alexander?*"

"And here I thought baseball players just wanted to watch *Fast & Furious*."

"You've been hanging out with the wrong baseball players," I said.

That knocked her silent. Shit. I hadn't meant to bring up Henderson at all. I *never* meant to bring up Henderson.

Scrambling for a way to take back my glib words, I reached for my computer keyboard. A couple of keystrokes cleared away the video I'd been reviewing, scouting reports on Atlanta that were key to this year's season. I tucked my phone between my shoulder and my ear and typed, "Bergman Seventh Seal."

There it was. On Foreign Film Forum. Ten bucks for a month-long subscription.

Katie still hadn't responded to my jibe about Henderson. I started talking a little too quickly, trying to sponge up the silence. "We're starting a new tradition. Monday Movie Night."

"What?"

"I'm picking first. Bergman's *Seventh Seal*. Here. I'll send you the link." I tapped the keyboard.

"I don't know… You gained so much ground with Angel on Friday. You're willing to risk it all on some old black-and-white movie?"

Now it was my turn to fall silent. I hadn't intended to invite along a chaperone. But what, exactly, did I think Katie was going to do with her grandmother? It wasn't like she could leave the woman alone for the night, not with her arm still out of commission. Not with most of the world shut down for coronavirus.

"Let me see what I can find in the way of Swedish restaurants near you," I said.

"You don't have to do that."

"I'm supposed to be the world's most attentive boyfriend, right?"

But Katie corrected me. "*We're* supposed to be the world's most devoted couple. It's not just you. It's us."

"Well, I can promise you won't find Swedish takeout for me, here in Coral Crest."

"I'm sure someone makes a great grouper sandwich, with a side of lutefisk."

"I'm afraid to ask what that is."

She laughed. "It's fish, cured in lye. A Swedish Christmas specialty."

I almost gagged. "How the hell do you know that?"

"My freshman-year roommate at Northwestern was from Minnesota. Her family made a big deal out of their holiday traditions—lutefisk, a crown of candles, the whole nine yards."

"Please tell me you don't still keep in touch. If there's even a chance you can land lye fish before Monday, I'm keeping my front door locked. Chained. Bolted shut."

"You're safe. I haven't spoken to her since graduation."

I breathed a mock sigh of relief.

"I *do* have her recipe for kardemummas, though," Katie said.

"What's that?" I didn't try hard to mask my suspicious tone.

"You're such a fraidy-cat!"

"Lye. Soaked. Fish."

I loved the sound of her laugh, low and throaty, with just a hint of a suggestive note, as if she were welcoming me into a private room. "They're cookies," she said. "Crispy cardamom cookies."

"That doesn't sound too dangerous." They actually sounded really good. "Why don't you make your cookies, and I'll do something Swedish here."

"'Something Swedish?'"

"I'll do some research. It's not like I have a freshman-year roommate to draw on. At least, not one from Sweden."

"Where was your freshman-year roommate from?"

"Wait," I said. "Is this us just talking? Or are you asking for your article?" It wasn't like my freshman-year roommate was some sort of secret. But I'd spent the better part of the day trying to figure out why I didn't want Katie writing about me. And why I'd said yes, despite my aversion. This was as good a time as any to test the new rules. "Are we on the record?"

She missed a beat, but then she laughed. "Why don't we just say this is on deep background. Deal?"

"Deal," I said. And then I answered, because my vague concerns were just some sort of bullshit, born out of having too many cameras shoved in my face over the course of my career. "He was a good ol' boy from Bayou Teche in Louisiana."

"Did he play baseball too?"

"Bubba?"

"Was that his name?"

"That's what everyone called him. And no. Bubba did *not* play baseball. If you called down to central casting and asked for a nose tackle, they'd send up Bubba Thibodeaux. So, if we decide to watch a movie set in Nawlins, I can track him down and get his grandmère's recipe for gumbo."

"Hmmm… Maybe we should rethink this Bergman thing… We could *both* get Bubba's recipe."

"You're not getting out of *The Seventh Seal* that easily," I said. And then, because that sounded like I was a controlling jerk, I said, "I mean, you *can* get out of it. If you really don't want to watch it. Or if you think your grandmother doesn't."

"For you, Angel would watch hour-long infomercials for Ginsu knives. I wasn't kidding when I said you've wrapped her around your little finger."

"Just her?" I pushed, and then I hated myself a little because she hesitated. Just another little stutter, nothing disastrous. I only noticed, because I was hanging on every word she said. Because this silly conversation was suddenly important to me. Because I *cared*, even though we were just mapping out the next campaign in the fake relationship Katie swore was making her grandmother perk up.

"You've got me thinking about baking," Katie finally said. "And that's something I've never done for any man."

"Be still my beating heart."

"Actually," she said. "You should probably be grateful Sean's so serious about flattening the curve. You'll never have to pretend my cookies are edible."

"The way your grandmother will."

Katie's laugh was a harsh bark. "Angel has never pretended *anything* I've done is better than it is."

There was a story there. A bitter one, from Katie's tone. But I didn't have any right to ask. And she might not be willing to tell. She might not want to air her family's laundry, even if *I* granted *her* off-the-record status. Besides, her grandmother might be in earshot.

I let her off the hook. "It's a date, then? Monday night?"

"It's a date."

I pumped my fist as if I'd just gotten the third out in the ninth. But as I ended the call, I realized I didn't want this game to be over. I was hoping it had only just begun.

27

KATIE

Stiffening my jaw, I tried not to yawn out loud. So far, Movie Night had lasted approximately seventy-two hours. I would have called it quits on *The Seventh Seal* about ten minutes in, if not for Angel's rapt attention.

I sneaked another glance at the clock on the cable box. 8:58. Precisely three minutes since the last time I'd checked.

But my grandmother was completely enraptured by the black-and-white film. This was the latest she'd stayed up in the three weeks since her fall, and she wasn't showing a hint of fatigue. Instead, she was following every line of the subtitles, gasping in surprise at some of lines, moaning in suppressed agony when characters were put at risk.

Another glance at the clock. 9:01. How much longer could I last?

And yet… And yet…

I glanced at my phone, which was once again open to FaceTime. Jason was sitting in his own living room, staring at his massive TV. The lights were off behind him, and the movie had silvered the blue of his eyes. The flicker of the film brought out the scruff along his jaw. My fingers flexed, as if I could reach out and touch his rough beard.

In theory, we had FaceTime open so we could comment on the movie. But Angel and Jason were so engrossed that I didn't dare make a peep. I had to be missing something major.

I forced my attention back to the film. Back to the medieval knight. Back to the plague. Why the hell had I agreed to watch this thing anyway?

9:05.

Resisting the urge to stab myself in the eyes with my knitting needles, I picked up the project I'd stashed in the living room before my ordeal began. I had a fresh skein of yarn, one Lucifer hadn't yet destroyed. I was making a sweater with two different colors of yarn, a complicated brioche stitch, and asymmetric cables down the front, back, and each sleeve. I didn't want to get bored part-way through.

The designer called it "rhythmic and soothing." I could use a little rhythm in my life. Something soothing, too.

But I'd already made three mistakes casting on, catching the yarn on the needles in unintended loops. Everyone said casting on was the hardest part of learning to knit. Why was I such an over-achiever, choosing a pattern that required me to cast on three hundred and twenty stitches?

The yarn was fraying from my oft-repeated attempts. I'd already cut off a couple of yards to make a fresh start. Winding the now-crimped wool back onto its ball, I checked the time again. 9:06.

Seriously? Had I discovered a breach in the space-time continuum?

I wrapped my yarn around my thumb and forefinger, making yet another try at casting on. Some people used knitting to relax. Some people found the motions calming.

I should knit a pincushion. A cat-shaped pincushion. A

cat-shaped pincushion with a name spelled out in yarn: L-U-C-I-F-E-R…

As if she could read my mind, Lucifer pounced on the tail of my yarn, needling ten claws into my thigh. I shouted in surprise and pain. The cat darted out of the room as Angel jumped half-way to the ceiling. "Katherine Anastasia McIntyre!"

I reacted exactly the way I had when I was called on the carpet as a kid. I tucked my chin into my chest and dug my toe into the thick rug. Looking up through my eyelashes, I barely masked a sulky snarl. "That hurt!" I said.

"She's a five-pound cat."

"She's a five-pound piece—" But I managed to lock my reflexive response into a cage of ice. Yelling at Angel wasn't going to ease my stinging leg. Shouting in anger would never turn Lucifer into a cute and cuddly kitty.

Besides, Jason was watching from his phone. Mortified, I forced myself to meet his gaze. He'd paused his version of the movie, and his face was framed by Death's massive black hood. I scrambled to freeze ours, so we stayed remotely in sync. "Hey," he said, pitching his voice in the sort of low, soothing tone that might comfort an injured animal. "Are you okay?"

"Yeah," I said, begrudgingly. "I was more surprised than hurt. Forget about it. Let's just finish watching."

But Angel was having none of that. "Rewind," she ordered.

"We're almost at the end," I said.

"Jason?" Angel queried, demanding his support.

And he *winked* at her. Jason Price *winked* at my grandmother.

Angel preened.

"Fine," I grumbled. "Have it your way." I hit the remote control, taking the movie back two full minutes before I paused on a view of the chess board. "Satisfied?" I asked Angel.

Instead of responding to me, she said, "Jason, dear. Can you find the same place?"

Of course he could. He probably spent half his life watching video of games. He hit the same frame on his first try.

"Ready?" he asked.

I nodded and hit Play at the same time he did. As Angel's attention was snared by the sonorous Swedish dialog, Jason fiddled with his phone. My cell buzzed with a message.

JASON

If I were there, I'd kiss it to make everything better.

If you were here, we wouldn't be watching this stupid movie.

I started to hit Send but decided I didn't want to sound like a shrew. I back-spaced and tried again.

KATIE

If you were here, we would have tucked Angel into bed an hour and a half ago.

Angel interrupted whatever Jason was typing in reply. "If you two lovebirds can't resist sweet-talking each other for the length of one simple movie…"

I rolled my eyes, but I switched my phone back to Face-Time. Jason was sitting up very straight, staring at his TV. A smile, though, quirked the corners of lips.

Making my own concerted effort to watch the end of the film, I shoved my hopeless knitting into its canvas bag. I waited an eternity until the scene changed before I checked the clock again. 9:16.

Fighting the urge to scream, I considered the plate of kardemummen I'd baked that afternoon. But even my desperation to escape the stultifying movie wasn't enough to risk eating a cookie.

Sean's oven must be broken. Or maybe the timer was off. There had to be *some* explanation for why half the cookies were charred, and the other half glistened with uncooked dough. Even from my seat on the couch, I could smell the piney cardamom, like menthol cough drops. The egg wash I'd applied looked like yellow slime.

Screw it. So much for baking. So much for knitting. And I sure as hell wasn't following a word of the Swedish film. Thank God for subtitles.

And thank God for Jason Price—even if he was the reason I was watching this never-ending movie. If a woman had to be trapped in a room with her mesmerized grandmother and a murderous demon cat, she could do a lot worse than having Jason Price to stare at.

After the last interruption, he'd placed his phone at an angle, so I had a good view of his profile. He had a strong chin, even with a few days of stubble.

The new perspective caught his Carver jersey in its frame, glass flickering in the TV's reflection. I pinned my lower lip between my teeth.

Yesterday, I'd written out a long list of questions for my article. I'd considered calling him and working through them one by one, but I was pretty sure I knew exactly where *that* would take us. He'd answer the first question, maybe two, and then he'd side-track me with some sly double entendre. Or not even that—he'd say *exactly* what he was thinking, and I'd catch my breath against that lazy, now-familiar flip deep inside me.

I was already skating on thin ice, writing about a guy I… What? Had a crush on? How very junior high… Had slept with? Well, yes… Was carrying on a fake relationship with because he was the only bright spot in the middle of a terrifying pandemic when I was trapped in a house with a grandmother who drove me stark, raving mad, just by breathing?

Yeah. That was sort of the problem.

Despite all that, I thought I could write an amazing article. But I'd decided to email all my questions. And I'd woken up that morning to find four and a half pages, of single-spaced, perfectly precise, grammatically correct responses in my inbox.

The bones were there for a good story. Jason was the first person in his family to leave Texas for college. He'd applied to Carver early-admission because it was the only school he really wanted to attend. He'd dropped by baseball tryouts because he'd been great at Little League, and he'd played varsity at Killeen High for four years.

Everything was there in his answers—how he'd fallen hard for philosophy after taking a freshman seminar. How he'd taken an extra course every single semester, even during baseball season, because he could never fit in everything he wanted to learn. How Stan Dixon had become like the father he'd never known.

It was great stuff. But even when I re-read it for the third time, I knew it was missing…*something*. I needed to find a spark. A new light to show something about Jason that had never been shown before.

"That was *marvelous!*" Angel broke into my thoughts. She looked like she was going to applaud, but she remembered her injured arm at the last possible moment. "Jason, dear. Thank you so much for sharing with us."

"My pleasure, ma'am."

As I tapped the remote, finally turning off the endless film, Angel wiped away actual tears. "I don't remember the last time a movie made me *think* like that! That noble soul… What he saw… What he suffered… And his acceptance in the end, his… Katie? What did you think?"

This was the part where I was obliged to say that Jason

had transformed me, wasn't it? That my so-called boyfriend had changed the way I thought about life, art, and the human spirit?

"It was, um, better than the kardemunnen."

Angel looked appalled, but Jason laughed. "Next Monday is your choice," he promised. "Now Mrs. McIntyre. What did you think about that last scene?"

As Angel enthused about the Dance of Death, I felt a warm glow. It didn't matter that my cookies were a failure, that my knitting was in knots, or that I couldn't remember a syllable of Swedish, not even the word for wolf.

My fake relationship with Jason was working. Angel was active and engaged. She looked less stressed and sounded less tired than she had at any time since we'd taken over Sean's home.

And best of all? Jason was on-board for at least another week. I'd have time to ask him follow-up questions, to make my article everything I knew it could be.

What fake relationship got better than that?

28

JASON

"Katherine Anastasia McIntyre?" I'd waited all day Tuesday for her to call. That was the problem with the "fake" part of our relationship. I didn't have a real excuse for picking up the phone, even to give her grief about her obviously deplorable taste in movies.

What the fuck was wrong with me? I'd never needed an excuse to talk to a woman before. But now, I actually caught my breath, waiting to see how she took my teasing tone.

If I was going to tie myself into knots about what a woman thought, I might as well be her *real* boyfriend.

At least Katie was laughing. "My mother had a thing for grandiose names."

I laughed too. And then I decided to take another risk. "You showed me the picture in Sean's office, but you don't talk about her much."

For a moment, I thought I'd pushed too far, fake boyfriend or not. But then she cleared her throat and said, "Turned out,

Mama only wanted babies. Not actual kids. She ducked out when I was five."

"I'm sorry," I said, and I meant it. I couldn't imagine what my own childhood would have been like, without Mom's stabilizing influence. "That must have been tough."

"It was harder on Sean. He was already starting to butt heads with our father when she ditched us."

"Yeah," I said. "I know a thing or two about *that* family dynamic."

I cringed a little as the words left my mouth. In Katie's eyes, I'd already killed off my father. How old was I when he'd died? I was pretty sure I'd said twelve. Not a lot of time for us to have butted heads.

This lying stuff was complicated. Maybe Mom was right when she said it was always easier to tell the truth.

Fortunately, Katie was still focused on her own chaotic family. "Sometimes I wonder who Sean would be, if Daddy hadn't died his freshman year in high school. My brother spoke at the funeral. Said he wanted to go to med school. It was like he could become a doctor and retroactively wipe out pancreatic cancer."

"Ouch. That's when you went to live with your grandmother?"

"Technically, she came to live with us. Daddy had kept the house after Mama left, and Angel thought…" Her voice trailed off.

How had we even gotten on this topic, just from my teasing about her name? "So, your current living arrangements must stir up a lot of crap."

"You don't know the half of it," she said.

I want to. Tell me. Tell me why you sound so sad. Tell me what you're thinking.

Instead, Katie said, "Let's just say Angel would have preferred a granddaughter more interested in Federalist antiques than baseball. Or football. Or hockey. Or the junior varsity jai alai team at Timbuktu U."

I laughed for her, a tiny little gift.

"Enough," Katie said. "You don't want to hear this ancient history. Tell me what you did today."

What I'd done… Aside from reaching for my phone half a dozen times to start this conversation?

"I ran down to Beach Reads. It's a bookstore on the Ave, the main street here in Coral Crest. They sent out an email saying foot traffic is way off, and I wanted to do something to help."

"Like what?"

I glanced at the new stack of books on the end table. "Like buying more books than I'll have time to read before the World Series. I also gave them a game-worn jersey from last year. They're setting up an auction. Maybe it'll help cover rent for next month."

"I'd love to get out to a bookstore," she said.

I made a mental note to send her some reading material. "My day wasn't all fun and games. I had a Zoom call this afternoon. Another team meeting."

"What is there to meet about so often?"

"You know we all voted to stay here, a couple of weeks ago?" She hummed agreement. "Well re-opening feels like a long way off now. A lot of guys are tired of hanging around. They've got family back home. Better gyms. More shit to do."

"So much for 'all for one and one for all?'"

"It just makes sense."

"What about you? Are you staying down there or heading back to Raleigh?"

Or Killeen. Jen must have had a spy planted on the team. She'd called before I clicked on the red button that said Leave Meeting. "My sister thinks I should visit her in Texas."

"And you're the type of brother who listens to his sister? I didn't think those exist."

"She's been my assistant for the last seven years, and I'm a little lost without her here. Today, she mostly called to remind me to leave a check for the kid who cleans the pool. She also knew I'm about to run out of soap for the dishwasher. And she told me to water the whatchamacallit, the plant in the kitchen with the purple flowers."

"The orchid? It's gorgeous. Or it would be, if you trimmed the dead leaves."

"Too late. The flowers fell off three nights ago. And the leaves pretty much crumbled when I shoved it under the faucet. I didn't have the heart to tell Jen."

"What about the peace lily in the living room? They're pretty forgiving."

Grimacing, I turned my phone around to snap a quick pic of the sprawling plant. Without a word, I sent it to Katie.

"Yeah," she said. "Not that forgiving. Why did Jen leave you in the lurch?"

"Family."

"Family?" she repeated. When I didn't elaborate, she said, "I told you *my* deep, dark secrets."

Christ. I didn't want to get into this. I'd have to tell more lies about Dad. Or tell the truth, at least some version of it. About pissing off Jen enough that she'd actually hung up on me, three hours ago.

Instead, I did my best to divert Katie, distracting her with the verbal equivalent of a suggestive leer. "All of them?"

"Seriously," she said. "What's going on with your family?"

"Off the record?"

"Okay."

I sighed and started building another lie. "It's not a big deal. Mom wants me home to help with the family business."

"Which is?"

"Making sports gear. Usually." I changed my nagging parent's gender. "Now, she's churning out PPE for first responders."

"That sounds like a great reason to be home."

"It would be, if there was one single thing I could contribute to the effort. Mom doesn't want me there to work. She wants me to glad-hand local politicians. Get her name on the nightly news."

Even though Katie was never going to meet my mother, I felt like shit for the lie. Mom was the only person in Killeen who really understood me. She may not have succeeded in getting Dad off my case, but she'd always been sympathetic. It wasn't fair to turn her into the bad guy just because I'd offed my father.

Katie, of course, was missing the point. It wasn't her fault. I'd buried the goddamn point beneath a shitload of lies. "Sometimes we have to do things we don't want to do. Remember, you're talking to a woman living with her grandmother and a psychotic beast from hell."

"Your grandmother's a sweetheart. And I don't know what you have against a *cat*."

"I'm serious!

"So am I."

"Does your mother run the company alone?"

There it was. A chance for me to backtrack. To straighten out the…misunderstanding I'd purposely created. I could give myself a stepfather. I could say Mom wasn't the problem. She'd been the only thing close to a solution since I'd been old enough to slam the door on my way out of my parents' house.

But in a totally fucked-up way, that would let my father crap all over whatever I was building here with Katie. So I took a deep breath and said, "Yeah. Since Dad died. And I know this sounds like I'm a controlling dick, but I really don't want to talk about this anymore."

"You're right."

"Thanks. I'm glad you understand."

"No. I mean you *do* sound like a controlling dick."

"Is this the part of the conversation where you get angry and hang up on me?"

"I told you before. I don't get angry."

And she was right. She didn't sound upset. Just *very* matter-of-fact. "Fine," I said. I changed my tone, making it self-mocking, as if I were the perfect 1950s housewife welcoming my hard-working spouse home from a long day at the office. "And how was your day, dear? Anything happen at the office?"

"Actually…" Katie said.

I could picture her teeth catching her lower lip. I'd seen her enough to know that's what she did when she hesitated, when she was steeling her nerve or taking a risk she wasn't certain would pay off. "This is going to be good," I said.

"Never mind."

"No. I want to know."

"It's nothing," she insisted, sharper than necessary. Or maybe exactly as sharp as she needed to be, because I let her change the subject. "I was just wondering what you'd say if next Monday's movie night was *The Princess Bride.*"

"What is it about women and that movie?"

"What is it about a smart and beautiful princess joining forces with a strong and brave hero to find true love?"

"Well, when you put it that way…"

"Plus, I think Angel might like it. She'll identify with Count Rugen. Can I tell her we'll watch *Princess Bride?*"

"As you wish," I said, because all my sisters loved the movie, and I'd actually thought the book was pretty funny when I'd read it years ago.

Plus, I got to hear Katie laugh. And I wanted to hear a lot more of that—even if she'd been thinking of asking me something completely different before she thought she'd diverted my attention.

Whatever it was, it must be bad. Because the Katie McIntyre I was coming to know didn't back down from anything. I'd learned that as I'd answered a dozen questions about every aspect of my career at Carver. I didn't want to know what could make her yield the playing field.

But just for today, I was willing to let her deflect me. We tried to figure out a menu that would complement the movie. And for the rest of our conversation, neither one of us brought up family, dead or alive, real or imagined. At least, I didn't. I had no way of knowing, for sure, if she was telling me the truth.

29

KATIE

I had my work cut out for me.

Every morning, I woke up with a to-do list a mile long. I was working on my story about Jason and his career at Carver. I'd organized my notes and started to plug in his answers. The result was a perfectly serviceable portrait of a college baseball star, but I wanted something more. Something deeper.

I kept going back to that quote from Coach Dixon, the one where he talked about most of his players majoring in Contemporary Studies. What the hell kind of major was that?

The program apparently didn't warrant a page on Carver's website. In fact, the only other references I found were articles where Carver's coaches—baseball, football, and basketball—mentioned the degree. Reading between the lines, there had to be at least one hundred student-athletes in the department. But there was no official record of Contemporary Studies anywhere.

My journo-judgment went on red alert.

Journo-judgment. I didn't have to be bitten by a radioactive spider to know when something was off in a story. I just knew when all the facts failed to add up. My superpower had served me well when I was a cub reporter for the *Springfield Examiner*—I'd uncovered an embezzlement scheme on the city council, and I'd laid bare a kickback scandal in the police motor pool. But this was the first time my journo-judgment had ever clicked into gear on a sports story.

I knew exactly what happened next. I brewed a pot of coffee. I curled up on the couch with a quilt over my shoulders and my laptop on my knees. I researched the crap out of my story until my eyes grew gritty and my fingers turned stiff, until the sun rose.

And I didn't ask Jason for details. He'd majored in philosophy. He explicitly wasn't connected to the Contemporary Studies program. I didn't want his perspective to taint whatever I actually found. And if I was going to discover something truly *off* about the program, I didn't want to put Jason in the middle.

Instead, I phoned Carver University. I started with the general information number on the university's website, falling into a phone tree that courteously advised me to listen closely because my options had recently changed. The hell with that. I pressed 0 and gritted out the word "Operator" until a human picked up.

Ultimately, I was transferred to another answering machine. At least this one was for the Department of Contemporary Studies. It allowed me to press 1 for the departmental secretary, to press 2 for Dr. Halliday, or to press 3 for all other matters. I wasn't sure who Dr. Halliday was, but I suspected he or she was the shortest path to the answers I needed. I pressed 2 and left my name and number, asking for a call-back.

After that excitement, I was primed to negotiate the

endless on-hold time with Virginia's unemployment office, trying to register for the benefits *Press Box* said I was due. While I waited, I ran searches for good-news articles I could write for *The Feel-Good Phoenix*.

Sure, I'd just tossed off the idea to Brittany, a glib suggestion to counter her cavalcade of side gigs. But I'd returned to the concept a dozen times, poking it, prodding it, and figuring out how I could make it work.

I'd said something to Timothy when he dropped off our groceries on Wednesday, and by Friday he'd built me a fantastic website. He left places for articles and photographs, automatically creating an archive for old features.

He even folded in space for ads, because every site he built was commercial. I promptly threw together a couple to make the page look legitimate. No one needed to know that Wag the Dog dog-walking was owned by my best friend. Same for Capit-hole Donuts.

Now, all I had to do was find some stories. I could conduct interviews by email and phone. After that, it would be a breeze to write the actual articles.

In fact, I posted one on Friday, officially making the site live. A fellow *Press Box* refugee put me on the trail of the perfect opening story. He had a cousin who'd set up a table on a street corner in a run-down part of Baltimore. The kid started out with half a dozen cartons of diapers he'd bought at one of the big-box stores outside of town. He gave them away in packs of four to anyone who needed them. His stash was gone by noon, but he'd taken in donations that let him buy twenty new boxes that afternoon, and his pastor drove him back to the store to stock up. The corner store was already in its third week, and gifts were keeping pace with community need.

The kid had a cell phone, and he answered my questions in between distributing stock. I got the money quote just before he headed out on his next shopping round: "Sometimes strangers gotta help each other, you know? Ain't no one else gonna do it, but it's the right thing for everyone." I asked him to send me a selfie to illustrate the story, and *The Feel-Good Phoenix* took flight.

Writing the story gave me energy in a way nothing else had since I'd moved in with Angel. It almost made me forget how little progress I was making on my other goals.

After *The Seventh Seal*, my Swedish lessons took a nose-dive. I'd only completed one new online unit, mastering *Björnarna kommer att äta vårt vintervete.* It was hard to care if the bears ate our winter wheat. At this rate, I was never going to make it through an entire gritty murder mystery. I'd be lucky to manage a menu. In a fast-food joint. That specialized in winter wheat.

I also needed a new knitting pattern. I'd clearly been overly ambitious, choosing a complicated sweater. Plus, I needed better yarn—the stuff I was working with split into fuzzy strands, and it twisted around itself if I set it down for longer than a second. I vowed to try a shawl instead, maybe an open lace pattern with a ruffled border.

My baking goals were stalled as well. I'd asked Timothy to pick up yeast at the grocery store, but he'd just laughed out loud. Apparently, the shelves had been bare for weeks. That, or he was uproariously entertained by the concept of my actually making a loaf of bread that could be used for anything other than a primer on carbon dating.

I found one recipe for a tidy little loaf that only required baking soda, and I tried it on Thursday afternoon. The dough, though, was so sticky I needed to scrape it off my hands with a butter knife. The so-called bread baked up as heavy as a brick, and it collapsed into a gummy mass when I tried to slice it. I dumped it in the trash before I even tried to inflict it on Angel.

Undaunted, I attempted a well-deserved treat—peanut butter cookies. I *nailed* the cross-hatch design with a fork, but the cookies turned out harder than concrete. Neither Angel nor I wanted to make an emergency visit to the dentist, so the rocks lingered in a Ziplock bag, like one of those spooky Internet stories about fast-food hamburgers that sat unchanged for decades. Every morning, I started to throw out the stark evidence of yet another cooking failure, but the damn things *smelled* amazing. Maybe I could soften them in milk. Or coffee. Maybe sulfuric acid.

New skills aside, the vast majority of my time was filled with all the tiny tasks that kept a household running for two. I threw together some semblance of food for us (I wouldn't say "cooked" because I really tried hard not to lie)—three meals a day, plus snacks. I washed countless dishes. I helped my grandmother shower and dress. I excavated kitty litter twice a day because Lucifer refused to use an even slightly sullied box. We always had a mountain of laundry—a lot more than I ever generated on my own, because Angel was awkward with her non-dominant hand and spills were constant. The bathrooms, the kitchen, the living room where we spent most of our waking hours—something in the house always needed cleaning.

I had a lot more sympathy for my friends with young children.

By Friday evening, I could barely keep my eyes open at the dinner table. Angel's high spirits from Monday night had gradually faded throughout the week. By the time she'd picked her way through my excuse for spaghetti and meatballs—overcooked noodles, sauce from a jar, and microwaved lumps of meat dumped out of a frozen package—she made an overtired toddler seem like Emily Post.

We snapped at each other while I cleared the dishes; apparently, I stacked the silverware incorrectly. While she stared sullenly at yet another *Law and Order* re-run, I took out the trash. When I returned to the kitchen, Lucifer yowled as if she were being skinned, and Angel immediately accused me of intentionally kicking the miserable animal. I hadn't, even when the devil cat pounced on my sock-clad foot, front claws doing their best to carve me into sushi. I almost cried with relief when Angel said she was going to bed, even though it was barely eight o'clock.

I wasn't a total monster. I checked the volume on the baby monitor before I opened my laptop on the living room couch. I couldn't end the week without making any progress on the Carver Contemporary Studies situation.

Better late than never. I tracked down Dr. Halliday—Leandra Halliday, it seemed, a tenured professor in the sociology department, on the Carver website, and I crafted a careful message.

From: Katie McIntyre

To: Dr. Leandra Halliday

Re: Contemporary Studies Department

Date: April 3, 2020

I hope this email finds you safe and healthy. While I left a message for you on the Contemporary Studies Department voicemail, I suspect you might not be checking those messages during this chaotic time.

I am researching an article about Carver alumnus Jason Price, and the Department of Contemporary Studies has come up. I'm looking for information about Carver's program, but I have been unable to locate any references on the university's website. Could you please phone me at your earliest convenience? My number is (202)…

Before I could close my computer, the doorbell rang.

Glancing down the hall at Angel's room and hoping my grandmother remained asleep, I hurried to the front door. I wasn't expecting anyone. Certainly Timothy wasn't dropping off groceries, not after Wednesday's delivery.

It might be Jason.

There was no reason for it to be Jason. Jason was in Florida, riding out the wait till spring training resumed. Or he was in Raleigh, his real home. Or he was in Texas, having caved to his mother's demands for help at the factory.

But my heart still hitched into double-time. I ran a hand through my hair, wishing I'd found time to shower during the day. I sneaked a sniff at my right armpit and was relieved to find I didn't stink. A quick puff of air against my palm confirmed I'd avoided garlic breath from dinner—not as grand a feat as it sounded, because the food had been completely flavorless.

Flipping on the outside light, I opened the door.

Brittany stood on the porch, brandishing a sweating bottle of rosé and a plastic bag from Cheesetique. "Who's your best friend in the entire world?"

Reality came crashing down. I hadn't talked to Jason in three days. Despite the lies I told Angel over breakfast every morning, he wasn't really my boyfriend. We didn't stay up late every night, chatting about our respective days. I'd made no excuse to call him, maybe because I didn't want to tell him about my digging into Carver's Contemporary Studies program. I was in a holding pattern until after the weekend, until our next Monday Movie Night, *The Princess Bride.*

Instead, my best friend, whom I'd explicitly told to stay away, was standing in Jason's place.

"What the hell, Brit?"

"It's Friday night. I'm not working. You're not crashing on a deadline. I thought we could drink some wine and eat some brie and make a list of all the men we want to invite to an orgy."

"Are you insane?" I asked. "Angel and I are social distancing."

A flash of emotion stitched together Brit's eyebrows. She actually sounded hurt as she said, "I thought you'd want some company."

"I'd love some company. But I'm a grown-up, and I know it's not safe."

"Timothy comes over."

"Yeah, he does. And he stays out on the sidewalk. Come on, Brit. Don't make me the bad guy here."

"You used to have fun breaking the rules."

"This isn't some game of creeping neogophilus!. Have you seen the pictures coming out of New York? My *brother* is one of those doctors. He's working back-to-backs. He's recycling his masks. The least you and I can do is try to flatten the curve." My voice had ratcheted higher, and my throat was suspiciously tight. I reined in my emotions as I tried to figure out what else I could say, how I could make her understand. I gave up, though, and settled on, "Good night, Brit."

She huffed and seemed to be thinking of a good parting line. But I didn't wait to hear it before I closed the door, turning the deadbolt for good measure. Only after I switched off the light did I realize my hands were shaking.

In fact, my entire body was trembling. How the hell could Brittany just show up, especially after I'd explained the situation multiple times over the past three weeks?

Yeah, it sucked. She shouldn't be out of work. Me neither. The world shouldn't be shut down because of a virus no one had ever anticipated.

I thought about that wine bottle, glinting in Brit's hand. Physical longing shot through me as my mouth filled with saliva. I *wanted* a glass of rosé.

No. I wanted something stronger.

Of course Sean kept a well-stocked bar, including a tall bottle of Glenlivet. I poured a healthy double and dropped in a single ice cube from the kitchen's freezer. The first mouthful jolted my spine like a lightning strike.

Brittany had been way out of line. She never should have shown up at the house. And she had no right at all to turn *me* into the villain.

Another slug of Scotch, though, and I realized another reason I was so disappointed. *Brit* had been the person standing outside. There'd been that moment, crystal-clear, when I'd imagined Jason was waiting for me.

I would have sent him away, too. No matter how much I wanted to see him. No matter how much I longed to talk to him in person. No matter how hard my heart had beaten at the thought that he'd come to see me.

One more gulp of Glenlivet, and the ice cube kissed my lips.

He didn't have to be my *actual* boyfriend for me to tap his number on my phone. Friends did that all the time, right? They called each other. It wasn't even strange to call on a Friday night, because coronavirus had everyone sitting at home.

But I didn't want to call him like a friend.

I closed my eyes, swaying as the alcohol sizzled into my blood. The swoop of Scotch felt like the swoop of something else, the heady, breathless twist as I'd opened the door to his suite at the Hotel Monaco. I felt his lips on mine, melting away the chill from the tumbler in my hand. His fingers set off tiny explosions as they traced the line of my jaw. His hands molded to my hips.

I tasted the Glenlivet on my fake boyfriend's lips.

There hadn't been anything fake about that night at the Monaco. No fake relationship. No fake desire. Certainly no fake orgasms.

What had I just told Brittany? I was a grown-up.

Well, grown-ups made their own decisions. And I was deciding to pour another drink. And I was deciding to head downstairs to the privacy of my own bedroom. And I was deciding to raise the sleek glass to my lips, to press the green icon on my phone, and to place a call to Jason Price.

30

JASON

I dropped my open book onto my comforter and yanked an extra pillow from the small of my back. I was one guy. Why the hell did I need six pillows?

But Jen had insisted on—what did she call them? The European shams. And the standard shams. And the pair of polyester-filled king-size pillows to "balance the decor." At first, she'd even insisted that I keep my down pillow, the one I actually used to *sleep*, in my closet, storing it away each morning when I made the bed.

I'd put an end to that shit. But I still had enough decorative foam on my bed to fill a department store. And—I settled against the headboard again, testing the new arrangement—none of it could make Gibbon's *History of the Decline and Fall of the Roman Empire* an interesting read.

I'd tried. Every night for the past three weeks, I'd forced my way through another thirty pages of the first volume.

When I finished it—*if* I ever finished it—there were five more to follow.

I read hard books all the time. I liked learning new things. I enjoyed checking off the classics, alternating literature and history and philosophy with the sci-fi I'd loved as a kid and the thrillers that had gotten me through countless airports.

Maybe it was the Mind-Fuck, making it hard to concentrate. Maybe it was the chaos of not knowing when I'd play ball again. But I was better than all that. I could finish off Gibbon's Chapter XII—The Reigns of Tacitus, Probus, Carus and his Sons—before I called it a night.

Maybe.

If I brewed a pot of coffee.

And shoved bamboo shoots under my fingernails.

Salvation came in the form of a phone call.

"Katie!" I cringed at the desperation in my tone, equal parts pleasure at seeing her name on the screen and relief at having a reason to set aside Gibbon. That was a lie. At least three quarters of my reaction was pleasure she was calling. Seven eighths.

Shit. I'd already pretty much decided to throw Gibbon into the pool. I was one hundred percent pleased to hear from Katie. I shut the book and shoved in my earbuds.

"Is this a bad time?"

If the phone hadn't shown me her name, I might have wondered who I was talking to. She sounded tentative. No, more than that. She sounded exhausted. Frustrated. Scared.

I swallowed my first impulse—to ply her with some seductive line. Instead, I let some sincerity soak into my reply. "Of course not. I'm glad you called."

She answered with a hopeless little sound, something squeezed between a laugh and a snort. "Let me guess. That's what you're supposed to say, according to chapter one of the fake boyfriend playbook."

"Damn," I said. "I've gone and I misplaced my copy. So you're stuck with my real response."

I heard something that didn't make sense until her audible swallow. Her phone had clinked against a glass. It sounded like she was grimacing when she said, "And *that's* what all the fake boyfriends say. Chapter two. Paragraph one."

She was the one who'd started the fake relationship game. I didn't have a clue what had soured her on the idea. But as long as I had her on the phone… "Sounds like I'm a drink or two behind. What are you pouring tonight?"

"Glenlivet," she said. "Want to join me?"

I could. Spring training was on hold. As I pushed off my bed and padded into the kitchen, I asked, "What are we drinking to?"

"How about the end of the world?"

I found a glass. "Sounds pretty dire."

"Isn't it?"

I poured a generous two fingers, watching the liquor ripple into the glass. For a moment, I thought I was caught in a flash of déjà vu, but then I realized I was remembering the last Scotch I'd drunk—at the Hotel Monaco, in DC.

Talons scraped across my abs. My body remembered *exactly* what had happened the last time I'd drunk Scotch with Katie. It didn't matter that this time I was only wearing boxers instead of a full tux.

I scowled at my dim reflection in the kitchen window. Katie hadn't called because I was a horndog with one thing on my mind. She obviously needed something. Support. Compassion. Fuck-all if I knew what else.

"What's up, Killer?" I asked.

And she told me. It didn't all make sense—Swedish bears and overcooked spaghetti and trying to track down sources for an article. But I understood that most of that was misplaced worry about her grandmother, who'd become more and more subdued as the week wore on. And Katie was crystal clear when she told me about chasing off her friend. She wrapped up her soliloquy with a gulp from her glass, and then she said, "This isn't the person I want to be."

She didn't want to be the responsible one. She didn't want to be the person nursing her elderly grandmother. The person rustling up meals. The person keeping the house safe from invasion in the middle of a pandemic, even if that meant cutting ties with her closest friend.

She wanted something else. Something more. And I had the power to give her exactly that.

Not forever. Not even for tomorrow. But for tonight, I could make things just a little better—if she'd let me.

I poured another slug of whisky and padded back to my bedroom. This time, the pile of pillows looked a hell of a lot more inviting. I leaned against the headboard and said, "Will you let me help you?"

Her laugh was harsh. "I don't think a Bergman movie will do the trick this time."

"Bergman wasn't what I had in mind."

She caught her breath, just as I'd hoped she would. That's why I'd lowered my voice, why I'd let my throat tighten around a growl.

"What were you thinking of instead?" As I'd hoped, her question was tinged with anticipation instead of the dismissal she'd offered the night I took her on a tour of my place.

I switched off the nightstand light, the better to concentrate. Time to fish or cut bait. "Tell me what you're wearing."

She laughed. "Tell me what *you're* wearing."

"Navy blue boxers," I said immediately. "I'm in my bedroom. It's dark in here, but the shades are open. The lights are on in the pool."

I imagined Katie standing beside the water. Her black hair would curl in the Florida humidity. Her eyes would look dark in the nighttime, green nearly lost in the shadows. I pictured her stepping into the pool, gliding down the steps, cupping her hands to embrace the warm, clear water.

"Katie," I breathed, desperate to know if she'd follow me.

"I'm in my bedroom, too," she said, and I almost groaned at the rush of blood into my cock. "I'm wearing yoga pants. And a gray fleece."

"What color are your panties?"

"Red," she said. "Scarlet. With lace at the top. Cut high on my hips."

My voice dropped half an octave. "And your bra?"

"I'm not wearing one."

Jesus Christ. For all I knew, she was actually standing in her grandmother's bedroom, wearing farmer's overalls and an armor-plated girdle. But she sounded like she was game, like she was hot and slick and ready for anything I could give her.

"Perfect," I said.

And then I told her what I'd do if I were there beside her. I said where I'd put my fingers. How I'd use my mouth. I guided her hands, slowing her down, giving her a chance to take her time, to give herself everything she wanted. What she needed. What she deserved.

After she came the first time, she set about paying me back. I followed her rules, only doing what she said I could, when she said, the way she said. I clutched my sheets with my free hand. I bit my lip hard enough to taste blood. I didn't last five minutes.

The second time, I had her describe what she was doing, how she moved, what she did to pleasure herself. Her moans had me hard again before she was done.

The third time, I wove a fantasy, describing how my belt would wrap around her wrists, pinning them above her head. "No," she said. "Not your belt. Not leather." It only took a moment to regroup. She was a hell of a lot more enthusiastic about the idea of a necktie. Silk. Gray. I described how I would wrap one around her left ankle, how I'd use another to secure her right foot. I told her how I'd test my knots. And then I told her every single thing I would do after she was tied to my bed.

The fourth time, she insisted I play along. We spoke over each other, laughing, catching our breath, hurrying, then holding back. I knew she was getting close when she whispered my name over and over, low and hard and steady. I matched her pace, faster, faster, until she cried out, loud enough and long enough that I hoped her grandmother was at least half-deaf. I groaned like something inside me was breaking as I collapsed onto my tangled sheets, swearing, sweaty, and absolutely sated.

"That," she said, minutes or hours or days later, "was a hell of a lot better than Bergman."

I laughed. But at the same time, something caught inside my chest.

I wanted to see her. I wanted to brush her hair off her face. I wanted to pad into the kitchen to get her a glass of water, to watch her throat as she swallowed, to collapse beside her and sleep through the rest of the night.

I wanted to wake beside her in the morning.

She murmured something, soft and sweet, and I realized she was drifting off to sleep. I said her name, just loud enough that I hoped she heard me, and I told her to turn off her phone. She hummed some sort of agreement, some sort of promise, and a few seconds later the call disconnected.

I turned off my own phone. I watched the reflected light from the swimming pool flicker on my bedroom ceiling. I twisted for my empty tumbler and realized that a new dose of Scotch had failed to materialize on its own. I sank back onto the sheets, covering my eyes with my forearm. My pulse was only now returning to normal.

Fuck this fake boyfriend game.

I was heading to DC.

31

KATIE

I woke just before my alarm went off. As I stretched for my phone, I felt a pleasant pull in my thighs, an echo of my tension the night before, as my toes had literally curled from the intensity of my orgasms.

Chalk up another win for the Professor.

Before last night, I'd never considered my phone an invaluable sex toy. In fact, I'd always rolled my eyes at scenes in books and movies where hot couples got each other off solely by the seductive tone of their voices.

Okay. Voices hadn't been the only thing in play last night. My wrist twinged, complaining about the most delicious repetitive stress injury I'd ever given myself.

Pushing back my covers, I eyed my clothes on the bedroom floor. My fleece was at the bottom of the pile, the first garment I'd shimmied out of as Jason raised the thermostat. My yoga pants had gone next. My bright blue sports bra was tangled into a ball—I'd lied about going braless. And my practical cotton undies were hardly the seductive lingerie I'd described.

A bit of fantasy never did any harm. Speaking of fantasy… I rubbed my sore wrist, imagining that my fingertips found welts from knotted silk. I'd never let anyone tie me up before, not in real life. I was a little surprised by how excited the idea had made me.

And by how loud I'd been when I came.

My gaze fell on the baby monitor, and a flicker of panic twisted my belly. What if the device had malfunctioned? What if it had somehow worked in reverse, transmitting every single sound I'd made last night, sending my filthy words and thoughts and deeds into the unit on Angel's dresser?

I glanced at my bedroom door. At least I'd had the sense to close it before I called Jason.

My throat was bone dry, as if I'd run a marathon in my sleep. I could remember crying out more than once, testifying to my faith in God, Jesus, and Jason, not necessarily in that order.

If Angel had heard…

I made short work of pulling on clean clothes, washing up, and scurrying upstairs, intending to collect the newspaper from the front porch before I started making breakfast. Angel already waited at the kitchen table.

"Morning," I said, swallowing the "good" that would have made a proper greeting. I avoided looking at my grandmother directly, but a definite chill emanated from her zip-up chenille robe. Maybe that was just Lucifer, broadcasting her evil aura from Angel's lap. "Toast okay?"

"Toast is fine," my grandmother said, pursing her lips like the Queen of England.

What the hell did she want? It wasn't like either of us would be pleased if I tried to deliver Eggs Benedict or Quiche Lorraine.

I loaded four pieces of bread into the toaster and pressed

the starter button with grim precision before I had the nerve to ask, "Did you sleep well?" I'd started each morning with the same question since I'd assumed my role of nurse and helpmate, but now the words were a hell of a lot more loaded.

"Lucy was out of sorts for hours," Angel announced, scratching the demon's chin.

I chickened out before I could devise a non-incriminating response. Instead, I opened the refrigerator and studied the shelves as if they displayed all the treasures of King Tut's tomb. "What do you think?" I asked, like a surgeon determining a life-or-death diagnosis. "Fig and apple preserves? Or some of Timothy's grapefruit marmalade?" When Angel didn't respond instantly, I filled the silence by moving jars around, pretending I was looking for something hidden at the back. "And what should we have for lunch? It's the weekend. Maybe I can whip up something special."

Yeah. Right. My "something special" added up to a shake or two of dried oregano, that *soupçon* to balance Campbell's excess of salt in its time-honored chicken noodle potage.

Angel answered as if she'd gulped a giant spoonful of grapefruit rind. "We could try a plate of vegetables and a dip. What do they call that? Crudity?"

My grandmother had mastered ordering in French restaurants long before I was born. But I only said, "Crudités! Great idea! That'll be something different."

Fuck. I guess the walls weren't as thick as I'd hoped.

At least the toaster cooperated by popping up before I had to come up with another line of conversation. And I'd never been more grateful for Sean and Timothy's print copy of the newspaper, which kept Angel and me in our separate corners until we finished our meal.

I thought I might redeem myself—at least a little—by offering Lucifer her stinkiest food, Sumptuous Swordfish Sauté. Alas, that sacrifice only gleaned a swish of a hairless tail as I set the crystal bowl on the floor.

I offered to wash Angel's hair—the most challenging of my caretaker duties—but my grandmother said, "We can do that tomorrow. I barely slept last night, and my neck is rather stiff."

Your neck is always stiff, I thought, but I wasn't suicidal enough to say it out loud. I considered offering Angel an apology, but I suspected that would only lead to mutual mortification. I also considered asking what, exactly, Angel found so offensive about an adult woman enjoying her adult body in time-honored adult ways. After all, my grandmother was thoroughly infatuated with the idea of Jason as my boyfriend. Fake boyfriend. Whatever.

I didn't want to think about *that* lie. Not in the weak light of morning. Not when I'd pretended he was a hell of a lot more last night.

So I made a huge fuss out of settling my grandmother in her wing chair in front of the TV. I tuned in an *NCIS: New Orleans* marathon. I counted out Angel's pills and brought her a fresh glass of ice water. I went back to the master bedroom and carried out Lucifer's cashmere-lined cat bed, taking care to position it on the side table so the devil could purr directly into Angel's ear.

The iron links in Angel's spine didn't begin to come loose.

Finally, I said, "I'll be back upstairs in a few minutes." I had to direct my statement to Scott Bakula's criticizing eyes. Clutching my phone, I retreated to the scene of my crime.

My first thought when I gained the refuge of my bedroom was to text Jason, sending something witty and cool to break the ice before we both started to feel weird about the night before. Okay. Weirder.

But I couldn't think of a single witty thing to type. I flipped through emojis, but cartoon drawings weren't exactly an articulate anchor for a relationship. Besides, most of the ones I considered sending reminded me of Aaron's skanky correspondent, the one who'd blown up his phone during the hockey game.

The more I thought about what to type, the more English-language words I forgot. Finally, I did what I should have done first thing that morning. I texted Brittany.

KATIE

Yikes! Phone sex with Jason last night. What do I say to him this morning?

My phone flashed a quick message: Delivered.

I caught my breath, realizing Brit might think the message was an invitation to show up at the front door again.

But that's what made the text perfect. It was the same sort of message I'd sent my best friend dozens of times in the past. Okay. Not exactly. I'd never asked for a phone sex consultation before. But it was a plea for help, a way for us to get past last night's tiff.

My phone flickered with another notification: Read. Three bubbles rose up, and I waited for Brit's reply. She'd ask for details. I had to decide how much to share. I had to figure out what was too important to dilute by telling it to anyone else, even someone who'd been pinky-sworn to secrecy for more than a decade.

The bubbles bounced. Brit was taking a long time to answer. Maybe she'd taken my question literally. Maybe she was typing out a script for me to use.

The three dots disappeared.

Brit might actually be more upset than I'd counted on. She might be looking for an apology, even though I had none to give.

There! The dots reappeared, dancing at the bottom of my screen.

Of course, we could talk it out. We'd never stayed mad at each other for more than a few minutes in the past.

Once again, the bubbles dissolved. And this time, they

didn't come back. I was left clutching my phone, wondering what I was supposed to do next—with Brittany, with Jason, and with my puritanical grandmother upstairs.

When in doubt… I ignored all of them and reached for my computer. My own life might be a hot mess, but that didn't mean I couldn't get some actual work done. I forgot about everything when I was submerged in researching a good article.

I started to prowl the Internet, looking for my next *Phoenix* story. Two hours later, I had half a dozen solid leads.

But still no reply from Brittany.

32

JASON

I grunted as I lifted my suitcases out of the Audi's trunk. Last month, I would have handed my keys to the hotel's valet and let a bellhop take my bags to my room, but today I'd parked my own damn car because it seemed safer. Hell, last month I'd traveled with nothing more than a carry-on duffel, relying on Jen to send my crap ahead. And I'd flown first class. Had a driver meet me and skipped the rest of the bullshit.

But Jen was back in Killeen, and I needed enough crap to last a couple of weeks. I'd ditched the idea of a quick flight from Coral Crest to DC after I'd thought about the plane's close quarters and questionable ventilation.

Another thing COVID had fucked up.

After hanging up the phone last night, I'd wasted a couple of hours staring at the pool, wondering if I was really going to do what I already knew I was going to do. This wasn't the Mind-Fuck driving me. This was my own decision.

I gave up acting like a moody teenager around two in the

morning. After that, it didn't take long to shower, fill two suitcases with clothes, books, a couple of baseballs, and a spare glove, and take a quick pass through the house, adjusting the thermostat and turning off the lights.

I'd thought about calling Katie, but it was too early when I left. I should have phoned mid-morning, but I was tangled in the fucked-up interchange near Savannah. By noon, I'd written too many conversations in my head, discarding version after version when I realized I didn't have a clue about Katie's lines, about what she would actually say.

She wasn't the type of woman who'd pretend to be happy to see me if she wasn't. She had a lot on her plate—her grandmother, her brother's home, trying to land a job now that *Press Box* was shut down, even the idiot article she was writing about my time at Carver. Sure, she'd shouted my name when she came, but that didn't mean she wanted me showing up on her doorstep. Not in the middle of a fucking pandemic.

I wasn't showing up on her doorstep. I had a better plan than that. But I still put off calling. She might think I was an asshole for a few more hours—it was fucked up not to acknowledge last night's crazy call—but I'd set things straight soon.

I was an hour into North Carolina when I finally remembered the plants. Jen would kill me when she found out I hadn't called the nursery. Screw it. I'd buy replacements before I let her back into the house. Besides, the only thing still living was the tree in the living room, and it had dropped a shit-ton of leaves.

I stopped for food three times during the fifteen-hour drive. I hit half a dozen interstate rest areas too, off-loading burnt-tasting coffee and restocking with twenty-ounce Styrofoam cups. Traffic was light the entire way, even as I worked across the grid of DC's streets.

Now, as I stepped up to the Hotel Monaco's front desk, I

was jittery from too much caffeine, short-tempered from too little food, and in desperate need of the john.

"Mr. Price!" The front desk clerk had a good memory. Or else he was a baseball fan. "I didn't see your name on our list of reservations."

I forced a smile. "I didn't know I was coming up here until late last night."

"And how long will you be staying with us?"

That depends on whether I have a snowball's chance in hell of converting a fake relationship into a real one… "I'm not sure. Let's say two weeks, but I might need to change things."

"Excellent!" The man started typing at his computer with all the enthusiasm of a kid set free for extra-long recess. "I think… Let's see… Let me check… We can… No… No… Wait a moment… There!"

I released a breath I didn't remember catching.

The clerk beamed. "We can put you right back in the Presidential Suite."

The thought of sleeping in that bed without Katie hit me hard behind the knees. But the alternative was locking myself into a single room, one without a kitchenette, one that might not be large enough for even the most basic workout.

I realized part of me had just *assumed* I'd end up in the suite. "Perfect," I said. "Is your restaurant open?"

The clerk lowered his voice as if he were speaking ill of the dead. "I'm afraid not. But we've put together a list of local restaurants doing takeout."

"Perfect," I said. It wasn't, but we were in the middle of a pandemic.

"And how many keys will you need for your stay?"

Two. I wanted Katie sleeping beside me that night. Or, even better, not sleeping. But you can't always get what you want. I said, "One."

There was a flurry of paperwork, followed by a half-ass offer to find someone to help me with my bags. I refused, of course, and was soon in the middle of the Presidential Suite. The curtains were closed, and the heat was on too high. I fixed both after a pit-stop in the marble-clad bathroom. Then I fished my phone out of my pocket, inhaled a deep, bracing breath, and tapped Katie's number.

Nothing.

I didn't have a signal. Swearing under my breath, I crossed to the window and tried again. One bar wavered for a second, but it quickly disappeared.

The Presidential Suite suddenly seemed a lot smaller. I made a tour, holding out my phone like Diogenes searching for an honest man. A single bar struggled to surface by the bedroom window, but when I tried to place an actual call, nothing went through.

I should have been angry, but instead I laughed. I'd driven fifteen hours to make a grand, heroic gesture, and a fucking cell phone was killing the mood. I crossed to the nightstand and picked up the landline, pressing nine to get an outside line. Sitting on the bed, I shifted my glance back and forth between my cell and the hotel phone's keypad, entering the ten digits of Katie's number.

One ring.

Two.

"Hello?" She sounded brusque. Irritated. Thank God she was a journalist. Most people wouldn't have answered a call from a stranger, but she had to stay available to sources.

"Guess where I am right now."

"Jason?"

"I'll give you three hints. One. I'm sitting on the edge of a bed."

"Angel and I are watching the news."

I grinned at her starched tone, a clear warning for me not to serve up a repeat of last night. "Two," I said. "I'm fully clothed. For now."

"I afraid I don't have time—"

"Three. This place could become a bad habit."

"You're at the Monaco?" Her voice went up on the last word, as incredulous as if I were in the *country* of Monaco. "Why— When— What are you doing there?"

"After last night, I realized I need to see you. To be with you. I'm off for a couple of weeks, while the league figures out a new schedule. I figured I could wait up here, just as easily as I can in Raleigh."

"But I can't… We can't…" Frustration was pushing surprise out of her tone.

"Check with your brother. He's a doctor, right? I'll do whatever he says is necessary."

"People need to quarantine!"

"There are worse places to be locked up than our suite at the Monaco."

"But it could be days. Weeks!"

"Call your brother," I said. "Tell me how long."

"This is nuts."

"While you're at it," I said. "Find out if I can see you now, if I stay outside. I'll shout from the curb. We can stand by a window and talk on our phones. I'll get surgical scrubs and a mask, and I'll wear rubber gloves. I'll track down one of those hazmat suits, like I'm going into a nuclear wasteland."

She laughed. "We need to save that stuff for the doctors who really need them."

"I'll tell Mom to make more. What else is a factory good for?" I'd nearly fucked up. I'd nearly said "Dad." As far as Katie knew, of course, my father was still dead.

"I'll call Sean right now."

I'd pay the guy a million bucks to give us the all-clear for tonight.

No.

I wouldn't.

I wanted to keep Katie safe. Katie and her grandmother

both. "Call me back at this number." I read the digits off the phone. "My cell doesn't work here."

"That sucks. Especially if you're going to be stuck there for a while."

"I've got books," I said. "And TV. I can even charge movies to the room."

"Jason…" Not quite the same way she'd said my name last night, but I'd take what I could get.

"Go on," I said. "Call. I'm running out to stock up on a few things, but I'll be back in half an hour. We can start the countdown then."

"I don't know what to say."

I grinned. "I can think of a few things." My tone made it clear that every single one of them was completely unapproved for grandmaternal ears.

The response I'd hoped for was drowned out by a shriek. "Ouch! Lucifer!" Then, "She just attacked my foot for no good reason!"

"Maybe she knows the dirty things you did last night. Gray silk knotted around your ankle…"

I hoped her wordless response wasn't merely an expression of frustration with the cat. I wanted her frustrated by the situation. Frustrated that I was five miles and a million light-years away. Frustrated that we couldn't continue our call the way we had last night.

"I'm hanging up now," she said, her voice halfway between laughter and a warning.

And she did.

I was left to tame my own frustration, making a run to the store for quarantine supplies.

33

From: Sean McIntyre
To: Katie McIntyre
Subject: COVID Quarantine

Katie—

I'm sorry our phone conversation went so poorly last night. Of course I understand that you're going a little stir crazy. Of course I understand that Angel can be a bit unreasonable at times. Of course I understand that you were only asking for my advice. I shouldn't have said this guy's visit is just a booty call.

But try to see things from my perspective: This is the first day off I've had in over three weeks. Two of our ER docs are in the ICU right now, both of them on ventilators. Numbers are going up in DC, Maryland, and Virginia, and nothing seems likely to change for the foreseeable future.

Anyway.

Here are the rules, if you insist on bringing that man into my house:

1. He must quarantine for fourteen days. That means no contact with any other people. No maid service. No room service. No visitors—including you.

2. He must clean any outside items he brings into his hotel room, including groceries and containers of takeout food, with disinfectant wipes.

3. He may leave his hotel room for drives in his car or for walks outside, IF he wears a surgical mask any time he comes within six feet of other people.

4. These requirements may change as we learn more about the virus.

If he shows any sign of infection during the fourteen days—a cough, a fever, fatigue, darkened toes, or—this is a new one—a loss of his sense of smell or taste, then all bets are off.

That's it.

Take it or leave it.

S.

P.S. I could hear you swearing while you read this. Careful, or Angel will wash your mouth out with soap.

P.P.S. I sent two canisters of Clorox wipes to the Hotel Monaco, with instructions for them to be delivered to Jason Price's room.

P.P.P.S. A couple of masks too.

P.P.P.P.S. I love you and want you and Angel to be around for a long, long time.

34

KATIE

I stared at the pantry shelves. *I* would have been perfectly content with cheese and crackers for dinner, but I was pretty sure Angel wouldn't call that a meal. Sean wouldn't either, and the last thing I needed was for my grandmother to rat me out to my brother. Not when he'd actually backed off from playing Dr. Tyrant and given me permission to see Jason. Or to get ready to see Jason. Or to think about seeing Jason in two freaking weeks.

Whatever.

The doorbell rang as the *Sixty Minutes* clock started ticking like a time bomb. I abandoned whatever passed for menu planning in my so-not-a-homemaker brain and headed to the front door.

A driver was climbing back into his gray Accord, his body already obscured by Uber's stylized U on his back window. He pointed toward a large manila envelope that was centered on the doormat, my name printed on the front in firm block letters.

I started to call out "Thank you!" but the words caught in my throat as Lucifer made a break for freedom. I planted an ankle and knee across the escape path and slammed the door into my leg, narrowly averting disaster. The feline demon rewarded my vigilance with a raking strike of her front claws across my calf before she strutted back to the family room, tail high in a show of disdain. At least this time she didn't draw blood.

The driver was gone by the time I opened the door again, and I retrieved the envelope. Puzzled, I carried it into the house. It was heavier than a mere letter.

As Angel glanced up from a story about the virus's ravages on the economy, I slipped my finger under the flap and pulled out a cheap daybook. Its flimsy plastic cover was designed to look like leather, and each ruled page was stamped with an over-size number to show the date. The pages were rippled, as if they'd been dipped in water. Or sanitized with a Clorox wipe. A binder clip held a chunk of pages at the beginning, letting me flip directly to today's date: April 5.

Someone had written "1" on the page, shading in the number with the glittery ink of a gold-color gel pen. Line drawings beside the numeral seemed to represent the Capitol, the Lincoln Memorial, and the Washington Monument. Or maybe someone had a really screwed-up idea of hand-drawn porn.

Angel snorted. "Who sends a calendar? In *April?*"

"Jason," I said.

Predictably, my grandmother's face softened. Whatever doghouse *I* was in for Friday night's phone sex, Jason was miraculously exonerated. Which, of course, wasn't fair. But I wasn't about to alienate Angel's affections any more than I already had. Not when I might need her on my side for future negotiations with Sean.

I turned to the next page. A giant "2" filled Monday, the crimson ink gleaming with embedded sparkles. A car filled the rest of the page. At least, I thought that's what the box was supposed to be, with four shaky circles at the corners. A glinting navy blue question asked at 9 a.m.: "Meet me at the sliding glass door?"

Of course he knew about the sliding door in the kitchen. I'd shown him when I gave him a FaceTime tour of the house.

I flipped to Tuesday, with its shaded "3" and a loose—very loose—interpretation of the blue rooster at the National Gallery of Art. Thursday, "4," included a green rectangle; I think it was supposed to be the National Mall, given the lopsided rectangles scattered around its edges, standing in for the Smithsonian museums.

I turned page after page until I came to April 19, a Sunday. That sheet was filled with a giant glittering "15," along with line drawings that looked like Independence Day gone mad—a shooting star, fireworks, and puffy explosions that resembled lopsided clouds. 7:45 p.m. was circled multiple times, and the word *Freedom* was written in capital letters.

"I don't understand," Angel said.

But I did. Jason was changing the ground rules. This went way beyond phone sex. In one fell swoop—well, in a drive of nine hundred miles—he'd thrown out every vestige of "fake" in our relationship.

He was here, actually in DC. And I couldn't wipe a silly grin off my face. Because I'd already let my daydreams go *way* beyond Fake Boyfriend Land. I'd wondered what it would be like to really be with Jason. More than quick sex. Real conversations. A real, live relationship.

And I was about to find out. The excitement that fluttered from my lips to my fingertips (and, if I were honest, considerably lower) told me just how pleased I was that Jason had taken this unexpected move.

"Katie?" Angel asked, and I realized I'd taken far too long to reply.

"It's the fifteenth day of quarantine. He's helping us count down. Like an advent calendar."

As if I'd flipped a switch, Angel started humming. *On the first day of Christmas…* As she drew out the line about the partridge and a pear tree, I took out my phone and tapped the number Jason had called from the night before.

"Hotel Monaco, how may I direct your call?"

"I'm trying to reach one of your guests. Jason Price."

The operator put me on hold. Jason answered on the first ring. "Price."

"Yes," I said.

He laughed. "I'm not sure what you're agreeing to, but I'll take whatever I can get."

"Is that a promise?" My coy tone peaked Angel's eyebrows even as she hummed *five go-old rings*. I immediately wished I'd waited to make my call. But now all I could do was clear my throat and say with business-like precision, "I was agreeing to our scheduled meeting. Tomorrow. 9:00. At the sliding glass door."

"Yes, ma'am." He sounded like an eager rookie reporting to the first day of spring training.

"Sorry," I said, knowing my fast-shifting tone must be confusing. "But…"

"But your grandmother's there, and you aren't really free to talk in front of her."

"Exactly."

"So you can't really respond, if I tell you I'm sitting all alone in our suite."

"Nope."

"And you're pretty much silenced if I say I dreamed about you last night."

I wanted to know if his dream had turned him on as much as mine had. If he'd woken with his legs tangled in his sheets.

If his heart had pounded in triple-time as his body caught up with his mind, finally realizing he was awake. That he was alone.

"Cat got your tongue?" he growled, hooking something deep inside me.

"Lucifer," I managed to say, snapping my fingers to get the cat's attention. The devil incarnate was gnawing on Timothy's carefully tended succulent garden, the one that sat in the center of the glass coffee table. Angel was up to ten leaping lords, so she wasn't a lot of help.

"Lucifer?" Jason asked.

"Lucifer could make better drawings! And what was with the glitter pens?"

"Slim pickings at the local CVS." He laughed before he asked, "I can see you tomorrow?"

"I'll leave the gate to the back yard unlocked."

"Sleep well."

"I'll try."

"Maybe it would help, if you picture me—"

"Gotta go!" I said, not trusting my response if he finished his sentence.

As it was, Angel was glaring as I hung up the phone. She cut off her humming to say, "In *my* day, a girl would never call her young man first."

"I'm not a girl, Angel." I didn't bother hiding my exasperation. My grandmother should know better by now.

"All the same," Angel said, her lips pursed. Before she could launch her next line of attack, Lucifer jumped onto her lap, arching her back before she curled into a tight, hairless circle.

"Sweet Lucy is ready for her dinner," Angel announced.

Then sweet Lucy better figure out how to open a goddamn can. But I didn't say that out loud. In fact, I wondered if I owed the arch-demon a favor. She'd successfully distracted Angel from Dating Etiquette Lecture Number 4,729.

"Let me see what I can put together." Even playing second fiddle to a bald cat couldn't dampen my mood as I carried the calendar into the kitchen. I glanced out the sliding glass door as I opened a reeking can of cat food.

I wondered if there was any way to speed the clock to tomorrow morning.

35

JASON

I waited in my car at the end of the block, eyeing my phone like it was a map to buried treasure. 8:58. I could start the engine now. I could park in front of Katie's house. I could walk through the side gate and make my way to the sliding glass door that led to the kitchen.

I forced myself to wait until exactly 9:00.

I wasn't playing games. Not exactly. If Katie asked, I'd admit that I barely slept last night, tossing and turning in *our* hotel bed, fruitlessly trying to punch the pillow into a more comfortable shape.

I'd tell her I moved to the living room an hour before sunrise. That I tried to read one of the books I'd carried north from Beach Reads, a mystery with a title I couldn't remember.

I'd tell her I'd waited till seven to begin an hour of strenuous exercise, following one of the workouts the team's trainers had sent when we all scattered to our homes. I took a shower. Got dressed. Ate a protein bar. Drove to suburban Virginia. Waited.

9:00.

Finally.

I picked up the paper bag on the passenger seat, resisting the urge to glance in the Audi's rear-view mirror. I already knew I didn't have anything stuck between my teeth.

The gate swung smoothly as I pushed my way through. I took time to latch it closed behind me, proving I wasn't a barbarian. Rounding the corner, though, I was rocked back on my heels.

Someone—*Katie, of course*—had set the scene.

A chair was pulled close to the sliding glass door. Its wrought-iron frame was cushioned with ample pads; it looked comfortable enough to sit in for hours. A matching table crouched between the chair and the door. A thermos sat on the table, next to a mug. A piece of paper had been tented in half and decorated with the words *Day Two*. It stood beside a bud vase that held a matching number of flowers.

Even *I* knew they were carnations. Pink. Jen would be proud of me.

The sliding door shone like a mirror as I approached. The sun was behind me, bright in a clear blue sky. I watched myself approach the house, the chair, the table, the note.

Only when I stepped past the eaves could I see into the kitchen. See Katie. I barely noticed her clothes—something dark. Instead, I zeroed in on her fingers, clutched tight around a mug. I saw her toes, pale against the dark floor. Her hair was messy, like she'd run her hands through it too many times.

I wasn't expecting the kick to my gut when I looked at her face. Her lower lip caught between her teeth. My breath hitched as she swallowed, hard, like she was making some sort of decision. I was surprised by the warmth that flooded my chest as I met her eyes.

I was a professional athlete. I knew exactly how my body

moved, what it took to flex my feet, how my hips followed, balanced and even. But I couldn't figure out how I'd closed the distance to the glass, how I'd set my palm against the door, how I'd spread my fingers.

She matched me, on her side. Her hand trembled, just a little, as she continued to hold my gaze.

Thank you for being here, she told me without saying a word.

I should have come sooner.

I could have stood there for hours. But something flickered near Katie's feet, and I glanced down to see a monster attacking her ankles. It was brown and wrinkled, like something that had been buried for a century or two. It opened its mouth to show hundreds of teeth, and its feet ended in razor-sharp claws.

I pounded the glass with the heel of my hand, and the creature arched its back and hissed. Before I could hit the door again, it streaked out of the room.

I turned my horrified gaze to Katie, only to see her laughing. She pulled her phone out of her pocket and touched the screen to make my cell buzz.

"What the fuck was that?" I asked.

"*That* was Angel's pride and joy. Lucifer. Lucy to the rest of the world."

"It's *bald*."

"It's a Canadian Sphynx."

"Can't you take it to a vet? Give it something to make its fur grow back?"

"It's bred that way."

I shuddered. I couldn't imagine touching the thing, much less letting it curl up in my lap. "You deserve combat pay," I said.

She laughed. "I can't tell you how much it means to hear you say that. Everyone else thinks she's the sweetest cat in the world."

"Everyone else is nuts."

Another laugh. I was getting good at this. "But anyway," she said, pointing with her chin toward the wrought-iron table. "I made you some coffee. I went online to find the manual for the machine and everything."

"I'm flattered."

Katie looked over her shoulder. I followed her gaze and watched her grandmother shuffle into the kitchen. The old woman said something I couldn't make out.

Katie said, "I told you Jason was coming to visit. He'll stay outside. Sean said it was okay."

I said to Katie, "Put me on speaker." After she fumbled with her phone, I said, "Good morning, Mrs. McIntyre. I brought a game I thought we could all play." I opened the bag I'd carried from the car. Apparently, it had taken the bellhop three tries to find it downtown. I'd tipped generously for the service.

"Boggle?" Katie asked, reading from the box.

"I figured it wouldn't matter if we were on opposite sides of the door. We just have to be able to see the board at the same time."

Her excitement was gratifying. Maybe she'd spent her own time worrying about what we would say to each other. How we would fill fourteen fucking days.

Her grandmother peered over her shoulder. "How do you play?" she asked.

I slit the plastic wrap on the package and removed the lid. Taking out the pieces, I said, "These sixteen dice have letters on every side. You shake them and let them fall into the grid. Each person tries to find as many words as possible in three minutes, going up, down, or diagonally. You get one point for every letter in every unique word, so cat is worth three points, if you're the only one who found it on the board. After five rounds, the person with the most points wins."

Mrs. McIntyre sniffed. "Sounds easy enough."

It took Katie a minute or two to find pads of paper. I'd

brought one from beside my hotel phone. I waited for Katie to pull two chairs over to the glass door, and then I shook the dice, placing the grid where all of us could see. I made a big show of displaying the timer and then I counted out, "Ready? Set… Go!"

The first ten words were easy: eat, ate, tea, eta—I bet I was the only one who got the Greek letter—pat, apt, tap, tape, pate, peat. I shifted my attention around the grid, spinning out the simple three- and four-letter words until I'd filled the first page of my notepad. After that, I worked on longer combinations.

My concentration sharpened. I forgot about the chill in the air and the faint cast of dew on the metal table, about the small, quick movements of the women inside the kitchen. I was competing, and the only things that mattered were the sixteen white dice and the sand flowing through the timer. In my final ten seconds, my gaze flashed from the grid to the hourglass and back again, as I confirmed I'd wrung every last word out of the board.

"Time!" Katie called, and I set down my pen. "Okay, Professor," she said, and I loved the flash in her eyes. "Read off your list."

Grinning, I worked through the easy words. Sure enough, neither of them had eta. But I'd missed lea, which Katie gleefully circled on her paper. I wrapped up with the longest word I'd found: "Palette," I said, not quite scrubbing the gloat from my tone.

"Got it," Katie said. "But didn't you see patella?" I whipped back to the grid and teased the word out of its sneaky diagonal connections. "Hmm," she said. "I guess that's seven points for me."

She made a big show out of creating a master scoresheet, writing each of our names in capital letters. Under KATIE, she wrote "10." Under JASON, she wrote "3."

I inclined my head, trying to demonstrate good sportsmanship, but I really regretted we weren't on the same side of the glass barrier. If we'd been together, I would have shaken the dice into a new grid before I reached out to tuck that errant strand of hair behind Katie's ear. I would have leaned close enough to feel the warmth of her cheek. I would have nuzzled the soft spot on her jaw, just below her ear, and when she was absolutely, completely distracted, I would have flipped the timer and dug into the new round.

Instead, I turned to Katie's grandmother with a respectful smile. "How about you, Mrs. McIntyre? How'd you do?"

"I got three," she said.

"Three points?" I asked, waiting for Katie to add them to her master scoresheet.

"Three words." She turned her pad of paper toward both of us. I could barely make out her spidery writing. Eat. Cat. Pat.

The sun drifted behind a cloud and the patio was suddenly shrouded in shadows. I swallowed a boulder of concern and quickly pasted a smile on my face. A quick glance at Katie confirmed that something was very, very wrong. I had to say something to ease the frown that was carving gullies beside her lips. "Maybe I didn't make the rules clear," I said. "The goal is to write down *all* the words you find."

"I did," Mrs. McIntyre said, her voice turning testy.

Katie cleared her throat. "It's a little hard for us to see the dice in here," she said. "Maybe if we bring them inside, and *you* can look through the glass?"

"Sure," I said. But Katie had had no trouble seeing the dice. "I— How do you want to do this?"

In the end, I pushed back my chair and walked across the garden, going to stand beside the bird feeder in the far corner of the yard. Katie opened the door and collected the game. I strode back to the patio as she started wiping down the pieces, running a Clorox towelette over all of them.

It only took a couple of minutes, and then she said, "Okay? Everyone ready?"

But she didn't sound ready. She didn't sound like she wanted to play the game at all. I nodded, and she flipped the timer.

As the grains of sand started to fall, I felt the familiar pressure to study the board, to write the words, to compete and win. But I kept looking up from the dice, letting my attention snag on the women inside the kitchen.

Mrs. McIntyre leaned over the board, her face tight with concentration. Twice, she wrote down words, but scrawling the letters seemed to take even more energy than studying the dice.

Katie didn't write at all. Instead, she watched her grandmother, only averting her gaze to her own paper when Mrs. McIntyre cast a look in her direction. Her shoulders looked like they were strung with thirty-gauge wire.

"Time," I finally said as the last grains of sand sifted into place.

"What words did you get, Angel?" Katie asked. It sounded like her throat was scraped with broken glass.

Mrs. McIntyre displayed her answers. T-H-E said the top line. Below that, she'd scrawled E-H-T.

Katie looked pale, but that could have been the reflection of sunlight off the door. "Maybe we should take a break," she said.

Mrs. McIntyre nodded. "I don't like missing my programs."

Katie turned to me, her face grave. "Do you mind? I just want to help her get settled."

I smiled like a jackass, trying to say I didn't mind at all, I was happy to sit here all day, I didn't have a care in the fucking world. Katie just nodded and picked up her grandmother's mug. They disappeared into the rest of the house.

Shit. I tried to keep my mind blank until Katie returned.

She picked up her cell and tapped the screen, taking me off speaker.

"I'm sorry," I said, the second she raised the phone to her ear. "I just thought it would be a fun game to take up sometime."

"It's not your fault," she said.

"Has she been like this before?"

Katie shook her head, but she said, "There've been a few things… She's seemed off. Confused. But I thought that was because she's eighty-seven years old, and she broke her arm, and she's living in a strange place."

"Why don't you call your brother?"

Katie sighed. "He's working. He's on days this whole week."

I tested my voice inside my head before I spoke. The last thing I wanted was to ride into town and start mansplaining. I couldn't sound like I was ordering her to do anything she didn't want to do. "You should leave him a message."

"I should."

"Go ahead," I said. "I'm not going anywhere."

When I said it, I meant *for the morning*. I wasn't going to leave the wrought-iron chair. I wasn't going to walk out of the back yard.

But when she met my gaze through the sliding glass door, something else snapped into place inside my skull. I felt like I'd just laced up new cleats, like my feet were suddenly held in perfect balance. My brain was scoured, as if the morning sunshine had boiled away the never-ending scum of the Mind-Fuck. I was on the mound for the first game of the season, all my stats re-set to zero, full of absolute potential.

Katie felt it too. I saw it in her face, in the way the skin beside her eyes relaxed, just a little. It rippled across her shoulders, unraveling something that had held her too tight, too stressed. Her lips curved into the tiniest of smiles and she nodded before she ended our call.

It only took a moment for her to leave the message. I couldn't make out her words through the glass, but she didn't bother with long explanations. When she was through, she bowed her head and took a long, slow breath.

She pursed her lips as she exhaled, clearly making a conscious decision to set aside her concern. Opening her eyes, she tapped her phone precisely. When I answered, she gave me a wicked grin that shot a jolt straight to my crotch. "Okay," she said. "No more kid gloves."

"Yeah, yeah," I said, because after the morning she'd had I wanted to keep things light.

"I'm serious. You're going to lose your shirt."

"So, now we're playing strip-Boggle?"

She flicked her gaze toward the other room, where her grandmother was presumably watching TV. "Don't you wish."

"I do," I said, my voice suddenly rough.

Her throat bobbed as she swallowed. "Sorry, babe." My cock twitched at the casual endearment. "The best we can do is a round of dirty words. And only if we *show* each other our lists, instead of reading them out loud."

"I'll show you mine, if you show me yours."

She grinned and shook the dice, turning over the timer before I had a chance to grab my pen.

36

KATIE

Dirty Boggle. The first grid I created by shaking the alphabet dice didn't have a single naughty word. Actually, it didn't have a lot of words, period, because half the letters were J, Q, W, and X, with a solitary E as the only vowel. By mutual agreement, I shook the dice again. That time, we lucked out because of the convenient placement of two Cs and a K.

Scribbling my words furiously, I thought about fifth grade health class, when the teacher told us to write down every dirty word we knew. (I think the idea was to write them down once, then never use them again. But the second half of the exercise never really took place.)

At the time, I was still Angel's idea of a good girl. But I'd spent a lot of time listening to Sean and his friends, and I had an *excellent* memory. I won the competition hands down, with more than ten pages of ruled paper, one word a line. I think even the teacher was impressed. Or a bit horrified.

Poor Jason didn't know what he was up against.

When the timer ran out, we both edged close to the sliding glass door, positioning our answer sheets so we could see who'd won. One by one, we crossed off our words. We were surprisingly evenly matched.

But in the end, I won by five points. That was because of the last word I'd written down, the one I wasn't sure even counted as dirty: COVID.

Jason nodded grimly as he conceded his loss. "Yeah. COVID counts." And then he recited a string of other words from our lists, saying exactly what he thought about the novel coronavirus.

We both started laughing—chuckles at first that somehow turned into the type of laughter that made tears stream down my face, leaving me gasping for breath with my cheeks stiff and my sides aching. "Katie?" Angel called from the other room. "Are you choking? Should I call 911?"

"I'm fine, Angel," I finally managed to gasp.

"Then when will you be making lunch?"

So much for maternal love and affection. Once she knew I wasn't in need of emergency treatment, any hint of coddling was gone. I looked up at Jason, who was folding his game sheet, tucking his Dirty Boggle answers into the breast pocket of his shirt.

"Ready for some lunch?" I asked.

"I brought a sandwich." I showed her the bag from the place across the street from the hotel. I'd ordered ahead, last night.

"Give me ten minutes to pull something together for us."

"I wish I could help."

"Thirteen days," I said. "And then I'll put you to work."

He sighed and leaned back in his chair, pulling up something on his phone as I turned back to the kitchen. I needed something quick. Something easy. Something even *I* couldn't ruin.

Peanut butter and jelly to the rescue. With a sliced apple, and a handful of chips.

Angel sniffed when I brought her meal into the living room. But she took a huge bite. "You should make this more often," she said, as soon as her mouth was unglued.

"Let me know if you need anything," I said, moving her glass of water closer.

"You go back to your young man."

For once, I listened to my grandmother without hesitation. "Sorry about that," I said to Jason, once I had him back on the phone.

"Hey. You've got a job to do."

"Speaking of which…"

"Ouch," he said. "*That* doesn't sound like a good conversational opening."

"No. I only mean… I'm thrilled you're here. You know that, don't you?"

"But…" He prompted, drawing out the word as his wariness turned it into a question.

"But I've got work to do at some point. I'm building a new website, *The Feel-Good Phoenix.*"

And I'm trying to track down more information about Carver. About the Contemporary Studies department. But I didn't say that. I'd only left the message for Dr. Halliday on Friday. I needed to give her a chance to respond. There was no reason to drag Jason into my research. Not yet.

I wanted him to know I was a competent journalist. I could do more than just email a list of questions to a guy and cut-and-paste his answers into an article. I wanted him to know that *Press Box* never should have cut me.

"That's fine," he said, completely missing all the dismissive thoughts I'd assigned to him. "I can always read a book while you write."

"But sometimes I need to make phone calls—interviewing witnesses, that kind of thing."

"Katie." I loved the way he said my name, calm and measured, like he'd known it forever. I was a total sucker for the way he looked at me through the sliding glass door, the light blue of his eyes distilled into something more intense in the shadows of the eaves. "I don't expect you to drop everything just to entertain me. You had a life long before I got here. Relax. I'm in this for the long haul."

There it was, more confirmation that our fake relationship had evaporated, that it had been replaced by something else, something different, something more. But even more important than that, I heard four words Jason had cast off as if they had no meaning: *You have a life.*

Aaron had never understood that. He'd always expected me to worship at the altar of all things Henderson. He'd certainly never recognized that I had my own career.

My throat thickened, and a slick of tears blurred my vision. I told myself not to be ridiculous, not to break down like a silly little girl. I also told myself not to blink, because those tears would go streaming down my cheeks, and I couldn't pretend I was fine.

As if he knew how desperately I needed to change the topic of conversation, Jason said, "Of course, I *do* expect you to take regular breaks. All work and no play..." He trailed off with a suggestive leer at my fleece top. The collar had slipped to bare my right shoulder, making it absolutely clear that I'd splurged on one of my lace bras that morning.

"Hush," I said, lowering my own voice to a whisper. "Not with Angel in the next room."

His face shone with a semblance of innocence. "I don't know what you're talking about. I was referring to the upcoming weekend. Can't you take a break from work over the weekend?"

My shoulders slumped. I'd already fought this battle with Brittany. The last thing I wanted was to have Jason go AWOL, the same way my so-called best friend had. I made my voice firm, even though I wanted to whine. “Our world is pretty shut down right now.”

“But there’s nothing that says I can’t bring the world to you.”

He made it sound so easy. But I had to shoot down his plans. “Nothing but Sean,” I said. “My brother wasn’t kidding when he set his quarantine rules.”

“And I don’t intend to break them.” Jason stepped closer, placing his left palm on the door, his long fingers flat against the glass.

My right hand moved like it had a mind of its own. Even stretching, my fingers weren’t as long as his, but I matched his palm with mine. The glass was too thick for me to feel the heat of his body, but my heart hitched at even that much contact.

“I won’t break them,” he repeated. “But we can still keep quarantine and order takeout from restaurants, can’t we? And we can watch movies together, right? While you’re working, I’ll do some research.”

“Research, huh?” I tried not to let him hear how I was melting, but I was pretty sure he could see.

“Let’s do something easy first. Italy. The three of us can go to Italy.”

“I’ve always been crazy for gnocchi,” I said.

“Nookie? *Now* who’s talking, with your grandmother in the next room?”

I gave a little gasp of indignation, but he had me trapped. I couldn’t exclaim in outrage, mock or real. I couldn’t punch his shoulder. I couldn’t lean in for a quick, teasing kiss, pulling back just in time to create a more thorough response from him. He laughed at what must have been my pretty obvious frustration.

“Nookie it is, Killer. Friday night.”

I raised my chin. “It’s a date.”

He grew serious as he studied my face. Then he repeated, "It's a date."

But I couldn't leave things there. Not with the very real frustration of the sliding door between us. So I stepped back. I planted my right fist on my hip, and I tilted my head—and my phone—to a more appraising angle. "Not so fast, buddy."

He accepted my change in mood, giving me a quizzical glance.

I stood very straight, trying to look imperious. "One week ago today, we spent about seventy-two hours watching *The Seventh Seal*. You owe me *The Princess Bride*. Tonight."

He looked around the yard behind him. "I don't know," he said. "It's going to get pretty cold out here, after the sun goes down."

"You can go back to your hotel," I allowed. "Get some dinner. But show time starts at seven thirty sharp. Deal?"

I waited for the argument, for the refusal to watch my choice, for the wriggling out of our bargain. But he only quirked his lips into a smile and nodded once. "Deal," he said. "Now go get your computer. You've got some work to do."

"And you?"

"Me?" He gestured with his phone. "I've got a book."

I smiled as I retrieved my laptop.

37

KATIE

The kitchen wasn't an ideal home office. This first day with Jason visiting, I resented having any distance at all between us. But a ladderback chair pulled up to the glass forced me to put my computer directly on my knees, which quickly became an ergonomic nightmare. And if I slouched against the door itself, my back was to the man waiting outside.

I finally realized I could put the torture chamber couch to perfect use. The unbearably hard, heavy cushions stacked into a perfect back rest when I placed them between the sliding door and the kitchen table. Before long, I was propped up, computer centered on my lap, with a glass of ice water by my side.

I had an unobstructed view of Jason's profile as he studiously read something on his phone. I knew from his Twitter feed that he preferred books in print, buying them from independent bookstores in the cities he frequented during the baseball season. But, like so many people during crazy corona times, he was making due. If he was willing to stick around for the afternoon, reading a book electronically, who was I to argue?

He must have felt my attention, because he looked up from his screen. Before I could glance away, he flashed me a brilliant smile. This wasn't the seductive gaze that had lured me to his Hotel Monaco suite. It wasn't the teasing grin that made me think of all the naughty things he'd urged me to do over the phone.

This smile was simple and uncomplicated. Easy to look at. Easy to be with forever.

What the hell was I doing here? What were the rules of this new game?

I offered my own smile, and he returned to his book. But I was left leaning against the couch cushions, trying to figure out how my world had just shifted on its foundation.

Jason's kindness… His patience… His willingness to suffer discomfort on my behalf… Hell, even the magical power he seemed to have over Angel, diluting her tart observations about the world and everything in it…

He was completely different from any real boyfriend I'd had before. Certainly night and day compared to Aaron Henderson's self-centered approach to just about everything.

But how was I supposed to think of him now? It had been easy to say he was my fake boyfriend when he was nine hundred miles away. Now that he'd driven all the way up I-95? Agreed to spend two weeks waiting for something as basic as an in-person chat?

Looking at Jason, I felt…

For a woman who made her living with words, I should be a hell of a lot better at choosing some. I forced myself to make a stab at it.

I felt full.

Complete.

Safe.

I felt a hell of a lot of things that I'd never felt before in my life, which was pretty sad for a twenty-nine-year-old woman to admit. Especially one who'd been half an hour away from saying "I do" to another man.

My hand shook as I picked up my phone. I needed to tell Brittany about this. She'd been with me through the disaster of Aaron. It was only fair that I let her in on whatever was growing between Jason and me.

Of course she didn't answer my text.

My flash of annoyance was tempered by the realization that she could be sick. She could have come down with COVID. She lived alone. Even now, she could be huddling under a stack of blankets, gasping for breath, her lips blue, her fingers cold…

Panicked, I opened Instagram. It only took a heartbeat to find her feed. She'd added half a dozen tiles that morning—bright pink donuts coated in Cap'n Crunch cereal, yellow ones lined with gummy bears, neon green dotted with Chiclet gum, the white squares lined up like tiny teeth. (Where did she even get that stuff? I hadn't seen it in ages.)

Brit was fine. She just wasn't talking to me.

I tried to believe it didn't matter. Her feelings were hurt, but she'd get over it. This stupid disease was making everyone miserable. But her refusal to answer my texts really stung.

Fine. I could sit here dwelling on things I couldn't change, or I could get some actual work done. Clenching my jaw, I opened my computer and dived into email.

Garbage. Garbage. Garbage. But there, between the spam and the only slightly more legitimate emails from vendors I'd actually used in the past was an email from LHalliday@Carver.edu. I clicked on the message.

From: Dr. Leandra Halliday

To: Katie McIntyre

Re: Contemporary Studies Department

Date: April 7, 2020

Thank you for your inquiry about Carver University's Contemporary Studies department. In addition to being the department head, I am privileged to teach our most popular course, Modern Cities and the Police State. More than forty fourth-year and fifth-year seniors are enrolled in our spring section.

I am attaching a copy of our current curriculum. This semester, we are not using a textbook or other book list; rather, our students are encouraged to purchase a packet of selections available exclusively through the university bookstore.

Sadly, my time is quite limited as I manage this seminar during the challenges presented by the novel coronavirus. While I will not be able to answer any more specific questions you might have, I encourage you to reach out to Carver University's Holmstead Library. The staff there can provide you with copies of senior theses submitted by students in the Contemporary Studies program, many of which draw on material from my seminar.

The email concluded with a link to the library's reference desk and an impersonal *Sincerely yours.*

I re-read the letter twice before I leaned back on my couch cushions. On the surface, Dr. Halliday had provided a perfectly reasonable reply to the message I'd sent her. Her words were civil. She provided specific information. She pointed me toward a resource to learn more.

But why hadn't she phoned, as I'd requested? And why did she make a point of mentioning fifth-year seniors? A number of elite athletes took five years to finish their education, sitting out their first two semesters for medical reasons or because league rules made them ineligible to play. They trained hard and honed their skills for four full years as bigger, more competitive athletes.

For that matter, why did she mention the substitute for standard textbooks? Reading packets were common supplements for reading-intensive classes, providing a broad range of excerpts that would be prohibitively expensive to purchase in their entirety. But to structure an entire seminar without *any* required reading?

The more I thought about it, the more the referral to the library raised additional questions. I'd asked about the department in general. Why was Dr. Halliday pointing me toward senior theses? Weren't those papers supposed to be the culmination of a student's work, based on more than a single course?

Was Dr. Halliday's reply some sort of secret message? Had she salted her email with seemingly innocuous details to get past any university officials who might be monitoring her email account?

It couldn't hurt to follow up, the way Dr. Halliday suggested. I clicked on her link to the library and submitted my request for Contemporary Studies theses, asking for ones that had won departmental awards.

After I hit Send, I looked up, only to find Jason watching me. My smile was automatic, but I closed out my email. I was probably making proverbial mountains out of molehills. Once I took a look at those senior theses, I'd share my baseless suspicions, and we'd both have a laugh.

I realized that I didn't know what Jason had written about in *his* senior thesis. I probably wouldn't understand a word of it, but I should ask. I reached for my phone, glad to have any excuse to interrupt his reading.

Before I could tap the screen, though, a call came in from Sean.

"Hey," I answered quickly. *My brother*, I mouthed to Jason through the window. He nodded, little lines of concern fanning out around his eyes.

"I got your message," Sean said. "It's not at all unusual for elderly patients to experience some disorientation after a major physical trauma."

"This wasn't *some disorientation,*" I protested, although I made an effort to keep my voice softer than *NCIS: Los Angeles*. "She couldn't put together three-letter words."

"She was competing. That stress could have inhibited her language skills as she tried to impress you."

"When has Angel ever worried about impressing *me*?"

I took his silence as agreement.

"It's not just the game," I said. "She's really focused on her TV shows. And she keeps humming, for no reason at all."

"Humming?"

"Christmas carols and stuff. Like she's got an earworm, but she doesn't remember to keep it to herself."

This time, my brother's silence didn't feel as reassuring.

"Sean?"

"She's not showing any sign of a stroke, is she? No slurred speech or trouble walking? Vision problems or complaining about numbness? No severe headaches?"

"None of that."

"And she's eating normally?"

"She complains about everything I cook."

"Well, *that's* normal."

"Thanks," I said.

"How about sleep? Is she up all night? Or sleeping around the clock?"

"I hear her snoring through the monitor when I wake up at night. And she's pretty much awake all day."

He sighed. "She's eighty-seven years old. It's not a surprise that she's slowing down. Add a broken arm… And she must be missing her friends from Oak Grove. She's cooped up with you…"

"Um, thanks?"

"You know what I mean." He sounded tired. "It sounds

like her reactions are within a range of normal. She's probably a little anxious. And situationally depressed."

"This is more than that." I rarely took such a decisive stand with my brother, especially about anything medical. But he wasn't here. I was. And I was the person responsible for Angel's well-being.

"Even if she's starting to slip, there's not a lot we can do. Not in the middle of a pandemic. Nothing you've said makes me think she needs to be on meds for Alzheimer's or any other form of dementia. Keep an eye on her, and let me know if things change."

I sighed. I knew Sean wasn't intentionally being difficult. He was just telling me the truth—the medical facts—to the best of his ability. But I wanted something more certain, more substantial as I navigated my time with Angel.

"Oh," Sean said, before I could ask for the impossible. "The CDC just issued an order saying people should wear masks when they're out in public."

"I thought we were saving them for doctors. Like you."

"They don't have to be surgical masks. The advisory calls for 'cloth face coverings.' Even a bandana is better than nothing. You're not going anywhere for the foreseeable future, but I'll have Timothy bring you a couple with the next load of groceries."

"Thanks," I said.

"What good is a medical degree if I'm not up to date on the latest and greatest from the CDC?"

It wasn't a very funny line, but I chuckled all the same. "You're okay?" I asked.

"I'm fine."

He answered too quickly, but I had to let him pretend. "And Timothy?"

"He's fine too. We've only been awake at the same time about three hours in the past week, but he's fine."

"Don't get too worn down."

"Don't worry about me, kiddo." I'd hated when he called me that while I was growing up. But somewhere along the way, it had started to sound pretty good. We said our good-byes, and I ended the call.

Jason was waiting for an update. His face was calm, patient, but he leaned toward me. Alert.

Without my saying a word, he clearly knew the stakes. He understood why it was so unsettling for me to think about Angel slipping. About her becoming sick. Dying.

The mere idea threw me back to the short, sharp days when my father lay in a hospital bed. He'd gone from healthy and *normal* to dead in a month, hastened along by my…

I shied away from the memories. They didn't matter now.

Jason had lost his own father—different circumstances, different regrets. But he knew the jagged edge of loss. So he was ready with words of comfort when I told him everything Sean had just said. And that made this whole nightmare a little bit better.

38

JASON

On Wednesday afternoon, Day Four, I paused at the end of a row, studying the even lines the lawn mower had made in the grass. I couldn't remember the last time I'd mowed a lawn. My last trip to Killeen?

It felt good to move. Good to walk in a space larger than the living room of my hotel suite. Good to breathe in the gold-green smell of fresh-cut grass, strong enough to penetrate the medical mask strapped across my face.

I'd been tempted to take it off while I worked. I was outside, far more than six feet from anyone else. But Katie's brother had gone to the trouble of getting the damn thing to my hotel room. And I didn't want her to think I was trying to avoid the guy's rules.

Even if I'd give my left nut to get inside that house right now, to get past the glass door so I could touch Katie, hear the little rustle as my fingers closed in her hair, taste her tooth-paste, smell her shampoo…

Of course, giving my left nut would make the rest of our time together a hell of a lot less worthwhile…

My phone buzzed before I could put the mower back in gear. Another thing that felt good about being here in Sean's back yard. My cell worked. The number on the screen was new to me, but I was pretty sure it was a call-back from a message I'd left that morning.

"Price," I answered, tersely enough to shut down anyone I didn't want to talk to.

"Patrizia Antonioli here," a lyrical voice replied, her Italian accent turning her words into a rhythmic song. "You left a message at Firenze? About a dinner delivery for Friday night?"

"Thanks for calling back." The online restaurant reviews had uniformly raved about the upscale place's menu and its attention to detail. "I'm visiting from out of town, and I haven't had the chance to eat at Firenze. I hope you can help me choose a menu for a small dinner party on Friday. Food that will stand up to delivery and reheating."

"My pleasure, *signore*. And how many people will be attending your party?"

Three, of course. But I was pretty sure no one would mind leftovers. "Six," I said.

"And did you have any preferences we should take into consideration?"

"Just the best on your menu."

She walked me through my options, emphasizing the restaurant's Tuscan traditions. I didn't know if Katie ate veal; a lot of people didn't. I suspected she'd eat her steak rare, but I wasn't sure about Mrs. McIntyre. I guessed that none of us wanted to deal with long pasta, trying to keep from dripping sauce down our fronts.

In the end, Patrizia recommended ziti to start, with a rich bolognese made from three cuts of pork. Our main dish would be a Tuscan steak carved fresh from the bone, prepared medium rare so we could offer Mrs. McIntyre the edges, if necessary. Patrizia insisted we should have white beans cooked with fresh rosemary, and our meal wouldn't be complete without the panzanella ("squished bread salad," she enthused.) For dessert, she suggested a crustless lemon tart brulée.

"One more thing," I said, after the menu was set. "Can you divide the order into two portions? Food for five people in one package and food for one person in another?"

"Of course," she said. "But it sounds as if one person will not be enjoying the party."

Oh no. I'd enjoy it. Not as much as if I were inside the house, but good things came to those who waited. At least that was the lie my mother told me when I was growing up.

I read off my credit card number and sealed the deal. Phase One of Operation Tuscan Travel Adventure was complete.

39

KATIE

COVID did strange things to time.

I stared at the day planner Jason had given me, with his bold number glittering on the page. Wednesday. April 8. Day 4. The calendar was decorated with red-and-white striped blobs that must be flags. And something—maybe a scroll? The Declaration of Independence? A sheep trapped under a bedsheet?

Today was lasting forever, minutes stretching impossibly into hours that spun out to centuries. Four separate times that morning, I'd committed to writing an article for the *Phoenix*, promising myself that if I typed for an hour, I could take a break. My piece was about a thirteen-year-old girl who'd planted a vegetable garden so she could share the harvest with her shut-in elderly neighbors.

Pounding away at my keyboard, I spewed out paragraph after paragraph, editing away my most egregious journalistic sins on the fly. I rearranged words and revised concepts, spinning out entirely new approaches to the story. I folded in quotes from the girl, from her mother, and from the neighbors who'd already received bags of fresh lettuce.

And when I looked at the clock, precisely fifteen minutes had passed.

Staring out the sliding glass door, I watched Jason take the last pass with the lawn mower. *He* was being productive. I should be too.

I'd get back to my article. But first, I should make an attempt at my long-neglected Swedish lessons. I logged into the website and donned my earbuds.

Snön har täckt taket på huset. The snow has covered the roof of the house.

Not exactly the most useful sentence I'd ever tried to memorize.

I sighed and watched Jason edge the flower beds. I'd told him not to bother, but he'd said it was the least he could do, since Sean and Timothy had given up their home.

I glanced at the calendar again. Still Day 4. I wasn't sure I could last another ten. At least not without having a Major Conversation.

Maybe I was supposed to play things cool. Some women would be coy. They'd hint at what they wanted, nudging a guy closer and closer to the edge of a cliff. I managed to wait until Jason was back at the hotel that night and Angel was in bed here at the house.

"Price," he answered his landline, voice calm and efficient.

"I need to make sure we're both on the same page."

He didn't miss a beat. Instead, his tone was round with amusement. "Which book are you looking at? *The Care and Feeding of Fake Boyfriends?*"

"I've got a new one," I said. "*Real Boyfriend 101.*"

"Huh," he said. "I must have left that one in Florida. What are the chapter titles?"

"Chapter One," I said. "'Knowing If It's Real.'"

"Signing up for two weeks on a back deck seems pretty real to me."

"I was hoping that would be your answer." But I needed to know more. "Chapter Two," I said. "'Moving In.'"

"COVID has things pretty fucked up. Quarantine means I either move in, or I spend the next fuck-knows-how-many-months on that same patio."

Of course he was right. And I'd reached the same conclusion. But I said, "That brings us to Chapter Three. 'Housemates or Roommates?'"

This time, he made me wait. Not long enough that I wondered if I'd misread every moment of the time we'd spent together—at the Monaco, on the phone, standing on either side of the damned sliding door. But I still felt a little twist of relief when he said, "I'll do what you want, Katie. But if I'm calling the shots, I'm sleeping in your bed."

"Thank God," I breathed. "Because the day bed in Timothy's office is directly over Angel's bedroom."

"And why would that be a problem?" he asked, his voice deceptively naive.

"My grandmother might be losing her mind. But her hearing seems to be perfectly intact."

He laughed. "Any other chapters you're worried about in that book of yours?"

Moving Too Fast in the Midst of a Pandemic. Secrets and Misdemeanors. Screwing Around and Recording the Evidence.

But Jason wasn't Aaron. And I wasn't the woman who'd ignored blatant warning signs for months. "I think that's about it. For now. But there might be a sequel—*Real Boyfriend 201*—down the road."

"If you've got questions, ask me. Any time. Any place."

"Oh, wait. I've got one more," I said. "What would you do if you walked into our bedroom and found me wearing a lace-up corset and thigh-high boots?"

His answer was a hell of a lot more specific than I'd imagined it would be. A hell of a lot more satisfying, too. I vowed to come up with more questions for the remaining nights of quarantine.

40

JASON

Thursday morning, I collected my towel from the floor of the suite's living room, breathing hard after the third rep of exercises the team's trainers had recommended. They called the routine "strength training." Half the guys would have rebelled if they found out we were doing Pilates and yoga, along with our usual mix of crunches and push-ups. I only knew because Jen had set me straight.

I had a few hours to kill before I could go over to Katie's. She was taking her grandmother to the doctor for a new cast. I'd wanted to drive them, but I knew better than to offer. We'd agreed I would come over for the afternoon.

That left me time to set up more for tomorrow's evening in Tuscany. I stalked into the bedroom and used the phone by the bed to call the independent bookstore closest to Katie's. According to their website, they sold books, wine, and chocolate. Sounded like a great place to get trapped during a pandemic. Even better—for my current purposes—they made deliveries.

"One More Page," a woman said, answering on the second ring.

"I'd like to place an order for delivery, for tomorrow afternoon."

"What did you have in mind?"

Under the Tuscan Sky was easy. And I trusted Robert and Jean Hollander's translation of the *Divine Comedy*, even though I wasn't sure if my marked up copy was in Florida or North Carolina. After we had those books squared away, I said, "I'm thinking we need some sort of coffee table book too. Something with a lot of photos." If Mrs. McIntyre wasn't up to reading, at least she'd enjoy the pictures.

"Perfect! We've got one of ten Tuscan hill towns." And then, like a good salesperson, she volunteered, "There's also a new biography of Lorenzo de Medici; it just came out last year."

"Add it to the stack," I said. "And do you have any Tuscan wines?"

"We've got a chianti and a brunello."

This was too easy. I took a bottle of each and told her to toss in a couple of candy bars too. They weren't Tuscan, or even Italian, but they were chocolate, so I was pretty sure they'd be a hit.

"I can enter your credit card, whenever you're ready."

I read off the number.

"And the name on the card?"

"Jason Price."

"Like the baseball player?"

Usually, I cringed at the recognition. But any person who stocked the Hollander *Divine Comedy* along with a new Medici biography probably wasn't going to squeal like a stuck pig if she met someone she'd read about in the paper. "Exactly like," I said.

"We follow your Twitter feed," she said. "Thanks for all you do for small bookstores. And this is *such* a great idea, building a vacation in the middle of a pandemic. Would you mind if we bundled some of these books and put them on our website?"

"Not at all," I said. "Just wait until tomorrow night before you post it, so I don't ruin my surprise."

"Of course," she said.

"And I'll be back next week, with another country. I just don't know which one yet."

When I hung up, I thought about Beach Reads, down in Coral Crest. They could set up something too.

Hell, why stop at that?

I knew a bunch of guys who were sitting on their asses, waiting to get back to the ballpark. No reason they couldn't do something to help their own local bookstores. Cantor was always interested in anything food-related; he'd have a great time choosing books to go with a menu. Durban's wife was a photographer; they could pull together another themed package. Hell, every guy on the team could come up with *something*.

I drafted an email. I knew my teammates well enough to set things up as a contest. I'd pay five thousand bucks to a food bank chosen by the guy whose local store sold the most books by June 1.

Some of them would roll their eyes, sure. They'd all have some smart-ass comment about my being the Professor.

But five large was enough to get everyone bragging about who had the biggest dick. At least some of them would follow through, and local small businesses would get the benefit of all that competition.

Time to hit the shower. And get dressed. And find something else to do to kill a few more hours of quarantine.

41

KATIE

Day 6, announced the day planner, with eye-numbing glitter and something that might have been the enormous stuffed elephant in the rotunda of the National Museum of Natural History.

Every individual hour crept by, but the days came together with remarkable speed. Before I knew it, it was Friday, and we dove into the fantasy of traveling to Italy.

Jason had thought of everything—food, wine, books, and entertainment. He'd tracked down Fellini's *La Dolce Vita*, but he let me sidetrack him to *The DaVinci Code*, which he watched on his phone while Angel and I settled in front of the TV in the living room.

Everything was perfect. I couldn't have asked for more tender steak. The wine complemented the meal as if it had been chosen by an expert sommelier. The books were a perfect balance of fun and thought-provoking, and Angel was already enchanted by the photos of Florence, even if the book was so heavy she could barely manage it with her arm in a cast.

Jason waved me off when I tried to thank him after Angel was in bed. We were settled on opposite sides of the glass door, me nursing a glass of chianti and him drinking water before his drive back to his hotel.

"It was fun," he said. "It gave me something to do during the week, setting things up."

"But I'm not doing anything in return."

"Life isn't a perfect trade-off." When I started to protest, he shook his head. "Things are shitty right now. We're on lock-down in the middle of a pandemic. You're working. You're taking care of your grandmother. Let me take care of you."

Every word he said was true. But I didn't like the way it made me feel. I didn't like depending on anyone.

But he talked about my work like it was something that mattered. There was nothing bad about that kind of support. And there was nothing bad about the glass of wine in my hand. There was nothing bad about the meal or the movie we'd enjoyed. And there was *definitely* nothing bad about the smoky look in Jason's eyes as he waited for me to reply.

"I don't know…" I finally said, because I had to say something.

"But I do. Relax," he said. "You'll make me famous, with that article you're writing."

I huffed a laugh at the notion that my piece would move the needle on his fame. Then I batted my eyelashes and pitched my voice to a Marilyn Monroe coo. "More famous than being the closing pitcher of the World Series champion Raleigh Rockets?"

He laughed and drained the last of his water bottle. "Enough," he said. "I'll see you tomorrow."

"Call me when you get back to the hotel. Better yet, take a

quick nap. You'll want all your strength for what I have in mind."

"That sounds like you're issuing a challenge, Killer."

"Huh," I said. "I thought it was more of a promise."

It *was* a promise. And later that night, I remembered to scream into my pillow so I wouldn't have to face Angel's condemnation in the morning.

The rest of the weekend flew by. On Saturday, we feasted on leftovers. Angel spent most of the day watching cooking shows, while Jason and I read. I sat near the sliding door in the kitchen, and we kept our phones on so we could pick out tidbits from our books to share.

Jason brought his own copy of *The Washington Post* on Sunday morning, and we both read every article in every section. I actually took a nap on Sunday afternoon. I'd thought about stretching out on some of the couch cushions, spread on the kitchen floor, but Jason convinced me that was a ridiculous idea.

When I came upstairs after my nap, he was dozing in his chair on the patio. I wanted to open the door and run my fingers through his rumpled hair.

We'd planned to have pizza for dinner on Sunday—individual pies from one of the local Neapolitan places to make it easier to maintain our glass-door distance. But it started to rain late Sunday afternoon, and Jason soon looked miserable, huddled beneath the eaves.

"Go home," I said.

"I'm fine."

"You're not fine. Your back is getting soaked."

"It's a warm rain."

It *was* warm, for April—in the low seventies—but that didn't make it much more comfortable for him. I said, "What are you trying to do? Win boyfriend of the year?"

"What's the prize for that?" he asked with a speculative leer.

"You'll find out in three days."

"Not tonight?" He drew out the two words, twisting something deep inside me.

My laugh was shakier than I wanted to admit. "Go back to the hotel," I said. "Dry off. And call me after Angel's gone to bed."

He pretended to look at a watch. "That's when? 5:30?"

"Go," I said.

"Oooh," he said. "I like it when you're strict."

"Jason!"

He left. And I knew we'd made the right decision. But sometimes being a grown-up sucked. Especially when Angel decided to stay awake till well past ten.

42

JASON

Day 9, and I was climbing the walls.

I woke to rain lashing the windows. I did my workout in the bleak morning light, pushing to complete an extra set of reps because I felt like crap. A shower didn't help. An extra cup of coffee either. I collapsed onto the couch and picked up *The Mirror and the Light*. Things weren't going to end well for Thomas Cromwell.

By noon, thunder and lightning had started. The living room lights flickered a few times.

It was ridiculous to even consider going over to Katie's. But I could sit at the curb in front of her house. Maybe I could catch a glimpse of her through the dining room curtains.

When the fuck had I turned into such a pathetic bastard?

I dug a fresh mask out of the envelope from Katie's brother and slipped the loops over my ears. Yeah, I was pathetic. But what the hell else was I going to do here in Quarantineville?

I was half-way across the lobby when my phone buzzed. After checking the screen, I said, "Hey Jen." I tried not to sound like I was disappointed.

"Move the phone closer to your mouth," she said. Even if I hadn't known she was in Killeen, I'd have guessed she was back in Texas. She lapsed into a drawl after twenty-four hours in the Lone Star State. "You sound like you're talking through mud."

"I'm wearing a mask."

"Working out at the stadium?"

"I'm, uh, not in Florida."

"You went back to Raleigh?" Her voice rose in pitch, and I predicted her next words before she said them. "Tell me you remembered to call Ms. Greenjeans so they could save the plants."

"Um, not exactly."

"You didn't call?"

I winced, but I wasn't going to lie to my own sister. "The plants were pretty much past saving."

"Even the peace lily?" she wailed.

I wasn't sure which one that was, but it didn't really matter. They were all goners. "Sorry," I said. "I'll buy new ones. I promise."

Someone else would have wasted a lot of time telling me how much I'd disappointed them. Jen, though, recovered quickly. After all, it wasn't like the plants would magically regenerate, just because she made me feel like shit. "Did you fly back to North Carolina?"

"I drove," I said. "But I'm in DC."

"D—" She cut herself off.

"What's up?" I asked, trying to head off her next cascade of questions. She was the one who'd booked my emergency flight after the Heart Foundation gala. It wouldn't take long for her to figure out why I was in DC now. "Why'd you call?"

"We think it would be a good idea if you came home," she said. "To Texas." And then, louder, before I could build up a head of steam: "You don't have to stay very long. Just a week. Maybe two."

"Who's 'we?'" I asked, because that was easier than explaining, all over again, why I wouldn't be caught dead within a thousand miles of Killeen. Especially now, when I was nine days into a two-week quarantine.

"Janine and Jackie and me." Before I could issue a flat denial, she pulled out the big gun. "And Mom."

My sisters never understood why I refused to visit Dad. But Mom did. And if she was in on this…

"What's going on, Jen?"

I could picture her finger twirling the end of her ponytail. She only did that when she was nervous. Or scared. And she sounded a little of both right now. "Daddy's pushing himself too hard. He was already working twenty-hour days to get everything changed over on the production line, and then four guys in the warehouse got sick. It took a week to get them tested and then Dr. Steele only did it as a favor to Daddy. They've got it, COVID, so the whole factory's shut down till April 20th. Daddy's still going in, though. He's running prototypes and changing specs and he hasn't come home the last three nights, and, and—"

"He's a big boy," I said. "He can take care of himself."

"Did you hear what I said? *Four people* tested positive! Daddy isn't playing games. This isn't a publicity stunt, just to get you down here."

It wasn't. Yet. But the second I set foot inside the factory, my father would be scheming about how to make money off me. I wouldn't let him do that to me. Never again.

"I'm sorry you're scared," I said to Jen. "But I can't help you. April 20th is only two days away."

"He needs you!"

"He doesn't need anyone. Certainly not me. And he doesn't deserve you."

"What can I tell Mom?"

I sighed. "Tell her I love her very much. Tell her to call me if she needs to talk. Tell her I'll send a check to cover medical care for the guys in the warehouse."

"That's it? You're just going to throw money at the problem and hope it'll go away?"

"Thanks for calling," I said.

"I didn't mean that," she said immediately.

"Don't forget to take care of yourself. If *you* get sick, you won't be able to help anyone."

"Jason—" she tried again.

"I've got to go," I said. "Love you. Bye."

I didn't hang up on her. I waited for her to say goodbye too. But the second she did, I cut the call.

My first thought was to phone Katie. But I couldn't drag her into the middle of my family drama, not without explaining that Dad was alive and well and as much of a bastard as he'd ever been.

That wouldn't be a huge deal. Not really. She'd have to understand. But the last thing I wanted to do was waste more time on this fucking rainy day talking about my father.

My face was wet beneath my mask, a nasty combination of sweat and trapped condensation. I felt like I needed another shower, which was stupid because I hadn't *done* anything since taking the first one. All the same, sitting in a closed car, staring through the rain at a house I couldn't get into felt like the stupidest idea I'd had in months.

I headed back to my room. And I turned on the TV. And I watched crappy movies for the rest of the day while it rained and rained and rained.

43

KATIE

Day 9 was going to last forever.

It was never going to stop raining. Angel was going to watch episode after episode of urban crime-solving, each murder wrapped up in a tidy forty-two-minute package. Lucifer was going to yowl for snacks or a meal or just because she knew it drove me nuts. I was going to flip through pictures of Tuscan hill towns, imagining I was somewhere where the sun baked terra cotta tiles, where bright red poppies waved in field after field, where I could sit in a town square and watch old men play bocce without a care in the world.

I published a *Phoenix* article, but my heart wasn't in the story about the NFL linebacker who'd started walking his elderly neighbor's teacup chihuahua because she couldn't get out of the house. I gave up on Swedish after one repetition of something inane about bears or wolves or snow. I found a dropped stitch two rows back in my knitting and set it aside until I could convince myself the mistake would make my shawl look authentically homemade.

I knew better than to try baking anything. We ate cheese and crackers for lunch. We had canned soup for dinner. I put Angel to bed early, and headed downstairs to my own bedroom.

I didn't want to call Jason. I didn't want to ruin a conversation with him, the way everything else was ruined on this miserable, rainy day. But while I was still debating what to do, my phone buzzed with a new call. Jason.

"Hey," I said, not bothering to fake enthusiasm about anything.

"Yeah," he said. "That's been my day, too."

"I'm sorry I didn't call earlier. I wanted to be in a better mood."

"I know what you mean," he said. "I got into a fight with Jen this morning."

"About what?"

I could almost see him shaking his head. "About nothing. About crap that isn't worth fighting over."

I tried to think of a good reply, but my brain was mired in thick, cold mud.

"Well," he said after too long of a pause. "At least this still counts as a quarantine day."

I sighed. "See you tomorrow?"

"Absolutely." He answered quickly enough that I actually smiled.

We didn't flirt. He didn't offer wry double entendres. But when I hung up the phone, I felt different than I had when I woke up that dark, dreary morning.

We'd weathered more than a rainstorm. We'd survived *normal*. And that meant more than any spectacular virtual weekend in Italy.

44

KATIE

Day 10.

The storm turned out to be a cold front. On Tuesday morning, Jason showed up in a hoodie. His breath fogged the air like cigarette smoke as he blew on his closed fists. His nose was red, as if he'd been drinking or crying. He shuffled from foot to foot, hunching his shoulders.

"You're going to freeze out there!" I said.

He jammed his left hand into the front pocket of his jeans, but he had to hold his phone with his right. "I'm fine," he said.

"You need a lot more layers."

He offered half a shrug. "These are the layers I have. Remember, I drove up here from Florida."

"Just a sec." I put my phone on the kitchen table as I headed to the other side of the house. Angel was already mesmerized in front of the TV. At least she'd set aside crime dramas in favor of some series about flipping tiny houses.

After an unsuccessful search in the master bedroom closets, I found what I wanted in the foyer. Several hangers were empty in the coat closet; Sean and Timothy must have taken most of their cold-weather gear over to my place. But my brother's old peacoat was there. I grabbed it and a Washington Nationals scarf and headed back to the kitchen.

"No way," Jason said, when he saw the rival team's logo.

Not surprised, I dropped the offending muffler on the table. But I was amused by Jason's speed as he sprinted to the far end of the yard, giving me ample space to open the sliding door and drape the coat over his chair. He barely waited for me to secure the door before he returned.

The sleeves were about three inches too short. His shoulders stretched the seams. But the borrowed coat was better than hypothermia.

"Thanks," Jason said before he poured a cup of coffee and settled into his chair, taking out his copy of the morning paper.

Smiling, I set about my morning routine. A quick scan of websites, looking for more *Phoenix* fodder. A flurry of emails, shooting interview questions to likely candidates for feel-good stories. Crossed fingers, as I hoped to hear from the Carver librarian, with no luck.

I ended with a quick run-through of Brittany's emerging donut empire on Instagram. I sent her a quick text every couple of days, but she still wasn't responding. Nevertheless, she was getting a lot of great feedback on her latest flavor combinations.

Today, she supplemented her usual baked-goods photos with pictures of face masks. She'd apparently gone into production over the weekend, attaching clever tie-on straps when she couldn't get elastic for the more traditional earloops. The fabric she'd used was gorgeous, a rainbow of batik prints that looked fun and fashionable instead of clinical.

I clicked Like on the photos, and I sent her a text. I even

added an email, just in case she'd reverted to the Stone Age for her personal communication.

Silence.

As expected.

And so the day unfolded. Angel seemed content. Lucifer was a bitch. Jason took a break from reading and jogged around the yard, warming up enough to shed Sean's coat. Then he threw a bucket of balls into the net he'd purchased for the purpose. I watched him collect the balls, bending and stretching with an ease that seemed more like ballet than baseball, and then he started to pitch again.

It would be so easy to open the door. To step out onto the patio. To wait for him to empty the bucket, then applaud his efforts.

My stomach dropped as I imagined him turning toward me. He'd take a single step forward, and we'd look at each other across the lawn.

"You shouldn't be here," he'd say.

"I couldn't wait," I'd say. "Not any more."

He'd close the distance between us, and his arms would wrap around me, and I'd breathe in the smell of his skin at the line where his throat met his shoulder. Neither of us would feel the chill of the spring day. Neither of us would care that Angel was inside, that Lucifer was pacing by the kitchen door. We'd laugh, and we'd both start to say something at the same time, and we'd both fall silent before we found better things to do than talk.

I opened my eyes, realizing I'd closed them to better feed my fantasy. Jason was looking at me from the middle of the yard, his chest heaving as if he'd done a hell of a lot more than retrieve a bucket of baseballs.

At first, I wondered how he knew I'd been watching him. Then, I saw my fingers on the glass door's latch. I'd flipped it to the Open position, without conscious thought. That noise must have been enough to snag his attention. He must have been as attuned to my presence as I was to him.

All I had to do was flex my wrist.

But I'd promised Sean. I was responsible for Angel. I had to keep all of us safe.

I pulled back to the table, knowing Jason wouldn't be able to see that far into the kitchen. He waited for a moment, perfectly still, as if he were giving me the chance to change my mind. When I didn't move back to the door, he spun around and plowed a perfect four-seam fastball into the deepest part of the net.

As I got a glass of ice water, I studied the day planner on the counter. Day Fucking Ten. I stared at my computer screen for an hour without typing a word.

45

JASON

Day 11.

April 15. Tax day. I told Katie I couldn't be there. I made some excuse about needing to go over documents with my accountant.

I *did* have to look at my filings. That took about fifteen minutes while I skimmed the numbers, pretending to make sure everything looked right. I didn't have a fucking clue what the papers were supposed to say. But Jen had signed off on the draft last month, before she bailed, and the overall total was in line with the past ten years.

I called my accountant and got her assistant. I authorized the filing. That left about fifteen hours before I could reasonably head back to bed.

I didn't want to spend fifteen hours sitting in Sean McIntyre's back yard. I didn't want to throw baseballs into a goddamn net. I didn't want to read another book. I didn't want to scroll through news on my phone, hoping to see some sort of breakthrough, some way that we could put eighteen men on a diamond and play a fucking game of baseball.

I *wanted* to throw myself against that goddamn glass door until Katie took pity on me and let me into the house. I wanted to bend her over that kitchen table and give her a piece of the dreams that left my crisp hotel sheets tied up in knots. I wanted to talk to her, face to face, without a fucking door between us.

I'd come close to calling off the whole deal yesterday. I'd almost told her I couldn't take it anymore. I'd almost said I'd take on her brother, the CDC, and anyone else who said I couldn't come inside.

But I'd made a promise. For four more days, I'd keep it.

I just couldn't be there today.

46

KATIE

Day 12.

Thursday.

I worked.

Jason read.

Angel napped.

Lucifer tried to raise the dead with a completely unprovoked symphony of yowls that only stopped when I gave her an extra serving of Swordfish Sauté.

Logically, I knew time would go faster if I distracted myself. I tried listening to one of my Swedish language lessons, but I couldn't figure out if the wolves were eating the children or if the children were eating the wolves.

I started to frog two rounds of knitting, ripping back stitches to get to the error I'd found earlier, but I accidentally pulled the shawl off one of the needles. After a frustrating half hour when Lucifer learned more human swear words than she'd ever been treated to before, I gave up and stripped the project from the second needle as well, winding all the yarn back into a lopsided ball. Lucifer promptly pounced on her new toy, carrying it away to Sean's closet.

I was desperate enough to consider baking something. A quick trip to the fridge, though, showed that we were out of eggs. For just a moment, I wondered if Angel had hidden them on purpose, trying to spare herself the results of my culinary handiwork.

Finally, I posted a quick *Phoenix* article about a neighborhood organizing a superhero car parade for a five-year-old leukemia patient returning home from treatment in a hospital. And I sent a reminder to the Carver librarian, asking if she could scare up those senior theses for me to review.

Jason left before sunset. Angel and I had poorly drained bowtie pasta for dinner, with pesto from a jar. Angel was in bed an hour after that, and I fell asleep before nine, feeling like I'd failed a test.

47

JASON

Day 13.

Friday morning, I had a team meeting on Zoom. I didn't want to make the call at Katie's—too many distractions, even if yesterday had seemed like an all-day screening of watching paint dry.

So, I begged off my morning torture on the back patio and logged in five minutes before ten, armed with a fresh cup of coffee. Ormond promptly called the meeting to order. It turned out, his news wasn't good.

"Right now, the league is looking at a shortened season starting May 1. No fans in the stands, at least until June. The goal is to keep everyone safe."

"Safe, my ass," DJ Thomas said. "They're trying to figure out how to screw us out of more money."

Ormond powered past complaints from half the team, repeating the arguments we'd been hearing for over a month. "If fans aren't allowed in, then owners don't get the gate.

They don't get concessions either, or parking or merch. And if money doesn't flow in, it can't flow out."

That brought on a new round of protests. Everyone knew the owners' biggest income came from TV. Ormond handled it well, letting everyone bitch for long enough that guys felt heard, but he cut it off before anyone dug in too deep. He said, "That's it, guys. Do your workouts. Stay safe. Stay sane."

"Hey," I cut in, before folks could sign off. "We're a week into the bookstore challenge. Five thousand bucks on the line."

A handful of guys left the call—no surprise. But others chimed in to boast about the jerseys and gloves they'd donated for auctions, bragging about reading lists they'd put together with the help of willing bookstore staff. Kyle Norton hadn't voluntarily cracked a book since twelfth grade, but he'd asked his wife to make a list of the novels her book group had read. Adam Sartain dug up his required reading list from fifth grade, figuring bookstores sold to kids as much as they did to adults.

"Nice try, guys," I said. "But if that's all you've got, I'm pretty sure my money's staying in Virginia."

"Since when do you live in Virginia?" Ormond asked.

My gut instinct was to wince, but I had to hide that too. The last thing I needed was a bunch of smartass guys monitoring my every move. "Just visiting a friend."

"Some friend," Ruiz said. "You're with the chick who was engaged to Henderson, right? The girl who dumped his ass on New Year's Eve?"

Before I could answer, Sartain chimed in. "The one Gonzalez hassled at the heart charity thing."

"Gonzalez hassled *her*?" Norton chimed in. "I heard she shut him up without breaking her stride."

"And looked damn good doing it, too," Thomas said.

My hands were below the desk, so none of the guys could see my fingers curl into fists. I didn't want them talking about

Katie—even if they sounded damned impressed. I made sure I didn't sound too concerned when I asked, "How the fuck do you morons know about any of that?"

Every one of the guys had heard about the gala from someone else. And half of them knew I'd left the joint with her. It was a miracle they hadn't raked me over the coals before.

"Come on, Professor," Thomas said. "How do you keep her from handing you your balls on a regular basis?"

"Fuck off," I said evenly.

"Looks like he's in a hotel room," Norton said. "I call bullshit on the whole story."

"Fuck all of you," I said, keeping the same tone but adding hand gestures for the aurally impaired. Then, before they could pile on more, I reminded them, "Five thousand bucks. June 1. May the best bookstore win."

I cut the connection before anyone gave me more shit. And then I reached for the phone on the end table, because I needed to confirm my order with One More Page about the books they were delivering to Katie that afternoon, for our imaginary weekend trip to France.

48

KATIE

Day 14.

I woke up slowly on Saturday morning. I was cocooned beneath my comforter, and my head was heavy on my pillow. I caught my breath and listened carefully to the baby monitor, trying to determine whether Angel was still asleep. I could just make out the soft sound of her breathing.

We'd stayed up late the night before—the latest since Angel's fall. Jason had arranged our virtual trip to France with his usual perfection. He'd found a bistro that delivered French onion soup and cassoulet along with a whole baguette and salted butter that tasted like heaven. Even better, he'd tracked down a bakery that created a box of pastries, each individual bite decorated like a precious jewel.

He'd supplemented the food with two excellent burgundies, *The Only Street in Paris*, *A Tale of Two Cities*, and a coffee table book filled with pictures of the city's churches. He'd even included another toy for Lucifer—a spiked plastic ring that looked like it came off a giant's milk jug. I was pretty sure the demon-beast only loved it because she could leave it in the middle of my bathroom floor, perfect for assaulting bare feet after I took a shower.

After we humans had gorged, Jason had returned to his hotel room so we could watch a double feature. He'd chosen Jean Renoir's *The Rules of the Game*. Predictably, he and Angel had a ball with the black-and-white classic. I barely managed to refrain from checking my emails.

I got a bit of revenge by choosing *The Hunchback of Notre Dame*. The animated one. From Disney. Angel fell asleep before the titles rolled. It had been difficult to rouse her and get her into bed, but I still felt vindicated.

Even more so later, when Jason and I used our phones for their God-given purpose. Jason seemed to find my mock French accent a turn-on.

Who was I kidding? By the explosive end of our little chat, I could have been speaking in ancient Sanskrit, and he wouldn't have known the difference.

Now, I flexed my wrist and took a quick shower—double-checking for killer cat toys—and headed upstairs for coffee. Only when I entered the kitchen did I realize it was raining. Again.

Jason texted while I waited for the space shuttle to churn out my first cup of caffeine.

JASON

Got a late start. See you in half an hour.

I just got up too. No reason to sit in the rain.

I'll sit in my car.

Stay warm and dry, at least for now. Angel isn't even awake yet.

All the more reason for me to get there now. No chaperone!

Ha, ha.

In the end, it rained until the middle of the afternoon. By the time the downpour stopped, the wind picked up, brisk enough to tear the blossoms off Timothy's prize Kanzan cherry tree.

Jason and I texted throughout, coming to the reluctant conclusion that it didn't make sense for him to come over at all —especially because we planned to watch the concert-opera version of *Les Misérables* that night. The show was almost four hours long, so we had to get an early start.

I didn't know what meal he had delivered to his hotel room, but Angel and I feasted on a reprise of the night before. I toasted the leftover baguette. The soup and cassoulet reheated perfectly, and I opened the second bottle of wine early enough to let it breathe. Maybe I was finally getting the hang of this cooking stuff.

Predictably, Angel fell asleep long before Jean Valjean reunited with Fantine. Lucifer yowled like one of the Thénardiers when I helped my grandmother get ready for bed, but she soon settled at the foot of the bed, alternately chewing her new plastic toy and attempting to embed it in the ceiling.

I called Jason after I climbed into my own bed. "You're spoiling us," I said.

"Not as much as I'd like to."

I knew I was supposed to say something amusing and seductive, but the wine was catching up with me. I yawned, thinking he wouldn't hear.

"Go to sleep," he said.

"I'm awake!" I protested.

"Get your sleep tonight," he said. "Because you might be up late tomorrow."

"Promise?"

His soft laugh folded around me. "You'll see, Killer."

"When will you get here?"

"Has to be after noon."

I was surprised by my sudden spike of jealousy. "What are you doing in the morning?"

"Pacing back and forth in the Presidential Suite. Throwing my clothes in a suitcase. Checking out by remote access."

"Then why not—"

"Fourteen days, your brother said. And I'm pretty sure that by 'day,' he meant a twenty-four hour period. I'll shave off a couple of hours for good behavior. But I don't want to piss him off by getting there too early."

Sean would never know. Unless Angel told him. But Jason was an honorable man. He'd made an agreement, and he was sticking with it.

"Fine," I said, doing my best not to sound like a spoiled brat. I didn't succeed.

"Go to sleep," he said again. "Soon enough, you'll be begging me to leave you alone."

I couldn't imagine that would ever happen, but I hung up the phone. And I spent hours staring at the ceiling, wondering if Jason's nerves were as fired up as mine about the thought of tomorrow.

49

JASON

By 7:00, I was awake and dressed and showered.

It was too early to show up on Katie's doorstep.

By 8:00, I'd eaten the last of my protein bars and downed my final cup of Keurig coffee.

It was too early to show up on Katie's doorstep.

By 9:00, I was pacing the room, double-checking the closet and bathroom to make sure I'd packed all my shit.

It was too early to show up on Katie's doorstep.

By 10:00, I hit the button on the remote checkout, carried my bags down to the lobby, and got my car out of hock for the last time.

It was too early to show up on Katie's doorstep.

I drove around DC like a tourist. The roads were almost empty. It was Saturday morning, and all non-essential businesses were shut down.

I headed toward the Capitol, with its massive dome, sitting on its hill like some weird cake decoration. I drove through a ghost town of white marble—House office buildings and Senate office buildings, the Supreme Court and the Library of Congress. I found a farmer's market, depleted stalls where a handful of people gathered, mostly wearing masks, mostly keeping their distance from one another. I didn't join them. I wasn't going to throw away two weeks of quarantine.

I drove down to Nationals Park, surrounded by hotels and offices and a few empty parking lots. I found the place the Rockets stayed when we played here, and I weathered the gut punch when I saw the Temporarily Closed sign taped to its front door.

The entire city felt empty. All of it felt *wrong*. DC should be teeming with thousands of people, tourists and locals alike.

And I should be making my way to a ballpark, here or in Raleigh or somewhere else where two teams were ready to slug it out for three hours, war that passed as entertainment. But we were fighting another type of war, against an enemy too small to see, a virus that had brought the world to its knees.

We'd all been drafted, willing or not. And I'd long ago agreed to the terms of engagement from Katie's brother. I'd washed my hands. I'd worn my masks. I'd kept my fucking distance.

11:00.

It was too early to show up on Katie's doorstep.

Screw that.

I drove across the bridge to Virginia.

50

KATIE

The sound of the doorbell ricocheted through me like a Taser lead. I'd been up since six and dressed since seven, bouncing around the house like a ghost on crack. Angel had finally ordered me to stay out of the living room. Even Lucifer had decided it wasn't worth her time to yowl every time I crossed her tracks.

Now I navigated the foyer like a prisoner going to my execution. I wasn't sure what to expect. How I was supposed to act. React. Jason and I had only spent a total of twelve hours together, actually in the same room. And now, courtesy of COVID, he was moving in.

We were nuts.

My lungs stopped when I touched the front door. Every cell in my body lit from the inside with a tiny red flame. My fingers were miniature broken machines, their gears slipping from their sprockets as I fought the deadbolt.

I opened the door and said, "Hey."

"Hey."

Two suitcases waited by his feet. His hands hung by his sides. Tiny lines crinkled beside his eyes as he smiled at me.

I didn't do shy. I didn't do embarrassed. But I felt…unsettled in a way I never had before. I wanted to look at him and I wanted to touch him and I wanted him inside the house, and I wanted him standing on the porch, framed in the sunlight forever.

I stepped back so he could come inside. The foyer was large enough that he could cross the threshold without brushing against me. I wished we were standing in the entry of my cramped sublet, where he'd have no choice but to touch me. But if we were in my apartment, we would have been free to get together two weeks ago. We wouldn't have had the past fourteen days of torture.

I wanted to jump his bones, right there in the foyer. But at the same time, I was terrified to say anything, to make any motion at all that might make him pick up his suitcases and leave.

I knew my fear was ridiculous. The man had just spent two weeks on my back porch, waiting for me. I'd have to stab him several times with a rusty carving knife if I wanted to make him leave.

But he seemed every bit as tentative as I was. Every bit as aware that our relationship had just changed in a huge and unpredictable way.

We stared at each other, carrying on a dozen different conversations without saying a word. And then, like a malevolent spirit rising from its rotting grave, Lucifer stalked into the room.

She arched her back. Her tail stood straight up, a jagged exclamation point. She hissed like a stockpot boiling over on the stove, and then she yowled like all the demons in hell.

"What the f—" Jason started to say.

At the same time, Angel called from the living room, "What are you doing to that poor creature now?"

"Welcome to the madhouse," I said. "Time to face the music."

I led him into my grandmother's throne room. "Angel," I said. "Jason's here."

She cut off mid-splutter, somewhere between reminding me that Lucifer was the sweetest cat in the world and asking me to fetch another cup of tea. "Jason!" she exclaimed, as if she were greeting a long-lost friend.

"Mrs. McIntyre," he said warmly before he crossed the room and bent to kiss her cheek.

She accepted the gesture before she clicked her tongue to chide him. "If you're staying here now, you might as well call me Angel."

"Angel," he confirmed. "How are you feeling this morning? How's the arm?"

I didn't register the specifics of my grandmother's response. The amazing thing was that she was talking. Full sentences. Voice rising and falling with emotion, responding appropriately to Jason's follow-up questions. She even volunteered that she'd been looking at the coffee-table book with pictures from France. She remembered the book. She remembered its content. And she remembered that Jason had given it to us on Friday.

Relief pooled behind my knees like melted butter.

"Now go on, dear," Angel finally said to him. "Take your things downstairs and get settled."

And that was another miracle. I'd been dreading the confrontation with my grandmother when I told her Jason was sleeping in my room. I fully expected her to relegate him to the day bed in Timothy's home office. Or, worse, dictate that he had to sleep on the chiropractor's dream-couch.

"Lead the way," Jason said to me. His smile was easy as he retrieved his suitcases.

I felt him behind me on the stairs, the heat of his body scorching my spine. I gestured toward the pool table that filled most of the rec room at the bottom of the stairs. "Here's the pool table," I said. Then I wanted to bite my lip because it was obviously a pool table. Any idiot could see it was a pool table. No one needed to be told it was a fucking pool table.

But I didn't learn my lesson. "And there's the bathroom." I pointed toward the half-open door. Yep. Toilet. Sink. Shower. Pretty much exactly what it appeared to be.

Might as well go for the trifecta. "And here's the bedroom."

He cocked his head, just a little. "And there's the bed."

I don't know which of us moved first. But his arms were around me, and they were every bit as strong as I remembered. His mouth on mine was hot, pressing, and when I parted my lips, his tongue was ready. He drank my moan, or I drank his, and we stumbled into the bedroom as if we were running a three-legged race.

One of us remembered to close the door. He toed off his shoes. He was already reaching for the button on his jeans when I worked the zipper.

I tugged at the waistband of my yoga pants, but his hands were already there, hooking beneath the waistband of my cotton panties for good measure. I shifted my focus to his jeans and boxers, frantically working them past the jut of his hip bones. Lycra and denim and cotton puddled on the floor.

We collapsed onto the bed together. I stretched for my nightstand, miraculously producing the Trojans I'd primly added to Timothy's last shopping list. One of us opened the box. One of us ripped the foil. Working together, we rolled the condom into place.

We laughed. We gasped. We writhed around each other, under each other, over. He fingered me, just enough to feel that I was ready, past ready. When he entered me, fast and hard, we both caught our breaths.

He groaned as he built a rhythm, but I planted my palm over his mouth. "Angel," I whispered, and he nodded, biting his lip.

We shifted our hips, working toward a better angle. We strained together, our muscles tightening toward the same goal. He got there before I did, but he lowered a hand between us, using his thumb to apply the perfect, driving pressure. He stroked me, teased me, and carried me over the edge.

I forgot my own rule, forgot to swallow my cry as I broke, but his mouth was hot on mine, drinking all the words I didn't shout out loud. After, we lay on our backs, staring at the ceiling, our fingers twined between us. "Wow," he said. "That's a much better greeting than I got from the Monaco concierge."

"It's amazing what two weeks of foreplay can do."

In a perfect world, we would have stayed there for the rest of the afternoon. But we didn't live in a perfect world. We lived in a world where a virus still ran rampant outside our house, where my grandmother waited upstairs, where I had to rustle up lunch.

Pushing up on my elbows, I said, "Duty calls. The top two drawers in the dresser are empty, and I left you half the closet. Unpack your stuff while I make us all some lunch."

I didn't give him a chance to argue. Instead, I brushed a quick kiss over his lips and scrambled to the edge of the bed. It only took a moment for me to untangle our clothes, and I shimmied into mine in record speed.

I stopped, though, when I got to the door. "Hey," I said. "I know you didn't have to do this. Come up here in the first place. Wait two weeks at the hotel. Thank you."

He said, "Wouldn't have missed it for the world." It could have been a joke. But the way he held my gaze made me think he meant it.

I chickened out before he did. "Let's see if you feel the same way after lunch."

His laughter followed me upstairs.

51

JASON

I didn't think there was a way to ruin a fried salami sandwich, but Katie managed to find one. For the record, she was trying to make things easier for Angel. She cut up the salami before tossing it into the skillet.

Maybe her knife skills were crap. Maybe Lucifer attacked her while she was supposed to be cooking. Maybe she owed some sort of karmic debt for a past life where she abused some kitchen goddess.

But half the salami was singed to charred flakes. And half was slimy from barely being heated in the pan. All the bread was stale.

I choked it down because I was a guest. Or because I didn't want Katie to feel bad. Or because I could have gotten off my own ass and made my own goddamn sandwich instead of waiting for food to materialize in front of me.

Angel smiled encouragingly as she chewed. "This is your

best meal yet, dear," she said. If only I'd recognized the warning when I heard it.

After lunch, Angel took a nap. Katie and I anchored opposite ends of the most uncomfortable couch in America, leaning against the arms and stretching our feet toward the middle. I took the inside and she took the outside. With Angel snoring softly down the hallway, we both actually got some reading done.

For about five minutes. Then, we high-tailed it downstairs and fucked like drunken weasels.

Katie waited until her grandmother was awake before she announced she was making dinner. I offered to help, but she said, "Why don't you keep Angel company?"

Reluctantly, I took her point. We should keep Angel on our side, instead of risking eviction from Brother Sean. Or, at the very least, a new letter, setting forth a superseding set of rules and regulations.

Plus, I was pretty sure Katie would make a noise like a ravished banshee if I followed through on half the things I thought about doing to her in that kitchen.

So I drew on lessons my mother had drilled into me when I was five years old. I made polite conversation, starting by asking about the deranged gargoyle that glared from Angel's lap.

"Lucy?" Angel stroked the animal's naked back, and a monstrous rumble filled the room. "She's the sweetest cat in the world! The only person she doesn't like is Katie."

Lucifer opened one eye and directed a hiss at me with the precision of a timber rattlesnake.

"Hmm," Angel said, after switching her attention to the hell-beast's chin. "It seems like she doesn't like you, either."

So much for talking about the cat. I asked Angel if she was keeping in touch with friends from her assisted living facility. She told me about chair yoga, and senior choir, and visits from therapy dogs. She covered Lucifer's ears when she got to that last bit.

While we talked, I couldn't help noticing that things were getting louder in the kitchen. Something large and metallic fell on the floor and rolled around for a while before Katie stopped it. Something heavy and wet dropped into the sink. A few drawers slammed closed, and it sounded like a Valkyrie was trying to pry the pantry door off its hinges.

After one particularly loud clatter, Angel's face creased into a worried frown. "Maybe you should go help your sister, Sean."

I froze. Was it better to correct her? Or to take her suggestion and escape to the kitchen?

I finally said, "I'm Jason, Mrs. McIntyre. Jason Price."

She must have tensed up, because Lucifer jumped from her lap. The cat glared at me as if I'd taken a crap in the middle of the room. Angel blinked hard, and then she said, "Of course you are, dear. Please. If you're going to be living here, you might as well call me Angel."

She offered the endearment as if we hadn't had the exact same conversation that afternoon. But that was probably my own fault, for reverting to her formal name. I was still trying to figure out the right way to respond when there was another heavy thud from the kitchen. Angel said, "Go on, now. Katie needs you. I'll just watch my programs out here."

The cat jumped back to her lap as she pointed her remote at the TV. I recognized dismissal when I heard it. Figuratively girding my loins, I headed into the war zone.

The kitchen looked like a serial killer had been set loose with a chain saw. A huge can of tomato sauce lay sideways on the counter. About half of it had made it into the stockpot on the stove; the rest was splattered on a cutting board, the sink, and the backsplash. The guts of fresh tomatoes sprayed across four burners. Onion peels and the cores of three bell peppers were scattered in the debris. A pot of water boiled on the back burner, churning with strands of spaghetti that clumped together like a tortured squid.

Once I'd taken in the extent of the devastation, I asked, "Need a hand?"

"Nope," Katie said, her voice tight. "Everything's under control."

"Great." I forced a smile. "Angel thinks TV is more interesting than conversation, so you're stuck with me."

"Perfect." She tossed her head, trying to remove a stray wisp of hair from her eyes. It looked like she was saying no. Emphatically.

Remembering that it was best to avoid eye contact with rabid dogs and terrified kittens, I leaned against the counter farthest from the killing zone. A Ziploc bag of peanut butter cookies was shoved into the corner so I helped myself to a couple. "These smell great," I said, noting the perfect crosshatch of fork tines as I closed the bag.

"Wait!" Katie said, a look of pure panic freezing her face. "You'll—"

I thought she was going to say *spoil your appetite*. I was actually *trying* to spoil my appetite, because I didn't think the upcoming meal was going to be very satisfying. But as my teeth closed around the lump in my mouth, nothing crumbled. I could—literally—have been chewing a rock.

Grimacing, I took the cookie out of my mouth. It looked exactly the same as it had in the bag; there weren't even indentations where my teeth had been.

Katie said, "Those, um, didn't turn out the way I wanted."

"What are you keeping them for? Ammunition?"

"I thought maybe they'd soften if I put them in a plastic bag."

"How long since you baked them?"

"Three weeks."

I laughed because I thought she was joking. Then I realized she was telling the truth. "They're not going to get any softer," I said.

Before she could answer, the spaghetti boiled over on the stove. Water sheeted down the sides of the pot, hissing louder than Lucifer. As Katie started to swear, the cascade extinguished its gas burner.

Without a flame, the water quickly settled back in its pot. Katie gave an awkward shrug and said, "At least it's not boiling over any more."

"Careful!" I said, leaping in front of her and turning off the burner before the still-flowing gas could be ignited by the flame under the sauce.

"Oh," Katie said, nonplussed. She retrieved a long-handled spoon and stirred the mixture of tomatoes, peppers, and onions that threatened to overflow its stockpot. "At least it's ready to eat now. Why don't you get Angel, while I serve up dinner?"

It didn't look ready to eat to me. But I was able to follow direct orders. I stood by Angel's wing chair while she climbed to her feet, and I kept a watchful eye as she made her way into the kitchen. After seeing her safely settled at the table, I made myself useful by feeding Lucifer. The traitor took one bite of her food and sashayed out of the kitchen, presumably heading out to wreak havoc somewhere else.

"There we go," Katie said, gesturing toward our waiting bowls of pasta.

I had every intention of eating my dinner. So what if the pasta had been boiled into lumpy mush? Who cared if it hadn't been drained thoroughly, so the sauce was now mixed with equal parts of starchy water? What difference did it make if that sauce had scarcely had time to come to a boil, much less cook down to a savory complement to spaghetti?

My first bite included a chunk of raw onion. The second was gritty with bell pepper seeds. I didn't try a third.

"What do you think?" Katie asked, pushing her fork around her own bowl morosely.

"Honestly?"

She nodded.

"I think I'm doing the cooking from here on out, Killer."

"Thank heavens!" Angel said, favoring me with a wide smile.

I'd seen Katie go cut-throat on a game of Boggle. I fully expected her to put up a fight when I impugned her cooking prowess. Instead, she said, "I'll wash dishes."

"Deal," I said. "Any chance there's anything edible in the fridge?"

We settled on a quick frittata, cooked in a skillet and finished in the oven. I melted some feta on top before I cut us each a healthy wedge, and I sliced a couple of apples to go on the side.

"How did you learn to do this?" Katie asked as she used the side of her fork to scrape up the last of her eggs.

"My father c—" I almost slipped up, but I changed the tense just in time. "Couldn't cook to save his soul. Mom insisted I had to learn, same as my sisters."

"Your mother sounds like a wise woman," Angel said.

"Very much so," I agreed. Except for the fact that she'd stuck by Dad all these years. But I wasn't about to open *that* can of worms. Instead, I asked Angel about the best meal she'd ever eaten. That turned into a conversation about restaurants, and *that* turned into a discussion of travel. The sky was jet-black outside the sliding glass door by the time I stood to clear our plates.

"That's my job," Katie said.

"I've got it tonight. You cooked."

"Not really." She gestured toward the mess on the stove. "What a waste!"

"Some of it's salvageable," I said. "I'll turn it into ratatouille."

"My, my, Mr. Price," she said, with a sly smile that made me wish Angel was a million miles away. "What other secrets have you been hiding?"

Before I could consider the wisdom of answering in front of our octogenarian chaperone, Angel yawned. She tried to cover her mouth with her good hand, but weariness got the better of her. "Go on," I said to Katie. "Help Angel get ready for bed. I'll clean up in here."

That's what we did—divide and conquer. Once Angel was down for the night, it didn't make sense for us to sit in the living room. We didn't want to keep her awake. And the spotless kitchen didn't invite lingering.

But Katie crossed her arms as she said, "We might as well head downstairs."

She might as well have placed a billboard in the center of the room. *No fucking allowed.*

She'd been every bit as enthusiastic as I was that afternoon. And she hadn't seemed embarrassed by her spectacular failure in the kitchen; instead, she acted relieved to be through with cooking.

But she wasn't happy now. And it didn't take a rocket scientist to figure out why.

If all she and I had was sex, we'd be sick of each other in…

Okay. Truth be told, I couldn't imagine getting sick of sex with Katie. But I understood her wanting something more. Something different. Something real. More real, at least, than the two fuck-fests we'd already had, with me in the house for less than twelve hours.

She needed to know I realized she was more than a body. A willing, creative, athletic, flexible body.

Fuck.

I nodded toward the bathroom. "Are you washing up first, or am I?"

"I'll go," she said, looking a little like a hobbit slouching toward Mt. Doom.

While she was gone, I exchanged my clothes for pajama bottoms. I gave it another thought and pulled on a plain black T-shirt too. When Katie came back, smelling like peppermint and soap, I eased past her, making sure we didn't touch.

I brushed my teeth. Flossed twice. Read the list of active ingredients on my toothpaste. Checked to make sure my shampoo was still centered on the shelf in the shower.

The container was down to about a third after my two-week stay at the Monaco. I knew what that meant. The Mind-Fuck came howling like a rabid dog when that bottle got empty.

Usually, just thinking about it made me tense, like I was testing a bad tooth with my tongue. But tonight, nothing started to jangle. Tonight, the Mind-Fuck stayed locked inside its kennel.

By the time I came back to the bedroom, Katie was under the covers on the right side of the bed, propped up with two pillows behind her back. She was checking something on her phone. "Is this okay?" she asked, her voice carefully casual. She set her phone on the nightstand. "I can sleep on the other side if you want."

"This is fine," I said. I got into bed to prove my point.

"Jason—" she started to say, but I overrode her, intent on making my own point.

"You and your brother seem like very different people," I said.

I'd caught her by surprise. "Wh—what?"

"Just for starters, he's got every kitchen appliance known to man," I said. "And you aren't exactly, um, Julia Child."

Her shoulders twitched, releasing a bit of tension. "He's been cooking since tenth grade. I think he started because he wanted to do chemistry experiments. Now, it's a stress-reliever, when he's not working in the ER."

"Sounds like he's always had a pretty good idea of what he wanted to do with his life."

She relaxed a little more, sinking deeper into her pillows. "He was first in line to get every animal they dissected in high school biology. How about you? When did you know you were going to play ball?"

"After I realized I wouldn't be a fireman. Santa brought me a glove for Christmas when I was six years old. Best present ever."

"At the *time*, I thought my best present was a rainbow unicorn backpack. I carried it with me everywhere, until the straps completely disintegrated."

"But your actual best present?"

She turned onto her side and propped her head up on her hand. I matched her position as she said, "Sean gave me his old laptop when he headed off to college. I began writing—short stories and little essays. And I started keeping a diary I knew Angel would never get into."

We started talking about privacy. She'd worried about her grandmother prying into her secrets, and I'd needed to protect myself from five nosy sisters.

After that, we talked about our dream families when we were kids. I would have given anything—except my baseball glove—to not be the youngest. She'd wanted a sister.

In the end, we talked till two. We didn't touch each other, not until she leaned in to brush a quick kiss across my lips, just before she turned out the light. In the darkness, she said, "Thank you."

I thought about pretending not to have heard. Instead I said, "I like this. Being here. With you."

"Me too," she said. And neither of us said another word before we fell asleep.

52

KATIE

Jason's arrival threw some sort of switch. I hadn't realized how tense I'd been, trying to serve up three edible meals a day. I also hadn't realized how many cans of soup Angel and I had eaten, how many times we'd made do with cheese and crackers, or how often we'd called a bowl of cereal dinner.

And another thing: I hadn't realized how much I missed touching another person. And being touched.

It wasn't just sex. It was a casual hand on my waist as I handed over a cup of coffee. It was a palm against the small of my back as I stepped off the patio into the lush grass of the backyard. It was a thumb pushing into the arch of my foot after I stretched on the couch, taking a break from staring at my computer screen.

Okay. It was sex, too. Stealing off in the afternoon for a quickie… Heading to bed half an hour after my invalid grandmother to maximize our time devising new, barely muffled, ways to please each other… Waking in the middle of the night to slow, leisurely lovemaking that faded seamlessly back into sleep…

More than all of that, though, it was discovering just how compatible I could be with another person. Like every female with a brain, I'd been indoctrinated by books and movies where characters gushed about being soulmates. Personally, I'd never felt it before. My high school and college boyfriends were too transitory to make that sort of impression. My relationship with Aaron had been built on lies.

But this thing with Jason… It didn't take effort. It just *was*. We understood each other—the little things and the big stuff too. Getting to know him better was like discovering a male version of me. We were both interested in sports. We both loved books. Our families were important to us, despite the fact—or maybe *because* of the fact—that we'd lost our fathers.

So Jason and I *talked*—another thing Aaron had never been interested in. We could debate who was the best catcher in the history of baseball—Johnny Bench, no matter how much Jason clung to the delusion that Yogi Berra deserved the prize.

But we could also discuss how social media affected the notion of community, building new norms even as it set fire to the old ones. We could talk about books and art and history. Reading the morning newspaper became a communal activity as we traded pages back and forth, commenting on articles in every section.

I listened to Jason's frustration with the Rockets, with team management and league officials who, according to leaked gossip, kept changing deadlines for when—if—the baseball season would be played. He scouted out stories for the *Phoenix*, following my website with an enthusiasm for my writing that —again—Aaron had never demonstrated.

We were a team. And for the first time since the pandemic began, I felt deeply, truly happy.

53

JASON

Moving in with Katie threw some kind of switch. It wasn't just getting out of the Monaco, having more than two rooms and a kitchenette to pace. I hadn't realized how confining the hotel had been, living without cell phone access, arranging my life around sitting on Katie's patio, putting life on hold day after day after day.

And another thing. I hadn't realized how much I missed touching another person. And being touched.

It wasn't just getting laid. It was Katie hip-checking me after I demonstrated perfect technique while dicing an onion. It was her hands settling on my shoulders for a quick squeeze before she cleared the dinner dishes, while I finished a conversation with Angel. It was her nudging a foot against my thigh as we shared the couch, reading.

Okay. It was getting laid, too. Dragging Katie downstairs for a hot, quick fuck while Angel watched her endless TV upstairs, totally unaware… Marathon sessions after dark, the kind of mind-blowing sex that beat every made-up letter ever written to a porno site… Quiet screwing in the middle of the night, half-way between a dream and a slow-motion movie…

But more than all of that, it was discovering just how compatible I could be with another person. I'd never before been tempted to shack up with a girlfriend. No woman had ever been worth giving up my privacy, compromising on the thermostat, having another person *there* day in, day out, twenty-four, seven.

Except there *was* a woman worth all of that and more.

Katie and I *talked.* Sometimes, she was totally off-base, like when she insisted Johnny Bench was the best catcher in baseball history. But whatever the topic, she had an opinion, an interesting one, and she was competitive enough to debate it for hours.

Or to let it go. Because every once in a while, even a champ knew to let things go.

We were a team. And for the first time since the pandemic began, I felt deeply, truly happy.

54

KATIE

Okay. Life wasn't *all* sunshine and roses.

I still worried about Angel. Her arm was healing as well as could be expected. Bones knit slowly in elderly patients. But she was sleeping more than when I'd first arrived, sometimes staying in bed until nine in the morning. She slipped into a nap most afternoons and turned in for the night by eight. Often, I caught her singing to herself, humming when she couldn't remember the words.

Still, she rallied every time Jason entered the room. She slipped sometimes and called him Sean, but she was a thousand times more alert when he was nearby.

The virus, of course, still continued to rage. Timothy had more and more trouble filling our grocery order. There were limits on the amount of meat he could buy, and canned goods were catch as catch can. Toilet paper and paper towels remained on back order. Jason's writing a check to my brother-in-law couldn't solve stocking problems.

And on a personal note, Brittany still refused to break her silence. I tried to take her distance as a challenge. Every morning, I checked her Instagram, "liking" every one of her posts with near-religious fervor. Every afternoon, as I wrapped up my own work day, I sent her a text—nothing urgent, nothing demanding, just a quick summary of my life or a non-judgmental comment about hers.

KATIE

Found the perfect Phoenix story about a rescue dog who shares her toys with all the neighbors.

Jason's making Thai chicken with basil for dinner tonight.

Saw your chocolate-mint donuts this morning. Those green sprinkles are super-cute!

My phone dutifully showed me that every text was delivered. It confirmed that each one was read. But Brit never, ever wrote back.

I told myself it was because of the pandemic. She was stressed. She was alone. Once this damn disease was gone, we'd go back to being friends, the way we always had been. But each day dug another little knife into the space between my ribs.

And then, one week into Jason's stay, I got an email that made me squeal with excitement:

From: Day in the Park Games

To: Katie McIntyre

Subject: Advertising on The Feel-Good Phoenix

Dear Ms. McIntyre:

Day in the Park Games creates and sells board games that promote cooperative play for children and adults, age 8 to 108. Our What Color is Your Rainbow *was recently featured in a* Washington Banner *article about games that will get families through the stress of COVID-19.*

Here at Day, we have become loyal fans of The Feel-Good Phoenix. *We eagerly await each new story of hope during these challenging times.*

We note that the Phoenix *currently serves a limited number of advertisements on each web page. Please send us your current list of ad rates, so we can determine whether Day in the Park and the* Phoenix *are the perfect match we think they are.*

I'd nearly forgotten about the ad console Timothy had installed for me. The images I'd thrown together for Wag the Dog and Capit-hole Donuts had become so familiar, I barely saw them when I visited the *Phoenix* site.

Now, someone wanted to pay me good money to replace those ads. I'd have to check them out, of course, to preserve the *Phoenix's* wholesome reputation. But I strongly suspected we could come to a business arrangement without a great deal of haggling.

As I started researching Day in the Park, Jason walked in from the bathroom. A towel was knotted around his waist, and his freshly washed hair stood in spikes. He hadn't shaved for a few days, and the dark scruff made his arctic blue eyes seem even lighter.

"Mmm," I said, as if I'd just tasted the world's most perfect dessert.

Laughing, he asked, "What has you in such a good mood?"

I told him about the email, enjoying the show as he exchanged his towel for boxers, well-fitting jeans, and a blue-striped hemp shirt. As I'd hoped, he immediately honed in on the business question Day in the Park presented. We spent the rest of the morning debating appropriate prices for ads.

Two days later, I was staring at another email.

From: Lisa Boudreaux, Carver University Reference Librarian

To: Katie McIntyre

Subject: Contemporary Studies Senior Theses

Dear Ms. McIntyre:

I apologize for my delay in responding to your recent request for copies of award-winning theses written by seniors in Carver University's Contemporary Studies department. As you are no doubt aware, we are currently working with reduced staff in light of the current coronavirus crisis.

Nevertheless, I have now had a chance to research the documents you requested. I am pleased to inform you that each is available in electronic format. The following links will take you to this valuable research. Please do not hesitate to let me know if you have any questions or encounter any difficulty in downloading the material you requested.

The links worked flawlessly. I downloaded all three of the documents.

After Dr. Halliday's cloak and dagger game, reinforced by the library's weeks of delays, I wasn't sure what I expected. Part of me feared the documents would be entirely blank, that the Contemporary Studies program was a sham operation created solely to offer academic shelter to so-called student-athletes. Part of me expected the papers to be riddled with errors, full of incomplete sentences, or written in crayon. Part of me believed the subject matter would be laughably inappropriate—notes from long-ago ball games masquerading as scholarship or endless repetitions of the official rules of various sports.

But the documents I downloaded appeared to be entirely legitimate academic endeavors. One looked at the effect of opiate addiction on teen mothers in Albany, New York.

Another studied transportation issues created by streetcar projects serving under-resourced neighborhoods in seven urban centers. The third analyzed arts funding, looking at the impact of grants to individual artists, as opposed to incorporated theaters, galleries, and museums.

All three were written by baseball players. All three thanked Coach Dixon explicitly.

My first instinct was to go to Jason, to ask him what was up. But I quickly squelched that urge.

Jason wasn't impartial. Sure, he supported my publishing career. But he was also a Carver alum and a Dixon protegé.

I'd muddied the journalistic waters the instant I proposed writing an article about the man I was sleeping with. I knew that now. I should have known that then. The Carver librarian's email underscored the mistake I'd made. My professors at journalism school would be appalled that I'd placed myself in this position.

On the one hand, my professional integrity said I had to run out this ball. I had to see what would crawl out from under the rock I'd turned over.

But on the other hand, my growing role as—what? Jason's lover? His girlfriend? His I-shied-away-from-setting-a-label-but-I-really-wanted-this-to-be-something-more? *That* growing role urged me to walk away from the entire article.

Trying to make the best of the crappy situation I'd created, I cobbled together an uneasy compromise. I'd complete my research without consulting Jason. I'd get independent confirmation of whatever Dr. Halliday thought I should find. I'd follow standard journalism practice, confirming my story with two independent sources. Two sources with absolutely no personal connection.

I'd share whatever I found with Jason before I went public; I owed him that. But I wouldn't let whatever we had stifle my still-tingling journo-judgment.

Decision made, I settled in for the long haul. Over the

next week, I worked my way through each of the theses. I had quibbles with the authors. One of them didn't know the difference between that and which. Another wasn't solid on lie, lay, and lain. Two deleted the Oxford comma, which offended my personal sense of readability but was hardly an academic crime.

It wasn't until Wednesday night that I realized what I'd downloaded to my computer.

Jason was in the kitchen, cooking something with chicken, garlic, and basil that smelled incredible. Angel was zombified by *Law and Order: Criminal Intent.* Lucifer was shredding a sock I'd been foolish enough to leave on the closet floor.

On TV, a new episode opened with the usual corpse. This time, it was a young woman, stabbed to death. As the details of her back-story were revealed, Angel turned to me with a beatific smile. "Look, Katie! She's a reporter. Just like you."

Hopefully, not *just* like me. I had a (slightly) better grasp on my finances than the murdered character. I certainly wasn't using drugs. I'd never come close to stealing from my employer to get my next fix.

But as I watched the five-act morality play, I realized I already knew the story. It was based on a famous journalism scandal. The dead girl's boyfriend was patterned after Jayson Blair, a reporter for *The New York Times* who had plagiarized dozens of stories.

Plagiarism.

Opening up the first thesis, the one about opiate addiction, I pulled up a free plagiarism checker on the Internet. I typed in a few sentences. Nothing. No original sources noted.

But then I created a paid account with the program. I gave it some personal information—my email address, my phone number, and my street address. I added a credit card number and braced for the ninety-five dollar cost, whether or not it found anything suspicious.

I clicked Search.

And there it was. The Carver student had copied a study written by a low-level City of Albany Department of Health employee.

It wasn't a perfect match. No single paragraph was lifted word for word. Sentence order was sometimes changed. Two-bit words were substituted for five-dollar ones.

But looking at the two documents side by side, there was no doubt the Carver paper was plagiarized. I ponied up another two hundred bucks and confirmed that the other theses were just as tainted.

I had my answer.

And now I wished I'd never asked the question. Because the obvious next step was finding out who knew what when.

It looked bad for Stan Dixon. The acknowledgments by his athletes implied that the coach was in on the scam.

But I was a lot less sure about Jason. He *believed* in education. He'd slaved over his own thesis, something I now knew was about Aristotle and game theory, whatever that meant. Players—even teammates—who cheated devalued everything he'd worked so hard to achieve.

Even beyond those lofty ideals, Jason had agreed to let me write my article in the first place. He never would have gone along with my reporting if he thought he—or Dixon, or Carver—had anything to hide.

I tried to take comfort in my professional standards. I had to work the story. I had to find unbiased sources. I had to confirm the facts.

But in my heart, I already knew how this would end. I would need to find a way to tell Jason that the man he loved like a father was a lying, cheating fraud.

55

JASON

"Whipped," Zach Ormond said, when we both signed on early for a team meeting on the first of May. "You are well and truly whipped."

"Says the man whose wife literally signs his pay checks."

He flipped me the bird, even as he conceded the point. "Anna's been riding my ass about your bookstore challenge. She's raffling off a pair of tickets to the owner's box for Opening Day. Every customer at Quail Ridge Books gets entered into the contest."

"Shit," I said. "Who says we're even *getting* to Opening Day?"

"She thought about that. The winner can push to next year."

A couple of other guys had signed on while we were talking. DJ Thomas asked Ormond, "You really think they'll shit-can the whole season?"

"The owners say they'll lose over six hundred grand for every game we play without fans in the park."

Almost out of range of his computer camera, DJ pumped his hand at his waist, demonstrating exactly how much credibility he gave our overlords and masters. "The owners'll poor-mouth us till we agree to play for free." He seemed to remember who he was talking to, because he made a hasty amendment. "Except for Anna."

Ormond let it go. By then most of the guys had signed on, so he delivered a dutiful update on the owners' negotiations. Everyone still hoped to fit in a hundred-game season, but no one could figure out how to make the pay cuts work.

Not surprisingly, most of the guys called bullshit. They were getting desperate. The season was slipping away, day by day, week by week. The risks of getting COVID felt abstract when careers were on the line.

As Ormond walked us through the details, I zoned out, making my own calculations. Today was the first of May. Ordinarily, we'd be a month into the season. I would've closed up the Coral Crest house and moved back to Raleigh. The team would have spent a couple of weeks in North Carolina and a couple of weeks on the road, hitting a new city every three or four nights.

I would have beaten the Mind-Fuck into submission by taking half a dozen trips through airports.

Instead, I'd spent almost a month in DC. I'd accepted Katie's offer of a full-size toothbrush instead of the crappy collapsible that kept me sane. I'd thrown out my squeezed-flat travel tube of toothpaste and started using hers. I'd finished my shampoo and shifted to something Timothy delivered. I'd sent checks to Sean and Timothy, trying to think of them as benevolent landlords instead of the potentially territorial brothers of the woman I took to bed every night.

And I hadn't felt the first twitch of restlessness. Not a hint of the itch that ate me from the inside out. I didn't feel even a whisper of the all-compelling *need* to move. Not once did I gasp like a drowning man pinned underwater…

I was free. I was a new man.

Katie had done that.

It was way too early to start throwing around labels. I'd scare the crap out of her if I said what I was thinking. But I tested words inside my head.

I…loved the way Katie freed me from the Mind-Fuck.

I…loved Katie's intensity when she was drafting a tough article.

I…loved…

The meeting was wrapping up when my phone buzzed. Jen. I muted audio and video for the team. "I've been meaning to call you," I said, which was actually true. I'd wanted to talk to her and to my other sisters and to Mom, but I couldn't risk letting Katie meet them, not while she still thought Dad was dead. Another reason to clear that up. Soon. For now, I said, "I'm doing a fund-raising thing with the team, getting the guys to support local bookstores. What do you think we should do to take it wider?"

"Whoa there, cowboy!" But she was laughing. "Back up. Tell me how this thing works."

I filled her in on the details, about how there *weren't* a lot of details. Each guy was responsible for finding his own store to support. Each guy had to figure out the best way to bring in customers.

"So when you say 'take it wider,' what do you mean?" Jen asked. "Each guy take on more bookstores? Or each guy add stores other than bookstores? Other guys on other baseball teams do the same thing? Or other guys on other Raleigh teams, other North Carolina teams?"

"I don't know. I just want to see how far we can push it."

"We?" she asked. "Last time I looked, I don't work for you anymore."

"You're my consultant," I said. "I'll send you a check."

She huffed out a breath, but I could tell she was smiling

when she said, "Let me think about it. I'll make a few calls. But you have to do something for me."

Shit. I walked into that one. And knowing Jen, she was already planning our family reunion. I gritted my teeth against the tension that slammed into my shoulders like a hundred pounds of barbells. "Jen—" I said.

"This isn't about Dad," she interrupted. "But the things he's doing at the plant are amazing. I've never seen him focused like this before. Consider yourself nagged. "

"Consider *yourself* shut down about Dad. Permanently." Like I'd ever succeeded in shutting Jen down about anything, permanently or not. But then, because she *had* agreed to think about the bookstore thing, I asked, "What's up?"

"Mary Ann Dixon called last night."

Guilt tasted like iron at the back of my throat. "I've been busy," I said, immediately lining up my usual excuses.

"She said she's left you a dozen messages."

Was it that many? I'd listened to each of her voice mails. That was the price for not picking up when I saw her name on my phone. "I don't know what to say when she calls," I said.

"You tell her you're sorry she's going through this. You say it must be tough, watching Stan get worse. Hell, tell her you don't know what to say. But you can't ghost her like this. It's not fair."

"I'll send her a check today."

"Don't be such an asshole!" Jen's shout was so loud I had to hold the phone away from my ear. "She doesn't want your money! She wants someone to tell her Coach has been important. That he's made a difference. She wants to know someone will remember him when he's gone."

"She knows that. They both do."

"Why is this so fucking hard? You've got issues with Dad. I get that. But news flash: Stan Dixon isn't Dad. He's the guy who stepped in when you ran away from home."

I hadn't run away from home, and she damn well knew it.

But I *had* learned a hell of a lot more from Coach than I'd ever learned from my own father. It took me a moment, but I finally relaxed my throat enough to say, "Okay. I'll call today."

"Don't put it off," Jen warned.

"I'll call!"

And I would. Right after I made lunch for Angel, Katie, and me. And finished the shopping list for Timothy, lining up groceries for next week. And sent out a text to the guys, reminding them they only had a month left in the bookstore challenge because Jen's call had kept me from chiming in at the end of the team meeting.

I'd call Coach soon. I just had to finish a few more pressing things first.

56

KATIE

I was sitting on a major story in the sports world.

The plagiarized Carver theses pointed me toward many more sources—supervising faculty, student advisors, tutors, and more. I found irregularities in the funding of professorial chairs for the Contemporary Studies department. I uncovered more questionable courses.

At least half a dozen professors were involved, mostly junior faculty. Leandra Halliday was tenured, though, and a dean had direct oversight of the multi-disciplinary aspects of the program.

I sent emails to Coach Dixon's faculty account. I left phone messages for him at the university. Every time I spoke to anyone official at Carver, I asked if they could get word to him, if they could urge him to get in touch.

But I remembered the articles I'd read when I started my research about Jason. Coach Dixon was dying of cancer.

The more I learned about Carver, the slower I worked.

There were the ordinary delays, waiting for people to get back to me, tracking down new leads, organizing the information I already had. But truth be told, my heart wasn't in completing the article. As the evidence piled up, I stifled my journo-judgment for one day at a time, then two, then three.

After all, I had plenty of other things to keep me busy, taking care of Angel and running our little household.

I knew that we were playing the pandemic game on the easiest setting. We didn't have kids to educate or entertain. We didn't have traditional jobs to manage. Despite Angel's pre-existing conditions, we were relatively healthy adults, living in a sumptuous home with high-speed wi-fi and a thousand channels of cable TV.

On May 11, the governor signed an order putting most of Virginia in Phase One of reopening. We were assured that Arlington would follow in a couple of weeks, just as soon as we got our infection rate down and confirmed there were sufficient hospital beds if anything went drastically wrong.

But I didn't want to move into Phase One.

On a practical basis, it would make no difference to us. Sean's edict stood fast. We remained on total lockdown for the foreseeable future.

But the rest of the world would start making decisions. Once businesses re-opened, people would have to weigh risks, deciding if it was worth it take the subway downtown, if it was safe to go to the gym, if it was time to get their teeth cleaned. Every action could result in disaster.

Or everything could be just fine.

It was the not knowing that frayed my nerves.

So I redoubled my efforts on *The Feel-Good Phoenix.* I'd taken on five more premium-level sponsors, and more than two dozen companies had paid for smaller ads. I'd already increased the cost of those advertisements, a move fully justified by an astronomical increase in readers.

Every morning, I checked my analytics, and the growth

curve swept up like the sides of the Washington Monument. I'd reached out to a few furloughed colleagues from *Press Box*, letting them know what I was doing and offering to pay flat rates for articles. Soon, I had enough content to post multiple items every day.

People wanted good news, and I felt great giving it to them.

I considered running a piece about Capit-hole Donuts. I saw from Brit's social media that she'd purchased a food truck in anticipation of Virginia entering Phase I. I had no idea where she got the financial backing or what she'd put up as collateral, but the pictures were amazing on her Instagram. I still texted every day.

KATIE

Great color scheme for the truck—love the orange and blue!

You are such a shrewd businesswoman, building two lines at once. Which do you think will make more money, donuts or masks?

Fun logo! Those donuts are going to sell themselves!

I never would have thought to use the masks as a loss leader. Can you really afford to give one away for every dozen donuts bought?

She never wrote back. Sometimes, when my thoughts bounced from the *Phoenix*, to Carver, to Jason and Coach Dixon, I wondered if Brit was even a friend worth keeping.

In ordinary, non-COVID times, I would have confronted her directly about her silence. I would have camped out on her doorstep until she *had* to speak with me. I would have told her how much it hurt, being cut off because of circumstances neither of us could control.

But these weren't ordinary times. COVID twisted everything. No one was absolutely rational. If I let the coronavirus take Brit from me, I'd be giving into the disease. The pandemic would have won.

Besides, if I wrote off Brittany, who would I confide in? Angel?

Fat chance.

So I worked some sort of Zen mind-magic, pretending Brit *couldn't* respond. She was out of the country, on some wild adventure that she'd tell me about over fancy cocktails and pancetta gougères, once the pandemic was history. And I started treating her silent phone like a diary, venting some of the worries that compressed my chest like a physical weight.

KATIE

Angel called me Abigail again today. Does she hate me as much as she hated my mother?

Lucifer went on a hunger strike. Now, the only thing she'll eat is frozen raw emu. Twenty-five dollars a pound. That cat eats better than I do.

Timothy brought a birthday cake for Angel today, chocolate with cream cheese frosting. It was sweet of him to remember, but you bake a better cake.

Major League postponed Opening Day again. My first thought, when I heard, was Jason gets to stay for longer. Guess I'm a pretty crappy girlfriend. Not to mention sports journalist.

Tonight, Jason replaced the toilet flapper while I did our laundry. It feels like we're playing house. Or maybe we're not playing.

Don't tell anyone. I'm not ready to say it out loud. But just between you and me, I'm falling pretty deeply in like with Jason.

Screw it. I've fallen in love.

On May 28, Arlington finally entered Phase I. I haunted Brit's Instagram as if I were a principal investor. All through the day, she added fun, artsy posts. The Caramel Crème Brûlées looked amazing. The Key Lime Kustards made my mouth water. She put a funny censoring bar over the Pink Velvet Down Belows (complete with a strategically placed candy pearl at the apex of each iced oval treat), and then she posted the empty tray later, saying they'd all been eaten.

That night, I got into bed while Jason brushed his teeth. When he came into the room, I was watching the video of Brit's first sale.

"We can pick up a dozen tomorrow," he said as the clip ended.

"Yeah. That'd be an immediate three strikes from Sean. First, we'd have to leave the house. Second, we'd be dealing with Brit, whom he still hasn't forgiven for a childhood prank. Third, we'd be getting *donuts*, pretty much heart attacks in a box, according to Dr. Doom."

"Who says he has to know?"

I looked up, startled, as another video began to auto-play. "I won't lie to my own brother."

"I'm not saying we should break out of jail."

Even as he said the words, my phone projected the sound of people shouting, the soundtrack to the new video. A trio of cops filled the screen. They were standing beside a black-and-white police SUV. One of them was kneeling on the neck of a man. "What the fuck…" I said.

"We could hire Uber Eats," Jason said. "Once we know where Brittany's parked for the day—"

"Look at this," I said, turning the phone so he could see the screen. "They're killing him."

I thought I was exaggerating. But almost nine minutes later, it was clear I'd actually spoken the truth. The kneeling policeman had killed the man on the ground. And the other guys in uniform had done nothing to stop him.

Sick to my stomach, I started looking for more information. It only took a moment to get the facts. "His name was George Floyd," I said. My voice sounded funny. Disconnected. It echoed weirdly in my ears. "He died on Monday."

57

JASON

I stood by the stove, stirring a five-bean chili and wishing I could have added the ancho and chipotles that would have made it perfect. But Angel had said anything spicier than bell pepper was out. She was a trouper with everything else I cooked, so I couldn't really complain.

At least I wasn't missing much in the living room. Angel was napping back in her bedroom, and she'd taken her miserable cat with her. Katie was sitting on the couch, shuffling a deck of index cards and laying them out on the coffee table.

I'd seen her do that before, planning stories for the *Phoenix*. She sketched out all the available articles, one to a card, then she arranged and re-arranged them until she found a good balance for the coming week.

She'd have to do a lot of shuffling this week, because the regular news was especially shitty. Even now, she'd taken advantage of Angel's nap to turn on coverage of the Black Lives Matter marches.

It felt wrong not to be out on the streets. I could wear a mask. I might make a difference.

But rules were rules. No protesting for us. We could only watch and grieve and wonder how 2020 could get any worse.

The landline rang and I grabbed it quickly, before Angel was disturbed. I just had time to catch the Caller Id. "Timothy! My man! Let me guess. You can't find any fish sauce."

"What?" He sounded confused.

"Fish sauce. It's on the back of the shopping list, along with lemongrass and rock sugar."

"I'm not at the store."

Now that he said it, I could hear an ambulance in the background. "Are you at the march?"

His voice cracked. "I'm at the hospital. It's Sean."

My hands moved automatically. I set down my wooden spoon. I turned off the burner beneath the chili. I slid open the drawer beneath the phone and took out paper and a pen so I could accurately record whatever he said next. I waited for him to tell me his husband was dead. "What happened?"

He lost it for a moment, collapsing into a huge, shuddering sob. "He just started to cough last night. We weren't even sure it was COVID. I brought him in because his lips were turning blue."

I was very aware that I had to keep my voice down. I couldn't let Katie and Angel hear me, not until I knew all the facts. "Are you with him now?"

"They won't let me in!" Panic was stark in his voice. "I can't even enter the ER. Dana, the attending… She said he was going straight to the ICU. They're probably putting him on a ventilator right now. She said they'll call me when they know more. Jesus Christ…"

"Listen to me, Timothy. They're taking care of him. They're doing everything they can. You need to go back home. Call your doctor. Tell them you've been exposed, and you need to be tested. Stay home until you know you're clear."

"I can't. I need to stay here. What if they change their minds? What if they say I can see him and I'm not here?"

"They won't change their minds. This is standard procedure. These are his friends, the people he works with every day. They'll take care of him. The best thing you can do is go home."

"I need to get your groceries first."

He wasn't thinking straight. "Screw our groceries. Go home. Call me when you get there."

He finally agreed, and I was left standing in the kitchen, wondering how the fuck I was going to break the hearts of two women.

Taking a deep breath, I settled into a familiar calm. It didn't matter that dinner was halfway cooked. It didn't matter that we were trapped inside the house, unable to join the folks marching for justice. It didn't matter that we couldn't storm the hospital, couldn't be with Sean, couldn't sit by his bed and tell him everything would be okay, even if that was all a fucking lie.

I had a job to do. Same as when I took the mound. Same as when I had to close out the game, make good on the runs my teammates had already put on the board.

I turned the key on the box that held my emotions, and I went into the living room.

Katie looked up from her work. "Who was— What's wrong?"

I flipped through the facts, same as I did in a ball game. As a closer, I chose the best pitch to annihilate the batter. Here, I chose the words that needed to be said first. "Everyone is fine, for now," I said, trying to keep her from jumping to the same conclusion I had.

"Who was on the phone?" She was scared.

I gave her the facts—crisp, clean, fast, like a soldier reporting for duty. "Timothy. Sean's in the hospital. It's COVID, but they're taking care of him."

She dropped her index cards, spraying them across the couch and onto the floor.

I closed out my account. “He’s in the ICU. He’s on a ventilator, or will be, soon. No one can visit, but they’ll get updates to Timothy.”

She glared at me. “That’s not right.”

“It is. I just got off the phone—”

“No,” she said, and her cheeks flushed. “It’s not fair. Sean’s a *doctor*. He *helps* people.”

“And now other people are helping him. He’ll be fine.”

“You have no way of knowing that!”

The night we met, Katie had said she didn’t get angry. But she was furious now, spluttering with a blinding, flash-point rage.

And she was right. I *didn’t* know he’d be fine. Instead of telling her another lie, I bent down to scoop up her notecards.

“Don’t touch those!” Katie shouted.

I held them awkwardly. When one started to slip, I looked down, trying to keep from messing up her order.

Stan Dixon, said the top card.

That was great, some idiot corner of my brain chirped. Katie was writing a *Phoenix* story about Coach. I looked at the next card, wondering which of his good deeds she would use.

Plagiarism, said the next card. *Dictionary definition.*

Department of Contemporary Studies.

Leandra Halliday.

And then, in Katie’s fast, angular writing, the letters I’d come to know well in the past two months: *Dixon in on scandal? Or so negligent he missed it?*

58

KATIE

"What the fuck is this?" Jason demanded.

My palms tingled as I stared at him. My breath was coming fast, and tears threatened to spill down my cheeks. I was so fucking angry.

Sean couldn't be sick. He was the one who followed the rules. He was the one who *made* the rules.

I waited for the ice to come, for my spine to freeze. I needed that strength. I needed that shield, so I could go into Angel's room and wake her and tell her about my brother.

Sean went into that hospital day after day, night after night, treating the sickest of the sick. He'd sacrificed so much —his time, his peace of mind, his home—and now he had COVID, and I was so mad I couldn't breathe. If I opened my mouth, I'd start to scream, and I would never, ever be able to stop.

Without the ice, bad things would happen. Without the ice, people would leave. People would die.

My fingertips burned. My eyes ached. My pulse pounded in my ears, each beat as loud as a gunshot. I wanted to throw something at the TV, to stop the stream of people marching, people chanting, people demanding that the world be fucking fair.

I couldn't find a single sliver of ice.

Jason was shaking my notecards in front of my face. "What the fuck are you writing about Stan Dixon?"

That was an easy question. A safe one. My anger couldn't hurt Carver University. My anger could only destroy people I loved.

"Student-athletes are breaking the rules," I said, but my voice sounded like it belonged to someone else, someone calm and distant and endlessly patient. "They're shunted onto a sweetheart academic track where the department looks the other way when they plagiarize their papers. Dixon either knows and he's helping them do it, or he doesn't know and he's an idiot."

It was the first time I'd said all the words out loud. They were simple and cold and logical and I wondered why I hadn't told Jason a long time ago.

He ripped my notecards in half. "You can't write that."

My fury about Sean boiled over. "Those are mine!" I tried to pry the crumpled pieces from his fists.

"Not anymore." He shoved them into his pockets before he swept up the cards on the couch. "Stan Dixon is a good man. A better father than my own dad has ever been."

"Ever was," I snapped, because this was a stupid fight, and maybe I could still somehow summon the ice if I focused on meaningless things like basic grammar.

Jason was flipping through the cards he hadn't shredded, his body spiraling tighter with every line of the case I'd proven. When he finally looked at me, his pale, pale eyes seemed white. "Ever *been*," he said. "Dad's alive and well in Killeen, Texas, the same asshole drunk he's always been. And even though Stan Dixon has cancer, even if he never coaches another inning of baseball, even if, God forbid, he drops dead tonight, Coach is worth a thousand of my father any day."

The lie detonated in the center of my brain.

Jason's father was alive.

Jason and I didn't share some secret, special past. We weren't destined to be together because we'd been shaped by the same trauma. He didn't know what it felt like to watch a father suffer, to watch a father *die,* to stand on the edge of that gaping hole and know it was never, ever going to be filled.

The betrayal was too huge. I couldn't imagine finding words to express the crater he'd just excavated in my world. So I said the only thing I knew was whole and right and true. "You can't tell me what to write."

I'd never said that to Aaron, all the times he'd laughed off my articles, all the times he'd patted me on my head and treated my career like a kid's cute game.

"If you publish that article," Jason said, "you'll destroy the best college coach who's ever lived."

I was a lot smarter now. A lot stronger. There was no way in hell I was backing down. I raised my chin and enunciated every syllable: "All the more reason for people to know the truth."

"Jesus, Katie! What the fuck is your problem?"

"My *problem* is—"

"You're balls to the wall on everything!"

"I'm not afraid to fight—"

"You can't, for one single second—"

"*You lied to me!*" The words ripped open my throat.

"—imagine that you're wrong."

"You *lied*!" I repeated. "And I'm not wrong about Carver. Stan Dixon is helping players cheat!"

"If you're so certain about your story, then why is this the first I'm hearing about it?"

"It doesn't have anything to do with you!"

"Now who's lying?" Realization narrowed his eyes to slits.

"I never—"

"If you really thought this wouldn't affect me, you would have told me you were writing it."

"I wanted to—"

"I answered your fucking questions. Every one."

"And that was great. But this is more important. People deserve to know the truth! Other athletes… Other Carver students… I'd expect you to *want* the story out there. You *worked* for your degree!"

"You can't write it now. Not with Coach—"

"When, then?"

"—dying."

The word sat there, ugly and stinking. But it didn't change a thing. "How long should I wait? A month after he's gone? Six? I'm a journalist, and you don't get to control my career. You don't get to say what I write and don't write."

"Jesus Christ. It's one fucking article. Look. I'll pay you for the rights. What would it be worth to *Press Box*? Five thousand? Ten? I'll write a check right now."

Scarlet waves broke over my head. I couldn't feel my fingers. I couldn't feel my toes. A voice that might have been mine a century ago said, "You think you can get anything you want by throwing your money around."

"You've been willing enough to catch it for the past two months."

"Stop," I said, enunciating the single syllable with perfect precision. "Think before you say one more word, because it sounds an awful lot like you're calling me a whore."

"You're the one who works with words. If that's the right one, you'll be sure to know it."

"Get the fuck out of my house."

"With pleasure." He turned on his heel and stalked down the hall, slamming the front door before I could tell him to go to hell.

59

KATIE

I was five years old, and my mother was insisting I wear my pink dress because we were going to dinner at Mr. Ballard's house. The dress was the only one I owned, and I hated it. Its lace collar scratched my throat, and the zipper always stuck at the back. I wasn't allowed to run or jump or climb when I wore it, because anyone could see my panties and nice girls didn't let people see their panties and why did I make such a big fuss about this because I didn't have to wear the dress very often.

I begged my mother to let me put on pants, even the new ones, the ones with three stiff buttons on the fly. When that didn't work, I pleaded to stay home, I'd be good, and Mommy and Daddy could even call the babysitter who smelled like cigarettes.

When Mommy refused *that*, I got angry.

I told her it wasn't fair, that boys never had to wear

dresses. I told her the dress was ugly. I told her only stupid people liked dresses.

The angrier I got, the louder I shouted, until my eyes were streaming and I was choking on snot and I could barely catch my breath. My father and Sean crowded into my bedroom doorway as I gulped like my goldfish when it jumped out of its bowl. Daddy said, "Jesus Christ, Abby. Let her wear the fucking pants."

I'd never heard Daddy swear before. From the look on Sean's face, he hadn't either.

Mommy said, "You always take her side."

Daddy answered almost before she finished talking. "*You* always turn things into a fight. Let. It. Go."

Mommy dropped the dress on the floor. She stepped on it as she walked out of my room. Daddy followed her down the hall and one of them slammed the door to their bedroom.

We didn't go to Mr. Ballard's party. But Mommy came out of her room with a suitcase. She carried it out to her car. She said goodbye to Sean and she gave him a kiss, but she didn't say anything to me, because I'd been angry. I'd been bad.

I never saw her again.

~

I was seven and Sean and I were watching some Japanese cartoon that he really liked but I never understood. Daddy came in and turned off the TV and asked us both to sit on the couch beside him.

His medicine made his voice hoarse. His fingers shook in his lap. He still looked funny without any hair.

When he told us we were all going to live with Angel, I got mad. Angel's house smelled like bathroom spray, and she always kept the shades pulled so all the rooms were dark. The only toys we had at Angel's were a bucket of crayons, most of them broken, and a Chutes and Ladders game that was for babies.

"I want to stay here," I yelled at my father. "I'm best friends with Stacy, and she lives next door. If you loved us, you wouldn't make us move!"

"I love you very much, Katie-bird. That's exactly why we're going to Angel's."

Sean tried to hush me, but I wouldn't shut up. "I hate you!" I screamed, and the words were scary because I'd never said them to a person before. Being scared made me even *more* angry, and I shouted as loud as I could, "I don't ever want to live with you again!"

We moved to Angel's house the next day. And Daddy got sick that night and had to go to the hospital in an ambulance. I visited him once, where he lay in a giant bed, barely able to stay awake. I begged him to get better. I told him I didn't mind living with Angel, that we could all live there together, and I would never, ever complain again.

The night Daddy died, Sean and I made promises to each other. He said he'd become a doctor, so he could keep other dads from dying. I said I'd never get angry again.

For twenty-two years, I'd kept that promise. I'd sharpened my tongue. Sharpened my wits. I'd learned to defuse situations with humor. I'd mastered hitting fast and hitting hard. I'd learned to submerge myself in ice, to freeze out the fire and the fury that had ruined my life when I was only seven years old.

Until now.

I'd let myself be angry with Jason. And I'd made another person I loved leave me forever.

60

JASON

I merged onto the freeway like a robot, automatically matching the speed of the sparse traffic. I checked my mirrors. I twisted to clear my blind spot. My hands were tight on the steering wheel, as if the car would turn itself back toward Katie if I yielded a fraction of an inch.

What had just happened back there? How the fuck did everything explode so quickly?

Yeah, I hadn't told her about Dad. But he didn't come up in conversation every goddamn day.

How's work going? How many times had I asked her that, while I rubbed her feet as she worked on the hard-as-a-board couch? While I swept her hair aside and kissed her neck? While I stood in the kitchen, cooking breakfast or lunch or dinner, because she was so goddamn focused on her writing she hadn't come up for air.

She could have told me when we watched that news story

about how people were getting a break from lockdown by golfing on Carver's eighteen-hole course. She could have brought it up after the *Banner* ran that feature on a Carver med school virologist, the one who explained how a rapid-development COVID vaccine would be built on an entirely new model.

A car honked, and I jerked the wheel, pulling back into my lane.

Fuck. Fuck, fuck, fuck, fuck, fuck.

I tapped the button on the steering wheel and told the impassive computer to call Jen.

"I was just thinking about you," she answered.

I bet she had a new plan to get me to talk to Dad. Screw that. "Have you got a few minutes?" I asked.

"A few minutes like I'm your favorite sister and you just want to talk? Or a few minutes like I'm your former assistant and you have a new load of scut-work to hand off?"

"I need a plane ticket to San Diego."

"When are you heading out there?" I could hear the approval in her voice. She'd finally won the campaign to get me to see Coach.

"I'll be at Dulles in twenty minutes."

"What—" She cut off her own question. I knew her well enough to picture the frown on her face. I could imagine her testing question after question, discarding each as soon as it came to mind. She finally settled on: "Are you okay?"

"I'm fine."

"Is Katie—"

"She's fine," I lied. "Angel's fine. Everyone is fucking fine."

"But you're heading to the airport on no notice, and you need a ticket to San Diego. Anything else I should know?"

I'd missed that saccharine tone, the one she used when I was being a total dick but she wasn't going to say so out loud. "I'll need a rental car. And a hotel—somewhere close to

Coach. I don't know how long I'll be there. Better get the room for a week."

"Okay," she said. I could already hear her fingers clacking on a keyboard. "Anything else?"

"I'll need clothes. Just the basics—jeans, some T-shirts, underwear. Toiletries too."

"You left without a suitcase?"

I ignored the question. "I'll need to show up with something," I said. "A bottle of booze. Chocolates. Whatever."

"Jase," she tried again.

"I travel light. You know that."

Jen was too good at her job to let my being an ass put her off her pace. "Give me a few minutes. I'll set up the flight first and get the rest while you're in the air."

As I thanked her and cut the call, the car tried to turn around. It was determined to take the next exit, to go back to Katie, to figure out a way to make everything right again. I tightened my hands on the steering wheel and merged onto the expressway that ended at the airport.

I'd never been a drunk, not like my father. I'd never gone to an AA meeting. But as the odometer ticked over each mile, I felt like I was closer and closer to throwing away two hard-earned months of sobriety, jettisoning my hard-won safety of COVID quarantine.

I could picture the cheap-ass day planner I'd picked up in the drugstore back in April. I could feel the plastic casings of the glitter gel pens when I drew the numbers to count down the days. I could smell the weak spring sunshine on the flagstone patio when I waited out those fourteen long days.

Sitting in my car, I was still in isolation. I hadn't broken the lock-down bubble. I could turn around, go back, and avoid the frustration and delay and boredom of another two-week wait. I didn't have to tear everything apart.

Overhead signs announced the airport's remote parking lots. They told me where I could ditch a rental car. They pointed me toward cargo services and airport administration. They gave me the choice of arrivals or departure.

I pulled up to the kiosk of a bored-looking valet attendant who presided over a nearly empty lot. I threw on a mask from the glove box, one of the ones from Sean that I'd stashed there during my two-week purgatory. I handed over my keys and took a numbered receipt. I probably only imagined that they guy looked at me funny when I didn't take luggage out of the trunk.

My phone buzzed as I paused by the door to the terminal. Jen was forwarding an electronic ticket for a United flight leaving in an hour, first class, window seat. Seemed like old times.

I could still turn around. I could get my car back. I could argue that I hadn't really broken the bubble; handing off my car key wasn't much different from picking up a delivery of food or wine or books from the front porch of Sean and Timothy's house.

I could drive back to Arlington. I could figure out what the hell had gone wrong back there, how Katie could have lied to me for months.

How I'd lied to her.

Screw it.

I tapped a quick note of thanks to Jen and pushed through the doorway.

The terminal was quiet, empty of the usual crowds of tourists heading into town, of businessmen leaving on trips. But a trio of redcaps clustered by the door, laughing behind their masks. And a woman rushed past, panting loudly as she dragged school-age twins by the hand. A young couple, maybe college kids, were making out by the plastic-shrouded water fountain, no masks in sight.

As I approached security, I saw that only one lane was open. It was monitored by a weary TSA officer in a bright blue shirt. Twenty or so people waited to X-ray their crap, mostly ignoring the circles that were taped six-feet apart on the floor.

I pulled my driver's license out of my wallet and got in line, trying to keep my breath slow and even as I acclimated to life in the coronavirus world.

61

KATIE

"Katie?" Angel's voice sounded disapproving. Her hair was disheveled, and the belt on her robe was twisted. "Is everything all right?"

I took a deep, fortifying breath. "Come sit down, Angel."

When I tried to lead her to her chair, she resisted. "Did I hear you fighting with Jason?"

"Come on, Angel. Just have a seat."

"Where is he?" She peered toward the kitchen. "Whatever he's cooking smells wonderful."

"Will you just sit down!"

I don't know which of us was more surprised. I'd spat the words as if another creature was working my mouth, manipulating me like a puppet. I was still shaking from the waves of anger that had washed over me while I fought with Jason. My mouth still tasted like rage, a stomach-churning acid I hadn't swallowed since I was seven.

Blinking hard, Angel sat.

"I'm sorry," I said, knowing it wouldn't do any good. Apologies didn't erase anger. Remorse didn't take back rage. Once the fury was released, no amount of regret would dilute its effect.

"What's wrong, Katie?" Angel's voice shook. All of a sudden, she looked very frightened. Very small.

I took a deep breath and decided which disaster to tell first. "Jason left."

"To go downstairs?" She sounded like a child, bargaining.

"No," I said, shoving down my annoyance. "He's left the house. Left us. Left me."

"What did you do to him?"

"I didn't do anything!"

How dare she take his side? How dare she assume this was *my* fault? *I* wasn't the one who'd lied about a dead father.

I'd told my own lie.

Fighting the urge to yell again, I answered more calmly. "He hurt my feelings. Badly. And when I called him on it, he doubled down."

"What could he possibly—"

"Angel, stop." Miracle of miracles, she did. "I have something else to tell you. Something worse."

"Worse than your driving out Jason?"

"Angel!" The rage was there before I could tamp it down. I was frightened by this new me. I didn't like her.

Before I could unload a weapon I'd always regret, I said, "Timothy called."

My tone warned her. She grew very, very still. She only managed a single syllable: "Why?"

"Sean is sick. He has COVID."

I watched Angel absorb the words. She couldn't make more than three-letter words out of Boggle dice, and she might not remember who was president, but she understood the threat of a pandemic.

I rushed to offer the only reassurance I could, the teeniest, tiniest sliver of hope. "He's at Memorial, where they're giving him the very best care."

"We have to go see him." She fought to get to her feet.

"We can't. They aren't allowing visitors."

"Then we should keep Timothy company. He shouldn't be alone right now."

"He's been exposed to the virus. He's self-quarantining at home until he finds out if he gets sick too."

"Well, we have to do *something!*"

"We are. We're keeping ourselves safe and healthy, so we don't add to anyone else's burden."

"But that's not…" She trailed off.

Angel stared at her hands in her lap for so long I wondered if she'd fallen into a trance. "Do you have any questions?" I finally asked, and she shook her head, just the faintest hint of a negative response.

I waited another century, but she didn't speak, didn't move, didn't give any sign of being alive. Finally, I reached over and turned on the television. Detectives Briscoe and Logan were better than painful, terrified silence.

Once Angel's attention was snagged by her old friends, I went into the kitchen. A pot of chili sat on the stove. I lit the burner and stirred before I tasted it. Once it heated through, it would make a good dinner.

I took down bowls. I grated cheese. I took a couple of biscuits out of the freezer and baked them, the way I'd seen Jason do so many nights in the past six weeks.

I'd told my own lie, at least by omission.

He'd lied in fact. He'd said, point-blank, that his father was dead. And when confronted, he'd called me a whore. I didn't want to be the type of woman who forgave that.

Angel and I ate dinner. Lucifer prowled the perimeter of the kitchen like she was harvesting lost souls so I fed her. I rinsed all the dishes, putting them in the dishwasher before I transferred the leftover chili to the fridge.

After, we watched mindless crap on TV. When Angel started to yawn, I helped her get ready for bed. I wondered if she was going to get any sleep that night. I knew I wasn't.

Alone in my bedroom, I found signs of Jason everywhere. He had five books stacked on his nightstand. A T-shirt lay on the floor of the closet where he'd missed the laundry hamper. A trio of oxford-cloth shirts hung from the rod.

I closed the closet door and flounced over to the bed. Pushing the pillows into a nest, I shoved his to the back, so I wouldn't have to smell his shampoo. That didn't work; I'd have to hold my breath to avoid the scent.

Fine. I'd strip the bed. I tugged off his pillowcase and threw it onto the floor. I started to tackle the fitted sheet, but stopped when my fingernail caught on the seam.

Furious, I pummeled the mattress with my fists. I gathered my own pillow and screamed into the down, over and over, ripping loose years of rage.

When I finally stopped, I was exhausted. Too tired to get undressed. Too tired to brush my teeth.

I pulled out my phone and realized I was hoping to find a text from Jason. I hated myself for the flicker of hope as I tapped the screen and hated myself more for feeling deflated when I saw he hadn't written.

I couldn't live like this. I swiped across one of his old messages, ordering myself not to read his coded words, sent while I was working on a *Phoenix* article:

JASON

LF. Meet you in the game room.

LF. Let's fuck. And I'd met him in the game room, and I'd reached for his zipper, and he'd bent me over the pool table, and—

I blocked him on my phone, guaranteeing I wouldn't get any more texts. I deleted the stream we had going, and then I deleted his record in my contacts.

I could use my phone for lots of things that didn't have anything to do with Jason. I opened Instagram and found Brit's latest creation: Meltaway Mint, festooned with chopped up Andes candy. I Liked it, because that's what I always did. And I opened the long string of texts to her, the ones I sent every night, like diary entries spinning into oblivion.

KATIE

Sean's got COVID. Jason left me.

I hit Send, because that's also what I always did. *Delivered* said my phone. Brittany must have been busy, because my phone didn't flash the next confirmation: *Read.*

I wondered what she could be doing. I wondered what a normal life was like. And I stared at the screen for an hour, feeling utterly alone.

62

From *Baseball's Inside Pitch*, Monday, June 2:

Major League Baseball and the Major League Baseball Players Association are entering their fourth week of negotiations regarding a shortened 2020 season. The players' current proposal calls for a 114-game season. Play would start on June 30 and end on October 31, with the postseason scheduled for November.

Under the current proposal, every player will have the right to opt out of play. Those with a high risk of contracting the coronavirus will receive their full salary, while others will be granted reduced pay.

Salary remains a sticking point, with owners demanding greater pay cuts than the ones players accepted in March. In addition, players and owners are not in agreement about the frequency of testing and other health protocols.

Negotiation during the coming week is crucial if the season is to get under way in a timely fashion…

COVID-19 statistics as of June 1, 2020:

Overall number of cases reported: 1.79 million cases

Overall number of deaths reported: 104,383 deaths

Seven-day average of new cases reported in all United States: 20,679 cases

Seven-day average of new deaths reported in all United States: 905 deaths

Seven-day average of new cases reported in California: 2635 cases

Seven-day average of new deaths reported in California: 65 deaths

Seven-day average of new cases reported in Texas: 1273 cases

Seven-day average of new deaths reported in Texas: 22 deaths

Seven-day average of new cases reported in Virginia: 1096 cases

Seven-day average of new deaths reported in Virginia: 26 deaths

Commonwealth of Virginia

Office of the Governor

Executive Order Number Sixty-Three (2020)

I order the following:

All patrons in the Commonwealth aged ten and over shall when entering, exiting, traveling through, and spending time inside the settings listed below cover their mouth and nose with a face covering, as described and recommended by the CDC…

63

JASON

Jen being Jen, a series of texts waited for me when I landed. My car was ready at Wheeler Rent-a-Car. I was booked into a suite at the Fairmont Grand Del Mar. Clothes were waiting in a canvas duffel, along with a selection of my favorite snacks.

And she'd taken the liberty of calling Mary Ann Dixon to tell her I was coming to town. Mary Ann was thrilled, but she made it clear Coach couldn't handle visitors after dinner, even *if* I'd flown all the way across country to see them.

Jen had promised I'd be there at nine the following morning. I'd wear double masks and we'd sit outside, with a fan blowing away from Coach. It wasn't as good as quarantine, but something told me we might not have two weeks to wait.

Jen had worked one more of her typical miracles and tracked down a bottle of Pappy Van Winkle, having it delivered in a gift box to my room. She'd sent along half a dozen books too, choosing from the current fiction bestseller list.

If she'd still been my assistant, I would have doubled her salary. As it was, I made a mental note to send her *something* as a thank you.

In fact, Jen had done her job a little too well. All too soon, I was penned in my room, itching to do *something*, eager to see someone, even though it was nearly midnight.

That was a formula for reviewing the wasteland I'd left behind in Virginia. I'd already spent the six hours of flight time replaying my fight with Katie. Yeah, it had been a dick move, letting her think Dad was dead. But in my defense, I'd had no idea how much she'd invested in my lie.

On the night we met, she'd told me she didn't get mad. I hadn't believed her. Everyone got mad.

But I couldn't remember any fight in my life that had gone incandescent as quickly as ours had. I knew she was scared about her brother, but she'd gone straight for the gonads, and she'd clamped down tight. And I'd pretty much responded in kind.

She'd never met Coach. She didn't know how much good he'd done—for me, sure, but for hundreds of other players who'd passed through Carver over the decades. In fact, he might have made a bigger impact on the guys who *hadn't* gone pro. They'd learned what it meant to work on a team, how to take responsibility when plays went bad, how to share glory when things broke right. We'd all learned how to be men.

Which was why I couldn't get my head around Katie's article. She was saying Coach had cheated, intentionally and repeatedly. She was saying he'd lied—to the university, to his players, to their families, and the world.

Not my Coach. Never.

I should climb into bed and get a good night's sleep so I was ready to face the morning. But I wasn't the least bit sleepy.

I turned on the TV and flipped through the channels,

stopping at random to numb my mind. It took me fifteen minutes to realize I was watching a *Law and Order* rerun. Shit.

I flipped over to one of the news channels. They were showing protests in Minneapolis, people marching in the streets, a grocery store engulfed in flames. Hastily made cardboard signs shouted about four hundred years of injustice. Other marches had formed in other cities, righteous people demanding an end to oppression.

It was too much. Too brutal. Too hopeless.

But it was the reality of life for millions of Americans.

I couldn't join a protest, even if people *were* gathering in downtown San Diego. Mary Ann had agreed to stretch the rules until they were close to shattering. I couldn't endanger her or Coach by meeting up with countless strangers.

So I did what I always did. I took out my wallet and I researched who was helping. Pulling up a handful of websites, I exercised my credit card. Color of Change. Black Movement Law Project. Black Lives Matter Network. Showing up for Racial Justice.

Google found me bookstores owned by people of color. I put in orders for a few dozen books by Black authors, about Black issues. I hesitated when I got to the screen asking where to ship them, but I ultimately put in Mom's address in Killeen. Jen could get them to me down the road.

Knowing I hadn't done enough but feeling trapped by the pandemic, I turned off the TV and roamed to the kitchen, where I picked up the top book from the stack on the counter. Stephen King's *If It Bleeds*. Perfect.

I carried it back to the living room. The couch in this luxury suite was a hell of a lot more comfortable than the monstrosity in Katie's house. So it didn't make sense that I kept shifting position, leaning back against the arm, slouching down with my head on a throw pillow, sitting up and leaning forward with my elbows planted on my knees.

Nothing was right. Nothing made sense. And when I realized I'd read the first three pages of the book three times through and I still wasn't retaining a word, I moved on to Jen's next choice. And the next. And the next. And the next.

Cross-country travel, combined with the time change, should have made it easy for me to sleep. But I'd spent years resetting my body's clock every ten days, more often on a busy road trip. Today's flight had been a breeze.

As I tossed the last book onto the floor, an electric jolt seared my fingertips. The Mind-Fuck. Here. After I'd just flown three thousand miles.

It made no fucking sense.

I took out my phone, desperate enough to anesthetize my brain by blowing away animated pixels in PUBG. As the screen read my face and unlocked, my eyes automatically traveled to my Message icon. I was waiting for a text from Katie. Hoping for one.

Screw it. One of us had to go first.

JASON

WTF happened back there?

I sent it, and the Delivered notice sprang up immediately. Of course she didn't read it. It was four in the morning in Virginia. But an irrational part of me was pissed when she didn't reply.

Closing my eyes, I leaned my head against the back of the couch. I tried to slow my breathing, tried to stop the squirrels from chewing away at my brainstem. But every time my mind drifted, I was back in Virginia, yelling at Katie, listening to her scream at me.

You think you can get anything you want by throwing your money around.

I didn't. I really, truly didn't. But as I lay awake in that suite, aware that the entire hotel was nearly empty around me,

I would have given the rest of my Rockets contract to fix the world.

Annihilate coronavirus.

Cure Coach's cancer.

And figure out how to make things right with Katie.

64

KATIE

My phone rang. Brittany. Calling a few minutes before midnight.

"I thought we weren't talking to each other," I said, by way of greeting.

"I figured I'd give you a call to see if you need anything at the grocery store. I've already got Timothy's list."

"You've got *Timothy's* list?"

"He could have stuff delivered, but I'm a lot better at choosing a ripe avocado than the other online shoppers."

She wasn't making any sense. I said, "Wait. Rewind. How did you get Timothy's number?"

"Sean gave it to me years ago. He wanted me to be able to reach both of them if anything ever happened to you."

"Hold on. I just want to be clear. We're talking about my brother Sean? Sean of the creeping neogophilus feud?"

"Hey," Brit said. "He wanted to know you'd be safe. Some

things are more important than holding on to old arguments. ”

I wasn't sure how to respond to that. Part of me wanted to explain how my brother was perpetuating the infantilization of women by the patriarchy. And part of me wanted to go all squishy inside, as I realized the grace I'd just been shown by my feuding brother and my best friend.

Grace or not, I couldn't let her get away with a tossed-off not-really-an-apology. "That's it?" I asked. "We're just going to wipe out the last two months? And the fact that you apparently called my brother-in-law before you talked to me?"

"I'm not sure what to say. I figured Timothy would be exhausted. *I* would be. So I wanted to catch him before he fell asleep."

"Uh-huh." My brother-in-law was important, but that wasn't the real question I'd wanted Brit to answer.

She must have figured that out, because she filled the awkward silence. "At first, I was really pissed that you wouldn't let me in the house. I didn't think I was doing anything wrong, and you were just trying to make me feel bad. I was legitimately busy with work, so I didn't have time—" She cut herself off before she continued. "I didn't *make* time to answer your texts. And then it felt like too many days had gone by, and I *couldn't* say anything. And then I realized how crappy I'd feel if a friend did what I'd done, so I decided I *shouldn't* say anything."

"But I Liked every one of your Instagram posts!"

"Which just made me feel more like a shitty friend."

"I sent you a text every night for the last two months!"

"What part of 'I was a jerk and I didn't know how to stop being a jerk and I'm really sorry, can you possibly forgive me' don't you understand?"

How could I refuse to accept an apology like that?

I didn't want her to feel worse. So I skipped over the part where I told her how much I'd missed her for the past two months, and how many times I'd started to pick up my phone to call her, and how happy I was that she'd finally reached out, and how I couldn't wait until we could see each other and hug each other and get back to how things had been before.

Instead, I said, "If you're really going to the store, I could use some soy sauce. And some rice vinegar. The unseasoned kind."

She laughed. "Yeah, right."

"I'm serious! I'm making a stir fry. We've got a lot of vegetables in the fridge."

"*You're* making a stir fry?"

"I watched Jason cook them often enough."

"Jason," she said, opening the door to whatever I wanted to say.

A raw hole gaped in the middle of my chest. "Yeah." But I was too tired to add anything else. Too tired to fill her in on how amazing the past eight weeks had been. How utterly, spectacularly craptastic our fight had been. How we'd both blown up anything and everything we'd ever had together. "I'll fill you in tomorrow."

"Okay," she said. Her voice was skeptical, but she honored my unspoken request. "So. Soy sauce."

"And rice vinegar."

"If you say so. That's it?"

"Hey," I said, because I wasn't ready to hang up yet. "I really *did* like your posts on Instagram. I could probably eat a dozen donuts right now."

"I'll bring some over with your groceries."

"That would be great. Angel's developed quite a sweet tooth."

She made a knowing sound. Angel had always liked desserts. Then she said, "Katie? The *Feel-Good Phoenix* is amazing."

"You've read it?" I was surprised by how pleased I felt.

"Every morning. These days, I need a bit of good news just to get out of bed."

"But you never—"

"You know what you should do?" she asked, cutting me off before I could once again challenge her former radio silence. "You should add a Like button."

"I don't want to police a bunch of comments—"

"Not comments. Just a simple Like. Don't even give people the chance to Not-like something. Build a community. Let people in."

It was a great idea. I was pretty sure Timothy could put it together in five minutes flat. Not that I'd bother him right now. He had enough on his mind. And he was probably asleep.

Instead, I said, "Brit? I've really missed you."

"Yeah," she said. "I've missed you too." Before either of us could get sappy, she said, "I'm heading out to the grocery store first thing tomorrow. Text me if you think of anything else you need. I promise I'll answer."

After hanging up, I resisted the urge to send her a message, just to get her reply. I trusted her. Despite everything, she'd never stopped being my person.

65

JASON

I tried not to stare as Coach fiddled with the cannula that was feeding oxygen to his nose. Mary Ann settled her palm on his forearm. "Leave it, Stan."

He dropped his hand back to his lap, but I couldn't tell if he was giving in to her, or if he was just too exhausted to continue adjusting the tube. No wonder Mary Ann had said he couldn't see me when I got in last night. He was a lot sicker than I'd ever imagined. It seemed like a miracle he was out of bed now.

The man I'd known as a tower of strength—the coach who'd kept twenty-five college students utterly rapt for a five-month season with his barked commands, the tireless bulldog who had paced dugouts for three hours without pausing for a sip of water—was reduced to a bundle of bones. He was cradled by pillows, beneath his sagging sweatpants, beside his heaving chest, behind his slumping back and his trembling head. A woven blanket had slipped down to his feet.

But he'd smiled when Mary Ann led me out to the patio. He'd opened the bourbon with a gleeful laugh. "Nurse Ratched will *have* to let me sample this!"

Mary Ann had sighed and said, "You'll do more than sample. But not at nine in the morning."

"Breakfast of champions," Coach got out before he had to fight for breath. "And Jason's my number one champ."

Fuck. I wiped my eyes with the edge of my hand, hoping they'd think the fan was blowing dust my way. My breath was coming faster beneath the pair of filtered masks I'd bought in the hotel lobby that morning, and I was grateful I didn't have to fake a smile.

Mary Ann said to me, her voice pointed, "He won't get his next meds for an hour or so. After that, he'll be out like a light."

Coach frowned, but he didn't waste the breath to grunt his exasperation.

An hour. To tell him about Katie's article. To give him time to clear his name. To say all the things I should have said a decade earlier.

I had three outs to get through in the bottom of the ninth. Time to bear down and get the job done.

"Coach," I said. "A friend of mine… This woman… A journalist I know is writing an article. It's about Carver. About the Contemporary Studies program. It's full of lies, but I want you to know I'll do everything I can to set things straight."

Somehow, he sank even deeper into the pillows. His body collapsed in on itself, as if someone had opened a hidden air valve. "No," he said, but he had to stop to cough. Mary Ann leaned forward with a glass of water, but he waved her off, scowling as he fought for breath.

"No," he finally repeated. "It's not lies."

"But she says the university is letting athletes cheat. She thinks there are special courses… Special tutors… She says players plagiarized papers, their senior theses!"

Coach gripped the arms of his chair and pulled himself to a more upright position. "It didn't start that way." Pause. Breath. Breath. "But that's what it became."

I knew my masks couldn't hide my dismay. I wanted to shout. I wanted to stand up and pace. I wanted to tell him he had to be wrong, because I'd torn up Katie's notecards.

But I gave him the only gift I could. I sat and listened.

He told me how things had started, with university-appointed tutors for the kids who needed extra help. Those specialists had recommended forming additional sections for the most challenging required courses, smaller classes where the TAs could have more control over their students' work. That led to the creation of new courses, classes with micro-focus, with—he didn't use the word—spoon-fed material. It was only natural to bring all those courses under one umbrella, a unified program. And over the years, the program became an official department.

Baseball wasn't the only sport to take advantage of Contemporary Studies. Football did too. So did basketball. The coaches and the athletic director knew exactly what was going on.

"I knew." The pauses were longer now, each phrase carved into its own space. "But it was better." Pause. "For kids to get." Pause. "A degree." Pause. "To help them." Pause. "Down the road."

He slumped even deeper into his chair. Mary Ann fluttered over him, plumping his pillows, adjusting the cannula, offering water, which he refused again. He asked her to go inside the house, to get his meds. She gave me a worried frown, but she left.

I'd gone to Carver because it was everything I wanted. A powerhouse university. A nationally ranked baseball program.

There were nights I didn't sleep because I stayed at practice till eight, grabbed something that resembled dinner, and then got started on a ten-page paper. I worked with my advisor in the philosophy department, choosing courses to complement the baseball schedule, doubling up on departmental requirements in the fall, when I knew I'd have more time. I dropped friends who weren't on the team because there weren't enough hours in the day. My only serious college girlfriend broke up with me when she got tired of always coming in last.

But all of that was a lie. I didn't need to bust my ass. I could've coasted like the others. I still would have ended up with a Carver diploma. I'd still be able to tell anyone who asked that I was a proud alum of the emerald and gold.

"I'm sorry," Coach said, and his voice was marginally stronger for having taken a few minutes' break. "I never meant… It wasn't supposed… We thought we were doing the best thing… For everyone."

"But your legacy—" I cut off the words once I realized what they admitted.

"It is…what it is… I was a good coach… And I made some mistakes…"

"You were the best coach," I said, my throat clutching around the words. "I've never thanked you enough for everything you taught me. Yesterday, I told s—someone you were more a father to me than my own dad."

There. That's why I'd flown cross-country. That's what I'd come to say. And if I stammered a little over *someone* I could say that was because I was exhausted, worn out from the flight and the sleepless night and the revelations Coach had made.

He extended a claw-like hand, trying to reach my fingers. To hell with COVID. It wouldn't have time to hurt Coach. I let him catch my hand, and when he squeezed, I barely felt the pressure. "You're a good boy… A good man… Make things right with your father."

He emphasized his command with another butterfly-squeeze of my hand. I nodded while I tried to swallow the baseball lodged in my throat.

"Do it," he said. "Captain's pledge."

Coach had always required more of his team captains than he had of other players. We promised to be first on the field at every practice and last to leave. We swore we'd help every teammate, whether that meant more hours at BP or fielding drills or running. We vowed to honor all the people who made the game possible but never saw the field—the managers, the statistics guys, the video coordinator, and everyone who sold tickets to our games.

His eyes glowed like embers, and this time when his fingers closed around mine, I felt it. "Captain's pledge," he said again.

"Captain's pledge," I agreed, resigned.

Mary Ann came out with his medicine. If she noticed his hand on mine, she didn't say a word. Instead, she placed a needleless syringe in his mouth and urged him to swallow. His body unwound within a minute, as if someone had pulled out the pins that had kept his joints together. His hand dropped back to his lap. His lips worked as Mary Ann wiped a bit of drool from the corner of his mouth.

Just when I thought he was asleep, he opened his eyes. He swiveled his head, and it took him a moment to find me. His pupils looked like opaque coins covering his eyes.

"Thank…you…"

I dashed my cheeks angrily. "Don't thank me," I said. "I shouldn't have come here. I shouldn't have bothered you. I shouldn't have said what I said."

I think he shook his head. I think he smiled. And then Mary Ann said, "He'll sleep for a few hours now. You can sit with him if you'd like."

I nodded. After Mary Ann went back inside, I shook out his blanket and spread it across his knees. I smoothed the collar of his pajamas, pressing out a wrinkle. I rested a hand on his shoulder.

And I started figuring out how soon I could get to Texas.

66

KATIE

I'd written enough features to know when I had a story worth telling. I'd edited my own work and the work of others. I'd wrestled with crappy articles, trying to make them mean something, pushing them to be better than they were.

My Carver article was good. I wouldn't say it wrote itself, because nothing ever does. But I saw its structure before I typed the first word. I knew how to use one of the fraudulent theses as a window into the entire sham. I understood intuitively where to include snippets from the course catalog and from Carver's own Honor Code.

Over the weeks, I'd gathered comments from current and former players. I'd tracked down a couple of tutors. I'd interviewed Dr. Halliday, and she'd pointed me toward a few other professors who agreed to speak on background.

No one in administration was willing to go on the record. I didn't have a coach. But my work was solid, and no one had offered up a hint of credible counter-argument.

On Monday, I made a list of my top ten markets. I'd met some of the editors at writers' conferences, so I sent them personalized query letters. I included my credentials, along with links to my strongest *Press Box* articles. I settled down to wait, knowing it could take weeks for a legitimate publication to make a decision.

And now that I was done, I couldn't put off the last project screaming for my attention. So far, I'd justified doing nothing because Angel needed me, and I had to be available in case Timothy called. But Angel was nearly self-sufficient, at least until it came to cutting meat or working buttons on a shirt. And Timothy was texting on the hour, giving constant updates that there were no updates. Sean was still on a ventilator, still in the ICU, still holding his own in a medically induced coma.

So I was officially out of excuses.

I headed downstairs and packed up Jason's things. I wasn't sure where he'd gone. Back to Florida maybe, although the stadiums were still shut down, with spring training on hiatus. Maybe he went to Raleigh, to wait out the siege in his primary home.

It wasn't like he needed the stuff he'd left behind—casual clothes, some toiletries, a broken-in baseball glove and a bucket of balls. But I couldn't leave them scattered around my room. I folded the clothes neatly and packed them into his two suitcases. I added his Dopp kit. And then I lugged both bags upstairs because I didn't want to see them ever again. I dumped them in Sean's home office, hiding them in the knee hole of his desk.

All day long, I found other things that belonged to Jason. He'd left a couple of books on the coffee table in the living room. A notepad from the Monaco was on the kitchen counter, with the beginnings of a shopping list. His running shoes were in the mud room, where he'd shed them by the back door.

I added everything I found to the shrine—I meant *stash*—

in Sean's office. After lunch, I brought up a nearly empty box of condoms and a belt I'd found beneath the bed.

As I stared at the pitiful pile—two months of a lifetime reduced to a few cubic feet—I told myself we would have ended up here even if we hadn't fought. He was a baseball player. He spent half his life on the road. He'd told me that the first night we met, warning me off of growing dependent.

With the league shut down for COVID, I'd spun out a fantasy life, one where Jason would always be by my side, in my kitchen, in my bed. But Jason Price was never going to stick around. He couldn't. That wasn't who he was.

67

JASON

I could have flown from San Diego to Killeen. The flight from California to Texas certainly wasn't any riskier than my cross-country trip had been. But I wasn't in any hurry to honor my captain's pledge. After the fight with Katie and the wrenching visit with Coach, a long, boring drive seemed like the perfect way to hit reset.

I called Wheeler and modified the reservation Jen had made for me. The drop-off fee to leave the car in Texas was exorbitant, but less than airfare would have been. Like I cared.

My phone told me I could make the trip in twenty hours—a day and a half of hard driving with enough sleep in between to keep from nodding off at the wheel. But I wasn't in any rush.

I put in five hours on Sunday and called it quits, pulling into a Courtyard by Marriott somewhere in the middle of Arizona. The June sun was bright enough to give me a headache, even through my sunglasses. The hotel's pool was drained, with a sign on the fence announcing it was closed, *cerrado*, because of COVID.

I'd tried texting Katie every few hours, but she didn't write back. I placed a couple of calls too, but they went straight to voicemail. I couldn't be one hundred percent certain, but I was pretty sure she'd blocked me.

So I holed up in the A/C, pretending I could concentrate on books. Mostly, though, I watched Black Lives Matter protests on TV. I walked across the street to a Wendy's for dinner and remembered that all fast-food salads were crap. Back in my room, the bed was too large and the shower was too small, and I spent hours staring at shadows moving on the ceiling before I finally fell asleep around three.

Monday morning, we had our weekly team meeting on Zoom. Halfway through Ormond telling us we were down to a 114-game season and the owners were still not budging on salary, I realized the bookstore contest had ended the day before.

When the official meeting wrapped up I roused enough to say, "Okay, slackers. Cards on the table. Let's hear about bookstore sales."

I wasn't expecting much. Since I'd hit the road, I'd totally forgotten to check in with One More Page. If Jen were running things, I'd be a hell of a lot better organized.

Ormond chimed in first. "Nine thousand four twenty-five, but half of that's in auction pledges. The total might go down."

Cantor said, "We never got the bookstore thing going, but we set up a competition for nine local restaurants, sort of 'order a baseball player's favorite meal' thing. We're up to seven thousand, give or take, but two places haven't reported last weekend's sales."

One by one, the other guys reported in. Some had stuck to

the script with book lists and signed gear. Others had come up with more creative approaches, teaming bookstores and restaurants, bookstores and liquor stores, bookstores and cinemas that were on the verge of going belly up.

Cruz slapped the table in front of him like he was back at one of the Coral Crest bars, lying through his teeth about women throwing themselves at his feet. "Sixteen thousand and change. Read it and weep, Professor. Get it? *Read it?*"

"Bullshit," called DJ Thomas.

"No, no, sixteen big ones."

"How the fuck did you do that?" I couldn't keep suspicion from my voice.

"I reached out to *compadres* on the Flash." Phoenix's major league soccer team.

"You've never set foot in a bookstore," Tyler Brock reminded the catcher.

"But I've gone to plenty of bars! We let them name drinks after all our players. Customers voted by ordering their favorites for takeout, and the profits were split with bookstores. Turns out, a lot of lonely women wanted a taste of Cruz's Love Juice." He tapped the side of his head. "You gotta think like a person trapped in a pandemic!"

Cantor protested. "Raleigh doesn't even allow takeout liquor sales!"

"You shouldn't live in a shithole, my friend," Cruz countered.

"Okay, okay," I said after some good-natured grousing died down. Most of the guys were just impressed by Cruz's ingenuity. "I'm sending five thousand bucks to a food bank in Phoenix. If you've got a favorite, Cruz, let me know. And thanks, guys. It helps to know that something good's coming out of all this crap."

And that was actually true. There *was* a silver lining to the virus, to the forty-eight games we'd already missed and the possibility of tanking the entire season if the owners didn't get their heads out of their collective asses.

I started scrawling notes on the back of a napkin I'd carried back from Wendy's, laying out details like I was scoring a game. My lawyer could handle a quick incorporation. We needed a snappy name or an acronym. I could hire a publicist, but there was a grassroots appeal to fellow athletes promoting their own efforts to support small business. Expanding our project would give the guys something to do if we lost the whole season.

We weren't like Katie. She'd worked like a dog and built her own newspaper. But there was no way out-of-work ballplayers could build our own league, no matter how much time, effort, and money we were willing to invest.

But reaching out to more small businesses? We could make a real difference there. And that felt good. No. It felt *great.*

When I signed off the call with my lawyer, I threw my crap in my duffel and got back on the road. Another five hours of driving felt like enough. I found a Holiday Inn Express with a McDonalds across the street, and I added large fries to my Big Mac.

Two more stages, and I made it to Killeen on Wednesday afternoon. I knew the way to Mom and Dad's house, but the thought of sleeping in anyone's guest room—especially theirs—during these COVID times sent the Mind-Fuck into overdrive.

Stupid, broken brain. I was on the road. It should know not to screw me over.

I checked into a Hampton Inn and called Wheeler to tell them I was keeping the car another week. "Make it two," I said, and then I agreed to balance the budget of a medium-size European principality, for the privilege.

I called Jen to tell her where I was staying. She said without hesitation, "You can quarantine at my place. I'll stay with Mom and Dad."

"I'm good," I said. "But thanks."

"Suit yourself. But I'd be failing in my sisterly role if I didn't ask when you're going to see them. We can all wear masks and meet on the porch."

"Point noted."

"Do you need anything?"

"I'm good," I said again.

On Thursday morning, she called from downstairs. "Parking lot. Now."

I knew I'd end up losing, so I cut my losses and said, "Give me a minute to get dressed."

I pulled on jeans and met her beside her Outback. She'd spread out a feast on the hood—a breakfast burrito and a gallon of coffee, displayed beside a bright green plant.

She tossed me a miniature bottle of Tabasco sauce as I approached. "You might be hiding out from everyone else, but I couldn't condemn my baby brother to another restaurant meal."

"You're a goddess," I said, doctoring the burrito. "What's with the plant?"

"It's your rehab program."

Out of habit, I flexed my left arm, making the crescent-shaped scar curl above my elbow. "What am I rehabbing?"

"Your life."

"That must be some plant. You're sure it's legal in the Lone Star State?"

She harrumphed and pointed me toward napkins just in time to save half my burrito from tumbling onto the asphalt. "It's a philodendron."

"If you say so."

"Here's the deal. I'm leaving this plant with you. It doesn't need any food. It doesn't need any sun. You can put it on a desk and forget about it completely."

"Except…" I could tell from her tone there was a catch.

"Except it needs water. Half a cup, once a week."

"A cup like a measuring cup? Or a cup like," I saluted with the strong coffee I was about to drink, "A coffee cup."

"Doesn't matter. Old Phil is a forgiving plant. Just water him once a week, and you'll see new leaves grow. Like this one. Here." She pointed to a light green bud near one of the heart-shaped leaves.

"Then what happens?"

"If you keep the plant alive for a month, you get goldfish."

"Goldfish? Like the crackers?"

"No, idiot. Not like the crackers. Like fish. Alive. In a bowl. Two of them, so they don't get lonely."

"And I give them water once a week."

"You change their water, once a month. But you feed them every day."

"And why am I going to do that?"

"Because if you keep the fish alive for three months, you get a puppy."

"A puppy!"

"Any breed. Or a mutt. You get to choose."

"I'm on the road two weeks out of every four. What the fuck am I going to do with a puppy?"

"Train it to come with you. Call it an emotional support dog."

"But since I don't actually need an emotional support dog, why am I getting a puppy?"

"To discover the joy of unconditional love."

"I'm going to love the puppy unconditionally?"

"Don't be an ass," she said, with all the love a sister could ever show. "The puppy's going to love *you* unconditionally."

"But I won't have to worry about the fish anymore? Or the plant?"

"You sound like a wimp. You'll be in charge of the plant *and* the fish *and* the puppy."

"That's it? That's my rehab program?"

She shook her head. "That's only the first phase. You keep

the plant for a month, the fish for three months, the puppy for a full year, and then you go out on a date."

"Who's the lucky woman?"

"I don't know yet. But you'll date her for three months before you take her to bed."

"Let me get this straight. Your rehab plan means I'm not getting any for fifteen months?"

"Maybe longer. If, you know. You don't find the puppy right on schedule. Or the woman."

"Your plan sucks."

"You're only saying that because you haven't tried it."

"No one in his right mind would try it! Who put you in charge of rehabbing my life, anyway?"

"You did," she said. "The second you decided to come back to Killeen."

"Maybe I'm just passing through. Killeen is on the way from San Diego to Raleigh."

"*Are* you just passing through?"

She asked the question casually, like it didn't matter what answer I gave. But I could see the twin lines deepen between her eyebrows. I knew she was frowning behind her mask.

I wadded up my napkin and shot for the trashcan at the edge of the lot. Two points. Nothing but net.

I gulped half the coffee and the caffeine seared my nerve endings.

I looked at the bright green plant and wondered if it would be kinder to throw it out now. I could leave it in the lobby. Maybe some merciful traveler would take pity on it and give it a good home.

Jen was still waiting.

"I don't know," I finally said. "I promised Coach I'd see Dad." But that wasn't true. Not exactly. "I told him I'd make things right."

Jen spoke before I could take back my words. "Come over to the house with me right now. You can catch up with

Mom. Be there when Dad gets home from the factory tonight."

I shook my head. "I'm not ready."

"When *will* you be ready?"

"I don't know, Jen." I let a little of my temper leak into my tone. "I'm here, okay? And I won't leave until I've seen him. Isn't that good enough for you? Can we stop talking about Dad?"

"Of course," she said, with a deceptive ease. "So, what happened in Virginia? Why'd you walk out on Katie?"

"I didn't—"

But I did. That wasn't the whole story, of course. I'd had good reasons to leave. Reasons that I'd carefully justified, on the plane across country, on my four-day drive to Texas, and every single time she ignored one of my texts or calls.

"Can we talk about something else?" I asked. "Something easy. Sex. Or politics. Or religion."

"I thought that's what we were doing. How was sex with Katie?"

"Je-en!" I drew her name out to two syllables, using my not-going-to-take-any-more-shit-even-if-you-*are*-my-sister tone.

"Fine," she said. "But it's over? You're not going back?"

I didn't see any way I could. "I'm not going back," I said. And then, because I needed to get the hell out of this conversation, I said, "Not for fifteen months, at least. Now can you get the hell back into your car so I can go back to my room and water this plant?"

She laughed, but then she asked about my visit with Coach. And she told me how Jackie was going nuts, keeping the kids busy on summer vacation, with no camp to break up the time at home. I asked about Janine, and she filled me in on that sister too. And somehow, without my actually agreeing, she got into her car and I got into mine, and we drove over to our parents' house so I could catch up with my mother, masked and six feet apart in the shade on the front porch.

I left before dinner. But Jen waved as she followed me back to my car, keeping an approximation of appropriate distance between us. "See you tomorrow," she said.

And I gave in, exactly like she knew I would. "Yeah, yeah," I said. "But only if you bribe me with another burrito."

68

KATIE

"Good morning, Angel," I said, watching closely as my grandmother came into the kitchen. Her cast had finally come off a week ago, but she still held her right arm stiffly. We'd attended a couple of online physical therapy appointments, but I hadn't been able to cajole her into doing exercises on her own.

In fact, I considered it a victory when she sat at the table without my prompting. She even put her napkin on her lap.

I turned to the tray of scones I'd taken out of the oven half an hour earlier. Sometime in the last few weeks, I'd come to the realization that recipes worked a lot better if you actually followed them.

Who was I kidding? I'd watched Jason cook, and I'd learned something. Most of the time, he'd gone with his instincts, but for baking, he always measured everything precisely. Miracle of miracles, when *I* scooped out the right amount of flour and sugar and waited for the oven to preheat before I shoved in a baking tray, the results were astronomically better than my earlier attempts.

Piling the scones on a plate, I said to Angel, "Help yourself to fruit salad." I'd made a special effort this morning, adding pineapple to strawberries, apricots, and the first peaches of the season.

Jason had taught me that, too. Choose the right size bowl. Select the proper knife for the job. Take time to line up the fruit. Curl the fingers of my left hand into a claw to make a guide for the blade with my knuckles.

Fuck. This entire breakfast was a stroll down memory lane. And I was doing great, *perfect*, except for the fact that I wasn't. I was pretty sure I'd never get used to how thoughts of Jason ignited strings of tiny fire up and down my spine. At least I was getting better at stamping out the flames with a quick trio of thoughts:

Jason would have left me anyway, as soon as the baseball season got back on track.

I would never let Jason kill my career, the way Aaron had tried to do.

Even if I wanted *to reach out to Jason now, it made more sense to wait until my article was published, until I could measure the backlash throughout the sports world.*

Jason. Jason. Jason. Would-have-left-kill-career-wait-wait-wait.

Sure enough, I didn't feel like shooting lasers out of my eyes anymore. And my chest no longer ached with the weight of held-back tears. I'd actually slept through the night twice in the past week, not waking from a single dream about him.

As I put the scones on the table, Angel became a little more focused. She scanned the table, her gaze skipping over the apricot jam and the apple-fig preserves. "No boysenberry?" she asked.

"You finished that yesterday."

She pouted as she sank back in her chair. "We always had boysenberry when Jason was here."

I was pretty sure that was a lie. But I couldn't remember for sure. I skipped through my litany anyway. Would-have-left-kill-career-wait-wait-wait.

I kept my voice even as I said, "We're only getting groceries every two weeks. Brit's too busy to come more often."

Angel sulked and poked at her scone with a knife.

"Sometimes we just have to be happy with what we've got," I snapped, angry that we'd somehow completed a switch. I was now the parent and my grandmother had become the child.

But even as I swallowed the rest of my fury, I didn't collapse into gibbering panic that my grandmother would leave me. I didn't stumble over myself, trying to take back my words. Three weeks of practice, and I was finally getting better at this anger stuff.

Plus, I realized I could solve this particular problem.

"Just a sec," I said, pushing my chair back from the table.

Downstairs, in my bedroom, I switched on the overhead light. I opened my nightstand drawer, but I didn't find what I was looking for. That was ridiculous, though. I was the only person who'd been down here since Jason left.

I shoved my hand all the way to the back of the drawer, and I found it—the tiny pot of marionberry preserves he'd given me after our night at the Hotel Monaco.

I stared at the gold lid and waited for the emotions to flood me. Sorrow that he'd lied to me. Hurt from the barbs he'd cast before he left. Anger—my dangerous new friend anger—that he'd let everything we had fall apart. But I was saved by would-have-left-kill-career-wait-wait-wait.

Why had I saved the jam? What was I going to do with it? What possible good could it do in my nightstand drawer?

I twisted off the lid as I walked upstairs, and I set it beside Angel's plate. She broke off her humming—*Seventy-six Trombones* from *The Music Man*— to say with surprise, "Thank you."

We ate our breakfast without further drama. I wasn't above deliberately putting things just out of Angel's reach so she'd have to stretch with her weak arm to get them. She didn't seem to catch on. We made small talk about articles in the newspaper, and I told her about the new *Phoenix* posts that had gone live that morning.

I'd debated, long and hard, about that morning's stories. But I finally realized the only reason not to write them was because of Jason. So I'd gritted my teeth—would-have-left-kill-career-wait-wait-wait—and posted half a dozen stories, each one covering the great work being done by ARC—Athletes Ruling COVID.

I included a paragraph in each article, explaining that ARC had been started by Jason's challenge to his Rockets teammates, that the brand-new non-profit was an extension of the thousands of dollars those baseball players had raised for local bookstores, restaurants, and other businesses.

Angel was amused, anyway. And she remembered not to ask when Jason would be coming home.

After breakfast, she took her usual place in front of the TV. I straightened the kitchen, and then I went to check on her. I could hear Lucifer scrambling across the floor before I entered the room. The demon cat was batting around the knitting needle from the scarf I'd been working on the night before.

"*För fan i helvete!*" I swore.

I'd given up on bears and wolves and snow-covered houses. Reading Swedish mysteries about brutal killers didn't seem nearly as attractive as it had at the beginning of COVID lockdown. But I'd learned a new Swedish curse word every day for the past two weeks. My accent was damn good, if I said so myself. *Förbannat bra.*

Another thing I'd given up on—my semi-circular, top-down, slipped-stitch lace shawl with a ruffled border. I was halfway through a simple garter-stitch scarf, and I hadn't made an error in rows. Well, no error I couldn't correct with a hastily applied crochet hook and a dose of Swedish swearing. Retrieving my needle from Lucifer, I vowed to get the scarf back on track.

The phone rang, though, before I could make an attempt. One glance confirmed it was the call I'd been waiting for: Timothy. Mentally crossing my fingers, I answered on speaker. "Hey there. Angel and I are both here."

My brother-in-law had tested positive for the virus two days after Sean went into the hospital, but he'd remained asymptomatic for weeks. Now, I realized I was holding my breath as I waited for him to speak. Glancing at Angel, I saw that she was staring at the phone with greater concentration than I'd seen her muster in weeks.

"He's coming home," Timothy said. Every muscle in my body turned to water. I started to laugh, matching the joy in Timothy's voice as he said, "I can pick him up this afternoon. He's got a lot of work ahead of him—OT and PT and he'll be on a bunch of different drugs, but he's coming home."

The three of us talked over each other, saying how wonderful it was, and how grateful we were, and how hard it would be for Sean. Timothy finally said, "I have to call Brit. We'll need more groceries, if two of us are going to be here."

When I hung up, I realized Angel was crying. I said, "You understood what Timothy told us, right? Sean's okay. They're releasing him from the hospital today."

She nodded. "I was just so worried…"

"We all were."

"I kept picturing him in that hospital bed. With all those machines. All those alarms."

"He was being taken care of by the best doctors in the city."

"That's what they said about your father," she said. "Michael had the best doctors, too."

I'd lived with Angel for twenty-two years. She'd fed me.

She'd clothed me. She'd paid my college tuition. But not once in all that time had she said my father's name out loud.

I was standing on the edge of a canyon. I was alone, utterly alone, because I didn't know anyone else who'd lost their father the way I had. No one understood the way I felt.

Would-have-left-kill-career-wait-wait-wait.

"Angel," I said, my voice nearly breaking. "Will you tell me about my dad?"

It took a moment. I thought she might have forgotten him, like she'd lost so many stories. But then she smiled as wide as a child on Christmas morning. "Your father loved the two of you so much." And once she started talking, the memories flowed like water.

69

JASON

The morning of June 22, three things happened.

One: Major League Baseball announced that a decision had been reached between the owners and the players' union. There'd be a sixty-game regular season, starting on July 1. It was a shitty compromise, but better than nothing. The moment I heard about it, I pictured the asterisks in the record books, and I wondered why we'd spent the past four months waiting if this was all we got.

Two: Katie's article about Carver was published by *Davis Monthly*. I found the piece when I got my usual subscriber notice of new content. By mid-morning, I'd received a dozen requests to comment on Katie's piece, but I didn't respond to any of them.

Three: Coach died.

Mary Ann called just as I finished reading Katie's article. We had a totally fucked-up conversation, because I thought she was calling about Carver being dragged through the mud, so I apologized before she got a chance to tell me Coach had passed. Then I realized she was crying, and I knew the truth.

He'd been sleeping for most of the past week and hospice had been a god-send and her sister was coming to stay with her, so really, it all was as easy as these things ever were. He'd wanted to be cremated. Hospice was helping coordinate that. There'd be a memorial sometime in the future, when it was safe for people to get together.

I couldn't think of anything to say, but I told her how much I missed him already. I let her know that a lot of people would be trying to reach her because of the *Davis* article, and I suggested she get someone to monitor her phone and email. The idea overwhelmed her, so I told her I'd find someone for her.

I called Carver's Office of Public Affairs, but I got shunted to voice-mail. I advised them to get someone assigned to Mary Ann immediately, that the twin blows of Coach's death and Katie's article were something they needed to manage without delay. I left a similar message for the university's athletic director, and another for Carver's president.

I knew Coach wouldn't want flowers. I could always donate to a cancer charity, but I figured a lot of people would do that. Instead, I pulled up a website and made a substantial gift to the Boys and Girls Club of Greater San Diego. It wasn't enough. But I didn't know what else to do.

Except I did.

I knew exactly what I had to do.

My face mask lay on the counter next to the TV, right beside the plant Jen had given me. I grabbed the mask quickly enough that a few brown leaves drifted to the floor. Fuck it. I'd been telling myself to water the damn thing every day for almost three weeks.

So much for Jen's rehab plan.

My keys felt heavy in my hand as I stalked out to the rental car. After almost a month of renegotiating with Wheeler, I could have used what I'd paid them to make a hefty down payment on my very own four-door mid-size sedan.

At least I'd used the car every day. I'd driven over to my parents' house mid-morning, when I knew Dad was busy at the factory. Baking on the front porch in the Texas heat, I'd spent hours talking with my mother, visiting my sisters, and playing catch with my nieces and nephews. I'd helped out with yard work and done a number of grocery-store runs. I'd taken countless calls from my lawyer, my teammates, and other athletes, guys who were willing to work on the small business support plan I'd sketched on the back of a napkin.

It sort of felt like my time in limbo with Katie. Except there wasn't any Katie on the far side of the glass. And my family could afford to be a lot more relaxed, COVID-wise, than Katie and Angel. No one was high risk. Masks and social distancing and fresh air let us spend more time together, in much closer proximity.

Today, though, I turned right when I pulled out of the hotel parking lot, instead of left. Today I drove to PriceGuard.

The parking lot was almost empty when I got there. A gray Silverado filled the spot marked President, right next to the empty one for Employee of the Month. Punishing sunshine beat the asphalt as I crossed to the factory door.

A sign announced that special precautions were in place, and I was invited to use the wall-mounted phone to call inside. I gave my name to the efficient woman who answered, and she said someone would be out in a moment. As I waited, a trickle of sweat wormed its way from the nape of my neck down my spine.

A moment turned into a minute, which stretched into five. I thought about going back to my car and getting the hell out of Dodge, but I couldn't quite manage to turn away.

Captain's pledge.

Finally, the door flew open like someone had shot it, and I backed off a step before I realized I'd moved. I was ready to explain what I was doing there. I expected to have someone aim a thermometer at my head, pulling the trigger to prove I wasn't a threat.

I didn't expect my father to walk out the door.

His jeans looked like they'd been through a battle. He wore a navy blue T-shirt with the PriceGuard logo over his heart. His steel-toed work boots could have been the same ones he'd worn during our last knock-down, drag-out, the one after he'd plastered the Rockets' name all over his parade float.

I had three or four inches on him, but he was wiry in a way that never let me forget the quick speed of his fists. The creases by his eyes were deeper, and his brush-cut hair had a lot more gray. He wore a plain black mask so I couldn't see his mouth. He didn't smell like booze.

The door clanged shut behind him. "Son," he said, squinting at the sun or at me or at the near-deserted parking lot.

"Sir," I answered automatically, hating myself a little for giving him the courtesy.

"Your mama said you've been hangin' around. Said you mowed the lawn last week."

"Yes, sir."

"I'd expect a son of mine to've learned to keep a straight line somewhere along the way."

I stiffened, but I didn't give him the satisfaction of fighting back. I'd mowed lawns for him once a week from the time I could yank the starter until I'd left for Carver. I'd never done it well enough to keep him from going back and fixing my mistakes. After a pause that made my clenched jaw ache, I said, "Jen says you retooled the factory? You're making PPE?"

He nodded like a sheriff sizing up a cattle rustler. "Had to do somethin'. No one's buyin' hockey masks. Baseball equipment either. Hospitals need visors."

"Great," I said. And then, before I could remember my

promise to Coach, I added, "You don't need my endorsement then."

His eyes were the same light blue as mine, bleached almost to silver by the brutal sun. "Not unless you picked up a medical degree in your spare time."

Coming from someone else, the line could have been funny. But my stomach tightened because I knew he was doing what he'd always done, putting his cards on the table. If I actually *had* gone to med school, he would've slapped my name on his new protective gear in one minute flat.

I was wasting my time here. I didn't have anything to say to him, and he had nothing left for me. I'd done my best. Given it—ironically—the old college try. Coach would have forgiven me, I was sure.

My father said, "Sorry to hear about Stan Dixon. He was a good man."

"How did you—"

"Your mama called. Said PriceGuard should send flowers. I had to call three different places before I found one to make 'em look like a baseball. A circle of white carnations, with red ones for the seams."

"Thanks," I said, trying to hide my surprise. "Mary Ann will be touched." She'd hate it. But there was no reason to tell Dad that.

"Shit luck he passed the same day that article ran."

I grimaced. "Jen should keep her big mouth shut."

"Your sister didn't say anything."

"Then how'd you know about the article?"

"I own and operate the third largest employer in Killeen. You think I can't set up a Google alert for my own son's name?"

I *didn't* think he could do that. And I definitely never thought he *would.* "My mistake," I said.

"It's true? All that crap about Carver?"

I nodded, because lying wasn't going to make things

better. "Pretty much. Plenty of guys did stuff the right way. But they set up the system to help the rest."

"I expect you're pretty pissed."

"She wrote what she had to write."

"She? Your girl?" Before I could correct him, he shook his head. "I meant you should be pissed at Carver. Your degree means less 'cause they let those guys cheat."

"We'll see," I said, because I was a lot more worried about what the scandal would mean to Coach's reputation. To the poor bastards who barely made it through Con Stud. The rest of us would survive.

"I'm just sayin'. If you came lookin' for a job, and I saw Carver baseball on your resumé, I'd wonder if you really earned your degree. See what I mean?"

Insanely, I pictured Angel sitting in her wing chair in front of her giant TV. "I'm only telling the truth," I heard her say. I shoved aside the memory with a conscious effort.

"I see, Dad." *Maybe that would keep you from splashing my name all over your ads.* But I kept from saying that last thought out loud. Captain's fucking pledge.

"So what d'you do now?" he asked. "Head back to DC to have it out with your girl before you report to trainin' camp?"

"How the fuck—" I cut off my question. "I know damn well Google didn't tell you about Katie and me." I knew, because I'd spent my own time searching her name. There was nothing online to link us together. Nothing before her article had appeared, and it hardly told the whole story.

"Well maybe that's somethin' your sister should've kept her mouth shut about."

"Jen doesn't know the first thing about Katie and me."

My father tilted his head, giving me the appraising glance that had always made me cave when I was a kid. I'd confess to taking spare change from his dresser. I'd admit to shirking work. I'd say up front that I'd eaten a candy bar five minutes before dinner, because he was going to find out the truth anyway. He always, always did.

But I wasn't a kid anymore. I'd won the fucking World Series. I stood my ground, my glare matching his cool gaze as new trickles of sweat etched my shoulder blades. I raised my chin and said, "There isn't anything to know."

"You high-tailed it out of Florida to see her," Dad said. "And you waited out some quarantine because of the virus. You spent weeks playin' house with her. And you put your tail between your legs and ran out to San Diego when she beat your ass in a fight. There. Have I got that about right?"

I gaped. Not so much that Jen had figured it all out. She pretty much knew what I was thinking before I knew it myself. But she'd told it all to Dad.

And he'd listened.

"Yeah," I said. "That's about right. But she didn't beat my ass."

"You fought?"

"Yes, sir."

"And you said a bunch of crap, both of you. Shit you wish you hadn't said. Shit that keeps you up nights, wishin' you could take it back?"

You're the one who works with words. If that's the right one, you'll be sure to know it.

"Yes, sir."

He shook his head slowly, like I was the most pitiful thing he'd seen in a lifetime of piss-poor things. "So what do you do now?"

There it was. The question I'd been asking myself since I walked into Dulles Airport. "I don't have a fucking clue."

Dad waited, giving me a chance to come up with something better. And when I didn't, he finally said, "Son, you need to make a searchin' and fearless moral inventory."

I recognized the language. There were enough guys—coaches mostly—who'd worked their way through Alcoholics

Anonymous to stay involved in baseball. He was quoting one of the steps. "Great," I said, trying not to sound sarcastic. "I'm sure that'll help."

"It will if you let it," he said. "But you can't stop there. You need to make amends."

I didn't even bother answering that. Coming from my father, from the man who'd drunk his way through my Little League career, through my four years of high school…

"Son," he said, and his gaze was suddenly riveted to my face. "I sincerely regret the shit that's gone between us. I missed too many of your games when you were young enough to care who sat in the stands. Once you hit the majors, I was wrong to use your name for PriceGuard. I didn't have the right to make those banners. To place those ads. I could have caused you a boatload of trouble with Major League. I can't ever go back and change what I did. But if you can think of a way for me to make it right, I'm willin' to do that now. I'm sorry. And I hope you can find it in your heart to forgive me."

It was the longest speech he'd ever made to me. He didn't take his eyes from mine the entire time he was talking. His voice shook a little, but not with his old anger, not with the rage I'd learned to hide from when I was a kid.

And when I stayed silent, he went on. "It's not an excuse. I'm not trying to say it is. But there's this devil that grabs hold of my brain. It tells me I need to be leavin'. Need to hit the road. It burns in my belly, hotter'n the sun in July. The drinkin', the whiskey, they shut it down. Not very well and not for very long. But they let me get some peace."

The Mind-Fuck. My father was telling me about the Mind-Fuck.

Only he never had the option of hopping a plane to another city. He'd had a family to raise. A factory to run. He couldn't skip out the way I had, fleeing before the Fuck ever got its claws in too deep.

So he'd drunk his way out.

"I'm powerless against it, Son. Against it and the booze. But there's a power greater than me. I see that now. That's why I needed to make changes. That's why I needed to tell you how sorry I am for the stupid shit I did."

He seemed to stand taller once the words were out. His face was relaxed, like the hands by his sides. He was patient. Calm. Sincere.

I'd held onto my anger for so long. I knew exactly how much it weighed. I knew its precise shape, just how much room it took up inside my head.

Dad's apology might not be real. He might go back to his old ways the second the plant was retooled to pump out sports equipment. But one look at his earnest expression told me he *thought* it was real. He'd dug all those words out of some place deep inside, and he meant every single one of them, whether I forgave him or not.

I swallowed hard. I locked my knees, standing a little straighter myself. I extended my right hand. And I said, "I accept your apology."

We shook, and both of us let some tension evaporate into the scorching air. "Thank you," he said. "Son."

And then, because he'd given me the most valuable thing he owned, I tried to give him something back. "This searching and fearless moral inventory… What does that mean in real terms? How would it work with Katie?"

He shrugged, and I realized he was just a guy on the far side of sixty, an exhausted plant manager who'd spent the past few months doing the impossible, building a wall to hold back a flood in the middle of a pandemic. "I can't tell you that," he said. "I've made my amends with your mother. And by the grace of God, she accepted them. But that's between her and me. None of you kids need to know the details."

I'd wanted too much. I'd thought he could tell me some secret formula, some magic words that would make everything right.

"But I can tell you one thing," he went on. "Forty-two years ago, when your mother agreed to marry me, I couldn't imagine keepin' secrets from her. I took her out to your grandfather's cabin, and we sat at the end of the dock. I was too nervous to look at her, but I told her everything I wanted to do in my life. I told her all my dreams, and I told her my fears. And I told her I could do it all, if I had her by my side."

"And Mom bought all that?"

"She did. I couldn't afford the type of ring she deserved. But I'd brought along this plant your Aunt Barb gave me. I pulled off one of those, what-d'you-call-it, vines from the plant, and I twisted it into a circle. I put it around your mother's finger, and the second she said she'd marry me, I threw the rest of that damn plant as far out into the lake as I could manage."

"Wait," I said. "Aunt Barb gave you a plant?"

He snorted. "She had this damn fool idea. When I'd fucked things up with your mother once before, she gave me one of those plants, the green ones, with the leaves that look like hearts."

"A philodendron."

"If you say so. She told me if I kept it alive for a month, then I could get goldfish."

"And if you kept *them* alive for three months, you could get a puppy."

"You've heard this story," he said.

"More or less. But you threw the philodendron into the lake?"

"The damn thing was half dead anyway."

"So you never got the goldfish?"

"What the hell would I do with goldfish?"

"Or a puppy?"

"You know damn well your mother's allergic to dogs. Wait," he said. "What's so funny?"

I shook my head, already reaching for my keys. "I'll tell you some other time."

"Come over for dinner tonight. I'll get out of here on time."

"I'd like to," I said, and I was surprised to discover that was the truth. "But I have somewhere else I have to be."

I was already weighing my options. It would take three days to drive to Virginia. But I could get to Austin in an hour and find a flight from there.

I could be in Arlington by dinnertime.

70

KATIE

I'd never realized how exhausting success could be.

The *Davis* article struck like lightning. My inbox exploded with comments from readers. Some applauded my leg-work in researching my article, my getting to the bottom of a scandal that had been decades in the making. Others, though, called me an intellectual elite, a woman writing from a position of privilege without understanding how I was harming a pool of dedicated athletes who were only doing their best to succeed in a world where all the cards were stacked against them.

As news of Coach Dixon's death spread, another group of letters started to arrive. People accused me of dancing on his grave. They said I should be ashamed of ruining his reputation. I was a monster for holding my article until he was no longer capable of telling his end of the story.

I knew the timing was only coincidental. *Davis Monthly* had needed to complete its fact check. They'd released the article the moment they felt secure about what I'd written. Besides, there were a lot of other people affected by the scandal. Coach Dixon had only been one cog in a massive wheel.

But I did grieve for the coach. For his family too, and all his players, even those who'd cheated. They'd lost a man they loved, and the Internet explosion was salt in their collective wounds.

As it was for Jason. I knew I'd hurt Jason.

Would-have-left-kill-career-wait-wait-wait.

The article kindled *The Feel-Good Phoenix*. Page-reads grew exponentially that first day, with more than half the readers taking the time to dig past the first page, going through older articles. I got notices from my Internet service provider that they were flipping switches behind the scenes, making more computer power available because of the volume of new readers.

I was grateful I'd already written articles for the rest of the week, and I'd made assignments to my handful of freelancers to make the site even more robust. Amusingly, I received nine resumés through the website from experienced journalists hoping to come aboard. Two of them looked promising, and I wrote back, asking for writing samples.

Just after noon, I got a phone call from Martin Schweitzer, my old editor at *Press Box*. "Great work you've been doing there, McIntyre. We always knew you had it in you."

"Thanks," I said, keeping my tone neutral.

"We're gearing up to reopen on July 1," he said. His voice was plummier than I remembered. He sounded like he was sharing a secret. "Baseball, basketball, and hockey will all be back by the end of the month. We'll have a lot of ground to cover, and you can have your pick of whichever beat you want. I'm authorized to offer you a ten percent raise. And of course you'll work from home for the foreseeable future."

"Thank you," I said. "I'll think about it seriously and get back to you in a few days." It was a generous offer. But I was pretty sure I'd turn it down. I was a lot more excited to build the *Phoenix* than I was to cover sports.

Brit called around two. "Which says baseball more? Lucky Charms cereal or Sour Patch candy?"

"Um, neither?"

"I heard that sportsball is coming back, so I'm making some new donuts," she said. "I bought a bunch of fabric for masks too. Football and tennis and that one with the ball and the net you use to clean the pool."

"Lacrosse," I said.

"I haven't figured out donuts for baseball or basketball. But for hockey, I thought I'd do something filled—a white glaze, like ice, with raspberry inside. You know. Like blood. There are lots of fights in hockey, right?"

"Right?" I realized my response sounded a lot like a question.

"I'll make it oval," she clarified. "Like a hockey field."

"Rink. Hockey's played on a rink. Baseball's on a diamond. Basketball's on a court."

"Oh!" Brit said. "Diamond! I can do something with that. I'll call you back."

I was still staring at my phone in bemusement when it rang again.

"Sean!" I said. "How are you feeling?"

"You know," my brother said. His voice still sounded like he was scraping words over broken glass. "Every day's a little better." Timothy had reported that Sean was down to two naps a day. And he'd managed to walk around the block twice over the weekend.

"I just got off the phone with Brit," I said. "Do you need her to bring you anything?"

"We're in good shape," he said. "She's been a lifesaver."

"She's a good friend," I said.

"The next time you talk to her, though?"

"Yeah?"

"Tell her she doesn't need to keep buying me 'get well soon' cards."

"I didn't know she was."

"She writes a personal note on each of them. Saying she hopes I'm getting over my creeping neogophilus."

I laughed. "That sounds like Brit."

Sean said, "I'm really calling because I was finally able to reach Rachel Thatcher. She can squeeze in an appointment with Angel at ten on Thursday morning."

I bit my lip. Dr. Thatcher was one of Sean's med school classmates. She was a neurologist, specializing in patients with dementia. "I'll get Angel there."

"This is a good thing," Sean said, his voice sounding even rougher because he was trying to be gentle.

"I know," I said. I took a deep breath and repeated, "I know."

We talked for a few more minutes, but I could tell he was getting tired. I sent my love to Timothy and signed off.

And five minutes later, my phone rang again. I'd just gone into the kitchen to start a bolognese sauce for dinner.

This time, the call was from a 202 number I didn't know. I considered letting it go to voicemail, but there were a lot of publications based in Washington DC. With the *Davis* article hot, I didn't want to miss a new freelance opportunity.

I put on my most professional voice, complete with a competent smile. "Katie McIntyre," I said.

"Great article, Killer."

I froze. "Jason?" And then, because I knew it was him, even if I'd cut him out of my contacts, even if I'd hoped he'd called, even if I'd dreaded ever talking to him again, I said, "I know it must have been hard for you to read. And today, especially. I'm sorry about Stan Dixon."

"Thank you," he said. "I saw him a couple of weeks ago. I told him about the article, what I knew about it anyway. He was ready for the story to come out. He thought it was best for everyone."

I closed my eyes. I hadn't realized how much I wanted to hear that. Not *needed* to hear it—the story had to be told, whether Coach Dixon was on board or not. But it was a surprising comfort to know he'd been at peace.

But that wasn't enough. I had to ask, "And you? What did you think when you read it?"

"It was fair. And you had your facts straight. You gave the university a chance to tell its side of the story. And it hurts like hell that I didn't know about it when I was at Carver. That I didn't do anything to stop it."

"You were just a student…"

"I had my head up my ass. I was too hell-bent on pitching to see what was going on around me. Or maybe I *did* see it, and I just didn't want to know."

I tried to think of the next thing to say, all the words and phrases that had become familiar as they circled through my brain when I tried to fall asleep. Would-have-left-kill-career-wait-wait-wait.

But the article was out now. I no longer had to wait. A third of my mantra was useless.

"Jason—" I said, at the same time he said my name. I laughed, because that was easier than saying what I was really thinking. "You go first."

I heard him take a deep breath. Hold it. Exhale long and slow, like he was standing on top of the mound, getting ready to make a perfect pitch. "Katie," he said again. "I was an asshole. I was scared of what you were writing, what it would mean to me and to Coach, to people I love. I didn't trust you to be fair, and even if you were, I didn't want to think about what the story really meant."

"I shouldn't have kept it secret," I said. Because that was the confession I'd made night after night, staring at the ceiling above my bed. "I started to tell you so many times. But I wasn't sure what I was going to find. And I didn't know how you'd react. And it was easier just to stay quiet until I knew what I had."

"I get that," he said. And after a moment, he went on. "My dad. Telling you he was dead. I just said it that first time, and I didn't realize what it would mean to you. There've been times, a lot of them, when I *wished* he was dead—"

"Don't say that," I interrupted.

"Wished," he repeated. "Past tense. There's a lot of fucked up stuff there, a lot of mistakes he made. And I made too. But I promised Coach I'd make it right with him. I did that this morning—right after I found out Coach…" He trailed off.

I said, "Sounds like you've had one hell of a day."

"Yeah. But I talked to Dad this morning, and we left things in a better place than they've been for a long, long time." His voice changed, became more determined. "But none of that changes what I did to you. I'm sorry. I never should have lied about Dad in the first place. And I shouldn't have kept lying after that."

His apology melted something inside me. "I've been pretty messed up," I said. "For years. I've talked to Sean about it, a little now. And to Angel too. Things got so screwed up in my mind. It was like *I* made the bad things happened. Mom leaving. Dad dying. When you said your own father was dead, it felt like you understood what a fucking mess I was… Like I wasn't really a freak…"

"You aren't a freak." He said it quickly. Without hesitation.

"I'm pretty much a freak," I contradicted. "I said terrible things to you that day. I don't even know why."

"You were angry."

"But I don't think you throw your money around. At least not without a reason."

"That's it. I try to solve problems. I try to help the people I love."

Whatever I was going to say next flew out of my head.

He must not have known, or maybe he didn't care, because he went right on talking. "I love you, Katie. I love you, and I hate that I hurt you. I hate that I said all that crap, and then I ran away, so I didn't have a chance to take it back. *We* didn't have a chance to make it better."

His words unlatched the deepest chambers of my heart. A bubble of light opened inside me, carrying me forward, giving me words I didn't know how to say. "I'm sorry, too. It's not an excuse, just an explanation, but I got so angry, and I was terrified of feeling that way, of being out of control. And then, after you were gone, it was safer to stay apart. Safer not to say anything. Not to say I love you too."

"God," he said. "We were both idiots."

I heard his rueful laugh, and I wanted to join him. I wanted to feel happy, without the weight that still swaddled my heart. But I couldn't. Because I knew that what I truly wanted wasn't possible.

I was fully aware that major league baseball players reported for training in eight days. That wasn't enough time to clear quarantine, even if—

"Wait," I said. "You called from a 202 number."

"My phone doesn't work here. Even if you hadn't blocked it."

"I know. I'm sorry. No, I'm not sorry, I just thought—" I cut myself off. "Wait," I said again, as if he were threatening to go somewhere I couldn't follow. "Where *are* you?"

He laughed. "I'm back in our suite. The Hotel Monaco says they'll name it after me, when the pandemic is over."

"But why— What— Aren't you heading down to Florida?"

"Nope. I've already talked to a lot of the guys. Most are planning to report. But a couple are trying to figure out what they should do because of George Floyd, because of Black Lives Matter. And one guy's mother has MS. He won't put her at risk by playing. Another has a pregnant wife. I'm taking the year off too."

"But your salary!"

"I'll manage," he said dryly. "This way, I can work on what really matters. There was this great article I read the other day, on this website called *The Feel-Good Phoenix*? It was about a bunch of athletes who are setting up challenges to help small businesses make it through the pandemic."

"So you read the *Phoenix*?"

"Every day," he said, and the words warmed me all the way down to my toes. And then he said, "Where are you?"

I looked around. "The kitchen. Angel's napping, and I was about to fix dinner."

"God save you both," he said.

"No! I've really learned to cook!"

He ignored my protests. "Go to the front door."

"Okay…" I walked to the foyer. For just a moment, I hoped that Jason was lying, that he wasn't really at the Monaco, that he was standing on the doorstep, waiting to hold me, to close his fingers in my hair, to match the kiss that I was suddenly desperate to give him.

But he wasn't lying. I opened the door to nothing. "What am I supposed to see?" I asked.

"Come on, Killer," he said. "Look down."

Centered on the welcome mat was a cheap day planner. Its plastic cover was stamped to look like leather, and a binder clip held all the pages to the middle of June. A gaudy "1" was drawn on June 23, with glitter pens that made my eyes cross. I turned the pages, counting off the numbers until I got to fourteen. The fifteenth day was filled with fireworks and rainbows and a pretty pitiful excuse for a unicorn.

"I know, I know," he said. "Your grandmother's cat draws better than I do."

"No," I said, automatically checking to see if Lucifer was making a break for freedom. The demon beast was nowhere in sight. I clutched the day planner to my chest. "It's perfect," I said. "It's absolutely perfect."

Fourteen days. Two weeks. A sliding glass door between us, with only a phone to bridge the gap.

This time, it would be a breeze.

Katie and Jason have found their Happy Ever After, but Jennifer Price Parker (Jason's indomitable sister) is still searching for true love during the pandemic. Because sometimes a holiday romance, falling for your boss, and a reality TV show aren't enough of a challenge!

Buy *Jennifer Price Lives a Charmed Life* today!

ACKNOWLEDGMENTS

Katie McIntyre Hits a Home Run grew out of conversations on social media, when people began talking about what a contemporary romance novel would look like during COVID. Some people argued that romance should always provide an escape, and that no author should ever mention the coronavirus. Others said that COVID was here to stay, and we had to find a way to tell stories about it, around it, and through it.

You can see where I came down on that debate.

The past year has been full of so many challenges and so much loss. But nearly every day, I've seen amazing examples of people helping people. I've laughed at memes that address our crisis head-on. I've cried at the heroism of health-care workers and essential personnel who have stepped up for days, weeks, and months, often without a break.

The coronavirus has made me marvel at the resiliency of people who found reserves they never knew they had. Artists and scholars have embraced our new world, allowing me to watch plays from my living room, to take courses with internationally renowned scholars from my couch, to view art exhibits and concerts and films that I might never have had the chance to see in ordinary times.

Amid all the loss and fear and suffering the coronavirus has brought, I hope we can embrace such glimmers of light in the darkness. And I hope *Katie McIntyre* can be one such bright point for readers.

The publishing world has changed dramatically since my

first book appeared in 2000, but one thing has remained constant: Authors never work alone. We always rely on the kindness and support of multitudes to complete our work.

Many thanks to Angelina M. Lopez, who listened to me as I fretted that I was never going to have another idea for another book (and who assured me I was wrong, and who clearly turned out to be right.)

Thank you to Patricia Rice, Maria V. Snyder, Pru Warren, and Sarah Zettel for their expert beta reading. Each of you poked and prodded in different ways, urging me to make Katie and Jason's story better. (And yes, sometimes the harshest criticism is the most productive!)

Thank you to Connie Barber and Diane Barber for their proofreading expertise. Of course, any errors that remain are mine.

Thank you to my family—Fallons and Johnsons, Klaskys and Maddreys and Timminses. When the writing is challenging, it's always a comfort to know I have your support.

And then there's Mark. I'm pretty sure no one else could have kept me sane throughout CoronaChaos. Thank you for…everything.

Mindy Klasky
Arlington, VA
January 2021

THANK YOU

I can't thank you enough for choosing *Katie McIntyre Hits a Home Run* from among all the romantic women's fiction out there! Without readers like you, I would never have my writing career.

You may not realize it, but *you* can be my hero. Study after study shows that the number one reason a person reads a book is because that book was recommended by a friend.

So will you tell one friend about *Katie McIntyre*?

Of course, if you're dead-set on reviewing my book where you bought it, I won't complain! Honest reviews are hugely helpful because many advertisers require me to have a certain number of reviews before I can buy ads.

Whatever you do, don't be a stranger! I'm mostly online at Facebook. I look forward to hearing from you soon!

www.mindyklasky.com
mindy@mindyklasky.com

ABOUT THE AUTHOR

Mindy Klasky learned to read when her parents shoved a book in her hands and told her she could travel anywhere in the world through stories. She never forgot that advice.

Mindy's travels took her through multiple careers—from litigator to librarian to full-time writer. Mindy's travels have also taken her through various literary genres, including romantic comedies, hot contemporary romance, and traditional fantasies. She is a *USA Today* bestselling author, and she has received the Career Achievement Award from the Washington Romance Writers.

In her spare time, Mindy knits, quilts, and tries to tame her endless to-be-read shelf. Her husband and cats do their best to fill the left-over minutes.

You can learn more about Mindy at her website, www.mindyklasky.com.

Made in the USA
Columbia, SC
03 December 2022

72599851R00248